KU-289-804

THE KILTERNAN LEGACY

Anne McCaffrey

 millington

© 1975 by Anne McCaffrey

All rights reserved

ISBN 0 86000 068 0

First published in Great Britain in 1976 by
Millington Books Limited
109 Southampton Row
London WC1B 4HH
also at
Wessex House, Blandford Heights
Blandford, Dorset DT11 7TS

Reproduced and printed by photolithography and bound in
Great Britain at Chapel River Press, Andover, Hants.

FK261760

WESTERN EDUCATION
AND LIBRARY BOARD

This story is admiringly
dedicated to
my Irish "fairy" godmother,
Hilda Whitton,
who made my fondest wish come true in
Mr. Ed.

Chapter 1

Aunt Irene Teasey, great aunt Teasey, solved my problem: She died. She died in Ireland, and left all that she died possessed of to me.

"Good heavens," my mother said when I phoned her to see if there was anything to be possessed, "I don't know. Your father used to say that Irene was the only smart female the Teaseys ever produced. Although why she'd leave you everything when she'd all those relatives . . . hmmm. Maybe that's why."

"Why what?" I asked—patiently, because Mother's thought processes had driven Father to an early grave, although he had once admitted to me in utter confusion that he found my mother's conclusions fascinatingly accurate.

"Why she did. I named you after her because your father liked her so much, and I *had* run out of interesting girl names [I've four sisters] and the one time I met Irene, I quite liked the old girl. Very independent sort, you know. Never married."

I wasn't certain from Mother's tone whether it was because of her independence that Irene had not married, or whether she'd developed the habit because she'd remained single.

"Well, is she likely to have left anything?"

"Quite possible. Doesn't the lawyer man give you any inkling?"

"No precise figures. I must establish my identity as Miss Teasey's great-niece first, and I'm executrix of the will, and there're death duties to pay, and—"

"You'd better go there, then. Always does to be on the spot, especially with lawyers—no, barristers—no, *they* plead cases before the bar, don't they? Solicitors is what you'd have to deal with. But she does solve your problem, Rene."

"By having to go to Ireland to consort with bewigged men?"

"*Men*, dear, is the relevant word."

"Oh, Mother!"

"Oh, Daughter! You were complaining only the other day that you didn't know who stood where in relation to you or Teddie-boy since the divorce. Why bother to find out? The ones who'll stay by you are too dull, or married and don't have the contacts you need, and the ones who side with Teddie you don't want to know."

She was, of course, massively correct.

"Besides, I read somewhere recently that a removal from the marital area is often a very constructive step. If taken in the proper direction."

I could tell that Mother now considered Ireland, of all places, to be the proper direction.

"There're men there," she said, again darkly suggestive.

"They're men everywhere, Mother."

"Not what *I'd* call men."

"Mother!"

"Nonsense, dear. Besides, think how broadening it would be for the twins!"

I gulped. "The twins are quite broadened enough."

"I don't mean precocious, love. I mean, broad in outlook and culture."

"You ought to know Teddie's opinion of Ireland by now."

"And I thank God that the jet set hasn't discovered Ireland yet. They do have good schools, and no drug problem."

"True, but they do have a minor religious war."

"Darling, it *isn't* religious. It's socioeconomic, hidden under clerical skirts, I read somewhere . . . And besides, you'd be in the south."

"Mother, I'm not certain that I want to go anywhere right now."

"What? Another six months in your lair licking your

wounds, dear?" Mother can be disconcertingly acute at times. "Consult the twins."

I did. I'll never figure out how she got to them before I did. After all, they were in school in Westfield, and she was in New York City. Their reaction was so affirmative that Simon was booking flights while Snow listed the clothes I had to bring. As she was constantly garbed in sweaters, shirts, and pants, her packing posed no mental exertions.

"But, children, you don't want to leave all your friends . . ."

"Why not?" asked Snow, her gorgeous, big, light-green eyes very adult in expression. "Everyone will be away for vacations in a week. It'd be great. You'll have to get some dresses, Mother. These are just too much!"

Snow was conventionally christened Sara Virginia, after Mother and my mother-in-law. At the party after the baptismal double-header, one of her uncles had observed the sleeping child, all lacy in the family christening gown, her wealth of curly black hair escaping the cap, and renamed her Snow White. She was only a half-hour younger than her brother, but the difference might have been two separate pregnancies. Simon was dark too, but not as dramatically so. His skin was ruddy, not white, and his eyes more gray than green. Curiously enough, their personalities belied their looks, for Simon tended to be the dreamer, and Snow had a fine sense of everyday expediencies. Teddie had complained that she was revoltingly precocious. She was. He had made her so by showing off his "fairy-tale princess" to bored sophisticates.

It was when Teddie began to . . . well, never mind. That sort of consideration was behind me now. And, fortunately, behind Snow. Yes, going to Ireland would solve many of my problems, all right. And pose others.

One of them was Teddie's reaction to having his children removed from his sphere of influence. Neither he nor that expensive and indolent lawyer of his had put any clause in the divorce papers restricting me to be domiciled exclusively in Westfield, New Jersey, or the continental U.S.A. I could not put the children in a boarding school, but that was the only restriction.

"What about my visitation rights?" Teddie had shouted.

"You haven't exercised those rights in three weeks!"

"Now see here, Irene, you can't just snatch my kids from under my nose without my permission—"

"I don't need your permission, and I'm courteously informing you of my summer plans. I'm going to Ireland for a month at the longest, and the children are going with me. I'm just telling you, and that's that."

Then, before I could become embroiled in one of those impossible arguments in which I always end up being wrong, ineffective, stupid or ludicrous, I hung up on him. It had taken me six months of divorced bliss to achieve such decisiveness. I'd always had the feeling that if only Teddie would really listen to my side of an argument, we might be able to patch up our faltering marriage. Only, my rebuttals had lacked the ingenuity of his ad-agency-trained responses, and I always lost.

Fortunately his lawyer had not discarded an iota of his laziness, and Simon and Snow overrode my hesitation, so we were on the plane to Ireland in ten days' time, the passport photos barely dry under the stamps. My lawyer had walked them through Immigration. I suppose Hank had had a notion of what Teddie might do if he were really as annoyed as he said he was about my taking *his* children from him. An injunction restraining me from removing Simon Richard and Sara Virginia Stanford from the continental U.S.A. was issued the day after we left. Had I known of it beforehand, I couldn't even have applied for passports for Snow and Simon. Later I wondered whether the children's efficiency had been prompted by a "get Mother moving" campaign or an inside knowledge of their father's reactions.

We were in Dublin at 11, and in a taxi to the hotel by 11:30. We'd been booked into the Hotel Montrose, typical Americana, but comfortable. I phoned the solicitor, Mr. Noonan, and was informed that he was in court.

"I thought he was a solicitor."

"He is indeed, but he's attending a client in court."

That didn't make much sense to me, but I was in no shape to pursue the subject. "Please tell him that Irene Teasey is at the Hotel Montrose, and I'd like to see him as soon as possible."

"Mrs. Teasey?" There was a startled squeak in the girl's soft voice.

"The American one. The great-niece." Silence. "I'm to see him about inheriting my great-aunt's property at Kilternan." Silence. "This is Noonan, Turner, and Pearsall's office, isn't it?"

"Oh, yes, it certainly is."

"Then please give Mr. Noonan my message and say that I'm anxious to see him as soon as possible." Again the rather stunned silence. "Is anything wrong?"

"No, no. Of course not, ma'am."

Well, I was too tired to chew that over.

So the twins thought, too, because Snow took the phone out of my hand, replaced it, and pushed me back onto the bed, and Simon shook a coverlet over me.

"You rest."

"But I can't leave you two alone in—"

"Why not? The natives sound friendly."

"And I'm hungry," added Snow.

"There's a grill downstairs, and a bank."

I'd given them each some money, American and Irish.

"You sleep!" said Simon in a stern, masculine voice.

I didn't really expect to, and was therefore more than a little annoyed to be roused from a very deep slumber by the insistent burring of a phone by my ear. Sleepily I grabbed at it to shut it up.

"Would I be speaking to Irene Teasey?"

"Yes?" I wasn't too sure myself, but the tone of the male voice implied that I'd better be Irene Teasey.

"I understand that Hillside Lodge is for sale," the man said.

"Hillside Lodge?" Where was that? Where was I? "Who is this speaking?"

"I'm Brian Kelley, of T K & B, and I've a client who's making a firm offer of—"

"Now, wait just a minute. I just got to Dublin this morning, and I haven't seen the place."

"Well, Miss Teasey, then I can be of service to you in several ways—by helping you wind up your business quickly, selling at a profit, and you'll have plenty of time to enjoy some sightseeing before you go back." The man had spoken with a wheedling psuedo-charm which I knew all too well.

"Mr. Kelley, you are rushing things."

"Why now, and I thought you Americans liked a direct approach."

Not when I'm half asleep I don't. "I have just had a tiring journey from the States, and I'm in no mood to discuss business at this moment. I suggest—"

"It's just evening now," he said with a conciliatory smoothness, and I glanced hurriedly at my watch, which read 3:30. "Let me welcome you to Ireland with a few jars. Say around nine? It would be worth your while, I assure you. Shall I ring your room?"

I stammered out an affirmative and then, when I realized that I had been guided into agreeing, I tried to retract and found the phone had gone dead.

Good Lord! I'd hardly expected such a problem, and I did wish that the solicitor had been in. I didn't have a clue as to whether I should even listen to offers. Grab the first sucker, or hang out for top development prices? Did they develop in Ireland? Ah, yes, I did recall rows of identical semidetached houses on the way from the airport.

Three-thirty is evening in Ireland? I rose, washed my face, put on eyebrows and lips, and decided that if this was evening in Ireland, there might be tea—preferably coffee—served somewhere. And where were my children?

That proved easiest to establish. They had gone out, the sweet-voiced receptionist told me, and gave me the impression that Snow and Simon had been laying on the charm right, left, and center. Good. There had to be some fringe benefits to life with Teddie . . . like public-relations-minded children. *"Preserve the Image!"*

Yes, I could have tea or coffee served in the lounge bar. So I had coffee and thin sandwiches while browsing through the Irish *Times*. A large section of the paper was devoted to real estate. The intelligence slowly penetrated my brain that "auctioneers" were also agents for selling and renting houses. T K & B translated into Thomas, Keogh, and Brennan, evidently a large and active firm, so friend Brian Kelley was a sharp operator, moving in quickly on a prime prospect. But wasn't it a shade too quickly? There seemed to be no dearth of houses in Dublin, or south Dublin. I did some hasty pounds-into-dollars conversions and found that many of the houses advertised were about $25,000. Not that that helped me, because, obviously, location had something to do with price, as did the age of the house. The range was all the way from £3,000 to £12,000.

And how had Brian Kelley known that Irene Teasey was in Dublin? And here only for the purpose of selling? Something Irene Teasey hadn't even decided.

After all, the only person who'd known I was here was . . . ah, was that why the girl in the solicitor's office had been so silent? Had she been tipped to report my arrival to "interested parties"? Surely Hillside Lodge couldn't be so valuable as to require such cloak-and-dagger tactics!

Mother never had been explicit on that score, but she'd been very disquieting about lots of relations who'd be unhappy about my inheriting. I'd tried several times to nail her down to specifics, without luck. Not even I can understand Mother's crypticisms. She'd interspersed her rambles with odd remarks and advice such as: "Her sisters were the worst—they'd greedy little clutching paws, and petty minds. Dublin's no more than a small town. Everyone knows everyone else, and all their business. You'll find that out. Never tell 'em anything. That's probably why your grandfather got out of Ireland. There was one other brother but he died. Your father often mentioned his uncle Beebee. His name was really Richard. At any rate, don't sell a thing, a stick, until you've had sound legal counsel. I expect the lawyer's good. Irene Teasey was no fool. Probably why she never married an Irishman. Or maybe *because* she never married an Irishman." This distinction puzzled Mother, and interrupted that particular discourse.

"This is, however, exactly what you need, Rene. A complete change, a new challenge. You're only thirty-six, the one advantage in marrying young."

I might be only thirty-six, but I felt a hundred even after two cups of strong coffee. As for the challenge of coming to Ireland, did I really need it? I sort of sank into my chair, feeling small.

Fortunately for my trend of thought, Snow and Simon came through the entrance, with Snow pointing at me dramatically in her "See? She's all right" gesture. Simon shrugged and then brandished something which turned out to be two maps, one of Dublin and one of Ireland.

"This is Dublin proper but Kilternan doesn't appear on it, much less Swann's Lane," Simon said, spreading out the map across the small lounge tables. "See, it's down in here," and he illustrated. "Nice country, I'm told."

"Who told you?" I asked, curious.

"We did a little adroit questioning," Snow said.

"Where?"

"Oh, up the road a piece is a largish shopping center," and Simon jerked his thumb over his shoulder rightishly.

"Not bad specialty shops, either," added Snow.

"How'd you get there?"

"Walked up, bused back." Simon flourished a bus schedule. "They're all double-deckers!" He beamed. "Thirsty work."

I got the hint and signaled the waiter. Snow did some flirt-practicing, and the man responded visibly until I gave her an adroit kick. She might be only fourteen but she looked much, much older. So did Simon, I realized, seeing him against an unfamiliar background. He'd shot up to a respectable five foot ten in the last six months, and recently complained that he had to shave. I suggested a beard, and he haughtily replied that everyone was bearded. Ergo, *he* couldn't be.

"And there's a rental-car place." Simon handed over another folder. "These are the rates."

"I should hire you as leg man," I said, but Simon knew I was grateful.

"They want your arm for new cars here," Simon said, shaking his head. I knew he'd had delusions about our driving a Mercedes or a Jaguar while we were here. "All those small foreign cars cost a fortune."

"All those small foreign cars are native, Simple Simon," his twin said with a remonstrating snort.

"Now, wait a minute, children, I'm not buying a car."

"Who suggested?" Simon was honestly surprised. "Just compared prices, that's all, but you will want something to get around in. This," and he tapped the bus schedule, "is supposedly an old Irish legend."

"What do you mean?"

Simon snorted, and Snow giggled. "You should have heard them at the bus stop! 'Sure now, an' I've been waiting the half-hour or more!' [Snow has an ear for dialect] I mean, Mom, and there's no route that takes us to our part of Kilternan."

"How do you know?" I waved at the Kilternanless map.

"Big area map in the Hertz place. Swann's Lane is"—and Simon walked his fingers down a road marked TO CABIN-TEELY—"approximately here," and his fingers hovered over a large rose in the carpet, five inches from the map edge.

"Hmmm."

"So, we'd need a car," Simon said.

"And you know the one I should have?"

"Well, you always liked Gammy's little Renault. They have the same model . . . Of course, it's right-hand drive, but you'd cope, Mother."

Simon has a most satisfactory way of assuming all kinds of abilities that I'm not so sure I possess until he indicates that I do, and then I do.

"And they've a Renault all ready and waiting for me to-morrow?"

Simon grinned. "Well, I didn't see any harm in asking. And they do."

"Garnet red," said Snow approvingly.

"Well, that's one thing settled. However . . ." and I told them about Mr. Kelley's call.

"I wouldn't see the man," said Snow autocratically.

"That's a bit quick, isn't it, Mother? Sounds fishy." Simon was giving me that too-intent look, which meant that he and Snow had been conspiring.

"Okay, what's with you two?"

"Well, we've all summer to do nothing in, why not do it in Ireland?" she asked guilelessly. "If that cottage is habit-able at all, it'll do as a base for any touring we want to do."

"You don't like the Westfield routine any more anyhow, Mom," Simon said. "Swimming club and that nonsense."

He didn't add "and running into your ex-husband and his new wife."

"You haven't been in Ireland more than . . ." I glanced at my watch, but Simon covered it, his expression very earnest.

"It's the feeling about it," Snow said, raising her hands in an unconscious effort to enfold the new experience, "and the people have time to talk to you, and answer questions, and *listen*."

"And give advice." Simon's grin was suddenly a faint echo of Teddie's I've-got-this-account-sewed-up smile. "I mean, they're *nice*, Mom."

"They know we're tourists," I said, to cushion their eventual disillusionment.

"Even if that's the case, it's a very welcome change!" Snow's eyes flashed, and her lips compressed against the increasingly frequent and distressing incidents that her young beauty provoked. If she felt less threatened in Ireland . . .

"Look, let's not go leaping without looking."

"Aw, Mom, Ireland's nice," Simon said, as if that were the definitive reason.

"I'm not saying no, I'm just—"

"Temporizing as usual," Snow finished for me.

"Really, Sara!"

She subsided, making a face, because usually she is not pert with me.

"Getting back to Mr. Kelley," Simon said adroitly, "you're not going to talk with him?"

"How can I avoid it? He was very insistent."

"Nine o'clock, you said? Well, you can be a number of places at nine. I think his insistence is a bit suspicious."

"So do I, but it doesn't hurt to listen."

The twins were dubious; they know how soft I am.

"Got an idea," said Snow. "You said he'd ring your room? Okay, nineishly, Sim sits in the lobby where he can hear. You sit in here, where you can see. Kelley announces himself at the desk, asks for you. Simon opens the map . . . wide. You see if you like Kelley's looks, and if you don't, when you get paged you don't answer. The girl at the desk can't find you if you're not here."

"That is rude. I mean, what if he is nice, and on the level . . ."

"So call him at T K & B and apologize. You were out for dinner and it took longer than you expected. Basic!" said the practical Snow.

I really wasn't up to meeting Mr. Kelley and being pressured, and the children knew it, so in the end I agreed that the plan was sensible.

Then we pored over the map to get some bearings. Dublin wasn't very big compared to New York (or, for that matter, Westfield, New Jersey), but the streets were irregular, and I could see that finding places might be a problem. And that led to looking at the full-scale map, and by the time we'd finished dinner the twins had plotted quite a tour of Ireland. Really, I could see their point. If we had a base, we could take short forays to historical sites, and it wouldn't be all that expensive—certainly no more than living in Westfield and shelling out five dollars a day at the pool—and more for air conditioning—or for trips to cousins. Well, I made no promises, but the twins knew me well enough to realize that they'd half persuaded me to stay.

"That is, if all goes well," I said, trying to be firm.

There were variables. For instance, how much cash would be left over after death duties and stuff from Aunt Irene's estate? I am *not* mercenary, but the trip over had taken most of my sinking fund. Of course, the support money from Teddie would be in on the first of July, and that would probably go further in Ireland than in New Jersey.

I suppose it was because everything was grown in a different soil, or maybe not to such homogeneous standards, but the peas at dinner were heavenly, the steak tender and delicious, and even the french fries ["Chips, Mom, chips," Simon corrected me] which I don't usually like, tasted superb!

"Maybe I was just hungry," I said, finishing the coffee with a sigh of repletion, and then saw my watch. "Oh, dear."

"Stations, everyone. Snow, you stay with Mother."

Simon put the maps under his arm and strode masterfully into the lobby and ensconced himself on the small sofa facing the entrance.

There weren't many people in the lounge yet as Snow solicitously ushered me in. We had a choice of seats, so I took one where, by leaning slightly forward, I could see anyone at the desk but I couldn't be seen from the desk. I was nervous, for I don't like deceptions of this sort.

"You wouldn't have Canadian Club whiskey, would you?" I heard Snow asking, and turned around in shocked surprise. "Oh, for you, Mom. Relax. Dutch courage."

"With ice?" asked the waiter.

"If you have it," replied Snow, at her most regal. Then she grinned impishly at the waiter, who winked back conspiratorially.

"Would you be wanting something, miss?"

"A Coke, please."

"How you can consume all that Coke and not blow up into a balloon, Snow, is beyond me." I remembered myself at her age, rather dumpy, and terrified of eating *anything*, for everything I ate seemed to go to my hips. If a mother is fortunate enough to have daughters (and that's what my mother *always* said, with the five girls and one boy), she is doubly blessed to have beautiful, slim, elegant ones. Eventually, I too made the grade.

"Oh, Mother," my darling daughter said airily, "I burn it off. That's what you always say."

"Snow!"

She grinned, and then I knew her impertinence had been to distract me. Just as well: Sim's map was flapping as if it would take off. Snow craned her neck beyond me to see the importunate Mr. Kelley.

His broad back was to us.

"Wouldn't you just know!" said Snow irascibly.

I put my glasses on, and the man was well-enough dressed from this distance: dark-haired, a mackintosh thrown over one arm. He turned his head slightly, and I could see long sideburns, slightly darker than his head hair, and the plane of his left cheek. Suddenly I was aware that Simon was shaking his head violently behind the map.

The barman came with our drinks, an ill-timed interruption. I couldn't seem to find the proper change, and finally Snow grabbed a pound note. By the time I could devote any attention to Mr. Kelley, he had turned his back fully toward us. And Simon kept shaking his head.

"Oh, dear." I mean, Simon is only fourteen, and, having lost that wonderful intuitive sense of judgment that small children have, he hadn't yet developed mature criteria.

Suddenly I was being paged, and I shriveled up against the overpadded seat. The waiter came back with the change.

"Aren't you being paged, Mrs. Teasey?"

"Yes, but we don't want to be bothered by that man," Snow said in a stern voice. "Do we, Mommy?"

"Well, that is, no. I'd rather not." I was horribly embarrassed.

"Well now. Not to worry," the waiter said, very understanding, and he walked quickly to the bar. To my continuing mortification, the waiter and the barman had a conversation, the barman picked up the phone, and in a few seconds Mr. Kelley had been given the word. I watched his reaction, and he seemed to be giving the nice receptionist a very hard time. Relenting, I was about to get to my feet when he suddenly turned, and I was very glad I'd refused to see him. He was an angry man with a sort of piggy face on which sideburns only increased the porcine resemblance. Yes, he was furious at this check in his sale. By the way he strode out of the hotel, fists clenched, mouth pursed, I'd the feeling that he'd be awfully persistent.

"You just leave it to us, missus. If anyone comes bothering you that you don't want to see, you just tell us," said the waiter, back again in front of the table.

"It's just that I'm so tired after the plane trip." I felt obliged to give some explanation—he'd been so cooperative —but I trailed off as he nodded understandingly.

"You look awfully tired, Mom," Snow said. "And we've such a lot to do tomorrow. You just finish that drink and off to bed with you."

"Really, Snow . . ."

But the waiter seemed to approve. Basically, so did I. Then Simon joined us, maps folded neatly under his arm.

"Hands," he said in cryptic disapproval.

"Really?" asked Snow. "He looked the type."

"Simon, *how* can you judge a person just by his hands?" I asked.

"Never wrong." Simon looked at me with mild rebuke. "Besides, you should've heard the time he gave the receptionist. He wanted seeing you bad!"

"Simon, please speak English."

"Why? You speak Amurrican."

"What's with you two tonight?" I was suddenly very tired, and the whole improbable trip became impossible.

"With us is you, Mom," replied Simon, knowing perfectly well what I meant. "C'mon, Sis, we better behave. She's plum tuckered out. Sorry, Mother." He slipped the map into his jacket pocket and stood up. "Let's get this wreck of the Hesperus to bed. We can watch the telly in the lounge."

With my children on either side of me, tugs for the wreck that I honestly felt myself to be, I left the lounge.

"Oh, here's Mrs. Teasey now," the receptionist was saying.

I groaned in horror and sagged against the children. Mr. Kelley *was* persistent. How had he known that I—

"It's a girl, Mother," Snow said.

If I hadn't wanted to meet Mr. Kelley, this young girl

certainly didn't want to meet me. She looked scared stiff.

"Here, Miss Teasey. The keys to Hillside Lodge." She held out at arm's length a ring of keys, some old, some shiny-new, attached by a thick string to a tag. "Mr. Noonan won't be free until half two tomorrow. He suggests that you might like to look at the property. Oh, the map." She fumbled in her pocket, an operation hampered by the fact that she had to juggle a motorcycle helmet and heavy gloves. I took the keys.

"Yes, I'd be relieved to see him. At two thirty?"

She nodded, still scared, got the map free of her pocket, and stepped up close. As she shoved the paper into my hand, she blurted out, "If Brian Kelley calls you, don't promise anything. Please! Not until you've spoken to Mr. Noonan. Oh dear!" With that she turned and ran from the lobby. In a matter of seconds we heard the explosive roar of a heavy motorcycle gunning, then varooming out of the parking lot.

"Get that!" Simon's eyes were wide with amazement.

"That was odd," Snow said. "What an elegant key!" She took the set from my limp hand, holding up an old key, long and wrought iron, with a curlicue in the handle and huge teeth in the business end: a real honest-to-God lock-the-door-against-invaders key. "What's the map say?" And she opened it, Simon craning his neck to look too. The mileage was clearly marked between checkpoints, and landmarks were indicated.

There was also a second small map, marked OFFICE, showing me how to get to Noonan's, just off the Grand Canal on Baggot Street.

"I didn't know Dublin had a canal," I remarked.

Snow shook her head dolefully. "The essential mother hath not changed. Let's put her to bed and hope for an improvement overnight."

They did. And oh, how quickly I was asleep, not troubling my conscience over the fact that I was leaving two fourteen-year-olds on their own in a hotel in a strange city.

Chapter II

Simon is a born organizer. The Renault was ready at the Hertz place at 9 in the morning. All I had to do was sign. I did try to explain how nervous I was about driving on the wrong side of the road, and that I'd be very careful, but Snow and Simon interrupted me. (Preserve the Image.)

So, planting Simon as map reader and conscience in the front seat, and sternly abjuring him to watch my left-hand side and keep me on and in the right, I drove off. And tried to shift with my right hand.

"Here, Mother, here," Simon said, grabbing my left hand and placing it on the gear shift.

By the time we were on a dual highway, I had the hang of shifting left-handedly and some notion of judging distance on the left side of the car. Just as well, because we turned off the wide road where minor errors were easily correctible onto a very narrow one with walls and high earthern banks, and winds and turns and cars coming down at me on the wrong side.

"There it is!" Simon cried, his arm across me indicating frantically to make a right turn.

"Where is what?" I cried, jamming on the brakes in reflex action. There was a screech behind me, and I shuddered, expecting the angry blast of a horn. When nothing happened, I bravely used the right-turn indicator and hastily did what I said I was going to do.

Swann's Lane was narrower and dirt.

"Are you positive it's Swann's Lane?" I had a glimpse of

incomprehensible syllables on a green-and-white sign imbedded in the low stone wall.

"Yeah, the first line's in Irish, Mother."

"This is nice!" Snow said.

I had the impression that it was, but I was watching the road to avoid the rocks and ruts.

"Look at the old horse! He's sweet!"

I got a glimpse of brown rump and tail, and then saw the cottages nestled into the cut of the hillside. And another one on the right side of the lane.

"Is that where we're going?" Snow was dismayed.

"Naw," Simon replied with contempt, "that one's where we're going," and he pointed to my left where a sandy-colored house loomed beyond some thick hedges and small trees, quite separate from the nest of cottages. As we drove up, a small sign at the corner of the wall confirmed that this was indeed Hillside Lodge.

The house had a forlorn look, unfinished sort of, despite the fact that (as I later learned) it was two hundred years old and a good example of farmhouse Georgian; I suppose I had envisioned a thatched cottage, charmingly rose-covered. There were gardens front and rear, and a lawn in front which had obviously been seeded when the house was built, because it had that velvet integrity so much prized. But the house wasn't at all what I had expected. Then I chided myself: Who was I to look gift houses in the face?

The front door was reached through a small glassed porch which was shelved with plants, all carefully potted and recently moistened. Someone was tending the place. There was a huge modern padlock on the front door and the older large keyhole. The door paint wasn't new, but it had been washed scrupulously clean.

Inside smelled musty. Well, Aunt Irene had been dead nearly two months. In front of us was a small hall with stairs, and doors on either side. To the right was a long sitting room, with fireplace, lace curtains, and the incredible combination of wall papers that I learned was an Irish failing. There wasn't much furniture: a Victorian two-seater, a modern fireside chair and hassock, a good mahogany table, a small desk, several lamps, an electric heater, and a few worn pieces of carpeting. Everything was immaculate, discounting the fine layer of dust.

"It's a pretty room," said Snow in a dubious tone.

"It could be."

To the left of the front door was a dining room with a nice old round table in its center, the buffet to one side, and a second fireplace with an enclosed stove. We could see beyond to the kitchen; the sink facing the front of the house was at a backbreaking height. Good God, how could any decent cook function? I groaned.

"Hey!" Snow stopped at the kitchen door in surprise.

I hurriedly joined her, and beheld a wonder. The sink might not have been altered, but beyond it were beautifully constructed cabinets, Formica-topped, a modern countertop fridge, a lovely gas range, and wall cabinets the length of the kitchen to the back door.

"Mom? More rooms back here," called Simon, and Snow and I, still flabbergasted by the splendid kitchen, turned back toward Simon's beckoning arm.

One of the two rooms was an office, with an old desk, an ancient file cabinet, several shelves of books (the dull-looking type), and some ledgers.

A snitch of carpet, well swept but its original motif dimmed by usage, led down the small hall to the solidly barred back door. Hooks and a boot rack held worn raiment of a durable farm type.

The second room was full of old trunks and boxes, a few discarded bits of harness, and a well-patched saddle and bridle.

"Maybe the old horse was hers?" asked Snow, her eyes brightening. I knew what she was thinking. She'd always wanted to ride.

High windows looked out on a back yard, the barn and stable, and the garage, in which the blue trunk of an old car was visible.

"Let's go upstairs," said Snow excitedly. I couldn't see why she was so eager, but I caught some of her contagion.

Except for the kitchen, there were evidences of what I'd call pride-poverty, and it distressed me to think that my great-aunt might have been in want during her last years. But that kitchen . . .

There were three bedrooms above.

"Three's all we need," cried Snow, bouncing up and down on the left-hand-room bed. "Wow! It's hard!" She was up and peeking into the little bathroom which fitted in the space over the front hall. "Well, everything we need."

The bathroom's fittings were old, except for the john. She flushed it experimentally, and a rush of water answered the summons.

"And indoors," I said. I'd half expected a privy out back.

The bedroom over the kitchen–dining room had obviously been my aunt's: the double bed was old cherry wood, with a beautifully crocheted spread, and the Victorian dresser and chair, the marble-topped, very shallow chests, and a huge ornate wardrobe were *good* pieces. The wide-planked floor was almost hidden by the one fine rug in the whole house: an Axminster with warm blues and reds. A good-sized electric heater stood against one wall, and Snow saw the electric-blanket attachment and whooped.

"How incongruous!"

"How practical!" I said, feeling relieved about Aunt Irene's last days.

The third bedroom was long and narrow, with a sloping ceiling. A recently built wardrobe stretched across one wall, but apart from that, only a narrow cot, a very small chest, and a chair occupied the room.

"I'd like this room," said Sim thoughtfully, his eyes roving about. He had to bend to see through the small rear window into the yard. "Say, there's a vegetable garden behind the stable. We eat!"

"I don't know if we can stay here yet, children."

"Why not?" asked Snow.

"There are such things as death duties, and I may be wise to take the first buyer that comes along with ready money in his hand."

"That girl didn't want you to talk to Kelley," Snow said.

"Mom has a point, Sis. We'll find out this afternoon from the lawyer. But I do like this room!"

"I'll switch beds with you," Snow said to her brother. "You like yours rock-hard."

"You sprawl." Simon pointed to the narrow cot. "You'd be on the floor half the time."

"Better than feeling like a corpse . . . whoops! Sorry, Mom."

For I'd given a shudder, not so much for her untimely simile as for my growing sense of trespass, unwelcome, and trouble. My right hand itched intolerably. I mastered the desire to scratch, because Sim and Snow would know I had one of my itches again.

A loud clanging, rattling, rumbling distracted us, and, curious, we all made for the front of the house. A huge construction bulldozer was churning up the lane, figuratively and literally, because you could see the tread marks on the unpaved road. I groaned. The springs on the Renault were not good enough to take that mess. Suddenly the bulldozer stopped. Or, I should say, was stopped. Craning my neck, I could see a stocky figure standing resolutely in its path.

Simon inched the window open. It was very tight, judging by his grunts and groans.

"This is a private road," Stalwart Defender was saying, "owned by Miss Teasey and not to be used by commercial vehicles."

"I was told to take Swann's Lane," said the driver, angrily gunning his engine for emphasis.

"By whom?"

"By Kerrigan. He owns the field there," and the man pointed up the lane. I couldn't see what lay at the end. But I'd all too often seen what havoc bulldozers made in fields before they got strewn with ticky-tacky boxes. Suddenly I very much did *not* want a development around this lovely pastoral setting.

"That wall also belongs to Miss Teasey."

"She's dead. Who're you?"

"I own that cottage. I also own a right of way on this lane. Kerrigan does not."

"I can't give a damn who owns what. I got orders to use this lane to get into that field!"

"Get out!" said Stalwart Defender. "Miss Teasey wouldn't give Kerrigan the right to spit on her land, much less use this lane. So get out!"

"You and who else'll make me?" and the driver began to fiddle ominously with his gears, activating the plow end.

"Hey, he'll run the guy down with that thing!" said Simon.

I started to reassure him, and then wasn't so certain myself. There was an obstinate jut to the driver's jaw, and he was beet-red with frustration.

"I'll make you, young man," I shouted from the window. "You just stay where you are!"

As I turned from the window, I heard a startled "Jasus, preserve me" from Stalwart Defender.

The three of us rattled down the steps. "Did either of you see a phone in the house?"

"There!" Simon pointed to a hand set on the small hall table. "And here!" He detached a shotgun from the wall above it.

I took the gun and started out the door, armed to defend my property, though I'd never held a weapon before in my life. I suppose the Irish air imbued me with this sort of courage and rebellion; certainly I'd never experienced it before.

"I'm Irene Teasey," I said, foursquare on the steps. Over the wall I could see the man on the seat of the bulldozer, but not Stalwart Defender. The driver looked startled at the sight of the gun in my hands, and my loyal cohorts. "That thing of yours is making a mess of my lane. You will kindly back down this instant or I'll have the police here immediately."

He was still goggling when I fumbled my way through the gate—rusty from long disuse—and onto the (*my*) lane. Maybe that's what added to my sense of power: owning the way into my own demesne.

"Now clear out! That thing's a mortal nuisance!"

He opened his mouth to protest.

"Simon, haven't you reached the police yet?"

That settled the driver, for he couldn't tell at this distance that Simon was only fourteen. A gun and two men to contend with, plus police interference, were more than he liked as odds. The bulldozer churned more mud as it rumblingly clanged its destructive way back down my lane.

"Your timing is fantastic, Mrs. Teasey," said the baritone voice of Stalwart Defender.

"Yes, thanks, even if I don't know the rest of the script," I replied, turning to get an eyeful of beard and body. Stalwart Defender was not much taller than I, and mostly shaggy beard and hair the last foot of that, but he looked big. He wore what I soon came to recognize as uniform for a lot of Irishmen: cord britches, heavy sweater, and a knit cap. He had very bright, light-green eyes, like Snow's, and well-shaped lips hidden in the face-fur. He also had hands!

"You spoke your lines with true conviction and have thus foiled the enemy!" I was accorded a slight bow and a wide grin.

"I'm the heir—heiress, I guess."

There was a startled blink of the green eyes.

"I really am Irene Teasey, you know."

"There's no doubt of it. I'm Kieron Thornton," only it sounded like "T'ornton." My hand was engulfed in one large, strong, scaly paw while the other neatly twitched the shotgun away from me. "Kerrigan may call the Garda. Swear on a stack of bibles that I had the shotgun. You've no permit."

"Huh?"

Snow and Simon now arrived to be presented.

"Say, how come we can stop that thing?" Snow asked, beaming at Stalwart Thornton, who politely ignored her and turned to me.

"You own the lane and you've the right to stop Kerrigan. I don't."

"Who's Kerrigan?" I asked.

Thornton hesitated. "You've not seen the solicitor?" He considered his next words. "He owns the fields beyond that wall," and Kieron pointed up the lane to its abrupt end. "He bought the property last fall, and was on to Irene to sell him the right of way through this lane. He's got prime development property there, and the owner of the only other way in, from the Glenamuck Road, is asking five thousand pounds for a right of way."

Simon whistled, and Thornton grinned at him.

"Yes, that's a lot of money. Irene suggested that if he paid *her* the five thousand pounds he'd save on the paving costs of a much shorter road."

"But you said my great-aunt wouldn't sell to him." I was rather confused.

Kieron Thornton grinned. "So I did. And so she wouldn't."

"Oh," I said, not much wiser.

"Then you don't intend to sell?"

"Sell what? The right of way?"

"No, the queendom."

"The queendom?"

Kieron Thornton frowned, as one will at an idiot child. "This"—his gesture included the lane, the house, the cottages, and the fields beyond—"is what your Great-aunt Irene called her queendom."

"I didn't know that." Then I caught his look of exasperated disapproval—so much like that mood of Teddie's that

I quaked and hastily began to explain. "Please, I only arrived yesterday. We've only just now looked through the house. I haven't a clue . . . And then there's this man bothering me with an offer."

Simon and Snow stepped closer to me, their protectiveness registering with Thornton, who made a slight bow of acknowledgment.

"I'm not talking out of turn by saying that this property is worth a great deal, Mrs. Teasey, to the wrong people. A great deal more, not necessarily in terms of money, to the right ones. I was very fond of your great-aunt. She asked me to protect her queendom"—and he smiled gently as he used the odd word—"until you got here. Then she asked me—" He stopped, changing his mind with a rueful smile.

"You were about to say, Mr. Thornton?"

"She asked me to help you, if I could and you would."

"My great-aunt and I never met. That's why I can't understand any of this."

"No more can others I could name."

"The relatives?" I asked, feeling sick with apprehension.

He nodded. "I won't say more on this subject, Mrs. Teasey. My judgments are colored by my partiality for your aunt. You may have an entirely different view."

"Wait . . ." I put my hand on his arm, for he'd given me a little bow and taken a step away. "At least show me what I've inherited, for good or bad. You'd know and, apart from the house, and this lane, I don't."

"Your solicitor can tell you."

"And undoubtedly will, but in an office with a surveyor's map or some such two-dimensionality. That doesn't tell me *what*," and I held up my hands to express a need for tactile assimilation.

He gave me a long look, then shrugged and turned toward the house. "As you will."

He led us back into the house long enough to replace the shotgun, warning the twins to stick to the story that he had held the weapon. I was to apply instantly at the local Garda station—by the traffic lights in Cabinteely—for a permit.

"If it was Aunt Irene's gun, how can you use it?"

"I've a permit. More than one person can have a permit on the same gun, you see, but everyone who uses the gun must have a permit for that gun. Complicated. And if the troubles up north get worse, you may be asked to surrender it to the Garda."

That made Simon bristle. "Surrender my gun to the police?"

Very politely, Kieron Thornton asked Simon how old he was, and then said that the age for gun permits was eighteen.

Simon muttered under his breath. He had been mad crazy to own a gun ever since that weekend in Pennsylvania with some of Teddie's friends who'd had a skeet shoot. Simon had shown a tremendous aptitude for marksmanship, outclassing his father, which hadn't set too well (Preserve the Image!). I'd managed to point out to Simon that he couldn't very well have a skeet shoot in suburban Westfield, but I'd been backed into promising that if he ever lived in the country, he could have a rifle. Well, we wouldn't be staying in Ireland that long.

Kieron Thornton knew the house and property well. He spared us the worst of the muddy parts and a very close look at the four cottages nestled in the hillside. These were rented, and he said that I'd have a chance to see the tenants later on. He owned the cottage he lived in and the land within its fences, having purchased the place from my great-aunt three years ago.

Now he led us past the house and the barn, which was well stocked with hay and straw, to the flourishing vegetable garden.

"I planted that for Irene. She wasn't well enough, and the lack worried her." His unspoken comment was that he'd known that my great-aunt wouldn't survive to enjoy the produce, but he'd humored her in the planting.

"Yummy. Fresh vegetables," said Snow. She was devastatingly pert all through the tour, ignoring my disapproving looks and Simon's disgusted snorts. However, she failed to attract Kieron Thornton's amused interest, and I was beginning to think that Ireland might be very beneficial for my precocious daughter if the males over twenty-one kept reminding Snow that she was still a child.

"Now," Kieron said, "the land extends another three acres beyond this," and he laid his hand on the earth-and-stone fence, "to the west, and down to the road, from there to the field across the lane. There're natural springs, plus the stream."

"Whose is the horse?" asked Snow, less affectedly.

"Your mother's . . . now. Horseface."

"Horseface?" Both Snow and Simon whooped with laughter.

Kieron laughed too, a nice rich real laugh. "I believe he has another name in the registry, but that's what 'he answers to."

"My aunt rode him?" He looked very big.

"Yes indeed, right up to her first stroke, and gently when she'd recovered completely from it. He's about twenty now, I'd say. In their prime, Irene hunted him." Kieron turned to me. "Call him. He answers to his name."

"Me?" But I raised my voice. To my utter surprise, the beast raised his head instantly, looked unerringly in my direction, and whinnied.

"You see, he does know his name," Thornton said as the horse trotted eagerly to the pasture fence.

"Hey, Horseface," called Snow, and she and Simon went off to meet him, gathering fresh handfuls of grass to feed him.

I caught a suspicious gleam in Thornton's eyes, which I couldn't account for. I was about to question him when we were startled by the angry blasting of a car horn.

"Hmmm. I was expecting that," said Thornton, taking me by the arm and guiding me back to the house. "The visitor is impatient," he added as the horn continued to break the pleasant soft noises of the countryside.

"Who is it?"

"Can't you guess?"

I stopped short. "Mr. Kerrigan?" Kelley and now Kerrigan? And with no real idea of what to do! "Mr. Thornton, couldn't you . . ."

"Mrs. Teasey," and he gave me a stern, reproving look, "you own this property. Admittedly, I 'have caused you an embarrassment by more or less forcing you to stop that bulldozer. But I knew that was what your aunt would have done. I did not know you were in the house. You may, after an appraisal of the situation, want to let Kerrigan have that right of way. I only ask that you wait until you've had time to arrive at a fair decision. Or maybe you Yanks like acres of houses all around you." He had managed to hurry me through the yard, and now he gave me a push toward the kitchen door.

"Oh, don't leave me!"

He gave me an amused look, disengaging my hands from his arm. "Believe me, you don't need *my* help." And he was away.

The car horn was still blaring, in a fashion guaranteed to irritate, and I was already annoyed at Kieron Thornton for landing me in such a compromising situation with an unknown and infuriated man. I raced around the side of the house to the front. A man was standing on the driver's side of a blue Jag, bent slightly so that he could lean on the horn. The car, the arrogance of the action, plus memories of other helpless moments like this, combined to give me unusual courage.

"Stop that infernal racket," I shouted, and it was cut off instantly.

The man who stared at me across the blue Jag top was as handsome as sin. Sandy-haired with a well-trimmed, slightly darker moustache and very black eyebrows, my importunate caller was elegantly dressed in a blazer and slim trousers, a trendy patterned shirt, and a solid-color cravat.

"You're not Irene Teasey," he said in a flat, surprised voice.

"I most certainly am."

Suddenly his angry expression turned into a smile. "Oh, but of course. You're the niece. The American."

"Yes, I'm the American *great*-niece."

"Well," and he walked toward me, all smiles, hand extended. "Welcome to Ireland—*cead mille failte*. That means a hundred thousand welcomes, Miss Teasey."

"Was that why you were blasting the horn? A royal salute?"

"I'm Shamus Kerrigan. I'm afraid there's been a bit of a misunderstanding."

"Was that your frightful bulldozer thing that tore up my lane?" I asked, trying hard to be severe, for Kerrigan had the sort of charm that is very difficult to resist.

He turned to survey the damage as if he hadn't just had to tool the Jaguar very carefully over the ruts.

"I do apologize. But it would only be the one transit.

Once the dozer is in the field, it wouldn't have to come out."

"Oh?" I looked pointedly at the stout stone wall. "How had you planned to get across that?"

"Well, rather, through it," he admitted, smiling ingenuously. "Of course, we'd build the wall back up again behind it."

"What comes in must go out, Mr. Kerrigan."

"Oh, I expect to get permission to use the other road."

"All the way from Glenamuck?" I asked, delighting in the surprise in his face at my knowledge, however spotty it was. "Surely you know that this is a private lane, Mr. Kerrigan, and that even one transit—much less knocking down my wall—constitutes trespass?"

He nodded and then smiled reassuringly. "Actually, I did have permission."

"From whom?" I was suddenly suspicious of Kieron Thornton. I'd only his word that my great-aunt hadn't wanted Kerrigan to have the right of way. Maybe the solicitor . . .

"From a relative. You see after Miss Teasey died . . ." and he looked appropriately regretful.

"No false condolences, please. I'd never met my great-aunt."

"I had, Mrs. Teasey," and there was suddenly nothing of the suppliant in Mr. Kerrigan's manner. "She was a most admirable woman."

Because she'd refused him? I wondered privately.

"I tried to find out who had inherited the property so I could have my solicitor make the proper application. I've got a lot of money tied up in that land."

There was now a flash of impatience in his voice, which he covered instantly with his facile charm.

"Yes, that would be a consideration," I said agreeably.

"So," and his smile was hearty again, "when I learned that it was yourself, and you in America and no one knew where, I tried to find someome in the family who could give me permission to use the lane."

"If *I* had inherited the property, Mr. Kerrigan, none of the relations here had any authority to give you permission for anything." I wasn't certain of that, but, by the expression in his eyes, I was within my rights.

"That's why I apologize," and he bowed with contrition.

"Because the relative assured me that he had the right to grant me the one use of the lane."

"Who was the so obliging relative?"

He smiled again. "I don't think that would be fair, do you, until this has all been sorted out?"

"Fair to whom, Mr. Kerrigan?"

He smiled more broadly. "You wouldn't consider my using the lane today, since I've the equipment laid on and all?"

I shook my head, smiling back. "I'm so sorry."

"Oh, you're a wise one, you are," he said finally, the grin still firmly in place. "But I feel we could sort the problems out," and he nodded at the battered road and the stone fence, "and very soon. Say, this evening? At half seven? Over dinner?"

"A very good suggestion." I emphasized the last word slightly, and saw that he took my meaning. "I'm at the Montrose." By the expression in his eyes, I guessed that he knew that.

"You're certain about the dozer?" he asked, with winning wistfulness.

"Positive. You're taking an unfair advantage of me, Mr. Kerrigan, for all your thousand welcomes."

"You Yanks!" I wasn't certain if that was a compliment or not. Nonetheless, he left, bumping the Jag carefully over the ruts.

Snow and Simon erupted out of the hedge where they'd been hiding.

"Who he?"

"Didn't you hear all?"

"Arrived late."

"And why didn't you come out?"

Simon shrugged. "You were handling him just great."

"Hmmmm."

"So we all get a free dinner tonight, huh?" asked Snow, her eyes wide.

"Yes indeedy. This pore li'l ol' Amurrican needs chaperones from that big Irish woof!"

Snow giggled.

"Sure has a beautiful Jag," and Simon whistled softly. "Say, Mom, that car in Aunt Irene's garage is a Mercedes! It's in beautiful condition inside. It's up on blocks and all, and the tires are there too."

"Really?"

"Horseface is just darling, Mom. Can I learn how to ride him? I mean, is twenty years too old for a horse to be ridden?"

Chapter III

I suppose our fate had already been decided that morning but I don't see such events with an awareness of their immediate and future significance. Teddie always did, and my obtuseness irritated him. Just as well he was safely three thousand miles from me—and someone else's problem now.

We went through the house again, peering into cupboards this time. And bare they were. I kept telling myself that it was because no one had been tenanting the place that there was only a dusting of sugar in the bowl, a half cup of flour in the canister, a small tin of curried beans, an inch of ketchup, a fingernail of salt and the same of pepper. The fridge had been cleared and unplugged. Snow turned it on with a dramatically uttered "There! We can shop later. That'll be fun."

"Expensive, too," I said, knowing my daughter's proclivity for impulse buying. However, we did have to eat.

Snow was rattling on enthusiastically about redecorating, which would mean more outlay of cash. I *could* see the merit of her suggestions (take a positive attitude, Rene). A touch here, some paint there, new curtains at those windows, some judiciously placed new carpet, and new vinyl and paint in the kitchen would give the house a much more cheerful atmosphere. Simon volunteered to paint the outside trim, Snow to weed the neat garden, and both were so generally enthusiastic that by lunchtime I could relax and appreciate the potential charm of the house.

I locked up and we piled into the car. As we bumped down the lane, Simon cursed the bulldozer and I wondered which of my relatives had had the audacity to give Shamus Kerrigan permission.

On the off chance that Brian Kelley would be haunting the hotel, we ate in town, at a charming restaurant just off St. Stephen's Green. Then we did some gawking down Grafton Street. People hurried, as on other streets, but as many more sort of lounged down the sidewalks, utterly unconcerned about reaching their ultimate destinations. Double-decker buses roared down the narrow street, occasionally puffing hot exhaust around our legs, but not with the horrid urgency of the New York counterpart. Altogether, Dublin was exercising much charm to soothe this savage colonial breast.

We arrived on the solicitor's street, and I suddenly felt very Georgette Heyer, looking at the beautiful Georgian fronts with the lovely fanlights above the doors. Finding the right number was not hard, but finding a spot to park the Renault did take time.

Michael Noonan looked more like a jet-set playboy than a solicitor, but, fortunately for my peace of mind, his manner and cogent explanations (as far as he went) dispelled any further comparison. He wore his dark hair short on top and close cut but long in the back, with well-trimmed sideburns, which added to his rakish appearance. His eyes behind the heavy black-framed glasses missed nothing of my appearance or my children's as he welcomed us each with a firm handshake. Despite myself, I looked down at his hands, as the children did, and knew their opinion before I saw it in their eyes. He had hands.

He also had brains.

Ceremoniously I tendered him my identification and my grandfather's naturalization papers, which clearly established Granda as the late Irene Teasey's brother Michael Maurice Teasey.

He handed me a parcel of long, folded documents. "Your copy of the will, which makes you principal heir and co-executrix with this office, myself in particular, the authenticated list of the belongings in the house and on the property, and their estimated value for death duties."

I dutifully opened the uppermost document, and flinched at the whereases and second parts and all that overwhelmingly confusing legalese.

"There were other bequests?"

"Some minor ones in the will, and I've a letter here for you which your great-aunt directed me to hand you personally," and I received a square envelope of heavy paper. "And here"—he was passing me another long, legal-feeling document—"is the trust-fund report."

"Trust fund?"

"Yes, and it ought to more than settle the death duties. We were exceedingly lucky with the appraisals, despite the fact that your great-aunt's property had appreciated a good deal over the past few years. The duties could have been atrocious, so I'm very relieved that the fund should prove ample." He saw my amazement and grinned. "I'm sure it's a common enough practice in the States too, Mrs. Teasey. Provided the trust is set up, as this one was, five years prior to decease, the money is tax-free."

"Excuse me, you mean I've been the heir that long?"

Mr. Noonan smiled very kindly. "Yes, Mrs. Teasey, you have. Certainly ever since I took over your great-aunt's affairs, seven years ago."

"Well!" The twins breathed out "Wows!"

"Mrs. Teasey? Don't ever feel that you have usurped anyone else's claims."

"Well, it was a great surprise to me. I never knew my great-aunt at all. I mean . . ."

"She knew about you. And she had good reasons for leaving her"—he smiled again, with mischief in his eyes—"her queendom to you. Now, we haven't received the exact figure for the death duties yet. They must be paid within this year, but not to worry. You've the trust."

"Then it's unlikely that I'd have to sell the property to satisfy the duties?" And why were there no supplies in the house?

He looked startled. "Good Lord, no. That was the whole purpose of the trust fund."

"Is the property intrinsically valuable, Mr. Noonan?"

"Yes, quite." He riffled some papers.

"I don't need the exact figure. I was just asking because Mr. Kelley—"

"Brian Kelley?" There was surprise as well as steel in Mr. Noonan's query.

"Yes. He was most insistent about seeing me."

"Did you?" Mr. Noonan's hands were suspended in 'his paper search.

"No. I decided against it. I didn't like his looks. Nor his insistence."

Relief smoothed the crows'-feet from the corners of Mr. Noonan's eyes. "How the devil did he know you were in town? You only arrived yesterday morning."

"I wouldn't know," I said, although all three of us had a fair idea from the pleading look in the receptionist's eyes. She had been the motorcyclist with the keys to my . . . queendom.

"If it had been at all possible, Mrs. Teasey, I would have met you at the airport. But you gave me no warning of your arrival." Mr. Noonan rattled the papers before him in a testy fashion.

"The children had finished school, there were seats on a flight, and so . . . we just came."

"As well you did. All things being equal, you'd best take possession of the house instantly. I mean by that, physical possession. There is a variety of conflicting interests."

"One of them named Kerrigan?" I asked.

He dropped the papers and slapped both palms against the desk, staring at me with amazement.

"Kelley *and* Kerrigan?"

"Hmmm. I assume that they're both prime contenders?"

He cleared his throat and said, with a slight, unhappy smile, "Essentially but not actually. To be blunt, Mrs. Teasey, almost every one of your great-aunt's adult relatives, and she had innumerable, believes that he or she should have been left the estate rather than yourself."

"Me too."

"Your great-aunt knew what she was doing, and, believe me, no matter what you might hear to the contrary, had every right to dispose of her property and possessions as she wished."

He was so emphatic that I was instantly more apprehensive. Teddie always said that I have no powers of dissembling, which he thought remarkable, since I had acted. He never could understand that I was playing a particular part then, whereas I was just me off the stage. My thoughts were, as usual, painfully obvious.

Mr. Noonan leaned toward me. "Now, not to worry, Mrs. Teasey. Your position is secure."

"It isn't her position that worries Mother," said Snow in her most protective manner. "We've just got her through a very messy divorce scene, and she doesn't need the greedy-relatives bit."

Mr. Noonan eyed my outspoken daughter with, I thought, more approval than prejudice.

"I think you've no cause for worry."

I heard, as clear as his spoken words, the tag "not yet."

He cleared his throat. "Now, how did you encounter Shay Kerrigan?"

"Trying to get a bulldozer up the lane."

"Oh. He did try."

"You knew he would?"

"Might. He was rather anxious to get in touch with the heir. My letter to you about his offer must have crossed your coming. I had arranged with one of the residents on the lane—"

"Mr. Thornton?"

"Naturally, you've had the chance to meet him, too."

"Oh yes, he actually stopped the bulldozer this morning. I just seconded it."

"And you landed here yesterday at noontime? Well!"

"I don't usually operate at such a high level, Mr. Noonan," I felt obliged to say, and then saw that he was more amused than critical.

"Mr. T'ornton showed us around the estate," Snow said, mimicking the accent. She went on, in one of her maliciously guileless moods, "He had a shotgun." I stared appreciatively at my daughter, and so did her brother. (Create the Image?) "But it was Mother who made the guy take that thing back down. You should've seen what it did to the lane."

"I'm sorry to hear that Shay Kerrigan would try that." Mr. Noonan was annoyed. He had the intense look of a man swearing silently.

"He came later . . . in person," Snow said brightly. "To apologize."

"Be quiet, dear," I said to her, and meant it. "I did have the right to refuse him the use, didn't I? He gave me some nonsense about having applied to a relative for permission."

"What?" Mr. Noonan was now furious. "Who?"

"He wouldn't say. But maybe I can find out at dinner tonight. He's taking"—I paused and then indicated the twins —"us."

Noonan was sharp, and his laughing eyes applauded my stratagem.

"If you can find out which relative it was, it might be helpful later."

"You mean, there may be litigation about this?"

"That's possible, Mrs. Teasey. As I said, your great-aunt's little queendom is now quite valuable. Where pounds and pence are concerned, blood has a tendency to curdle."

I groaned. I wasn't certain that I was up to more nasty court proceedings and complaints and countercharges. Not twice in one year!

"You can, of course, sell out as soon as the will is probated."

His expression plainly told me that he'd be disappointed if I chose that course.

"Your great-aunt rather hoped that you'd like to take your time about selling—if that was your final decision."

The letter from Great-aunt Irene burned in my hand. I was both reluctant and eager to open it.

"Mr. Noonan? About my great-aunt . . . Did she . . . I mean . . . she didn't linger or go without anything?"

He shook his head. "No. The final stroke was quick. She'd had one last December. Thornton found her and rushed her to hospital. Saved her life. She'd pretty well recovered by March, and was getting around much as usual when she'd the second stroke. That disabled her completely, and a week later the third one took her life. She was a delightful person," and Mr. Noonan's smile was that of regret.

"You liked her," said Snow.

"Yes, Miss Stanford, I liked her very much. She was a most unusual woman."

Then he turned his keen eyes on me. "I know substantially what's in that letter, Mrs. Teasey. I hope that you'll find it agreeable to you, and possible, but I am required to advise you that you are in no way legally constrained to follow those instructions. As soon as the will is probated, you can sell the estate to whomever you choose."

"And I do have the right to refuse Mr. Kerrigan the use of the lane?"

"Yes, indeed. That's private property. Yours . . . or yours legally . . . when the will has been probated."

"Until then?"

"The use of the lane was denied Kerrigan by Miss Teasey, and her order stands until yours rescinds or reinforces it. But you can't do anything until the will is probated."

"Mr. Noonan, in simple language, how much is the property worth?"

"It's still not simple, Mrs. Teasey. You could probably sell the house and its immediate gardens, the stableyard, and the back field for, roughly, say twenty-five thousand pounds." Snow whistled, and I shushed her. "Mr. Thornton owns his cottage and the two roods of land on which it stands. There are four other cottages, now renting from one to seven pounds a month. I do know that Mrs. Teasey was offered three thousand pounds for one of them recently, but with sitting tenants in all four the value is considerably reduced."

I thought dazedly of the sturdy cottages and then of the modern semidetached places selling for twice that and wondered.

Snow frowned. "A pound a month is less than three bucks!" She was round-eyed with indignant surprise.

I gathered from Mr. Noonan's expression that the rent *was* ridiculously low.

"I believe Miss Teasey mentions that offer in her letter to you. Now, the acreage on the roadside would bring in about three thousand pounds an acre."

"Three thousand pounds?" I was stunned at the difference in three dollars a month rent for a cottage already built that might *sell* for three thousand pounds, and then the same sum for just the land!

"That's sixty-five hundred dollars an acre, Mom," Snow said helpfully. "And you could charge Mr. Kerrigan a bundle for a right of way if he's getting that kind of money for houses."

"Hush, Snow, you're distracting me."

"Mother isn't interested in the *money*," Simon said, entering the discussion.

"I'll bet all the relatives are, not to mention Kelley and Kerrigan," continued my irrepressible daughter. "Those Jags cost money."

Mr. Noonan chuckled again. "Your daughter has the way of it, Mrs. Teasey. Of course, nothing can be done until the will has been probated."

"You keep saying that, Mr. Noonan. Is there another problem?"

"Technically, no." He leaned forward, his eyes intent on my face, an exercise I found rather disconcerting. "Read your great-aunt's letter, Mrs. Teasey, before you make any further assumptions or decisions. Think carefully about what she asks of you. Miss Teasey was a wonderful person. She was ahead of her times in some ways, but she had certain . . . shall we say, peeves, with which you may not be in sympathy. You are, you say, seeing Shamus Kerrigan this evening. Undoubtedly Mr. Kelley will be on to you again with his proposition. I don't know whom he represents in this matter, but there's no harm in listening to both of them. And you can do nothing until probate is filed." He smiled reassuringly.

"Which is my defense and alibi?"

"If you choose."

"How do I get a permit for the shotgun?"

He looked startled.

"I come from pioneer stock. There may be Injuns," I said in a deadpan voice. "No, actually, Mr. Thornton said that I shouldn't wave the gun about until I have a permit."

"I don't believe you'll need a gun against Shay Kerrigan, Mrs. Teasey," and his eyes were dancing with suppressed amusement. "However, speak to the sergeant at the Cabinteely Garda station. You're over twenty-one, and you have a place to shoot. There'll be no problem. Miss Teasey felt obliged to . . . discourage . . . ah . . . ."

"Invaders?" asked Snow. "Invaders of our queendom, threatening to lay siege?"

"With only a shotgun?" asked Simon. "Nuts!"

Michael Noonan chuckled as he rose, and extended his hand to me. "After you've read the letter and the will, please don't hesitate to phone me if you've any questions."

"That's kind of you, Mr. Noonan, because I've a feeling that I've inherited a lot of problems and will need many answers."

His smile corroborated my assumption and did my morale no good. Then he courteously ushered us out.

"You know, Mom," said Snow as we got into the Renault, "we don't know that much more than we did when we got here."

"He does," said Simon with a laugh. "Maybe the letter tells all."

"Hmmmm. I'm not, I repeat, *not* opening that letter till we get back to the hotel."

"And close to some Dutch courage," said Snow, as I gave first Simon and then her a forbidding look.

When we got back to the hotel, there were five messages from Brian Kelley asking me to phone him as soon as possible. The last was timed three minutes before our return.

"Read the letter first, Mom," said Snow, frowning at the message slips.

I turned to the girl at the desk. "If Mr. Kelley calls before I get a chance to catch my breath . . . please, I'm still not in?"

"Ah, not to worry, Mrs. Teasey." Obviously she did not much care for Mr. Kelley.

The twins ensconced themselves on either side of me on the lounge settee so that we all read the letter together.

The letter, dated March 3, was penned in such a beautiful copperplate handwriting that I admired the look of it before I got down to the reading.

My dear Namesake,

I had so hoped to be able to meet you, for it was my intention to invite you and your children to visit me this summer. But dear Mr. Fleetwood is so cheerful, and careful to say nothing to the point, that I realize I will not have another reprieve.

Now I must let dry pen and ink speak lines I had so often rehearsed. We have much more in common, my dear Irene, than our names. Originally I willed you my little property for the sake of our mutual name. You were the only child in three generations and five lots named for me. I confess I was inordinately pleased that you resumed your maiden name after your divorce. Thank goodness such relief was permitted *you*.

"What does she mean by that?" asked Snow, who was reading faster than Simon and I.

"Hush and read!" said her brother.

"Hush, the pair of you!"

I am now more sure than ever of the fitness of making you heir to my queendom. I shall try to set as much in order as I can in the time left to me, but you are American and I am confident that your upbringing will help you solve what problems remain with good Yankee common sense.

You could do worse, dear Irene, than to make this queendom your home and to remain here in Ireland. You will not need to depend on any man. Carefully managed, this realm can give you independence wherever you wish to live, if not in Ireland.

If you are not of a mind to stay, however, do me three favours: do not sell my faithful horse to the knackers but have him put down and buried in the back pasture. Ann Purdee will know how to go about that. Unlike the horse, you cannot shoot my Mercedes, which is a valuable old car. But do sell it to someone who cares for the car herself, not merely her monetary value. Gerry Hegarty, for instance.

My third request may seem to you to be spiteful. I am not at liberty to divulge the reasons behind this, since they affect someone else's reputation, but do not give access up the lane to Shamus Kerrigan.

"Wow!" said Snow. "That's laying it on the line."
"Yeah, but not why," said Simon.
What Aunt Irene hadn't said, but what I felt, was a curious anger in her wording.

If you decide to stay and circumstances permit, please continue the present tenants of Swallow and Lark cottages for as long as need be. You will understand very quickly and, if you are the girl I take you to be, agree. George Boardman, however, is quite willing, and able, to give £3,000 for Finch or Thrush cottages, whichever comes vacant first. Michael Noonan can help you secure them, but I have had to let the proceedings drop to keep death duties down.

I know that you will meet discord among the relatives—yours too, though mercifully removed by distance and marriage—for few will be pleased with the disposition of my property. There were several of the youngest generation who deserve something of me for their kindness and friendship, but for me to single

them out would be unkind. When the swearing ceases
and they have turned to other trivia, you may care to
ease circumstances. By that time, you'll know who I
mean.

You are, my dear Irene, the only logical successor
to my queendom. God bless and keep you.

Your affectionate aunt,
Irene.

"Long live Queen Irene the Second," said Snow, but her
tone was by no means facetious.

"She didn't want that bulldozer up the lane."

"Yeah, but I wonder why," said Snow darkly. "As if we'd
put down that lovely Horseface! I couldn't!" She glared
dramatically at me.

"I like her," said Simon, having deliberated on the matter.
"I mean, a woman who can recognize that a car has a personality, isn't just a mechanical object. I don't like this bit
about the relatives, though. Five lots? That sounds like too
many, and we've got a horde as it is."

"Cheer up, Simon, maybe they'll stay away in their droves
and dozenses. And besides, we're not staying long."

"Ah, Mom, you promised." They both rounded on me.

"*I* did no such thing." Before I knew it, I was embroiled in
a series of entreaties and promises and evasions (on my part)
that lasted through checking out of the hotel and driving
back to Hillside Lodge. But I held up the stream of argument long enough to tell the nice desk clerk to inform Mr.
Kelley that I had checked out and would phone him tomorrow.

"He may want to know where he can reach you," she said
with diplomatic subtlety.

"Then tell him I'm staying at the home of a relative."

I was halfway to Hillside Lodge before I realized that I'd
told Shamus Kerrigan to meet me at the Montrose. Snow
said that was no big problem—we'd get settled in and go
back and meet Mr. Kerrigan in the lobby.

We found a small general store and picked up milk in plastic bottles (you had to give glass ones to get glass ones),
eggs, butter, bread (a crescent loaf that smelled delectable
and some good Irish brown bread), bacon, Coke, and instant coffee. We'd do a major shopping the next morning.

And so, bag and baggage, we took possession of a queendom.

Fortunately, the lights worked, and so did the telephone. (I found out much later that I owed those services to the motorcycle girl—penance?) We all made beds together from lavender-scented linens found in the closet with the hot-water tank. It was stone cold, and I couldn't figure out where it got heated.

"Simon," I said in despair, for I longed for a hot bath before braving Kerrigan, "go ask Mr. Thornton how to get hot water. He's likely to know."

"May I help you, Mrs. Teasey?" asked a soft voice from the back door.

In America one hears that the typical Irish colleen is a reasonably buxom, apple-cheeked miss, constantly smiling, so this slim, tiny, solemn girl with the delicate features and coloring of an equally typical Dresden shepherdess was a surprise. In fact, nothing about Ann Purdee was ever what it seemed.

"If you know how to get the water hot, yes," I told her.

She smiled in a brief, polite way and stepped quickly past us into the dining room, where she knelt by the fireplace.

"This stove will heat the boiler," she said, lighting a match from the package on the top of the enclosed fireplace and deftly inserting it. Flames licked around white cubes. "If you open the door in a few moments, so, once the firelighters have taken, the draft will start a nice blaze. You'll have hot water in an hour. If you aren't going to use too much, you must bank the fire with slack." She saw the uncomprehending look on our faces. "To the left of the kitchen door is the coal bunker. The small pebbly stuff is slack, and you use it for slowing a fire down." She plunged the shovel into the coal bucket and showed us the fine stuff. "Would you be wanting the beds made and all?" she asked, wiping her hands carefully on her apron.

I expect the twins had checked those hands first off, but I was appalled at how bone-thin they were, red and cracked from hard work and cold water. A thin gold band on the third finger rolled loosely up and down between the knuckles.

"That much we figured out," Snow said with a little giggle, and there was an answering gleam in Ann Purdee's lovely blue eyes.

"We've old-fashioned ways of doing things here, don't you know? No bother once you've the way of it, but strangelike at first. Kieron T'ornton said you'd been by this morning."

What she was hoping to hear was as plain as day to me.

"We'll be staying on a while, Mrs. Purdee," and I was surprised when she flushed. "I want to take my time before I decide what to do."

"I want to learn how to ride Horseface," said Snow, bubbling into the sudden, rather awkward silence. "He isn't too old, is he?"

Some of the stiff stillness went out of Mrs. Purdee's body as she looked at Snow. "I can teach you for sure, he's not that old. I used to exercise Horseface," she told me, "when Miss Teasey couldn't. I've been taking care of him till you came. Not that there's much taking care like, with him on grass now. He's a grand old lad, you know."

Abruptly she reached into the pocket of her housecoat. "I have the rent for you, Mrs. Teasey. I was going to send it on to Mr. Noonan again, but as *you're* here . . . " and she put a pound note and a column of coins on the dining-room table.

"Oh, thank you." I was somehow embarrassed, never having been a landlady before. "Do you need a receipt or anything?"

Ann Purdee was watching me with a very disconcerting keenness. She swallowed now before she answered.

"No." She gulped. "There's no lease, you see."

"Is one needed? I mean, if my great-aunt rented to you . . . and I don't know anything about horse keeping, and . . . " The relief in her eyes was so intense that I became almost as upset as she'd been. "Besides, Aunt Irene specifically said that you should stay on."

"That's what worries me, Mrs. Teasey. You shouldn't feel yourself bound by what herself said."

"And why not? My aunt seems to have had good reasons for most of the things she did. I don't know the setup here, and I'm not about to make arbitrary changes."

From Ann Purdee's expression, I gathered that reassurance didn't reassure.

"I can't stop long now, for the bahbee's waking any time now. May I come back tomorrow? For there're some things I'm to tell yourself alone. But sure, you've only to step down to the cottage if you need to know anything like, where things are and all."

When she'd slipped out, I looked down at the money. Two pounds was roughly five dollars, and that didn't seem like a lot of money for a cottage that'd sell for three thousand pounds cash, but I knew that two pounds was a great deal of money to Ann Purdee.

I didn't have time to think about that now. It was almost seven o'clock. I sent the children scurrying to change into something elegant, and I slipped into what Snow considered the most acceptable of my new clothes. "You gotta be a Merry Widow, Ma!" (Construct the Image?)

We arrived at the Montrose at 7:20, parking the Renault. The receptionist told me that Mr. Kelley had indeed phoned back, and had been rather upset about my sudden departure. He'd wanted to know which relative had picked us up and what she had looked like.

"Ahha," said Snow with a chortle, "a 'she' he suspects." She made another of those incredible noises acquired from watching too many late horror shows.

The receptionist tried not to giggle.

"I'm sorry if he was unpleasant," I told the girl.

She shrugged. "Not to worry, Mrs. Teasey. I'm used to his sort."

Simon saw the blue Jag before I did, and dug me in the ribs warningly.

"Honey, you'll break my ribs doing that one day," I told him, rather more irritably than the situation warranted. "You're so strong . . . " I was scared stiff about meeting Shamus-Shay Kerrigan. Unless I have the lines, I can't act the part. And I'm never at ease with ruthless men. When I realized that Kerrigan must have a lot of money tied up in acres that he couldn't reach, I could see myself being ruthlessed. Probably not in front of my children . . . I was very glad to have their supporting presence.

Kerrigan was not. In fact, he was dumbfounded, a condition he undoubtedly seldom found himself in. He covered quickly, I'll give him credit, and professed to be delighted, saying all kinds of flattering things about my youth with two such adult children, and yes of course, he realized that I couldn't very well leave them alone on their second night in Ireland, but if he'd known he'd've brought his young

nephew as company. So I was doubly glad that I hadn't told
him.

He seated Snow in the Jag with the same courtesy he accorded me—a ploy which went down well with her—and
chatted amiably with Simon about the performance level of
the Jaguar as opposed to a Mercedes 220, which my son
had previously considered his favorite foreign car.

"We're dining at the Lamb Doyle's," Shamus Kerrigan
said as we wound past slower traffic. "Superb view of Dublin in the evening. You haven't been in Ireland before, have
you, Mrs. Teasey?"

I told him no, and then we bandied the usual "Good
flight? No customs problems?" et cetera back and forth until
we turned on to a less settled road and began to climb up
the hill, which he identified as Ticknock, the site of a
mysterious murder in the twenties. Then we were at the restaurant, which did have a commanding view of the city.
And of all the developments sprouting up in the near val-
ley: row after row after appalling row with postage-stamp
sized space between them.

I began to see why someone would offer £3,000 for one
of my aunt's—no, my—cottages. Shamus Kerrigan's bulldozer simply wasn't going to rape the land around me if I
could stop it.

Lamb Doyle's was not, thank goodness, modern Americana. We went upstairs to the cocktail bar and settled down
to admire the panorama and have a pre-dinner drink. The
handsome headwaiter came around with leatherbound men-
us, and Snow assumed her blasé act. I could see that Simon
wanted to kick her too, but I managed to catch her eye before her brother's critical expression irritated her. She got
my message loud and clear, and subsided.

All the while Mr. Kerrigan set out to charm us. And he
did. I noticed that Simon was watching the man's hands,
and realized that this criterion was evidently not giving the
expected result. Well, there's always an exception.

"Have you any vacation plans in mind, Mrs. Teasey?"
Shay Kerrigan asked me when he'd given our orders.

"Oh, we let our fingers do some walking—on the maps
—last night," I told him.

"I hope you'll do more than that," he said eagerly, leaning
toward me across the table. In his enthusiasm, his deep

blue eyes sparkled, crinkling at their corners when he smiled and widening for emphasis as he talked. He was a great one for the wide hand gesture. (*Must* Snow stare at his hands so?) "We're a poor country, industrially speaking, Mrs. Teasey, and way behind the rest of the world, but we've got some of the most beautiful scenery. If you go nowhere else, you ought to go down to Dingle, do the Ring of Kerry, particularly this time of year, though it's beautiful year long. Then turn north toward Galway—don't let the song turn you off, because it's all true. Sunset in Galway Bay has to be seen. Oh, grand"—he broke off to return a greeting—"how's yourself?" When the man smiled pleasantly at us and moved on, Shamus Kerrigan remarked that he owned the restaurant. "I used to race motorbikes with Reg, before he gave it up."

If Simon wanted anything in the world more than a gun, it was a motorbike.

"*You* ride motorcycles?" Simon shot me a glance that said "You see, good guys ride bikes too."

Kerrigan grinned at Simon's reaction. "Got a Bultaco 250 cc right now."

"A trial bike?" Simon was ecstatic.

"Spot on."

"Would there be any scrambles or trials going on here soon?"

Kerrigan was grinning more broadly now, with sideways glances at my reaction. "Every Saturday and Sunday, somewhere in Ireland, there's something going on. In fact, there's a trial on at the Curragh this Saturday. If you'd really like to go . . . "

Simon turned pleading eyes to me, his face screwing up the way he had had as a small boy desperately wanting what seemed unreachable. I groaned inwardly, wondering what expression on my face was being read by the others. Conflicting emotions, I hoped. Certainly Simon must realize the awkwardness in my being beholden to this man. And it would be—for Simon—a slap at his father, for Teddie had been almost apopleptic that *his* son could be interested in anything so plebeian and disreputable as motorbikes. Evidently bike racing was in better odor in Ireland than in the States.

"I've promised to take my nephew, Mrs. Teasey," Kerrigan was saying, his expression bland and innocent. Then he winked at Snow. "He's fifteen. If you'd like to come too, Snow?"

She played it cool. "Thank you very much, Mr. Kerrigan, but if Simon cares to go, I think I ought to keep Mother company."

"If we could persuade your mother to join us, would you come then?" That dratted man was clever enough not to condescend to my daughter but to approach her on a conspiritorial level that suggested I'd be missing a treat by refusing.

Snow rolled me a look of "What can we lose, Mom?"

"The Curragh is really worth the trip, Mrs. Teasey. I'd be obliged if you came. Think of me outnumbered by *three* teen-agers!"

He was a guileful soul, was Shamus Kerrigan. I'd half a mind to say no thank you, but both children were so intense suddenly that I stammered out an acceptance. No sooner had I done so than I saw the gleam of what could only be triumph in his eyes, and regretted my capitulation. I might have stymied him from talking business at dinner tonight, but he'd neatly manuevered me into a more vulnerable position.

Then he and Simon got into a discussion about motorbikes until the headwaiter announced that our table was ready.

"Are your children too young for bike races?" I asked him after we were settled.

Kerrigan gave me a stunned look before he smiled. "I'm not married yet, Mrs. Teasey." His smile became self-mocking. "You'll find that Irishmen tend to marry fairly late, sometimes not till they're forty, forty-five."

"They should be old enough to know better, then," said Simon with unexpected bitterness. He'd started making such remarks even before I'd given the twins any idea that I was thinking of divorce. They'd always seemed fond of their father, which was one reason I'd hesitated long after I knew our marriage had turned into a sham. But suddenly their affections for Teddie had suffered quite a change. Ever since the night of the Harrisons' party . . .

"I shan't marry until I'm at least thirty," said Snow loftily. "And only if I've known the man a long, long time and can assess his weaknesses."

Simon snorted, but Shay Kerrigan, to my surprise, took

Snow's comment seriously and agreed that it was very wise to look for weaknesses. If you loved someone in spite of such flaws, the affection must be secure.

"Of course, you have to be able to *admit* you can make mistakes, which is a mature attitude," she went on, while Simon rolled his eyes in exasperation at her present role. "Oh, cut it out," she said to him irritably.

My feelings were rather mixed. I wished she hadn't come out with such statements in front of a complete stranger; she was using phrases with which I had explained my divorce plans to my children, and Shamus Kerrigan was regarding her with a good deal of interest.

"They don't have divorce here in Ireland, do they?" she went on to Kerrigan. "Say, Mother, is your divorce legal in Ireland?"

"Shut up, Snow," said Simon. "Mother?" He appealed to me to assert maternal authority.

"I could ask, if you'd like," Shamus said, studiously avoiding my eyes.

"If she isn't, then if Daddy came to Ireland with that gushy woman he married, he'd be a bigamist and could be arrested, couldn't he?" And she gave a funny little laugh, not at all the sound of a fourteen-year-old girl. I got the feeling that Snow would very much like to see her father in jail!

"Here's the food," said Simon. "Stop jabbering and eat. This is too good to waste."

As though to prevent any more shock waves in the social situation, Shamus Kerrigan initiated other conversational gambits. He was good at it without being heavy-handed in directing the talk. If only I hadn't been bothered by the fact that he was doing the pretty only to get me to give him access up the lane, I'd've throughly enjoyed myself. To give him his due, not once did a hint of the matter arise during dinner. Nor on the drive home. I mean, to the hotel.

The twins and I were properly appreciative of the evening, and he confirmed the Saturday date. Then, as he tooled the big Jag slowly out of the parking lot, we swept into the hotel just as if we ought to. When I figured he must be clear of the intersection, we ducked back out and into the parking lot for the Renault.

Chapter IV

I don't sleep well in strange houses on unfamiliar beds. At least, that's what I told myself when I was still wide awake at three. I was damned well lying to myself. I disliked taking the sleeping pills which my doctor had sympathetically given me after I'd innocently complained about insomnia. I'd been rather aghast when he'd obliquely advised me to "get around more," meet new people, form new attachments, "however brief." Mother'd suggested that she was very broad-minded and this was a permissive society. I'd not been nearly as horrified at her tacit advice to take a lover as I had been at Dr. Grimeson's. After that, however, I couldn't chalk up my sleeplessness to nerves or not enough exercise: I had to admit it was the lack of sex.

Sex, or lack of it, had never been a problem while I was married to Teddie. He liked to exercise his rights and occasionally was rather brutal about exercising them, even after I tumbled to the fact that he was having affairs and in no pain. I'm not a prude—well, not for *other* people—but I wasn't going to play the suburban game, particularly after I'd decided to divorce him. I certainly wouldn't give him a chance to get custody of the twins because of any indiscretion he could lay on me. So I sweated it out. Then—and now.

I'd about dulled my sex drive before coming to Ireland, so it was heartily discouraging to find a resurgence after just a few hours in the company of an attractive man. It just wasn't fair.

While I was prowling about the first floor of the house,

trying to wear out my restlessness, I noticed two other
patches of light in the darkness: one at Thornton's cottage
and the other at Ann Purdee's. I also heard the thin wail of
a sick child. That brought back other memories: of me desperately trying to cope with two screaming, teething infants
while Teddie snored on in oblivion and then berated me the
next day for looking haggard.

I forced myself away from such reminiscenses. "Remember the good times," I'd been advised by another divorced
friend. "Hating him, or the if-I-had-he-might-not-have routine, is a waste of think-energy," Betty had told me. "You
loved him enough once to marry him, so you must have
seen something good in the man—remember that! And let
the trivia decay. Otherwise, you end up with a fine case of
soul-pollution. Which, honey, is a good way to scare off *any*
decent chance at remarriage."

"I don't want to get married again, Betty," I'd told her
vehemently.

She'd given me a sideways glance and ostentatiously fin-
gered her new wedding band. "Oh yeah? Convince me!"

Betty'd had a singularly dirty divorce (and given me tips
on how *not* to have one), picked herself up, joined a singles
club in Westfield, and married a widower with five children.
She had four of her own, and they bought a huge house
and all got on extremely well.

"Oh, you're at the I-hate-all-men stage right now," she'd
said. "Can't blame you. But it passes, lassie, it passes. And
then everything and anything in pants stimulates the old sex
appeal." She caught my astonished look and laughed. She
was tall and rather gangly, inclined to wear old tweed skirts
or blue jeans. "Even this old mare! At least you're not one
of those I-can't-cope-alone wailers! Soon enough you'll begin to wish you did have a male around. It's awfully nice to
have a shoulder to cry on when you damned well know
you've been stupid."

"Teddie was never cried on."

"I don't doubt it," and she rolled her eyes, for she'd
known Teddie rather well. "Which is to your advantage
right now. You've been used to coping."

"That doesn't mean I make the right decisions," I said,
thinking glumly of the horror of an apartment I'd taken.
The walls were paper-thin. The next-door neighbors had
whining kids and played their stereo so loud that we didn't

need to turn ours on except when their choice of music left
a lot to be desired. The apartment had been the best of a
bad selection, but I'd been so obsessed with the desire to
leave the "matrimonial home" and all its associations that
I'd taken the first available accommodation. The twins had
been very tolerant, and we'd moved as soon as possible into
an old, thick-walled house, newly converted into apart-
ments.

"That doesn't mean a man will decide right the first time
either," Betty had said in her droll way. "Say, why don't
you join a singles club?"

"Betty!" and I gave her a warning look.

"Honey, you don't have to *marry* the first man. You'd be
a fool if you did. That's how mistakes get compounded.
No, you need to get back into circulation, and by that I
mean just seeing a lot of different people, women and
men." Then she regarded me thoughtfully. "Your big problem, Rene, will be pleasing yourself for a change."

"I don't understand."

"I mean, don't try to be what you *think* the guy wants in
a woman. Just be yourself."

"I still don't understand you."

She gave me another long, searching look. "What-your-
best-friend-had-better-tell-you department," she said with a
sigh. "Now, look, I'm not the only one who thought you
were getting the bad end of the stick from Teddie-boy. I
don't mean the fact that he was sleeping around. I wanted
to bash him in the teeth for the way he'd speak to you. My
God, who did he think he was? The Pasha of Persia? And
you were too well-mannered to retaliate." Betty's breath
started to get rough with suppressed anger. "And I *am* taking you to the next meeting at the singles club!"

Betty would have—if it'd meant dragging me all the way
—but news of the legacy arrived, and she was jubilant for
my sake—and aligned herself with my kids to see that I
didn't back out at the last moment.

"Irishmen are gorgeous," she told me enthusiastically.
"Just what you need to get back into practice."

In the dead of night, I wondered if she had foreseen
someone like Shay Kerrigan. I'd have to write her. She'd be
highly entertained. And at this distance she couldn't match-
make very actively. But such thoughts were not soothing
me to sleep.

I went back to the kitchen and started the kettle. A hot toddy might help. Damn! No whiskey. Well, hot milk would be okay.

The pots fell out of the cupboard with a clatter. I nearly joined them when I heard a tap at the back door.

"Whoooo . . . who is it?"

"Kieron T'ornton, Mrs. Teasey."

"Oh, good grief! Come in."

As he entered, he looked down at the door latch. "You'd best be locking that door at night, Mrs. Teasey. We've a lot of tinkers on the long acre, and you could lose the best things in the house for sleeping."

I stood there, pot in hand, staring at him because he'd a brown bottle, unmistakably the kind which held spirits, in his hand. He noticed my gaze and grinned.

"The bahbee's teething, and a little of this helps."

"I'm not teething, but if you could spare a thimbleful. . ."

He strode into the room, looking blockier and shaggier than ever in the small space.

"If you'll permit me to drink with you? A pretty woman shouldn't ever have to drink alone." Then he chuckled. "That's what I'd tell your aunt."

"My aunt drank?"

He threw back his head to roar with laughter, but I made hushing noises and pointed up to indicate he shouldn't wake my kids. He covered his mouth until the laughter subsided. "Sure and she did!"

"Hmm. I didn't mean to imply that she was prudish . . . but somehow one doesn't think of old-lady aunts as drinkers."

"Don't think of your great-aunt Irene as an old-lady aunt," and there was strong feeling in the grin on his face. "She was a grand gal. Had she been younger or I older . . ." He gave me a mischievous wink and, with accustomed ease, slipped into a chair at the small table.

Strangely enough, I didn't feel the least bit embarrassed by Kieron Thornton's presence in my kitchen. What harm could I come to with a man who succored teething babies and distraught mothers at all hours?

"Is it Ann Purdee's baby?" I asked.

He hesitated before he said, "Poor little tike."

Then I nearly let the milk boil over, because it suddenly

struck me as odd that Kieron Thornton was at Ann Purdee's. Had she no husband?

"She's no man in the house, you know," he said in a slow drawl, and I wondered if I'd been thinking aloud again. "Which is as well," he added slowly, his eyes on mine. "One more such beating and there'd've been bloody little left of her, there being not much of her except willpower anyway."

"She dropped in on us this afternoon," I said, matching his casualness. "To pay the rent."

He caught and held my eyes. *"You've* no objection to her staying on then?" There was something he didn't add.

I shook my head, and he smiled with relief and approval.

"There's a story about Ann Purdee?"

"I'm not wide in the mouth, Mrs. Teasey, not about other people's affairs. Irene, your aunt, was satisfied, let's say, and helped out a bit now and again. No more than was neighborlylike."

I caught the hint and nodded. Ann Purdee had already struck me as a proud person whom well-meant but ill-timed generosities could wound deeply.

"I'm pleased you thought to move in right away," he said, taking a judicious sip of the hot milk and whiskey. "Hmmm. Very tasty." I'd doctored it with a bit of nutmeg and sugar. "Possession is nine points of the law in any country."

"And there'll be trouble?"

"Have you spoken with Mihall Noonan?"

"Yes, for all the good it did. I'm just as confused. And then, my aunt left a letter of instruction."

He was nodding, so I gathered he'd known about it. After all, Mr. Noonan had said he'd saved her life.

"Do you think," I asked him urgently, "that there'll be trouble with the relatives?"

"Not to worry, Mrs. Teasey. You were always to inherit, or so she told us time and again. God rest Queen Irene! God save Queen Irene!" And he raised the mug in a toast. "Not to worry, I said. You've loyal subjects here." He inclined the upper part of his body in a bow. "Given half the chance, we'll defend you to the death."

"Good God, it won't come to that?" I was half teasing, and yet I could hear the warning, the resolution to defend, in his tone.

"Finish your drink, pet. Get the good of it," he said in a sort of paternal tone, and lifted my hand off the table. "It's chilly, and you should be abed."

I could feel the cold even with the warm, laced milk in my tummy. And I could see the lightening of the sky through the kitchen window. "Good Lord, what time is it?"

"Half three. We've short nights in the summers here." He downed his drink and rose, pocketing the bottle of liquor. "Sleep sound, and God bless!"

He was out the door, softly humming a tune that was vaguely familiar.

I did sleep soundly. Very soundly. Until the thudding on the front door penetrated my sleep, and I felt Simon shaking my shoulder urgently.

"Mom, it's that Kelley guy."

The presumptuous manner of knocking added to my fury at his unheralded arrival. Perhaps it was close to ten in the morning, but I don't fancy being awakened by people I'm avoiding. I tried to open the window, but it was too tight.

"I'll tell him to go away," Simon said, starting down the stairs.

"No, I'll handle him!" I grabbed up my coat, more concealing than my flimsy dressing gown, and nearly tripped down the steep, short stairs. "What do you mean by pounding on my door in that fashion?" I demanded as I threw it open.

Brian Kelley, hand poised for another whack on the panels, stared at me, popeyed, his face gone white. Only for a moment, though, for he rapidly recovered his poise, his ruddy complexion, and his accumulated frustration.

"Are *you* Irene Teasey?"

"And whom else were you expecting in this house? And why have you been pursuing me? I left specific instructions that *I* would contact *you*." Then I belatedly realized that I shouldn't know what Brian Kelley looked like. "I assume, that is, that you *are* the persistent Brian Kelley."

"I am." He made a movement as if to enter the house, and I closed the door just slightly to emphasize unwelcome. Simon and Snow had ranged themselves on the stairs, and I was glad of their moral support.

"Well?" I said, tapping my foot.

"I have been trying to get in touch with you, Miss Teasey, to present a very fair offer."

"For what?"

"Why, for this," and he spread his chunky-fingered hand to indicate the house and grounds. "A very good offer, considering there are sitting tenants, and your circumstances."

"Which circumstances?"

"Why, that you have to sell."

"Who told you that I have to sell?"

"Well, you've the death duties to be paid. I happen to know that they'll be pretty stiff on a property like this."

"Will they?"

He wasn't liking my attitude at all. "I've a firm offer of twenty-five thousand pounds. That would be sixty-five thousand dollars!" He seemed impressed, and I refused to be. "You'd still get home with money in your pocket."

"Mr. Kelley, you seem to know a lot more about my affairs and my plans than I do. Among other points, you've neglected to take into consideration that my great-aunt's will has not yet been probated. Until it is, nothing can be done about buying or selling."

"If you accept this offer, Miss Teasey, you might find that probate is only a question of time." He was unctuously implying aid.

"I'm given to understand that it's only a question of time anyhow."

"You're in Ireland now, Miss Teasey." The threat was stated now.

"So I am, come to take up my inheritance, and comply with the terms of my great-aunt's will . . ." The piggy eyes informed me that Mr. Kelley knew the terms of that will. ". . . And her letter of specific instruction, which I intend to follow to the spirit and law." Well, he didn't know about any letter, that was certain. "Now, if you do not leave my premises I shall be forced to get the shotgun for which I obtained a license from the Cabinteely Gardai yesterday." That really shook him, and he backed out of the doorway and the small porch.

"You'll be sorry you turned that offer down, miss."

I slammed the door behind him, and while Simon was shaking the clasped hands of victory above his head, we heard the choleric Mr. Kelley stalling his car.

"Mom, you were great!" Snow said, chortling with pleasure.

"Who does he think he is, threatening you? Could he

really hold up probate, Mom?" Simon wasn't the least bit upset about that prospect.

"Don't know and I don't care, but I'll ask Mr. Noonan," I said, inordinately pleased that I had actually outfaced a man.

"Among other things, you'd better get that license today," Snow said, then sighed. "If only you'd stood up to Dad like that once in a while . . ."

"It would only have delayed matters," Simon said, glaring angrily at his sister. "Besides, Dad would have made Mother sell Kelley this place for sixty-five thousand bucks!"

"Oh no!" Snow didn't fancy that alternative.

My sudden triumph turned to doubt. "Do *you* think I did the right thing?"

"About Kelley?" Simon's outraged response answered the wrong question. "Oh . . ." and then he realized what I had meant and put both arms awkwardly but sweetly about me. My, he was getting tall. I had to look up at him. "Mother, you did exactly the right thing. With Kelley and with Dad. Sara and I have no regrets. None!" His serious face was suddenly split by an inimitably Simonesque grin. "Hell, Dad had no real use for us except to show off 'his twins' or prove his authority by snapping his fingers and having us, and you, waiting on him hand and foot. And I will *never* forgive him for that night in December—"

"Simon!" Snow's voice was sharp and scared.

I'd known that something had happened to the children the night they'd gone with their father to the Harrisons' party, but they'd never talked about it. I'd been flat on my back with one of those sudden, terribly debilitating stomach viruses. Teddie'd been furious with me because he'd wanted to go to the Harrisons' "do"; they always "did" so extravagantly. I knew he hated going to parties alone, as he was at his best scoring off a foil—like me. In desperation, and because the Harrisons had a daughter the twins' age, I suggested that he take the children. They'd come home about midnight: I'd been listening for their return, but they'd whispered in the hall outside my room without coming in. Which was unusual in itself, but I'd chalked it up that night to their concern about my health. I didn't know until much later that Teddie hadn't brought them home. Indeed, I didn't learn until after I'd initiated divorce proceedings that Teddie'd been put to bed at the Harrisons' stoned out of his mind, and was never invited there again. Something devastating had indeed happened, which the children were determined to keep from me.

Now Simon's face softened, and he patted me on the shoulder.

"No, Mother dearest of them all, you did the right thing. *We're* not sorry. You're a real tough mother!" And he kissed me.

"And I'm starved!" Snow said, as if Simon's overt show of affection irritated her. She was the less-demonstrative child. Now she marched toward the kitchen.

"Say, who does that Kelley character think he is," asked Snow into a pause at the breakfast table. "This place is worth a lot more than any old twenty-five thousand pounds."

"Did Kelley mean just the house, Mom? Because it would be a pretty good price that way."

"No, Simon, he meant the whole property."

Simon considered that momentarily. "Then he's a crook. Particularly threatening you with no probate unless you played his game."

"You don't suppose he's acting for Shay Kerrigan, do you?" asked Snow. "No," she answered herself, even as Simon exploded with a negative.

"Shamus Kerrigan's not that sort of guy. He wouldn't sneak about—"

"Well, he tried to sneak a bulldozer up our lane."

"Children, children!" I called them to order, but I had to admit that Snow's suggestion of Shay Kerrigan as Kelley's client had also occurred to me—and been discarded. "I agree with Simon, as far as Mr. Kerrigan's concerned, Snow. But that Mr. Kelley knew too much . . ."

"He didn't know about the trust fund, did he?" said Simon. "And that Mom wouldn't *have* to sell to pay the death duties!"

"Come to think of it, I don't know what's in the will."

"You said you did."

"I said I'd comply with it . . . Where *did* I put it down?"

Snow swished from the kitchen and flounced back again in very short order with the document and Aunt Irene's letter.

The will was considerably less dramatic, and fairly straightforward, once you discounted all those whereases and thingies. I was named co-executrix with a representative of the solicitors. We were to pay all her just debts and death duties. I was to administer the Brandel trust as long as necessary. Otherwise, everything, lock, stock, and barrel, was left to me, Irene Teasey Stanford.

As I could plainly see, the will had been signed ten years ago. That had been rather a hellish year for me. If I'd known of Aunt Irene's bequest, I'd've endured it with a stouter heart. That was the year I'd been sure I couldn't stick marriage with Teddie, when he'd flaunted that Joan creature all over town. However, you can put up with rather more than you think you can.

"What's the Brandel trust? Mr. Noonan said nothing about that yesterday," said Snow.

"That's another thing I'll have to ask him."

"If this Kelley character can hold up probate, do we get to stay on in Ireland?" asked Simon, eyes wide with hopefulness.

"*If* he can hold it up, we'll have to see how long . . . but however long, you two have to be back in school come September ninth, and don't forget it."

That unholy pair exchanged glances, and I had the suspicion that I'd already acceded too much.

"I don't know why you're so keen to stay here when obviously there's a lot of trouble brewing," I said, feeling a bit put out with their connivery.

"Aw, Mom, it's a lot better here than Westfield."

"Right *now*." I hinted at their well-known boredom.

"Ha!" Simon was contemptuous of my skepticism. "With trials and scrambles on every weekend?"

"And a horse for me to ride?" piped up Snow.

"We'll see, we'll see! Now let's get organized."

We'd tidied up and dressed and were going out the front door when I heard the phone ringing.

"Damn!"

"Mom!" Snow's tone was exasperated. "It's probably that Kelley character."

It was nearly noon, and though I honestly doubted that Kelley would be presumptuous enough to beard me again, I didn't want to put it to the test. So I left the phone ringing.

We found the nearest supermarket, which was more a discount house than a grocery. You could buy everything, including a TV. We had two huge shopping carts full, and I forked over £32 and odd pence, which didn't seem like much to me until Snow did a rapid calculation and said we'd spent over $75. I was flabbergasted, but, as Snow pointed out, it was cheaper than eating out.

I must say, it was fun putting things away in our new kitchen, making discoveries in the dining room like the beautiful Staffordshire dinner set and the delicate Beleek tea service. We kept some of the table linens for our use and carried the rest upstairs to store. The closets were already fairly full of my great-aunt's clothing. She couldn't have been a very large person, and certainly hadn't been given to frivolous clothes: Everything had a hard, durable look, though nothing appeared worn. Snow went into hysterics over the long-john winter drawers and knitted vests, but I advised her not to laugh.

"I wonder how much it would cost to put in central heating," said Snow when I explained about Irish winters.

"A bundle probably, and don't start planning a winter here, too, my girl. School beckons in September."

Snow gave me one of her wide-eyed innocent looks.

"Surely they have schools in Ireland, Mother."

"We all need some lunch," I said firmly, and went downstairs.

We grilled chops, made french fries out of the best frying potatoes I'd ever tasted, had marvelous frozen but fresh-tasting peas and a smallish green melon that was very sweet. We were all in such good moods that the meal became an event; even the washing up afterward went painlessly. Had I known how much the Staffordshire was worth, I don't think I'd've let Simon do the washing. But no harm was done.

I did call Michael Nooman, but he was engaged at court. The children wanted to do some sightseeing in Dublin, but I wanted to write Mother to inform her of our address and all the news, so I sent the twins out exploring until I could finish. I made a bet with myself as I heard them clattering out the back door. By the time I got upstairs and could peek out Simon's window, I'd won. He was in the garage examining the Mercedes, and Snow was halfway down the track to Horseface's pasture, the plastic bag of sugar lumps swinging from one hand.

Chapter V

When we got back from our tour at eight o'clock, there was a card pushed through the mail slot.

" 'Called to see you. Will call again.' signed 'Imelda.' " I turned to the children. "Have you met an Imelda you haven't told me about?"

Snow took the card from my hand, turned it over, and pointed to the printed name.

"Mrs. Robert Maginnis. Who she?"

"I haven't a clue."

"Maybe Kieron has," Simon said, and we took ourselves down to Kieron's cottage.

I don't know what I expected, but when he insisted that we come in and sit down awhile, I was stunned, and not a little embarrassed, by the unexpected charm of the room. The walls were finished off in a creamy paint, the beams darkened for contrast. There was an old-fashioned settee, and a beautiful small teak chest whose design was echoed by the bookcase and side tables. There was, of all things, a rocking chair, from which Kieron Thornton must 'have just risen, for it rocked to and fro on the braided rug. Pewter, copper, and brass ornaments gleamed on the mantel and table tops. It was a very finished room for a bachelor. He must have seen that opinion in my reaction, but he was gracious.

"This is embarrassing," I said, getting down to the reason for our visit. "We don't know who this is, and ought we to?"

He glanced at the message and the name, and snorted.

"One of your great-aunts, Irene's older sister." He handed back the card, and I could tell that while he was amused, he was also annoyed. At Mrs. Maginnis, not us.

"You seem surprised."

"I am. That's the first time she's called at that house in twenty years."

"Twenty years? Her own sister? Why?" I might wish that at least one of my sisters would make herself that scarce.

Kieron's eyes twinkled as he replied. "Originally I believe it was because Irene was stupid enough to buy property so far from the city."

"Originally?" I asked, hoping he'd go on. "Oh, please, you do know? And I'm dumped here in a real bag of weasels and Aunt Irene said that you'd help me. In her letter."

That obliged him to answer, although he was reluctant. "Irene's sisters didn't like the company she kept, nor her tenants."

I thought of Ann Purdee's delicate features, her work-roughened hands, and the two pounds, which was a lot of money to her.

"My aunt's letter expressly instructed me to keep on the present tenants in Swallow and Lark cottages." He was nodding, so that wasn't news to him. "Unless I find very good reasons for disobeying those instructions, I intend to honor them."

Something close to relief passed quickly across his face.

"Do you mean to tell us," began Snow indignantly, "that her sisters didn't come here when she was sick last winter?"

Kieron's expression was not friendly. "I believe they did visit her in hospital."

"Probably to see if she was dying and if they could get her money and property," Snow went on, disgusted. Her surmise was accurate, judging by the slight narrowing of Kieron's eyes. "It was *you* who saved her life. Mr. Noonan told us."

"Irene Teasey . . ." and he stopped, grinning at me, the second Irene Teasey.

"Wouldn't it be easier if you called me Rene?"

He nodded, smiling warmly, and began again. "Irene Teasey was a remarkable woman for her own age, and even this one. She had tremendous vitality and compassion—not the treacly sort, but down-to-earth, practical compassion—"

He broke off, hesitating as he tried to explain. "Ireland's a good fifty years behind the rest of the world, you know."

"Part of its charm," I murmured as he paused again.

"Not necessarily, Rene," and he was critical.

"Are you trying to tell us that Irene wasn't convention-al?" I asked.

"And that she liked her own sort of people on her queen-dom instead of the stuffy petty ones like her sisters?" piped up Snow.

Kieron nodded vigorously.

"Well!" said my daughter, as if that settled her prefer-ence. "And I'll just bet it made them stinking mad to think her place was worth more than theirs."

"Yes, but it wasn't until Shay Kerrigan paid an atrocious price for the Donnigan land . . ."

"Why wouldn't my aunt give Mr. Kerrigan access to the lane?" I asked, and he gave me such an intense, alert look that I added, "She specifically instructed me, in that letter, not to, even if it seemed spiteful."

"Just that?"

I wondered what else she could have said, but then he asked if we'd driven around the county very much, if we'd seen the housing schemes.

"Oh no, not ticky-tacky boxes," groaned Snow.

Kieron was nodding, but, to be honest, I wouldn't't've thought squashed-up building developments were Shamus Kerrigan's thing. He was very elegant himself. I *could* see Brian Kelley's type throwing up ticky-tacky.

"Is that why Brian Kelley's so mad-keen to buy this place?" I asked.

"Kelley?" Kieron was irritated. "How'd he know about you?"

"What do you mean?"

"Irene chased him away no end of times. And I threw him out of the house last February."

"He offered Mom a lousy twenty-five thousand pounds," said Snow scornfully. "The place's worth much more than *that!*"

"Sure and it is." Then he laughed. "And when you know that Irene paid five hundred pounds for the thirty acres in 1945 . . ."

"Wow!" Snow was impressed, and Simon whistled.

"No wonder her relatives were annoyed," I said. "But, if

they also didn't like her tenants, you weren't one then, were you?"

"My mother was." And there was a shadow of old anger and sadness in his eyes, and hurt.

"What is it that the relatives don't like about Ann Purdee?" asked Snow belligerently.

"You're in Ireland now, young lady, and people have different ways of looking at things."

Snow made a grimace.

"What matters is that the relatives, for reasons best known to . . . and appreciated by . . . themselves, did not approve of my great-aunt's way of life," I said, and Kieron nodded. "It also didn't sit well with them that she was the smarter businesswoman." Kieron nodded again. "Well, I could see being annoyed, but not cutting off the association . . . even if it is Ireland and they do things differently . . ." Ah, yes, there was more that Kieron Thornton wasn't telling me. "So I suppose," and I brandished the calling card, "they're going to see if I'm more amenable." Kieron nodded; he was beginning to look like one of those stupid drinking birds. "So if you'd be so kind as to tell me who my relatives are, then I can separate them from the real-estate people who want to con my land out of me."

"Irene kept the family bible up to date, but let's see. Irene had two sisters, Imelda Maginnis and Alice Hegarty, and two brothers, your own grandfather, Michael, and Richard. He's dead now but his widow's alive, Winnie. Each of them had about six kids apiece . . ."

"So did Great-granddad's," said Snow with a long-suffering groan. "And none of 'em are Catholics."

"None of them here are either," said Kieron. "You could take tea with a different set of cousins for a month or two."

Snow rolled her eyes. "Who'd want to?"

"Sara! Really, Kieron, I'd no idea we had so much family left in Ireland."

"I thought you Yanks prided yourselves on your Irish ancestry."

"Not all of us can claim a Timahogue or two," I said, a bit annoyed. "In America, it's more what you can do—"

"Or who you know," chimed in Snow.

"—than where you came from and who's your family."

"It's who you know here too," Kieron said, grinning at

Snow for her impudent observation. "Imelda and Alice are the ones to be right careful with. Winnie's a good sort; she means well."

"Are the sisters in bad circumstances? Financially?" I asked, still feeling guilty over inheriting from someone I'd never met.

"Jasus, no. Even Winnie's well-off. She watches the family fish business like a gull. None of 'em's pinched. They're just greedy. They can't take it in that Irene could possibly leave her property to a rich Yank simply because the gel was named after her."

"To begin with, I'm not rich."

"You are now," Kieron said.

"Not until probate. Which reminds me—Brian Kelley hinted I'd get probate a lot faster if I accepted his offer."

"Could he really do something nasty and obstructive?" asked Snow. We didn't need a verbal answer with the look on Kieron's face.

"I'd speak to Mihall Noonan on that point, as soon as possible. I don't know who Brian Kelley knows. But Alice's daughter's husband works for the same firm. *It's* reputable enough, but Kelley . . ."

"Is not," Snow said, making grubbing gestures with her fingers. "Sausage fingers and sweating palms and a piggy face to go with it."

"Would you fancy a cup of coffee and some biscuits?" asked Kieron, rising and politely changing the conversation.

I started to refuse, but Snow informed Kieron that I took coffee any time, anywhere, but I was choosy about my company, and while I was getting my breath back she boldly asked if she could peek through the rest of his beautiful home. She'd never been in a real Irish cottage before.

Any thought of resemblance between his home and a "real Irish cottage" was corrected. I wondered how Kieron Thornton supported himself, but by the time we got to his kitchen, through the beautifully appointed dining room, I did know that he'd made the cabinets in Aunt Irene's house and all the furnishings in this one. He said flatly that he worked only when and on what he wished to, and for whom he chose. I began to understand how charges of unconventionality could be leveled at this one of Aunt Irene's friends.

"You're too neat," said Snow approvingly as we continued upstairs and into Kieron's room.

"Why can't men be neat?" asked Simon, bristling.

"No reason for them not to, they're just too used to having a woman do it all for them," she said condescendingly.

"I was in the army," said Kieron, to interrupt the skirmishing. "And I happen to like things in order."

"So there," said Simon.

"He'll make some woman a good husband, then," his sister went on, determined to have the last word.

"The kettle's boiled." Our host hurried down the stairs, urging us to join him.

"Sara, you are impossible sometimes," I said, giving her arm a painful pinch. Ouching, she went down the stairs, well in front of both of us.

"What's that for?" she asked, pointing to a large copper cylinder and an electrical motor in the pantry.

"Heating water and pumping it out of the well. Irene had well water piped into all the cottages."

"Doesn't everybody?"

"Not in Ireland."

"Good grief!" Snow was amazed, but then, so was I.

Then Simon spotted the motorcycle in the lean-to. "Hey, what is it?"

"Honda 250. You like bikes?"

"Do I like bikes?"

"Simon is mad-crazy for bikes," Snow said rapidly, because both of us could sense that Simon was about to mention Saturday's outing, and in the present company, with the most recent disclosures, that seemed a sort of treachery. I'd have to figure out how to withdraw courteously from that invitation.

"Know how to ride?"

"No," Simon replied glumly.

"If your mother is willing, I'll teach you."

"But he can't drive it. He's only fourteen."

"You'd never know it to look at him. And in his own lane it doesn't matter." Kieron warmed to the idea. "Look, Rene, I'll give him a few lessons, he can't hurt himself. And he is on holiday."

With Simon looking so pleadingly wistful and Kieron's half smile egging him on, I was weakening.

As Kieron Thornton brewed the coffee in a filter pot, Simon was restlessly poking around the living room.

"Hey, this one isn't finished," he said, picking up an eight-inch carved figure à la chinoise from a group with several others which were completed and stained.

"Why, they're chess pieces," said Snow, jumping up to examine them. "*You're* doing 'em!" she said, pointing an accusing finger at Kieron.

They were lovely indeed: a queen and two bishops, and Simon had picked up the embryo knight. I stared at Kieron with awed respect.

"Good things to have on hand when you can't sleep," he said, without so much as a glance in my direction.

"Well, get her!" said Snow, affecting a haughty face like the queen's and then dissolving into giggles as she handed the piece to me. It was a delightful face, giving the queen a definite personality.

"Do you play chess, too?" asked Simon because his sister was getting on his nerves.

Kieron did, and Simon forthwith challenged him to a game, but they didn't start until we had spent a good bit of time admiring the individual figures.

"Are these ancient Celts?" I asked, trying to identify the costumes.

Kieron grinned approvingly at me and stroked his beard. "You got Brian Boru, and Conchobuir's there."

"Which one's Cuchulain?"

"So you know your Irish legends?"

"Some of them. Is the Red Queen Deirdre of the Sorrows?"

"Indeed and she is, and the white one's Maeve."

As I passed them from the box to the board, glancing at each pawn and major piece, I realized that they had quite distinct faces and expressions. Maeve, of course, was positively malevolent, and looked about to weep. Cuchulain was a knight with a sort of Steve McQueenish visage; I wondered if Cuchulain would have ridden a motorbike instead of a chariot. His opposite red number bore a marked resemblance to John Wayne.

"Cuchulain *could* have looked like Steve McQueen," began Snow thoughtfully.

"You mean the other way round, don't you? Cuchulain came first," said Simon, "by a couple of thousand years."

"Who knows?" said Kieron. "There're only so many basic facial types, and, certain temperaments are attracted to certain occupations. And then, temperament stamps a face with distinctive lines: the blandness of the politician, the alertness of the competitive businessman, the stance of the professional athlete, the jowls of a singer, the—"

"The long hair of the singer, you mean." Simon grinned.

"Not pop, *trained* singer."

"You mean, you don't *like* rock and roll?" Snow began to bristle.

"I said 'trained singer,' and that's what I meant, so don't be bold, pet. Most rock and roll singers, until they get very good, don't bother to protect their biggest asset. By the time half of them are thirty, they won't be able to sing a note because they've misused their voices."

"You aren't a trained singer yourself, are you?" I asked.

Kieron turned to me, his eyes laughing, his lips twitching the corner of his beard. "No, but your aunt was."

"Aunt Irene? Sang?" Was that part of the unconventionality that had annoyed her relatives?

"You didn't know?" Kieron frowned.

"No. I told you that I didn't know anything about her. Look, my mother met Aunt Irene once, when she was abroad before the war. She liked her. I've four older sisters, and a brother, all married now, with bundles of kids. Mother came from a large family, and so did my father, and I can't keep *them* straight. So when I came along, Mother'd run out of interesting names and thought it fun to name me after my great-aunt Irene." I flushed, because my initials had made me an IT girl, a plaguey nuisance in high school. "That's why I was so dumbfounded when she left everything to me." I stood up. "Oh, I'll just turn it over to—"

There were shocked cries of "Mother!" "You couldn't!" and Kieron Thornton leaned forward to grab my hand, and pulled me, rather hard, back into the chair.

"That's enough foolishness. Irene had very sound reasons for doing as she did. I've no right to fault you for not knowing about her, and I don't. But I was surprised that you didn't know of her career. That's how she was able to buy this land and keep it."

"What did she sing? Opera?" asked Snow.

Kieron's eyes twinkled. "Guess again." He looked at me. Then suddenly, I remembered what Mother had said.

"Good Lord, she sang Gilbert and Sullivan. At Covent Garden!"

"Bang on!" And Kieron laughed at the shock on the twins' faces.

"She didn't?"

"She did," Kieron and I said together.

Snow and Simon both turned to stare at me, mouths slightly agape.

"Mother sang G and S, too, before we arrived."

"I know," said Kieron blithely. "Check," he added, having caught Simon's king in a well-laid trap.

"Hey!"

"I'll give you the chance to beat me again," Kieron said, standing up. "I'd like to make it now, but I've an engagement at half nine."

We hastily thanked him for the hospitality, the gossip, and the game, and walked back up the slight rise to the Lodge. I was even beginning to think of it as home.

"Nine thirty and the sun's still up," Simon said. "Crazy country! Crazy country!"

Chapter VI

We were enjoying a nice leisurely breakfast when there was a knock at the back door, which Simon answered.

"Come on in, Mrs. Purdee."

She gave him a very solemn greeting and then came straight to me, holding out a small cardboard box and a key.

"You were out yesterday when I came by, Mrs. Teasey. And I know the tax appraisers have been here, so it's safe to give you these now. This," and she put the box on the table, "is the missing carburetor"—she pronounced it with a different accent, so that at first I didn't know what she meant—"for the Mercedes," and she nodded toward the garage. "And this is the key to the boot. We put the silver tea service and flatware there."

"Why?"

Mrs. Purdee eyed me very solemnly, as one does an idiot. "Sure, the silver's worth a small fortune, Mrs. Teasey, which your great-auntie didn't want to give the government. And Kieron told 'em the car wouldn't go for want of a carburetor and that part not available, but perhaps the new owner could sell it for parts."

Simon began to whoop and clap, appreciating the subterfuge, but I (they say I am occasionally square) was aghast.

"Your auntie wanted us to do it—*before* they came to lock up the house. And before the *others* got here."

Tax officials came off with a slightly better odor than my relatives if I correctly interpreted her pronouns; she plainly had little use for either.

"Will that Mercedes run if the carburetor's put back?" Simon asked.

"Oh, it will so." Her slight smile was tinged with a bit of malice. "There were only about three hundred made of that particular model, you see, and your auntie kept it in super condition. Kieron'll fix it for you if you want him to. You're to say that you ordered the part from the States." Then she started toward the door.

"Is your baby better?"

"My baby?" She whirled, startled.

"Yes, Kieron said it was teething the other night. I'd heard a child crying, you see."

"Oh, yes, well, you know how it is and all. She's easy now."

She couldn't get out of the house fast enough, and Simon and Snow both noticed it. I hadn't told them what Kieron had said about Ann being beaten by her husband, so I distracted their questions by suggesting we all go find our treasure.

And treasure it was! A superb tea service, complete with an immense tray, and an enormous box of tableware: place settings for twelve, and the most confusing array of forks, spoons, knives that I've ever seen.

The intelligence that the Mercedes was operable was very good news, and before we unloaded the silver from the boot, we took a closer look at the car.

It was curiously modern for a car built in 1956, and, to again rearrange my mental picture of Great-aunt Irene, it was a sports coupe, undoubtedly very dashing when it first came out. There wasn't a blemish on the leather upholstery —under the dust—and only signs of key-scratch on the dashboard. There seemed to be more dial faces than were familiar, but Simon told me—nonchalantly preserving his own image—that there were tachometers and things that measure motor revolutions per minute for rally driving and . . .

"If it runs, that's the only important thing," I told him, and banged at the neatly stored tires.

We were wondering where to store all the silver when Simon discovered that the center portion of the buffet obviously accommodated the silver chest. So in it went. The silver tea service could repose importantly on the buffet top, and suddenly the rather drab room took on elegance.

"Now, Mother," said Snow in her let's-get-down-to-brass-tacks voice, "if this room were, say, a soft Wedgwood green . . ."

"Yes, yes, you're right," I agreed, with unsimulated enthusiasm, and ran an experimental hand along the wallpaper. It was old and brittle. A good steaming ought to lift it.

An odd rasping sound penetrated my concentration. Snow looked up from her arrangement of the tea and coffee pots . . . they must be Georgian . . . and then her face cleared. "It's the doorbell, Mother!"

"Kelley?" I groaned.

"Simon, we need you," said Snow. "Who else would be calling at eleven thirty?"

As I marched to the door I took a deep breath to support my anger, and exhaled it hastily in the face of a shortish woman wearing one of those matronly knit combinations in a deadly blue, which did not compliment her frizzy blondish hair and florid complexion. Her eyes, a faded green, missed nothing, giving my tunic-slack outfit a quick and disapproving once-over. She arranged her mouth in a smile, which her eyes didn't echo.

"I'd know you anywhere. You're so obviously Michael's child."

"Michael's grandchild," I replied, correcting her because she was the sort of person you have to correct, want to correct. "And you are . . . ?"

"My dear, I'm your . . . ah . . . Auntie Imelda," and she shifted her feet for a forward movement.

"Oh, you left your card yesterday."

"Indeed and I did, because I'd only just learned that my dear dead sister's namesake was actually here in Ireland." She looked reproachfully at me. I found her sorrowful "dear dead sister" routine to be overdone.

"I'm pleased to meet you, but I'm afraid we're in such a mess inside . . . unpacking, you know . . ."

"Not to worry in the least, my dear Irene," and with that she brushed by me into the small hall.

It wasn't entirely the surprise of encountering the twins which halted her forward motion. I *knew* that she'd never been in this house before. Score #1. The coup obscurely pleased me.

"Your children, my dear?" She was clearly astounded at the size and beauty of my offspring. Score #2.

"This way to the living room, Mrs. Maginnis," I said, smoothly leading the way. Simon followed her, and Snow caught my nod and closed the half-open dining-room door, then brought up the rear of the procession.

"This is my son, Simon Stanford, and my daughter, Sara."

Mrs. Imelda Maginnis was far more interested in her surroundings than in my introduction. She acknowledged them with a cursory bob of her head. She managed to look down a very short nose as if it were a Medici hook. I could see her mentally inventorying the value of the furnishings. When I urged her to take the small settee, she settled herself tentatively on the edge with an almost audible sniff, as if she expected dust to billow out. Then she asked Snow how old she was, in a condescending tone that made me want to spit.

I could see Simon closing his eyes and cringing as we both wondered how Snow was going to respond. She behaved herself, undoubtedly for some malicious purpose.

"My," said Mrs. Maginnis in that arch tone, "you're well grown for fourteen. And how old are you, Simon?"

"Fourteen."

Mrs. Maginnis pursed her lips, uncertain whether she was being mocked.

"They're twins, Mrs. Maginnis. Don't let their looks or size fool you."

"How very intr'usting!"

Good heavens, I wondered, didn't "nice" people in Ireland have twins?

"Well, now, you've cousins the same age as yourselves who would be so glad to take you about while you're in Dublin," said their great-great-aunt, again insufferably patronizing. It was obvious that she felt we wouldn't, or shouldn't, be staying here very long.

I caught Snow's eye warningly.

"Sure and we'd like that so very much," said my dutiful daughter with an alarmingly Irish brogue. "We hope to do such a lot of sightseeing . . . while we're here."

"In fact, my dear," and Mrs. Maginnis turned to me, shifting her buttocks on the slippery sofa upholstery, "my sisters and I would like to give you a little welcome party. At *my* house."

So, her house was the best of the lot? I mumbled something appropriate and wondered how I could graciously decline. Then I realized that I was overreacting. They *were* my relations; Mrs. Maginnis was obviously trying to be hospitable, however much against her better judgment. And Aunt Irene had said that I should "do" something for the younger ones who'd been kind to her.

"It's not proper, of course, to do much entertaining, like. With Irene gone so soon." She sniffed pathetically as she eyed the carpet. Her nose wiggled to acquaint us with her low opinion of the thing. "Would Sunday suit? For tea?"

I was forced to say how kind she was, how thoughtful.

"We must do what we can to make you welcome while you're in Ireland, even in such sad circumstances. And then too, my dear, you'll need help settling and selling up the estate, won't you?"

"Actually, Mrs. Maginnis—"

"Please, Irene—Auntie Imelda."

I choked out the syllables as directed. ". . . I can't do anything about selling until the will has been probated, you know."

Clearly she didn't, and her eyes went very round and dissatisfied.

"Oh, but of course," she recovered quickly, with a nervous giggle. "Well, you'll be able to rely on us, you know, because you'll want to clear all the cottages of those tenants." She managed a ladylike shudder of revulsion. "And there're more deserving—"

"My great-aunt specifically requested me to keep on most of the present tenants."

"She what?" Great-aunt Imelda was not pleased to learn of instructions beyond the grave. "My dear sister had suffered several strokes, you know," and then she tapped her forehead, nodding her head significantly.

"This letter predates her illness," I replied mendaciously.

"Well, this isn't the time to discuss such delicate matters. And the men are not here to give you the benefit of their good advice. You'll need it, my dear Irene. Ireland's a man's country!" She rose; I wasn't quite sure if it was in deference to Ireland's being a man's country. There was, at any rate, a disagreeable hint of smugness in her expression as she glanced around her again, as if she were obliquely pleased by the spartan furnishings. "I can't imagine why you're not stopping at the Montrose. Such a nice hotel. So American."

"That's why we're staying here," Snow said.

As Mrs. Maginnis stomped to the door, her expression said plainly, "And that won't be for long."

Somehow Snow got between her great-great-aunt and the dining-room door. The woman undoubtedly had every intention of looking in. Foiled, she smiled sourly at me, and glanced up the stairs, which told her nothing.

"Until Sunday, then?"

"What time is Irish tea on Sunday?" asked Snow in her little-girl voice.

"Why, half four, of course."

"Oh?" In that one surprised, haughty syllable, Snow managed to convey how unaccustomed she was to taking tea at such an unfashionable hour. Nor was the implication lost on our relative.

"You mustn't go to too much trouble for our sake," I felt obliged to say, but I would not be hypocritical and reprimand Snow. It had been too delicious of her.

"My husband will collect you, for sure you'd never find your way." And Mrs. Robert Maginnis stalked down the lane.

"Well, ain't she somethin'?" Snow said, glaring at the portly retreating figure. "She was dying of curiosity about the house. I wonder who she thinks ought to inherit."

"One of the 'more deserving'?" asked Simon. He altered his voice to a falsetto imitation of his great-great-aunt: " 'And there're cousins the same ages as yourselves' . . . Yeah." He went bass again. "I can just imagine. Do we *have* to, Mother?"

"Well, yes, we do. We accepted, for one thing. For another, *we* might find out more than they want to." I shook a warning finger at my daughter. "And you'd better watch your manners, missy. I gather that children are seen and not heard here."

"I'll behave . . . if I can."

"You know, she's the second person who's suggested that we'd be selling . . . I must get hold of Michael Noonan." But he was out.

"You know something," Snow said musingly as she sat on the steps and peered at me through the rail, "she didn't take her gloves off, but I'll just bet anything she's got grabby little fat-fingered paws."

"Oh, let's not start *that* one again," I begged, which reminded me that Shay Kerrigan's long-fingered, well-shaped hands did *not* obey the twins' much-vaunted criterion.

"Say, Mom, didn't Kieron mention something about Aunt Irene keeping tabs on our kith and kin in the family bible?"

"Yes, he did, Sim."

"We might as well have the sheet to keep score on."

We found the family bible readily enough in the little desk in the living room, complete with family-tree chart, branches, twigs, and leaves all neatly name-tagged. I could only hope that we weren't going to meet *all* the relatives listed. Objectively, I could appreciate why Imelda Maginnis might be miffed with the property going out of the immediate family . . . the immediate Irish family.

"How was it Great-great Irene put it?" asked Snow. " 'Out of three generations and five lots'? Well, there sure isn't another Irene. And look, she knew about cousin Linda's baby! Who could've told her?"

I followed Snow's pointing finger. Aunt Irene had been up-to-date, all right. I knew Mother had too much else to do to correspond with anyone regularly. Then Simon thought of looking for any mail in the back-room office desk.

We didn't find any correspondence, but there were receipted bills from previous years, all neatly bound, as well as old ledgers—but none for the previous and current years.

"Probably the tax people took them away. Or Mr. Noonan," Snow said. Which seemed logical. Then she found the worn leather address book and the problem was solved. My eldest sister, Jenny, was listed with all her changes of address.

"That figures," said Snow. "No, it doesn't. Why would Aunt Jen be so big with letters?"

"I dunno. Except she's the clubwoman type. Organized," said her twin.

Simon was still pondering the family tree. "Grandpa wasn't the only wild goose to leave the family nest. There's a slew of others, if this 'E' means emigrated. It's after a lot of names."

"Unless it means 'E' for egress and they'd died."

"Naw! Boy, look at how Imelda produced. Six!"

"Alice and Winnie were as good. Now where would you put six kids in a house this size?" Snow wanted to know.

"I wonder what did happen to her letters," I said, noticing a good supply of nice notepaper. It probably *was* Mr. Noonan. I tried reaching him again, but this time he was engaged with a client, so I didn't think it would do any harm to ask his secretary what had happened to my aunt's private papers.

"Anything to do with the estate, or income taxes, is here, Mrs. Teasey, and will be returned to you. I believe that one of the tenants burned all Miss Teasey's private correspondence, at her request. Shall I have Mr. Noonan return your call when he's free?"

I said yes, because I wanted to find out about this probate business and Kelley's threat. Just as I hung up, a leather-bound scrapbook was thrust at me. I held it off far enough to distinguish a headline and realized that this contained my aunt's professional clippings.

"Wow!"

Irene Teasey in a hundred photographs . . . costumed and made up for her stage performances as one of the leading lyric sopranos of the Covent Garden D'Oyly Carte Operetta Company.

"Gee, she was pretty!" said Snow.

"And small. Look at her. Who was she here, Mom?"

"Probably Mabel in *Pirates*," I said, considering the parasol and the pantalettes.

Some rather lovely—and painful—memories surged up out of storage. I had a vivid recollection of Mother's expression when she saw me costumed as Mabel for my first performance in *Pirates*.

"I suppose it just skipped generations, dear, but you manage to sound exactly like your aunt Irene Teasey. She was *good!*" Until now, sitting in Great-aunt Irene's living room, I really hadn't thought past the approving note in Mother's voice (for Mother has very high standards in theater). "Odd that that break in both your speaking voices never occurs when you sing. You did very well, my dear. Very well."

That was the trouble. I did do very well. The Jan Hus

production of *Pirates of Penzance* was extremely well received by the off-Broadway critics. There was talk of the group turning into a professional repertory company and doing tours of G & S. Teddie was just starting with the agency, and he was torn between wondering if my career was good for his, and pride that he could show off a wife of star caliber. I certainly wasn't making any money at it. And I wasn't really any good at anything else musical. I had the perfect G & S ingenue voice, I looked Victorian, especially my figure, and, I was often told, I had the natural style of G & S. When the craze in musical tent circuses for summer circuit was going strong, I had one very exhausting, nerve-wracking, divine summer before I happily discovered I was pregnant. In spite of the fact that Simon was his spittin' image, Teddie had had a drunken habit of casting doubt on the paternity of the twins, acidly remarking that bitches could get pups from a number of dogs and I'd had plenty of opportunities to be unfaithful to him with my stage cronies. I don't know where he thought I'd've got the energy, with the schedule we had: rehearsals during the day and just enough time to bathe, eat dinner, and get made up for the evening's show, after which we were too tired to do much more than eat a hurried supper and fall into bed— alone. Of course, I had much the same routine once the twins were born—only, no applause. And the cruel criticism of a frustrated husband.

"You don't suppose she made any recordings, do you?" asked Snow, hauling me back to the present.

"She didn't sing in the Dark Ages, love, and there *are* recordings of Caruso, you know."

My great-aunt had done all the lead roles from Angela to Yum-Yum. There were press clippings, including those of a tour, until a final notice, a few sentences really, dated March 1944, which told me why my aunt's career had been ended. She'd been injured in a buzz-bomb blast.

"How?" asked Snow.

"It doesn't say."

"Must have been bad," suggested Simon. "Remember, Kieron said she bought the queendom in 1945."

"Her face?" asked Snow, flipping through the final pages. "No. Here she is, standing in front of the house. We could ask Ann Purdee."

"We could, but should we?"

"Why not? It's not your fault that we don't *know* very much about Aunt Irene. I think we *should* be curious now. It's only grateful."

"Aw, c'mon, stop the yammering," said Simon, and shooed us out of the house before him.

Then we all stopped, our progress impeded by ignorance. "Which is Swallow cottage?" asked Snow.

"She comes to the back door," Simon said, and pointed to the path and the small pasture gate. "That way, George!"

It seemed logical, and it was. When we had gone through the little gate and started down the steep path to the row of cottages, I had sudden second thoughts about the venture.

Three cottages were in a line, terrace cottages, they call them, the fourth (which I sincerely hoped was Ann Purdee's) at right angles to the others. Each cottage had a fenced-off rear yard, but only one looked cared for at all. The other two were junk heaps, with all sorts of rusting, molding, decaying garbage. The right-angled cottage was completely different: The palings had been secured, and there was a flourishing garden. Neat lines held a variety of children's garments flapping in the breeze. We had to go all the way around the house to get to the first of the two doors.

In the kitchen, Ann Purdee was up to her elbows in flour. Two very small and beautiful children were sitting on a braided rug, playing with cooking utensils and a cocoa can. A carry-cot on a small chest wobbled from its occupant's motion. Kieron Thornton's handiwork was obvious in the cupboards, the table and banquette benches, the shelving by the cooking range.

Ann Purdee and I stared at each other, and I was somehow embarrassed. She seemed surprised and apprehensive.

"I'm so sorry to bother you," I said, and tried to back us out.

"Don't *go!*" She hurriedly dusted her hands. Then Snow saw the children and started to squeal with compliments, demanding of Ann if the children minded strangers, could she play with them, weren't they gorgeous, and what a lovely kitchen, was it bread she was baking? Real Irish brown bread?

Snow's exuberance is infectious, and Ann Purdee's initial shock dissolved.

"We have come at a bad time, Snow . . ."

"To be sure, you're always welcome here, Mrs. Teasey." The emphasis was unmistakable.

I couldn't help wondering who *wasn't* welcome. However, it wasn't something I could ask Ann Purdee . . . yet.

"Please don't stop what you're doing," I said, for she'd been about to wash her hands, and that bread still required kneading. "We only dropped in because . . . I mean . . ."

"What Mother's stumbling over is that we want to gossip a bit with you. No one tells us anything!" Snow rolled her eyes in exaggeration and then beamed at the small child she'd placed in her lap. "What's her name?"

"Fiona."

"Such magnificient eyes! See, Mom?"

Simon and I had taken places at the table. I nodded vigorous approval.

"What was it you wanted to know?" Ann asked me, pounding the dough expertly.

"For starters," Snow began, seeing me floundering again, "the accident Aunt Irene had, the one that ended her career —why did it make her give up singing?"

Of all the questions in the world that we could have asked, that was evidently the one Ann least expected, for her hands poised a long moment above the dough. She also looked relieved.

"It was a terrible thing that, and would have been no bother to anyone but your auntie. She was hit by splinters of glass from a shattering window."

"But there's no mark on her face."

"She protected her face like, and her eyes with her arms. They were scarred, but the splinters pierced her throat."

"Her vocal cords!" I cried, and my hand went to my throat protectingly. I had that awful stomach-sinking of utter regret. "How awful for her!"

Ann shrugged. "She *said* it was as well. She'd had the best of the cream, and had no fancy to do character roles."

"Did she ever make recordings?" asked Snow.

"I believe so, but she'd none in the house, nor player."

"By preference?" I could see that it would be easier to give up music altogether.

"I 'spect so. She never did mention the matter."

"Did any of her relatives visit her often?"

Ann's expression became angry. "Neither of her sisters

bothered their barneys about her until the solicitor phoned to say she was in hospital. Then they flocked up the lane like . . ."

"Vultures?" Snow suggested helpfully when Ann faltered.

"Yes. And when . . . she died . . . why, they'd've stripped the house and turned—" She stopped, snapping her teeth closed over what she'd been about to say. But I heard it. " '. . . turned us out.' " Why on earth would Ann Purdee be considered an undesirable tenant?

"But you and Kieron had hidden the silver by then, hadn't you?" Snow was asking.

There were defiant tears in Ann's eyes, which she blinked away furiously. "She'd told us over and over that we were to hide it all from the tax people. Just as well. Had *they* ever seen it . . ."

"None of her relatives were ever in the house to see the silver?" I asked that so very innocently that Simon gave me an odd look.

"No, I couldn't say that. There were several came around often . . ."

"Which ones?"

Ann Purdee looked at me sternly. "I'm in no state to cast stones." She sighed, and gave the bread a punch.

"Well, then," said Snow, her resigned voice at variance with the grin she was giving the child she held, "we have to enter the Maginnis den without knowing friend from foe."

"Maginnis?" Ann was startled enough so that all the color left her face. "Mrs. Robert Maginnis?"

"None other, in her best bib and knit suit," said Snow. "Commanding us to tea on Sunday at *her* house."

"She was here?" Ann could not absorb the information.

"And has gone," Simon put in, "with a grinding of gears."

"Oh!" All the life had drained out of her.

I went on briskly. "Mrs. Maginnis—I cannot for the life of me bring myself to call her Auntie Imelda—"

At my exasperated tone, Ann seemed to pull herself together.

"Whoever named *her*?" Snow wanted to know.

"She can't drive worth a dime," Simon added, sensing what we were trying to do.

"At any rate, she seems to think that I'll oust my perfectly good tenants on her say-so because I'm in Ireland now and the men in the family will tell me how to go on."

Snow hooted with derision, and then Simon leaped to his feet and advanced ominously toward Ann. "So, my gel, behave with me!" He twirled an imaginary mustache and leered down at her, until she had to smile. "I'm the *man* in *this* family, you know."

"You are not to worry over what Mrs. Maginnis may say, Ann Purdee."

" 'My, you're well grown for fourteen,' " said my irrepressible daughter in Mrs. Maginnis's bright accent, " 'Twins? How intrusting!' " She went on, although she accidentally slipped into the role of Lady Bracknell discussing handbags and railway stations, but she had Ann Purdee actually laughing, getting her face all floury when she raised her hand to cover her mouth.

I decided we had said enough on that subject and rose. "The other thing was, did someone dispose of my aunt's old letters and correspondence?"

"She told me to burn all her letters. She made me promise I would . . . "

"Oh, please don't misunderstand me, Mrs. Purdee. We just noticed the absence of letters in the desk. We were looking for the family bible." I didn't want her to think we were pawing through my aunt's things.

"She'd burned a great lot herself when she recovered from the first stroke, you see. Said she didn't want anyone laughing at her mementoes."

"I'll bet Great-great's mail would have made fab reading," said Snow.

I reprimanded her, but Ann Purdee smiled and went on shaping the loaves, slapping them negligently on the baking tray before she deftly sliced the tops with a heavy knife.

"I'll be bold American—may I buy a loaf from you when they're done?"

"Sure, and I'm baking one with your name on for welcome!"

"Wow!" came from Snow and Simon.

"C'mon, kids," and I signaled them. "We've got a lot to do, and so does Mrs. Purdee."

Ann didn't try to stop us, so I knew my guess was accurate. Snow pleaded to stay with the babies and keep them out of Ann's way, but I insisted on her coming with me. Ann Purdee was a well-organized body, and I'd bet her children kept out of her way, young as they were, until she had time for them. Just as we were about to leave, I heard the sleepy cry of a young child upstairs, so I hurried my twins out the door. When Ann Purdee realized that we were going to walk down the front of the cottage row, she —almost frantically—suggested that it was shorter the way we had come.

"I thought I'd see if I could meet the other tenants," I explained. "Which one is Lark?"

"Ah, oh, the end one, but Mary'd be at work. And no one else is at home either."

I wondered why she was apprehensive, but the child cried again and Ann just closed the kitchen door.

"Great-great only said Swallow and Lark cottages should stay, and I can see why the others could go," Snow said, pointing to the litter in front of the one immediately to the right of Ann's.

The back seats of two cars, stuffing coming out through the rents in the upholstery fabric, were propped up against the wall, under the two dirty windows. Muddy bottles crowded the windowsills; cracked pots held dead branches and assortments of rusty tools and shredded paintbrushes. Propping up one end of a wooden bench were several rusty, corroded gallon paint buckets. The only door was bare of paint in places. I wasn't very happy with the appearance, and wondered how Aunt Irene had let the tenant get away with such slovenliness. Although I knocked on the door, I hoped that no one was in.

"Hey, Mom, we gotta do something about this," Simon said, and I agreed. "Maybe this is who Auntie Imelda meant as 'those' tenants . . ."

"Nonsense, I distinctly remember she said *all* the cottages," said Snow.

"Well, their days here are numbered," I said, glaring at the disreputable place.

The next cottage was not as bad, although the tenant was still no great shakes as a householder. I knocked on the door and was surprised to hear a querulous voice telling me to go away.

"It's Irene Teasey, your landlady. I'd like to speak to you."

"Who?" The voice was terror-stricken. "Who? Go away!

For the love of God, go away!" And I caught fragments of a feverish recited prayer litany. "Go away!"

"Well!"

"No sale there, Mom. I'd better try next time," said Simon. "They may think you're Aunt Irene back to haunt them!"

"If I were, I would."

The last cottage was more in the style of Ann Purdee's, with two doors, but there was sufficient evidence of order to reassure me that Lark cottage would suffer no change of occupant. No one was at home.

"So much for making like a landlady," said Snow. "C'mon, I'm hungry."

"You just had breakfast."

"If breakfast is over, can lunch be far away? I can't wait to taste Mrs. Purdee's bread!"

When we got into the house, Simon elected to see if Irish chopped meat (minced steak?) made suitable American burgers. Snow volunteered to do the french fries, and I could just see myself getting hog-fat and wondered if I cared.

Suddenly there was an unmerciful pounding at the front door, and a loud and abusive shouting for me to open the door.

"Now just a living minute!" Simon roared back. He pushed me out of the way and jerked open the front door. "Who the hell do you think you are using such language?"

Simon doesn't look fourteen, and Teddie's training had given him a good deal of self-assurance beyond that chronological age. He's also a responsible young man, and considers himself the man of our house. He has never used vulgar language in my presence, though I've heard him curse in Teddie's best manner when Sim thought I wasn't within hearing distance.

"And who the hell might you be?" asked the big, flame-faced man belligerently poised on my threshold, sizing up my son.

"I'm Simon Stanford. What's your business here?"

"I want to know who's been frightening the hell out of my old mother. What kind of people are you to frighten an old woman with ghosts? What business have you here in the first place? Where's the bitch who's playing that fucking trick on my poor mammy?"

"No trick was played on your mother," I said, coming to the door.

The man's eyes bugged out at the sound of my voice, and he turned very pale. "Who are you?" he demanded in a hoarse whisper.

"I'm Irene Teasey."

"You're not!" He said it emphatically, denying my existence with a wild wave of his arms. He took two steps backward, stumbling against the potted plants as I stepped beside Simon.

"I most certainly am Irene Teasey. My great-aunt willed me this property, and I only called at your cottage to introduce myself. I'm not a ghost, and I don't go about frightening people. Besides, Mrs. Purdee——"

"Her!" and the color flooded back into his now contemptuous face. "We've no dealings with the likes of them two." He stepped forward now, leaning toward me with a confidential air. He reeked of beer and cigarette smoke. "You wouldn't, a'course, know about *them* yet. But you'd do well to turf her out of that cottage and put in decent folk. I was on to your great-auntie about it many's the time. I don't want me old mammy having to——"

"My great-aunt specifically requested me to keep the tenant of Swallow cottage," I said, and had the satisfaction of knowing that he caught my emphasis.

He gave me a slit-eyed look. He had a mean mouth, I thought and tried not to glance at his hands. What I saw of his stained jacket, dirty sweater, and oily tie were sufficient character references.

"Truth be known, missus, your auntie wasn't all that right in the head after her first attack. Aye, that's the truth of the matter." He jerked his chin to his chest two or three times to give weight to his statement. "I can see you're a respectable lady and all, and you shouldn't associate with that lot."

"Mr. . . . ?"

"Slaney's the name, missus. Tom Slaney."

"Will you please explain to your mother, Mr. Slaney, how sorry I am that I caused her a moment's alarm? I only wanted to get to know her."

His eyes, which had been wandering over me, came back to my face, and his whole body was still a moment. Then he relaxed and began to smirk.

"Sure now, and you won't be staying on any longer an' you sell the place? With all them wanting it so?"

"Mr. Slaney, I've made no plans at all. Now, if you'll excuse me, my lunch is ready."

He touched his forehead. "Sure'n I'm only home meself fer me dinner."

There was more he wanted to add, but I closed the door firmly.

"He's something, isn't he, Mom? Did you hear his language?"

"All too clearly." I gave my son a big hug, very grateful for his presence and his size. If I'd been there on my own, I doubt that I'd have had an easy time with Mr. Tom Slaney.

After lunch, we were poring over the map to see where we would wander that afternoon when the phone rang. It was Mr. Noonan.

"It's kind of you to ring, and I'm glad you did, because something else has come up," I said. After he'd confirmed having all the business correspondence and records, I went on. "That Brian Kelley character was back again, offering twenty-five thousand pounds for the entire place. He intimated that if I didn't accept his offer . . . "

"You did mention that the will had not yet been probated and you couldn't sell?"

"Yes, and he intimated that probate wouldn't occur unless I did accept the offer."

"Oh, did he so?"

"He did! Can he?"

"Ah, it is possible to delay probate," he finally said, slowly. "But two can play at that game, Mrs. Teasey. Not to worry."

"With someone like Mr. Kelley, I do."

He chuckled, but the sound wasn't as reassuring as I'd have liked. Still, I did trust Michael Noonan.

"I'd also like to know who my tenants are, besides Ann Purdee. And she's paid me the rent direct. What about the others?"

"Ah yes, Mrs, Teasey."

"Oh dear." His tone clearly said "problem."

"Not to worry. Something can be done about them, you know."

"I hope so. Two of the cottages look as if pigs live there."

"Slaneys and Faheys."

"I don't know about Faheys, but I've met Tom Slaney." I gave the solicitor the details.

"Good Lord!" And then Mr. Noonan began to laugh. He'd a very nice one, rich and deep. "To be truthful, Mrs. Teasey, you do sound extraordinarily like your great-aunt. You startled my receptionist out of her wits, so it's easy to see the effect you'd have, knocking up Mrs. Slaney. The poor ol' thing's half-witted as it is."

"You mean, my aunt tolerated *him* for her sake?"

"He made himself bloody scarce while your aunt was alive."

"Well, can you contrive to make him bloody scarce again? What are the Faheys like?" I'd better get all the bad news at once.

"The trouble with them is more absence than presence. Your aunt had initiated proceedings to have the cottage returned to her, but she died and the matter was not pursued. You've met Ann Purdee?"

"Yes. Now, she's charming. And she gave us the silver and the carburetor."

"Silver? Silver? I don't know anyting about any silver, Mrs. Teasey." That's what he said, but the laugh in his voice indicated that that was only his official position.

"Slaney's not very complimentary about 'the likes of her.' "

"Slaney wouldn't be," and Noonan's voice turned hard. "Also, his mother is five months in arrears on the rent."

"He looks the type to drink up every cent in the house."

"You can do something about him. But I think we'd better arrange a conference so that you understand the entire position."

"Oh dear, problems!"

"Not really, Mrs. Teasey. And the tenants of Lark are absolutely reliable. The Cuniffs, a mother and daughter. No worry there."

"Two out of four isn't a good batting average."

"I beg your pardon?"

"An Americanism, I'm sorry."

"Would tomorrow, Friday, at half twelve be convenient?"

"I've nothing planned. Yes."

"Fair enough. See you then."

Chapter VII

Since I'd be seeing Noonan tomorrow, we decided to leave Trinity College viewing until the next day and fare south by road now.

We were just piling into the Renault when a squat and stolid black Morris Minor pulled past the gate. So we piled out and intercepted a dumpy, short woman whose faded features nevertheless bore a familial resemblance to Imelda Maginnis. For the life of me, I couldn't remember this one's name.

"She's the Alice, I'll bet," Snow told me sotto voce, and then assumed her little-girl-innocent pose.

Just as the aunt saw us, another woman came through the gate, turning around and craning her neck in such a way as to suggest that this was her first visit here, and something more.

"May I help you?" I inquired.

Both women stopped, mouths dropping open, and stared at me. I sighed. This was getting to be the stock reaction to me, or at least to the sound of my voice.

"You're Michael's child."

"Grandchild. And you'd be my Aunt Alice."

Thanks to Snow's memory, the identification was accurate. Ignorance would have been tantamount to insult to one of Alice's nature.

"Of course I am." She didn't introduce the other woman, who seemed accustomed to such treatment—or should I know who she was? Aunt Alice also didn't offer to shake hands, or, fortunately, to kiss me. She stood on the pathway, we on the grass—a demilitarized zone, as Simon later styled it.

"We were just about to leave . . ."

"Dublin?" Hope livened Great-aunt Alice's faded features.

"No," said Snow, all surprise. "Sightseeing."

Aunt Alice's lips pursed. "We *had* expected that you would get in touch with us."

"Oh?"

"We didn't know your address, and there are so many Hegartys in the phone book," said my clever daughter.

That was not quite enough justification to suit Aunt Alice's sense of self-consequence. That anyone should fail to know the address of chief relatives was unthinkable.

"*We* [there was never a more regal pronoun] have arranged a family gathering on Sunday, at teatime, so that you can meet with your cousins and get proper advice."

I couldn't resist the temptation. "Proper advice on what?"

"Why, the arrangements that must be made for this!" She gestured with contempt at the house and land. "It wouldn't do to leave the house unoccupied while probate is pending. Tinkers! I think it's possible that Jimmy and Maeve here might move in. They need a large house." So that was the unidentified quality to Mouse-face's look: seeing if she liked the house her mother had promised her.

Snow was having some sort of spasm beside me. I think Simon had kicked her.

"And once those . . . those . . . persons are turfed out of the cottages, I don't doubt but what you'd get a decent return from the properties instead of the pittance that satisfied Irene. Certainly you could realize enough to pay the rates until you can sell up."

"Sell up?"

"Well, you'll have to sell up to pay the death duties." Then my dear great-aunt stopped and stared hard at me. "I suppose that *you* could pay that out-of-pocket and never miss it."

"No, I couldn't pay those death duties out-of-pocket and not miss it. I don't know why you should think all Americans have gold mines."

"Michael did very well in America. Everyone knows that."

"My grandfather's business is none of mine."

She sniffed and crossed her hands—oh dear, they were paws—at her waist, as if girding her loins for another attack.

"You'd be well advised to listen to what the men have to say to you on Sunday. Property values being what they are, you'd do well to take the first decent offer you get."

"I have to wait until probate . . ."

"So you do, but if, for instance, Jimmy made you an offer on the place, it being in the family and all, the details could be worked out to everyone's satisfaction."

The last person I'd sell my house to was vacant-eyed mousy Maeve.

"So far, my solicitor has been quite capable of advising me, though you're very kind."

"That young man is too bold by half," said my great-aunt, so firmly that I suspected she'd run up against Michael Noonan's unrufflable intelligence already. "These are *your* children?" she continued.

"No one else's."

She snorted at my flippancy as I performed the introductions. She gave another snort but made no attempt to introduce Maeve properly.

"And you'll need someone very keen to break that ridiculous Brandel trust! Well, you're to be collected Sunday afternoon. Be sure you're ready at half four sharp."

She wheeled, made a peremptory gesture to the shadow Maeve, and was gone before I could get breath enough to say that I found I had other arrangements for Sunday. And what was the Brandel trust anyway, that I should break it? I'd forgotten to ask Michael. Oh, well, I was seeing that bold young man tomorrow.

"Wow!" was Simon's heartfelt response. "With relatives like that,who needs enemies?"

"That poor Maeve," said Snow.

"Poor Maeve nothing!" replied Simon. "She's panting to get into our house."

"Well, she won't!" I said definitively.

This time we got as far as the turn into the . . . my lane. And the car was an Austin, which was hurriedly

braked, as much to avoid ramming us as because the driver
was in a flap to stop us.

"Oh, wait, please wait!" the woman cried, and raced
around her car to me. "Please, I know my sister-in-law was
just here. I saw her car in the lane and pulled out of sight
till she'd gone. I'm Winnie Teasey, your uncle Richard's
widow. And please, please, do say you'll come Sunday? I'd
be glad to collect you. No, Bob is to do that. I've wanted so
to meet you. You *are* Irene Stanford, aren't you?" And suddenly the flustered woman was blushing with additional
confusion. There was something very appealing and sweet
about her disorganization. One had the urge to reassure her
at all costs.

"Yes, I'm Irene, and I'm very pleased to meet you."

"Oh, Alice has been *that* way." Her face contorted with
distress. "I knew it. You see, she'd been certain that it
would all come to her, being the oldest surviving sister like,
and she'd already decided that Maeve and Jimmy must
have the Lodge, and Tom and Michael would have the row
cottages, and Betty the big end one. Oh dear, I probably
shouldn't have said that, but you'd find out soon enough *anyhow*. But I mean, Alice has very *good* qualities . . . she's
a pillar of the church, it's just that *tact* was never her long
suit, and she gives such a different impression than she
should." She paused long enough to take a breath, and
seemed to notice Snow beside me for the first time. Then
Simon.

"Are you Sara? And that must be Simon. How clever of
you to have twins. And how charming you are! And only
fourteen? My, whatever do you feed your children to make
them so big? Now please don't let Alice put you off coming
this Sunday. There are so many of us who *want* to make
your acquaintance that you can simply ignore her and talk
to us. And Tom—that's Alice's husband—doesn't let her run
on so when he's about. But we all want to meet Michael's
children. Not that I knew Michael, you understand . . ."

In a way, Winnie was as overwhelming as her sister-in-
law.

"Michael'd left before Beebee—that's what Richard was
called—married me."

"I'll be truthful, Aunt Winnie, I never heard anything
about my Irish relatives, except that I had some, until Aunt
Irene left me her queendom."

Winnie's still pretty face illuminated in a rather astonishing way, showing us that she must have been a lovely young woman.

"Irene's queendom!" Tears filled her eyes. "She was such a good person. So understanding of people's problems. And I *told* them that Irene was quite right in the head when she made you her heiress, for I can just *imagine* what would have happened had she chosen any one of us. I mean to say, it would have been just desperate. If only Beebee had been alive!" She sighed. "Oh dear, there I go on, but I did *try* to get out early before Alice was likely to come."

"Auntie Imelda beat Auntie Alice," said Snow in a sweet voice that dripped acid.

Winnie's mouth opened in an "oh" of surprise. "Imelda's been here?"

"Between you and me, Aunt Winnie," my daughter went on before I could answer, "there's not much to choose between 'em."

"Oh, there is, there is!" Winnie was plainly upset that both sisters-in-law had had the jump on her. "Oh dear, oh dear, and really they're not *like* that."

"Money's involved," remarked Snow in a knowing tone.

"Oh, and you couldn't be more right. How clever you are. Oh, but please do come. I've a granddaughter, just your age, not nearly as pretty, and a grandson, *my* Betty's oldest, who's Simon's age. I suppose you're wild about motorbikes too?"

She couldn't have uttered wiser words to change Simon's mind about going to the tea.

"And don't ever tell Alice's Betty, but her second boy has a motorbike. He hides it in a friend's shed." Aunt Winnie said this as if she were certain Alice's ears were still tuned to the happenings on Swann's Lane. "So please *do* come."

"We'll come, Aunt Winnie. I promise."

Her relief was so intense that tears started in her eyes again. "Oh, you are good. Just like dear Irene. I miss her so much. Now I must run. I've these things to give Ann for the children. Such darlings!"

She dragged clothing out of the back of the Austin, and, with her arms full, she paused once more by the window. "Ann's related, too, you know."

Before I could ask how, why, when, where, because I

was quite delighted to claim a relationship with Ann Purdee, Winnie was off down the lane at a shamble-run.

"Well, will surprises never cease!" said Snow, grinning with delight.

"Mom, get the hell outa here before someone else descends on us," said Simon in a long-suffering tone of voice.

We did.

Chapter VIII

"Your position is somewhat difficult in this, Mrs. Teasey," Michael Noonan said as he began riffling through a bulky file of papers. "In September of last year, the elder Mr. Fahey informed your aunt that he was relinquishing the cottage, but he did not hand over the key. Your aunt telephoned him at his new address, and he said he'd mail it to her, only he never did so. By then George Boardman had offered her three thousand pounds.

"After your aunt suffered the first stroke, she asked me to press Fahey for the key. He again refused, saying . . ." Mr. Noonan cleared his throat and gave us an expurgated edition of the saying. ". . . He'd changed his mind and would keep the cottage as a summer residence. Legally he is not entitled to do so, since he is a veteran, living now in veterans' housing, and he can't hold two properties at once."

"Can't you evict people here in Ireland for non-payment of rent?" asked Snow.

"But of course you can. However, Fahey has paid the rent on the cottage until September. The amount is twelve pounds per annum."

"Twelve pounds? And Great-great was offered three thousand?" Snow's practical mind rebelled.

"In addition, he is claiming the amount that he had paid out for a new roof."

"To be blunt about it, is he by any chance blackmailing us for a lump sum, after which he'd quit?" I asked.

"That's about the size of it."

"Don't let him get away with it, Mom. The way they've left the place, they ought to pay *us* to get out of the lease."

"Slaney's is worse," said Snow.

"But Slaney is not the leaseholder," Michael Noonan explained. "His mother is. And the rent has been overdue since Tom Slaney returned."

"Since he returned?"

"He's a thoroughly bad lot, drinks heavily, is out of work more often than he's in, but his mother was Miss Teasey's cook until she became too feeble. Then she stayed on in the cottage."

"Aunt Irene said nothing about keeping on the tenant in that cottage," I said.

"Not surprising. Old Mrs. Slaney was very ill last winter, and not expected to last. Of course, you can do as you wish. Actually, it might be a blessing to put the old lady in an old-people's home, out of the reach of her son."

"I'd have to think about that," I said, feeling Ugly American.

"The Cuniffs in Lark are no problem. The rent is paid monthly by banker's order into your aunt's account, and there's never been a lapse."

"How much do they pay?" asked Snow.

"Seven pounds a month."

"That's still not much against a purchase price of three thousand pounds. You'd get more interest with your money in a savings account. Or would you?"

"Good heavens, Snow. What will Mr. Noonan think?"

"That Americans raise their children to be practical, Mrs. Teasey," he replied, with a twinkle in his eyes. "She's right, you know. The rents are absurd, due partly to the Rent Control Act and partly to your aunt, who had her own reasons."

"Which she didn't vouchsafe to us, and no one else will tell us."

"As soon as the will has been probated, you can sell any of those cottages and let the new owner worry about eviction. And as for Brian Kelley, that may be all wind and stuff. He even badgered your great-aunt when she was in hospital—until T'ornton"—he dropped h's too—"turfed him out."

"Mr. Noonan, in my situation, about which none of the

relatives are happy, could probate be contested? Aside from
Brian Kelley's threats, I mean."

Reluctantly he conceded that it could.

"Because I've been getting clues."

"We've been inundated by elderly disapproving auntie relatives," explained Snow, with complete disgust.

Michael Noonan's expressive lips twitched, suggesting
that he knew exactly whom she meant.

"We've been commanded to a family tea on Sunday, at
half past four," my daughter continued. "It seems we've
cousins our ages." She sounded so thoroughly bored that
Michael Noonan did chuckle.

"Well, Mr. Noonan? I've already had broad hints that,
when I go back to the States, Jimmy and Maeve might be
willing to caretake the house for me, or buy it, and that
once 'those' tenants have been chucked out of the cottages,
decent rents might be earned. And they know tenants who
are desirable, respectable, and solvent."

"We do things a little differently in Ireland, Mrs. Teasey."

"I've been apprised of that fact too."

"Please. I can appreciate how uncomfortable it could be
for you but, as my client, you should be aware that there is
a very good chance that one or another of your great-aunt's
relatives may decide to contest the will formally—unless
you'd be willing to *seem* to give them what they want until
probate has been secured."

"I gather they think I have to sell it to pay the death duties, so they're counting on my accepting a very low offer."

Michael Noonan chuckled again as he leaned forward
across his desk in a decisive manner. "Fair enough. Give
them no indication to the contrary. The trust fund is *not*
public information. And if they become too insistent, refer
them to me."

I sighed. Snow, however, gave one of her giggles, and
then composed her face into a mask oddly resembling her
Great-great-auntie Alice.

" 'That young man is too bold by half!' " she said, in
such an excellent imitation that Mr. Noonan roared with
laughter. "You've met her!"

"I'm just no good at dissembling, Mr. Noonan," I said,
worried.

"Ah, Mom, it'll be fun stringing them along. You let me and Simon handle it."

Our solicitor cleared his throat.

"Yeah, yeah, I know," Snow went on, "children are seen and not heard in Ireland, but *that's* an advantage."

"Mom?" said Simon in that "she's off again" tone.

"Oh, Sim, we'll *help* Mother. I mean, you don't want Auntie Alice's Maeve in our house, do you?"

"Actually, Mrs. Teasey, simply say that you can do nothing until the will is probated."

However, I saw Michael Noonan and my conniving daughter exchange understanding glances.

"Naw, Mom, just slide away from the question," said Simon, making the proper gesture with his hand. "You do *that* very well."

I knew what he meant, and I *could* evade very well. Teddie had taught me how, but I didn't want to discuss that any more.

"Mr. Noonan, there was mention in the will of the Brandel trust."

"That's the one Great-great-auntie Alice wants you to break," said Snow to me.

"She couldn't an' she wanted to, Miss Stanford," said Michael Noonan, the sharpness in his tone directed against Aunt Alice. "The Ladies Brandel are sisters, very old friends of your great-aunt's," and it was patent that he thought them charming. "They're well into their nineties, and as spry as sparrows. Both have their eyesight and hearing, and although they walk slowly, they still get about under their own steam."

"They're not relatives?" asked Snow, hopefully but suspiciously.

"Not at all!" He rocked back and forth in his chair. "No, they're devotees of Gilbert and Sullivan. I believe that they encouraged your aunt when she was first considering a stage career. I know that she always sent them tickets to the Rathmines-Rathgar G-and-S shows, said they'd been going since Gilbert first met Sullivan. For them *not* to see their annual operettas would mean that the end of the world had at last come. Irene Teasey inaugurated the trust under my father. I believe she discovered that they were existing on the produce of their garden patch and tinned cat food."

"But—but—" Snow was sputtering with indignation. "What about welfare?"

"The Brandel Ladies dispensed charity, Miss Stanford, they didn't receive it." You could see that he was repeating someone else's gently intoned dictum.

"But old-age assistance isn't charity."

"In their book, the same thing," He gave a very gentle shudder at such a degrading notion. Mr. Noonan was unfolding as a very interesting personality. "Such Old World principles are very much alive in Ireland, Miss Stanford. There's never a winter goes by but some elderly person is discovered dead of starvation, too proud to appeal to the agencies set up to help."

"And my aunt helped?" I asked.

"Subtly. She unearthed a distant cousin. That was necessary, because there's nothing stupid about the Ladies Maud and Mary Brandel."

"It would be Maud and Mary," said Snow, with an appreciative giggle. "And are they really 'ladies'?"

"Oh, indeed they are. They consulted the family bible," Mr. Noonan continued, "to see if there was indeed a Robert Esquith Brandel. Of course, there was, because Irene had done her research first. He had just died. Without a will, too. So Irene Teasey and my father connived to set up a fund, allegedly the estate of this deceased cousin. The monies came from several sources, actually, all masterminded by Miss Teasey: benefit performances, their legal old-age pension, which my father applied for without their knowledge, and some"—he gave that sly grin again—"windfalls which Miss Teasey contributed."

"And they've never caught on?" asked Snow. "I like that. I think I'd've loved my Great-great-aunt Irene, Mother."

"Me too."

"It is a grave shame you never met," said Mr. Noonan, and then rattled his papers as if he'd said too much.

"Can we meet the Brandels?" I asked, as much to rescue him as to divert my returned sense of guilt.

"I do wish you would. In fact, you should, as you now administer the trust. However, you must never reveal that."

"Will Aunt Alice spill the beans?" asked Snow, horrified.

"I'm inclined to doubt that she is received by the Ladies Brandel," said Mr. Noonan blandly. "Miss Teasey, of course, had the excuse of long acquaintanceship and a mutual interest in G and S."

"Mother sang G and S in the States," said Snow with the air of one springing a tremendous surprise.

"Yes, I know."

"You do?" Snow was utterly downed.

"Miss Teasey told me. And, as her heiress and also someone keen on G and S, it would be quite normal for you to pay them a call. Incidentally, the G and S Society here is very good. They give a season every year in December."

"Mom, think of the effect if Irene Teasey appeared again." Snow's eyes went round in anticipation of the reaction.

"For mercy's sake, Snow, we won't *be* here in December. But, Mr. Noonan, suppose they do contest the will . . ."

"Let's worry about that if they do, Mrs. Teasey." Just then his phone rang. "Yes, please, tell them I'll be with them shortly." He turned back to me. "They might try to contest the will, but succeeding is another matter entirely."

"How long would probate take?"

"A month or two more, with luck."

"Good heavens. That long?"

"In Ireland, the only thing that moves quickly is the weather." He shook my hand, very warmly, and Snow's, with a grin, and Simon's, man-to-man. "Don't hesitate to ring me if you've anything else that puzzles you about the way we do things in Ireland."

"Where do the Ladies Brandel live?" asked Simon.

Mr. Noonan grinned. "In Stepaside, in a cottage called Innisfree. It's rose-covered, with a blue gate set in a yew hedge." There followed a rather complicated set of directions, ending with the usual "You can't miss it."

I could and did. As Simon pointed out the third time we retraced the route, if we'd been walking we'd've seen the neat little gate, but in a car, zip, turn your head, and you're past.

One of the Ladies was in the garden, weeding the roses, and the other quickly appeared from the house. They were undeniably twins: Lady Maud the elder, we were soon apprised. They were tiny, coming no higher than Snow's shoulder, with bright faces, smooth-skinned despite their advanced years, and sparkling eyes that twinkled young. Their welcome, when they discovered our identity (indeed, once the twins appeared, they seemed to assume who we must be), was ecstatic.

"But, my dear, I nearly fainted when I heard your voice . . . that dear familiar tone . . ." I think it was Lady Maud—yes, Lady Maud had been weeding . . .

"So like dear Irene's. How extraordinary!" Lady Mary chimed in, her voice slightly deeper than her sister's. "That's why I *rushed* to the door. Because, although we *know* dear Irene has passed on," and there was a delicate dab at her eyes, "you sounded so like her . . . The heart does hope . . ."

"We do miss her visits so much . . ."

Nothing would do but that we come in and take a cup of tea.

"One only needs the excuse, my dears, and I've done my chore for the day," said Lady Maud, briskly stripping off her gardening gloves and placing them neatly in the wicker basket with her tools. "If you'd just drop these in the potting shed, dear," and she handed the basket to Simon, who trotted off. "On the bench, dear boy," she called after him, then beamed at me. "Such a nice child. So kind, so handsome."

I caught Snow's eyes as we entered, for I had a feeling of Brobdingnagian trespass into another era, a wonderland. Everything in the room was scaled to the size of its residents, from the diminutive Victorian sofa and chairs to the slightly lower tables with their exquisite pieces of Dresden china and silver ornaments. Even the fireplace was miniature.

As one, Snow and I moved to the sofa, which looked sturdier than the delicate chairs. A miniature Empire clock daintily chimed the half-hour. Before I could summon up a reason not to partake of their hospitality, Lady Mary and Lady Maud had each brought out a small tray, one with tea accouterments, the other with plates of bread and butter (sliced by the millimeter), fruitcake, and tiny iced lady cakes.

Simon loomed massively in the doorway and instinctively seemed to fold up his large and manly frame. I didn't know how to warn him tactfully from the delicate furniture but then Lady Maud was having him clear one small table for the tea and place another on her right for the goodies.

Lady Maud smiled her thanks. "Such a nicely mannered

young man, you must be very proud of him, Mrs. Teasey —or do we still address you as 'Mrs. Stanford'?"

"Don't you remember, Maud dear? Young Irene *resumed* her maiden name," said Lady Mary, her smile approving. "Remember how *thrilled* Irene was. *Such* a compliment, my dear, you've no *idea* how *gratified* Irene was that you wanted to be Irene *Teasey* again." Lady Mary spoke with a lilting quality.

"It's almost as if—if you'll pardon me, dear Mrs. Teasey —Queen Irene is dead! Long live Queen Irene!" Lady Maud's tiny hand was raised in a regal gesture.

"Long live the queen on her queendom!" cried Simon and Snow with outrageous spontaneity, and the Sisters Brandel applauded, their small hands pattering.

"Irene was overjoyed, my dear," said Lady Maud, her lovely eyes swimming with unshed tears, "to think that you too would occupy her queendom."

"I'm actually very humble and embarrassed, Lady Maud," I said, because I'd become increasingly uncomfortable in the midst of this gentle jubilation. "I mean, I'd never even met my great-aunt. And for her to leave me everything . . ."

"To whom else would she leave her queendom?" they demanded in indignant duet.

"To those grasping sisters?" asked Lady Maud.

"Or *their* namby-pamby daughters?" Lady Mary was appalled.

"Now, Mary, there's that quite charming child . . ."

"*She's* a granddaughter."

"Of course, how could I forget . . ."

"When you've seen as many generations as you must have," said Snow, "it must be awfully difficult to keep them straight."

The two ladies beamed at my daughter; then Lady Mary leaned over and patted one of the long black curls.

"Snow White—how very, very like the illustrations in our nursery books, so many years ago."

Snow was startled. "How did you know my nickname?"

"Oh, my dear child, we *know* so *much* about you." Lady Mary's twinkle now included Simon. "So to speak, we are *very* close despite only *meeting* today. Twins are *that* way, you *must* know."

Then all four of them began one of those disjointed dia-

logues in what I had long ago termed "twin short-speech."
For a bit I was totally ignored, and pleased to be.

"My dear, if you had to be burdened with children," said
Lady Maud, "at least you managed the felicity of twins. In
our day it was a shocking breech of etiquette for any
well-born lady to produce twins."

"*Nanny* was mortified," said Lady Mary.

"Not half as much as Papa," added Lady Maud, and
there was a dry, almost harsh quality to her voice. She
turned to me. "You must never reproach yourself, my dear,
over the terms of Irene's will. Ah, I see it has worried you."

"I had no idea of her intentions."

"*She* didn't intend that *you* should, my dear Irene . . . if
I may . . ." Lady Mary picked up the conversation, laying
a gentle hand on mine for permission to address me famil-
iarly. "She wanted it to be such a *surprise*. A *welcome* surprise. Your being *another* Irene Teasey, your children, not
to *mention* the fact that you *too* had sung Gilbert and Sullivan operettas, *all* and every *single* one of these considera-
tions served to reinforce her sense of the fitness of her bequest."

"She'd never the least intention of any other course,"
said Lady Maud, "once you were named for her."

"That far back?" I was astounded. "But the will—"

"Pshaw!" said Lady Maud. "More tea, dear?" she asked
Simon, who held out his cup.

"Irene *gave* them *all* a chance," said Lady Mary, unchar-
acteristically stern. "*Such* a *commotion* when *she* went on
the *stage!*"

"More of a commotion when she refused to live with
any of them after the accident . . ."

"With *each* of the sisters *certain* that *all* Irene *could* do
was mind *their* children . . ."

"She accepted our hospitality," said Lady Maud, "when
she first returned from England." An expression of intense
sorrow robbed her face of all youthfulness and joy. "Her
voice"—a hand gestured with ineffable, graceful regret—
"was gone."

"Yet we *never* heard a single *word* of complaint for what
she had so *tragically, needlessly* lost. That's *why* it was such
a *reviving* thought to her that *you* also *sang* Gilbert and
Sullivan."

"It was as if," Lady Maud said, pausing dramatically, "her voice had not been lost, merely passed on."

"But you see, Lady Maud, I didn't even know she was a singer."

"It was in your blood, my dear Irene. You couldn't deny the promptings of your inheritance any more than you should now deny the rightfulness of inheriting."

"I see you've a phonograph, Lady Maud," said Simon quickly.

I hadn't noticed one, and followed his glance to the shadow on the far wall: a horned, crank-type gramophone.

Lady Mary bounced to her feet. *"Indeed* we do. And *we've all* Irene's records! She was *so* generous to us in that *respect."*

"Could we hear one? Please?" begged Snow.

"Certainly," said Lady Maud, airily gesturing her permission. "It's so nice to have someone who can wind it, for, truth to tell, the spring is much too tight for either of us any more."

Simon was on his feet, carefully picking his way past the small-scale furniture, like a giant in a doll's house.

"What is your favorite?" Lady Maud asked me courteously.

"My favorite of Mother's is 'Poor Wandr'ing One,'" said Snow, and when I hastily agreed, Lady Mary told Simon where to find that album. (Afterward Simon told me that the Ladies Brandel's 78 albums would make a collector flip his wig. "Mom, they had Caruso imprints worth a fortune!")

He found the right side of the heavy old record, which he handled with awed care, where Frederick is entreating "one whose homely face and bad complection/have caused all hope to disappear/of ever winning man's affection."

"Not one!"

"Not one?" pleads Frederick.

"Yes, one," and I gasped with shock at the voice. What one hears of one's own voice differs from what others hear out in front. I'd thought I was accustomed enough to hearing my recorded voice. And there was "I" singing as I had always wanted to. For, to be utterly candid, I simply hadn't the training or the great natural voice that my great-aunt had had. I could hear the difference.

I recovered enough from the shock to smile reassuringly at the delighted ladies.

"I *knew* you'd be *amazed* that you *sound* so *much* alike!" said Lady Mary in a hoarse whisper.

"Do listen, Mary dear," said Lady Maud with gentle reproach.

Talk about infatuation with the sound of one's own voice! I only wished it *were* my voice.

They insisted that we hear the rest of the first act. And there was more tea in our cups, and more bread and butter, until I worried that we might be eating the dear ladies out of house and home. I hadn't a clue how fat the trust fund was, but at one point Snow leaped to answer the kettle's summons, and on her return caught my anxious eye and reassured me. I made a mental note to find out the exact details from Mr. Noonan. These ladies must be preserved as long as possible, although they seemed to be doing a good job by themselves.

With considerable reluctance, we made our adieus at six o'clock.

Chapter IX

I felt relieved about the circumstances of my inheritance. The good Ladies had reasserted Kieron's valid reasons for Aunt Irene's decision, eccentric as they seemed to me and unfair in the eyes of her disappointed relatives.

Irene Teasey had dared to be what she wanted—a singer when such a profession was not *quite* respectable—she'd made money doing so (which was construed in some oblique way to be wrong in the eyes of her conventional family), and she had managed—despite her femininity—to have invested it so wisely that she was now condemned for the success of that perspicacity. That figured, as Simon would say.

To add insult to injury, she had left her so much despised and unexpectedly valuable property outside the immediate family. The gesture was not so much of spite as a wish to continue the tradition of her independent spirit with the only one of her relatives (me?) whom she felt qualified to ascend. Well, she had earned the right to dispose of her possessions any way she chose. And she had chosen me.

I would go on Sunday to the relative tea and observe. I would nod, smile, and ooze (as Snow said) from any commitments. I'd see if I could spot those of the younger generation whom Irene had wanted to assist. I was beginning to comprehend why she hadn't named them . . . with specimens like Imelda and Alice looming large and rapacious on the horizon.

Yes, we'd do the pretty on Sunday and then forget about the whole kit and caboodle. We'd tour until the probate was accomplished, and get home in time for the twins' school opening. We'd've had a relatively inexpensive holiday. I'd half decided not to sell the queendom—at least not this year. I could rent the main house and have Ann and Kieron keep their eyes open—even make Ann my agent, with a small stipend to ease her situation. Such fun I'd have in Westfield, talking about my Irish holdings. And Teddie would be livid at my luck. (Preserve the Image!) I did want to evict the Faheys, and I would see if I liked George Boardman and could make a deal with him. I wanted to meet the Cuniffs, and I'd better brief Simon and Snow and have *them* speak with old Mrs. Slaney.

Really, the similarity between our singing voices was uncanny, I'd *have* to try to find copies of those recordings. Of course, I wouldn't actually say they were of *my* voice . . . and while I thought that, I could feel the temptation to perform welling up. Ah, well! If only I *could* sing like that . . . And, at thirty-six, I was far too old to be a G and S ingenue.

"Hey, Mom! Mom!"

Simon's voice jerked me out of my reverie.

"Telephone. For you."

"Who?"

"It's safe. It's Shamus Kerrigan."

I had been bombarded with so many new impressions that day that I had to stop a moment and think who might Shamus Kerrigan be. Then I hurriedly took the phone.

He was a smoothie! My half-formed notion to evade his invitation was neatly spiked. He said that if I were still game enough to be seen in his company, he'd collect us at half ten, and that we should bring raincoats just in case the weather blessed us.

"Which in Ireland is a certainty," he added with a laugh, and then rang off before I could demur.

"You were going to cancel," said Simon in a very stern mood.

I gulped. "Well, yes. Because he's just one more complication on top of the relatives."

"Ah, Mom, cool it! He won't bother you about the lane. I'm sure of it."

I knew that he had no way of substantiating that opinion except that he would will Shay Kerrigan not to.

"Well, even if he does, it won't get him anywhere until after probate."

"Then why are you looking under the K's in the phone book?"

"Well, that won't do me any good anyhow, there are too many S. Kerrigans," I said, closing the book with a *sssshlap*. "I yearn to see a Schwartz or Chang in the phone book."

"Too many damned Irishmen, huh?" said Simon, grinning, and he put his arms around me. "Now don't you worry, Mother."

"You're so good to me, Simon!"

He gave a self-deprecating snort and a quick, awkward kiss.

"I'm hungry. Bread and butter is *not* enough."

"You know, so am I."

"Maybe that's what's wrong with you. I'll peel the spuds."

I was fixing cabbage with caraway seeds when I heard Snow babbling away in her luring tone of voice. "Good Lord, who's she found?" I asked Simon.

He looked up from peeling his spuds and shrugged his shoulders. Then Snow appeared in the back door.

"Mother," she called in the "highbred" tone she can affect, "you'll never guess who's surfaced."

"Really, I am intruding," said a very male, deliciously baritone voice, and then my darling daughter was hauling a complete stranger into the room.

I've always been fascinated by prematurely silver hair, which is apparently a Celtic trait. Snow's victim had a head of wavy, shiningly silver hair, set off by very black eyebrows and a gorgeously trimmed black-and-silver handlebar moustache. He was laughing as she dragged him into the kitchen, reluctant to intrude.

"Oh no, you're not. We've been wanting to meet you. Mother, this is the man who wants to buy the cottage."

"Oh, good Lord, Sara . . ."

"I told you, young lady, that I didn't think this was the time to intrude, and I still think so. If you'll excuse me, Mrs. Teasey . . ."

"No, please, Mr. Boardman . . ."

"No, please, Mrs. Teasey," and his eyes were bright with amusement. "I've the habit of looking in on Horseface of a

Friday evening, and your charming daughter apprehended me."

"He's *hunted* Horseface." There was no quelling Snow. "*And* he sings Gilbert and Sullivan!"

The upshot of that was that George Boardman, who was as nice as his looks, joined us for supper. He reassured Snow that twenty was far from being decrepit in a horse and that he had indeed hunted the beast last year, albeit a fairly quiet hunt, but that Horseface had a good few years in him, in which Snow could learn how to ride. He'd become acquainted with my great-aunt when she'd still been active in the Rathmines & Rathgar Gilbert & Sullivan Society. He was forced by Snow to admit that he'd sung with them—still sang with them, for that matter. I wasn't surprised—his speaking voice hinted at musicality.

"She coached me," he said, warmly reminiscent, "in Covent Garden's best fashion, and she was superb! How she could imitate a baritone!" He laughed at some outrageous memory. "It's such a shame that you never met."

"Now, Mother," said Simon, patting my hand. "Cut it out. Mother feels guilty."

"She oughtn't," replied George Boardman flatly. "Irene was pleased as punch to have a relative who sang G and S. Those sisters of hers never saw her on stage, and they'd the gall to criticize her for it. No, don't you worry your head over inheriting. Just follow in Irene's footsteps. Her loss is sorely felt."

I thought he was hinting at something, but Snow interrupted the flow of the feeling.

"You want to buy one of the cottages, don't you?" She said it more than asked.

George Boardman glanced quickly from her to me.

"Aunt Irene said you did," Snow went on. "Well, don't you? Mother wants to get the Slaneys and the Faheys out."

"You're a bold miss for sure," he said, not altogether approvingly.

"Snow has a good practical head on her shoulders, if little tact," I said, seeing my daughter's flush. "She's not jumping the gun, because I have already asked Mr. Noonan to find out if you still want to buy. Aunt Irene left me a letter, and I should like to comply with her instructions."

Ah, that was it. He knew about the letter.

"Of course," I went on, "there's all this business about

probate, but Mr. Noonan said that possibly you'd buy now and pay later on a caretaker basis."

"I'd like to buy on any terms you think best."

"Even with the place as big a mess as it looks?" asked Snow.

He gave her another long look, and she flushed again, subsiding into the chair. I saw Simon give George Boardman a look of intense respect. Simon, poor dear, often felt at a loss as to how to handle two women at once.

"The place has tremendous potential, Mrs. Teasey."

"Rene, please."

He smiled wryly. "It seems odd to hear such a request in that voice. You do realize that you and your great-aunt sound fantastically alike."

"Yes. I seem to have scared poor old Mrs. Slaney into thinking I was the ghost of Irene Teasey."

He sat up, startled. "Yes, you would. The poor old thing. Have you reassured her?"

"More or less," said Simon. "Her son—"

"Tom Slaney's about?" For some reason this irritated George. "I'll look in on her myself. Poor old wight."

"Wouldn't she be better off in an old-people's home?" I asked hopefully. I'd already had doubts about putting out any tenant Aunt Irene had favored.

"She'd certainly be safer, and her bit of money wouldn't be spent on drink . . ." but I could tell George Boardman didn't really think I should evict the poor old lady.

There followed one of those awkward pauses, which Simon broke by remarking that we'd heard the Ladies Brandel's recordings of Irene.

"Aren't they pets?" George said, his face lighting up with a smile of extraordinary delight. "I was going to suggest that you visit them. Which album did you hear?"

"Pirates."

"I say, did you ever sing Mabel?"

"Yes."

" 'I am a pirate king . . .' " he sang, and he had a very good rich baritone. With his looks, he'd've made a fine Pirate King.

We got a trifle off the subject of his buying the cottage with a discussion of which roles he and I had sung. We ended up singing snitches and snatches of arias and choruses. I hadn't sung in so long that my voice tightened up quickly, but if he noticed, he gave no sign. Then too, Simon and Snow know as much G & S as I, and so we were all singing away, fairly shouting out the Policeman's Chorus.

"You've got to audition this fall for the Society," he said. "I'd give anything to see their faces when Irene Teasey appears on stage!"

"Oh, but we're only here to settle the estate," I said.

"Oh, I hadn't realized. Then you'll be selling up?"

"Oh, no. Just the cottage to you. I'll probably get a good tenant for the house here."

"You're not selling anything else?" He was very intent.

"Oh, no."

"I think Mother's getting used to the notion of a queendom of her own," said Simon teasingly.

"Mother's stubborn too," said Snow, unaffectedly this time. "Too many people want her to sell."

"Oh?" And George Boardman very much wanted to know who.

"You wouldn't happen to know of a Brian Kelley?" I asked.

"Indeed I do. Kieron usually bounces him off the place as soon as he shows up."

"Kieron can't play my watchdog all the time," I said, a little glumly, because I didn't want to run into Tom Slaney again.

"Not to worry. Slaney comes floating in about the first of the month, gets fluttered, and ends up in the nick."

"Make an edict, Queen Irene," said Snow with a giggle. "No Slaneys, Kelleys, and bulldozers welcome here!"

"Bulldozers?"

"Yes," said Simon before I could, "we warned off a bulldozer our first day here. Do you know a guy named Shamus Kerrigan?"

George was very serious as he looked toward me. "I know Shay Kerrigan very well. So did your great-aunt. In fact, he bought that property because she'd give him access up this lane."

"What?" we all said in chorus.

"But—but—in her letter to Mother she said *not* to give Shamus Kerrigan access to the lane."

"*Was* he going to put ticky-tacky boxes on that land?" asked Snow, rather more aggressively than need be.

"No, he most certainly was not, because I'm his architect

and I won't design that sort of house." George Boardman was equally adamant.

"That's a relief!" said Snow, heaving an appropriate sigh.

"Your great-aunt knew of our intention," George said to me. "That's why her sudden reversal was such a surprise. I tried to speak about it, and she wouldn't even hear Shay's name. Then she had those strokes, and neither of us cared to pursue the matter. Shay's about shelved the whole project." George looked at me thoughtfully. "I suppose that's why it's such a relief to know she'd still let me have the cottage. Frankly, I was beginning to think we were both in her black book, and neither of us could figure out why." He rose. "I really must be going now. I've an engagement."

While it was a relief to me to have him go after that unfortunate turn of conversation, we all tried to make him feel that his return would be very welcome. He assured me that we'd see a lot of him, one way or another.

Chapter X

The Curragh was a topologically astonishing area, and
the "soft" air (that means very fine misty drizzle) lent it an
additional mystery. We had come down an ordinary road
which wound through typical small Irish towns, and were
thrust onto a smooth, rolling plain, a vast prospect, at first
seeming to flow limitlessly into the mist-obscured distance.

The "softness" of the day was lifting, giving deceptive
prominence to sheep grazing at the top of the next rise, so
that they stood in bold relief against the brightening sky,
looking much larger than they actually were. To our right
was the distant raceground of the Curragh, also limned bigger than actual size.

"This is where the high kings of Ireland used to hold
chariot races," said Jimmy Kerrigan, Shay's engagingly per-
sonable nephew. "You get out here early enough and you
can see them training the race horses."

Shay Kerrigan had arrived on our lane only fifteen minutes late, charming and rather overpoweringly attractive in
an Arran sweater, matching cap, old corduroys, and heavy
boots. His slightly built nephew, a dark curly-haired lad
with traces of his uncle's charm in his smile, was also regu-
lation-Arran-sweatered, wearing bell bottom pants of which
Snow and Simon instantly approved. Jimmy's fascination
with Snow was patent, but his readiness to align himself
with Simon against her became apparent in the first exchanges. Jimmy had been as apprehensive about meeting
Snow and Simon as they had been about him, but all shy-
ness dissolved with an adroit comment or two by Shay. The

three hadn't stopped talking since we'd left Dublin proper and headed southwest toward Naas and Kildare.

I had entertained the hope that Kieron Thornton and Ann Purdee might not be abroad when Shay Kerrigan picked us up. I did not want to disrupt the fragile friendships developing by appearing to associate with a man who'd been in my aunt's black book. George Boardman had indicated that Shay had once enjoyed her favor, and I was consumed with curiosity to discover why he had fallen from grace.

However, Rene's Law came crashingly into operation: In short, anything that could go wrong did. No sooner was Shay Kerrigan's Jag driving up the lane than Kieron Thornton emerged from his cottage.

To confound me further, Kieron waved cheerfully at Shay, who hollered a greeting back. Both were smiling in the friendliest fashion. I had no chance to comment, what with the bustle of introductions and settling us in the Jag. Shay was deftly turning the Jag when Ann Purdee, astride her bicycle, came whizzing down from the cottages. I had a glimpse of her startled, even fearful expression, and then we were away. The fat, fer sure, was in the fire.

Fortunately, the children were babbling away at such a rate that my silence wasn't—I hoped—noticeable. I managed to smile amiably and made any responses in monosyllables. Kerrigan must have seen Ann Purdee—he'd swerved to give her clearance, but his expression had been "driver concentration" rather than concern. Oh well, I'd have to explain later. Right now I was determined to enjoy the day. The twins were in such good spirits. And as a passenger I'd get to see some sights, instead of just road signs.

Shay Kerrigan was a considerate driver. To my relief, he was not the sort of driver who keeps up a running commentary on, or swears under his breath at, the erratic movements of other drivers. He just drove, handling the big Jag easily. He did, it's true, jam down the gas pedal on the big double highway beyond Clondalkin, but that was a road engineered for speed, and it was fun to sail along. I could relax with such driving.

The twins had embarked on one of their duet stories, and Jimmy was utterly entranced, looking from one to the other (he sat between them on the bump) as the twins switched the story-ball. Before Simon's voice changed, you couldn't tell which one was speaking, a circumstance which had disconcerted their father to the point of fury. But then, Teddie hated anyone interrupting him and, I supposed, thought everyone had the same dislike. I don't think the twins even noticed who said what in their favorite stories.

"Do you two always carry on like this?" asked Jimmy when he'd stopped laughing over the punch line.

"Like what?" asked Simon, all innocence.

"Like that. One saying half a sentence and the other the other."

The two shrugged together. "We're twins, you know."

"Yes, but that's not going on forever, is it?" said Jimmy.

"Look at Lady Maud and Lady Mary," said Shay, glancing in the rear-view mirror at his passengers.

"Do you know *them?*" asked the twins in concert.

"Of course," replied Jimmy with a "doesn't everyone?" look. "Uncle Shay's their chauffeur for all state occasions."

I don't know which of us three was the most startled.

"Have *you* met them?" asked Jimmy.

"Yes," said Simon with, I thought, admirable sang-froid. "Took tea with them yesterday."

"They're a gas, aren't they? Do you know *why* they live in a teeny cottage like that? They used to live in a castle."

"No, why?" Snow was dying to find out.

"Well, Lady Maud got betrothed"—Jimmy stumbled a bit on the archaic term—"to a chap she didn't like. Her father did it. Fathers could when *they* were young . . ." Jimmy made the good Ladies centuries old. "And she refused to marry away from her sister. So he disowned her. And Lady Mary walked out too. They bought that little cottage, and they've lived there ever since. They used to have more money, and a huge old touring car, and a gardener and a maid, but Mum says that was before the war. And they used to be invited to all the big balls and official functions, because they were related to Queen Victoria somehow or other. That was before the war too." Then Jimmy stopped, as if he'd been about to say something he wasn't certain he could discuss.

"The Brandel trust stops only with their deaths, Jimmy. I told you that," said Shay Kerrigan. "Apart from that, Jimmy-lad, I believe that this Irene Teasey isn't the sort of person who would disobey her great-aunt's last wishes." He took his eyes from the road long enough to give me a very cryptic look. "Would you?"

"No one can revoke it. It continues."

"You just bet it does," Simon said emphatically.

"If *we* had to eat cat food, they'd eat meat," finished Snow. "Aren't they terrific? I mean, fairy godmothers should look like them, so dainty and so valiant. They're unique."

We were entering the Curragh now, and fell silent with wonder. Sheep grazed by the unfenced road, nibbling so disastrously close to the flow of traffic that I gasped a couple of times. Jimmy regaled us with the near misses they'd had. True, Shay slowed the car and wore a very alert expression. Then he turned off the road and we went beyond the rolling ground into very rough country. We came around a bend, and there were twenty or thirty cars, some with trailer frames, pulled up in a rough line.

"Here we are," Shay said, and a heavy motorbike varoomed an echo.

I was glad of my heavy sweater and slacks as Shay and I followed the young people toward the spot where the riders were readying their bikes. There was a chilliness in the air that seemed to ignore clothing: It felt more like autumn than nearly summer. When I recalled the stifling heat we'd had in New Jersey in early June, I resolved to enjoy all this coolth. Suddenly the sun broke through the clouds. Faces turned toward the brightness, and Shamus muttered something about it's not lasting. Which it didn't. I had no desire to complain, since we'd had good weather all week, when I'd been told to expect nothing but rain in Ireland.

I wouldn't have thought that my darling daughter knew anything about motorbikes, but she was chattering with her brother and Jimmy as if she'd osmosed pertinent knowledge from her twin's brain.

"That pair of yours is incredible, Mrs. Teasey."

"Would you make it Rene, please?"

"Rene?" Shay Kerrigan stopped being distant for a moment and actually saw me.

"Yes, that's what my family calls me. Irenes are supposed to be tall and stately."

"They are?" and the twinkle in his eyes reminded me that my Aunt Irene had not been tall.

"Well, in the States they are."

"Rene, then. Jimmy's rather odd man out in his family. Hates sports, loves to read, and he doesn't usually talk much."

We grinned at each other at the way he'd babbled on the trip.

"Simon's more introverted than Snow, but when they're both on the same wave length . . . ." I raised my hands in surrender, and Shay Kerrigan chuckled.

He put a hand under my elbow to steer me across some stony footing, and I was suddenly struck by a curious observation: His gesture was protective, helpful without any of the "you're too stupid or clumsy to do it properly on your own" attitude that had marked such gestures of Teddie's.

"I brought along a picnic basket, because there's no place about that serves a quick meal. Oh, the Jockey, if you'd want several hours to enjoy the food, but the Red House doesn't do lunches any more. I hope you don't mind."

Of course I didn't, but again Shay Kerrigan's attitude was the reverse of what I'd expected; if I protested, I was sure, he would take me along to the Jockey for my lunch —no, the Irish eat dinner midday.

The picnic, as far as I was concerned, was a real feast: cold chicken and ham and sliced roast beef, three types of cake, Cokes for the kids, hot coffee from a huge thermos flask for us.

By then a huge number of spectators, mainly males of assorted ages, had gathered and a few more bikes had arrived to be tuned up. Jimmy and Shay explained the course to me, and it looked frightening. I mean, straight up rocky slopes and down steep, curving tracks that goats would have had trouble with.

And "scramble" was the operative word. My goodness, how those riders stayed aboard their bikes, I don't know. Glue, I privately suspected, but where? because half of them rode in a standing position. Maybe they had suction cups on their knees, but I'll bet they had blisters and bruises, particularly when they bounced and banged up slopes. The going down was obviously easier, and unnervingly faster. I had to close my eyes several times.

Simon and Snow cheered and scrambled from one vantage point to another. I think the spectators were more active than the riders. I noticed one group which had walkie-talkie units, with members at strategic points so that what one person missed seeing he at least heard about.

I gave up counting to see if all the contestants made each checkpoint, but, all in all, it was a stimulating way to spend an afternoon. I certainly ended the experience with a great deal more respect for motorbike riders than I'd've thought possible. Hell's Angels these people were not.

While the scramble had been going on we'd had to move about a good deal, but once the events were over I began to feel the chill.

"I say, that won't do," Shay said with real solicitude, and he immediately rounded up the young people, ignoring their pleas to speak to this racer or find out if that bike had been badly damaged.

The heater in the Jag was very effective, and I was beginning to thaw out and enjoy the countryside when we pulled into a pub parking lot.

The place was called The Hideaway, in the town of Kilcullen. The pride of the establishment was someone's dessicated, mummified arm. The man had been a renowned boxer with an extraordinary reach. (I'd rather been told than shown, but Simon and Snow were not so squeamish.) We had a few drinks and then supper, and didn't get back to our house until the sun was out of the sky—which was, I discovered to my amazement, half past ten.

"I didn't mean to impose on you for the whole day," I told Shay, rather appalled.

He had my hand in his, and his very strong fingers managed to caress as well as hold.

"Impose? Sure and you didn't," he said, sounding excessively Irish for a moment instead of well-bred English. "For all of that, it's a pleasure to see young Jim getting on so well. You'll probably have him round in the morning again. He doesn't live that far away."

"Jimmy's welcome any time," I assured his uncle. "And the morning's fine, but we've got to go to tea with those relatives."

"What?" Shay's expression was amusement and concern. "The haughty sisters?"

"They all came to invite me the other morning."

"Came here?" He was surprised.

"Yes, and I gather that was a first."

"Not for Winnie. She was here now and then."

"You know them all?"

He nodded.

"You're not distantly related to me too, are you?"

Shay threw back his head with laughter and stroked my hand reassuringly. "God love you, no."

"Then how do you know so much about them? And how come Aunt Irene wouldn't give you right of way up the lane?" I just blurted it out.

The amusement drained out of his face. "I don't know, Rene. We were good friends until just before her stroke. I don't know what happened to turn her so against me. At first I thought it was the aftereffects of the stroke. Jasus, I bought the land up there only because I thought we could work out a deal about the access. And then . . ." He made a disappearing gesture with his fingers.

"So what are you going to do now?"

"That's for me to know and you to guess, pet." He raised my hand to his lips, and the salute was rather disconcerting. "Come along, James. I'll be on to you again during the week, Rene."

My children ranged beside me to say their farewells and give their thanks. We truly had had a marvelous day.

Chapter XI

Sunday started out so peacefully that perhaps I hadn't caught up with myself by the time we got to the tea. Which was just as well. I suppose.

I awoke around eleven to hear voices below and outside: Snow's excited soprano rang clear above the others—children's voices and something male. *That* had better be Kieron Thornton. Whose children? Ann Purdee's surely weren't old enough.

"Hey, Mom, did you sleep well?" asked Simon as I appeared in the kitchen door. Jimmy Kerrigan shot to his feet.

"I hope you don't mind, Mrs. Teasey, my coming back so soon . . ."

"Good heavens, no!"

Simon was plugging in the electric kettle, and it must have been warm, because I had a steaming cup of coffee in front of me in moments.

"What is Snow up to?"

The boys grinned. "Her first riding lesson," said Simon, and I heard that he had something else, momentous, that he wasn't saying.

"Well?"

He gave Jimmy a jab in the ribs. "What did I tell you? Mom hears what I don't say." He grinned bigger. "It'll be more fun if you find out yourself."

"Simon Stanford, Sunday morning is no time for unexpected surprises. We've had quite enough for one week."

"Oh, Snow'll tell all. Soon as she claps eyes on you. First have some coffee."

Except for the Slaneys and Faheys, the resident population of my queendom was assembled at the small pasture gate. I already knew Kieron Thornton and Ann Purdee. There were two other women, one holding a small baby, the other with her hands on the shoulders of a girl about eight or nine. Snow was astride Horseface, who was bridled but not saddled, and she had one child in front, clinging to the mane, and another behind her with a death grip on Snow's already tight jeans. The old horse was walking most sedately around the pasture, his neck gracefully bowed and his tail switching in a manner that I thought indicated satisfaction. His lovely small ears were twitching back and forth to the sound of the laughing children. But he was taking his task seriously. I had the additional impression that he was placing his feet very precisely so as not to dislodge his giggling riders.

Kieron saw me first, touched Ann Purdee on the arm, and pointed in my direction. The movement caught the attention of the other two women. One smiled welcomingly; the other tried to.

Ann Purdee, as one determined to face an unpleasant task squarely, took the darker woman's arm, and they both advanced on me. Kieron angled himself as their rear guard. Or that's the impression I received.

"Oh dear, you look so solemn, Mrs. Purdee. Whatever is the matter?" And I instantly remembered her seeing Shay Kerrigan.

"I told you," said Kieron, encouragingly cryptic.

"Mrs. Teasey, may I introduce my housemate, Sally Hanahoe."

"I'm very pleased to meet you, Mrs. Hanahoe," I said, holding out my hand.

The young woman blushed all shades, looked about to die, and then jerked her chin up bravely. "I'm not a 'Mrs.' "

I stared at her a moment, mystified, and then several matters became clear. "Those" tenants, "that lot," Aunt Irene setting up the tenants of *her* queendom as she chose, with very low rents. The baby Sally held was the little one in the carry cot, who'd been teething. I had been unconsciously wondering how Ann Purdee could have three so-young children, even in a Catholic country. And it also struck me that an unmarried girl with a baby in holy Ireland might have a very rough time of it. That accounted for Sally's defensiveness.

"Well! Well, I think you're a very brave girl to keep your baby. You must love her very much. And I think it's marvelous of you, Mrs. Purdee, to help her. Or are you related?"

"Only by trouble," said Ann in a rather grim voice. "Then you don't object?"

"To what? Why should I? Aunt Irene knew?"

"Irene knew," said Kieron, stepping forward. "She knew whom she wanted in her queendom."

"That's more or less why Molly and I are here, too," said the other woman, coming forward with her hand outstretched. She had a mature, serene face, but the lines at her mouth and her eyes spoke of deep sorrows past. "I'm Mary Cuniff and this is my daughter, Molly. I was a little luckier than Sally. I do have marriage lines, for all the good they do me." She gave Sally a cryptic smile.

"Well, I appreciate your telling me, but I can't see that it matters much—at least to me."

"What worries Ann at the moment is that you're taking tea with the relatives," Kieron said, and nodded toward Snow as his source of information.

"And? Winnie Teasey brought you clothes," I said to Ann, "and seems to know you—" I started to ask what degree of kinship we enjoyed but Ann interrupted.

"Winnie Teasey is a good woman with a guilty conscience." Then she caught herself. "Oh, that sounds nasty, but she knows I need the clothes and all, and it makes her feel better to give them to me than to the tinkers."

I cast about for something to say to ease the dreadful bitterness in Ann Purdee's voice.

"We're well met, then, Ann, Sally, Mary. I'm scarcely in a position to cast a stone. After all, I got rid of my husband only because I'm lucky enough to live in a country where separation and divorce are possible. And where a woman can bring up a child without too much censure. Furthermore, I'm not about to undo what my Aunt Irene did without very good reason. More than just those greedy relations' opinions of you." Kieron was giving Sally a reassuring hug. "And how did you get in, Kieron? Or were you a deserted husband?" I asked, trying for a lighthearted note.

"Oh, I suspect I'm useful as a gatekeeper, chucker-out, and odd-jobs body."

"Don't believe him," said Ann sharply. "He came back to take care of his mother when his sisters turfed her out as useless. You've a collection of outcasts in your cottages, Mrs. Teasey: unwed mothers, deserted wives, and"—she flashed another look at Kieron—"layabouts. And Tom Slaney's been back again. You're not even doing that job right."

"No, I threw him out on the roadway yesterday evening. Drink-taken."

"He's only dared to be back here because he knew Irene was dead. She'd have the Gardai on him!" Ann said.

"You know, I think my great-aunt was women's lib!" I said.

Mary Cuniff laughed, a very warm contralto sound. Sally Hanahoe was first startled and then giggled, but Ann Purdee looked upset.

"No," she said slowly, thoughtfully. "She didn't like them all that much. She believed that when you had made a decision you had to stick by it. You had to accept all the responsibility for your actions and never blame anyone else. Like your mother spoiled you, or your father didn't understand, or this or that. She felt that a lot of the women's-lib movement was trying to evade responsibility by saying men put them down."

"Ann, you're simplifying it again," said Mary gently. "You know what a desperate situation we [and she meant women] have in Ireland. You know what I'm paid and what that lout Feeney gets, and I do most of his work."

"There, that's just what Irene meant."

"Girls, girls!" said Kieron. "Sure and 'tis the Sabbath! And that's not what Irene meant."

"A squeaky wheel gets oiled," said Mary, and from the look on Ann's face I thought the next argument would be launched immediately.

"Hey, Mom, look at me! I'm riding a horse!" cried my daughter as the circle Horseface had been following brought her around to where she saw me.

Dutifully, and thankfully, we all went to the fence to make appropriate comments. Ann didn't seem at all nervous that her children were in the keeping of an absolute novice.

"Don't bang so with your heels, Snow. And sit very straight. That's better. Shorten your reins. You need more contact." Ann slipped in under the rail and shortened the reins to suit herself.

Kieron stepped closer to me and said in a quiet voice, as if commenting on the lesson, "You won't be taken in by the relatives and their notions of how you should dispose of your property, now, would you?"

"You own your house, so why should you care?"

"Those girls've all had desperate hard times. They don't complain, but it would be cruel to see what they've built so carefully together destroyed by that group of biddies." He put his hand under my arm and led me away. I wondered what he'd look like without all the face fur. He had such nice eyes. He was guiding me toward the garden patch, as if we were discussing that. "You see, Ann can't work away from home. There's no one to leave the children with, and she'd lose her Deserted Wives' Allowance. Not that it's much. Sally works in the supermarket. She pays board to Ann for herself and the bahbee. Ann minds Molly for Mary, who's a cashier at the Montrose. They all look after Mrs. Slaney, who's a desperate poor creature, can barely see or walk . . ."

"Would Mrs. Slaney be better off in a home?"

"No. She knows us and all. Leave her be the while." He glanced over toward Faheys'. "But them . . ."

"Mr. Noonan's getting them out. And how does George Boardman get into this queendom?"

Kieron laughed. "Sure an' haven't you guessed yet?" His twinkling eyes enjoyed my puzzlement. "Irene was immensely practical too. Go on, give a guess."

"I can't."

"I'm the tenor . . ." And when he saw my amazement: "Ann's the soprano, Mary the alto . . ."

"And George is the baritone? But Irene's dead, why have a quartet?"

"Why not? Long winter evenings, you know. Good crack. No, now, I'm teasin'. Irene liked George, and Fahey'd turned so sour in his old age he was no more use to her at all. It's only to be nasty he's kept on there." Kieron waved at the messy garden. "So when George offered her three thousand for the place, she told Mihall to get Fahey out. I'm not here as often as Ann makes out, and there

should be someone about the place. You see," and Kieron
turned dead serious again, "there could be desperate trouble
for Ann, and maybe Mary. We know Ann's husband's been
looking for her when his ship's in. He's a right bastard, and
he'd move in on her just so's she'd lose her allowance,
which she would do, even if he spent only one night. And
he'd beat her again."

Not if Kieron saw him first, I heard plain as day.

"Is he in Ireland?"

"No, he took the boat."

"Took the boat?"

"That's an Irish divorce," Kieron said with a bitter snort.
"Fella takes the boat from Ireland to England and he can't
be forced to pay support for a wife in Ireland."

"Good Lord." I wondered for a frantic moment if Teddie-boy might get some ideas. But Hank wouldn't let that
happen. "They can get away with that?"

"Oh, indeed they can. The last time was two years ago,
when she was pregnant with Michael. Winnie brought her
here. The big cottage had just gone vacant." He gave a
wicked grin. "Never have figured out if Irene approved or
disapproved of her girl graduates. But it saved Ann's life,
no question."

"You're on her side?"

"Don't sound so surprised. Fair's fair. Add to that, I owe
the girls a trick or two." A muscle began to jump in his
cheek. "They cared for my mother until I got home."

I started to inquire about his sisters, pure curiosity on my
part while Kieron was in this expansive mood, but a wild
shriek interrupted me. It was only Snow, sliding off the
shoulder of the horse. She wasn't hurt; in fact, she was
howling with laughter as we dusted her off and hoisted her
onto Horseface again. The horse dipped his soft muzzle
into my hand, sort of inquiringly, and made the most en-
dearing whicker. I patted his smooth nose encouragingly
and said something affectionate. He snorted with more
force.

"He likes you," said Snow, almost resentfully.

"He thinks he recognizes my voice, that's all. But I don't
seem to smell right."

"You do sound much like Irene," said Ann. Then, as if
she'd said too much, she turned briskly to my daughter.
The littler ones had gone off to play with Molly Cuniff.

Mary wasn't anywhere in sight, but just then Kieron saw the two boys peering around the Mercedes and excused himself. That was just as well. I had quite enough to digest right now.

If Aunt Irene had wanted to protect her subjects, it was logical to choose as successor someone whose ways were not as inflexible as the relatives'. But how could she be sure I'd not be as hard-nosed? On the basis of our names? Or an interest in G & S? Good heavens! Simply because one sang G & S didn't necessarily mean one went along with their sniping at Victorian mores.

I had just turned two eggs into the plate for my belated breakfast when Snow came bouncing in, declaring that she was about to expire from starvation. She was also full of incidental information.

"Great-great didn't like men—"

"With Kieron on the property?"

"—in general," and her expression chided me for interrupting. "Particularly Irishmen. Can't be trusted. Always believe the worst of a man and you won't be disappointed." She tried to snag a piece of eggy toast from my plate until I signaled her to make her own.

"Was she crossed in love?"

Snow shrugged. "Probably, but Ann said that she'd heard that Great-great always had a lot of beaux, and turned 'em all away. Ann said it was because they were after her money, and she always said *her* money wasn't for any man to drink up. Sally's not married, didja know?" I nodded. "Mary's been here since before Molly was born. *Her* husband was a bigamist, only he wasn't because the Church annulled his first marriage. Mary knew about that, but what she didn't know was that the State didn't recognize the annulment, so now she's married only as far as the Church is concerned, not the State."

"Why doesn't she get an annulment from him because he married her under false pretenses?"

"I dunno. I suspect it costs money, and he went through most of hers and then started going with someone else and she found them in bed together—"

"Sara Virginia! They haven't been talking—"

"Heavens no, Mother. They're too square, but I can hear just as well as you what people don't say. Anyway, Mary up and left him when she was seven months gone with Molly. I mean, gee, that takes real guts. Do you know what divorce Irish-style is, Mom?" asked my all-too-precocious daughter. "Taking the boat!"

"Oh, you mean skipping to England, where the man doesn't have to pay support?"

"Oh!" That deflated Snow. "You were smart to be an American, Mom. Daddy can't do that." Her eyes widened. "Can he?"

"I don't think he could slip anything past Hank van Vliet." It was easier to reassure Snow than it was to quell that niggle of fearful worry in my own breast.

"Mommy, aren't there any nice Irishmen?"

"Heavens, yes. Look at Kieron and George and Shay and Mr. Noonan."

"Yeah! But there's something that Ann doesn't like about Shay Kerrigan."

"Ohhhh?"

"She sorta tried to find out if he'd be coming around much. I told her you weren't giving him any right of way, because you didn't want a lot of traffic and ticky-tacky boxes lousing up the queendom, and that *seemed* to be what she wanted to hear. Then Sally appeared and Ann clammed up. Did you know Ann knits Arrans like zappo, it's finished? Only the Deserted Wives people can't find out, or they'd reduce what they give her. She does get medical free, but with the price of things going up so . . . Sally's got a friend who's a fisherman, and he always brings up a sack full of fresh-caught stuff Saturdays, and Sally brings in bruised vegs and stuff from the supermarket, but, honest, Mom . . .

"So then when Ann heard we were all going to this relative tea this afternoon, she flipped. *They* had big notions of a clean sweep in this quarter before Great-great was even in the ground. And the relative who was supposed to get Ann's cottage would only sell it anyway, because she's already got a luxury-type bungalow in Cabinteely. And Ann didn't say it, but she's still scared you'll change your mind, or you'll be coerced by the death duties to sell hunks of the queendom."

Snow's vivacity suddenly drained from her face, and she looked woebegone.

"Sara Virginia, you know perfectly well I won't. Certainly not to that crowd. But we do have to put in an appearance today. Besides, there're the young people that Aunt Irene wanted to help. How're we going to know who they are if we don't go where they are?"

"I hope they're there. Unrelieved Great-aunts Alice and Imelda are indigestion-making. Ugh!" She gave an expressive shudder, but her spirits did not revive.

Nothing will make me rise to battle stations faster than the need to cheer up Snow. I hurriedly distracted her by asking how we should redecorate the kitchen. This worked like a charm, although I wasn't certain that Aunt Irene would have liked purple trim.

"Fer Pete's sake, Mother, are we always going to be dominated by what Great-great would have wanted, done, said?"

"Well, no, of course not. I was just making—"

"Definitely." She ignored me and pivoted slowly about the room. "Purple in the kitchen, and we'll find a purple design—they *must* have contact paper in Ireland."

Simon strolled in, saying that he was hungry and were we going out to dinner or did we have to wait to stock up at the tea.

"What color do you want in your room?" Snow asked.

By the time we'd figuratively redecorated the entire house it was almost four o'clock, and we scattered to get suitably attired for the relative tea.

Robert Maginnis drove a sober black Ford Zodiac. "Not that he drove it well," Simon said later. For my own peace of mind, Robert Maginnis was a most pleasant-spoken, amiable man, with a ruddy complexion, a shock of rumpled white hair, and a very sweet manner.

"By golly," he said, "You do sound like Irene." He placed a hand under my elbow to guide me to the car. "You put quite a fright up Melly, I can tell you." I had to quell the twins with a stern eye, because his accent, not to mention his calling Imelda "Melly," made the phrases rhyme. "Hope we won't be too much for you all at one blow, like. We're a long-tailed family, we are."

Uncle Bob, as he asked to be called by the time we were halfway up the Kilternan Road, was a beef merchant, buying from farmers, fattening steers, and selling to local independent butchers. He had a chain of meat shops, but said he preferred the buying end.

"Gets me up early, like, to attend the auctions. Keeps me feeling young, y'know."

He was so affable, so jolly, so completely different from what I'd expected Aunt Imelda's husband to be that I was glad he was so talkative. I was too surprised to do more than make the proper responses.

I couldn't have found my way to the Maginnis house, and whether I'd want to find my way back there again would remain a moot point. The house was distinctive, set in its own grounds, surrounded by fields and a high stone wall. We drove into the stableyard, past nearly empty hay barns and cattle sheds, onto a flagged drive that led to the two-storied house of such varied design that I guessed amateur architects had enlarged it to suit their particular tastes.

We entered through the kitchen, which had been extended to incorporate a back room; the separating beams were a constant danger to six-footers, of whom there soon appeared to be many. There were seven people seated at the round table chatting with Aunt Imelda, who rose to greet us most effusively. Just as she was introducing me and explaining the degree of cousinship to the people at the table, Alice came barging in, two steps ahead of an anxious-faced Winnie. Winnie hovered for a moment, seemed to be reassured, and made off with the twins, whom she wanted to introduce to the younger set in the parlor. Uncle Bob was asking me what I'd like to drink. I thought tea or coffee, and there was a large guffaw from one of the men. I was then apprised that tea in Ireland does not necessarily mean the beverage tea; it can very easily—as this evening proved —be an excuse to have a party.

One of the men at the table had risen when Alice and Winnie arrived—I couldn't remember his name just then— and he took me by the shoulders and guided me to the seat next to him, rather beyond Alice's conversational arc.

"I'm your second cousin at a couple of removes, Gerry Hegarty, and you stay by me and I'll protect you," he said, with an engaging grin and the most incredible blue eyes.

"Watch out now for Gerry," said the black-moustachioed man across from me, offering me a cigarette. "I'll protect you from him."

"And who's to protect her from you?" asked Gerry as he lit my cigarette, waving aside the other man's lighter.

"My wife!"

"I'll see that my dad doesn't slip you any poteen," said Gerry with mischievous solemnity.

"What's poteen?"

"What's that she says?" Gerry repeated as if amazed. "Sure and you don't know what poteen is?"

"Mountain dew!" said the other man, rolling his eyes wildly to indicate potency.

Well, I knew what that was, so I eyed the drink set before me with suspicion. Gerry sniffed it and handed it back to me with a reassuring shake of his head.

"Safe! Weak Irish!"

Encouraged, I took a sip. "Safe?" I cried when I could speak again, wondering what form of distilled lightning I'd got.

"Stir it" was Gerry's suggestion.

I did, and took a very cautious sip. Evidently no one had stirred the mixer properly: I'd got a mouthful of pure Irish.

"You'll not be telling me this is the first drink you've had in Ireland?" Gerry asked, having watched my performance with intent curiosity.

I was framing a reply when I heard the black-moustachioed man speaking to Aunt Alice, who was leaning toward him with all the attitude of a private conversation.

"Sure and I'll have a chat with her soon's Gerry gives me the chance. Isn't that Maureen coming now?" And he pointed out the window.

With that, Aunt Alice muttered something under her breath and then flounced off—if a woman of that build and age could be said to flounce.

"What're you and Mammy cooking up there?" Gerry asked the man.

"Aunt Alice is your mother?" I was astounded, dismayed, and mortally glad I'd not had the chance to put my foot in my mouth.

"I'm her bahbee," he said draping his hands across his chest and giving me the eye, for all the world like a bashful three-year-old.

"I'm Jim Kenny," said black-moustaches beside me, "for I'm sure you'd not manage to remember all the names flung at you before. And I want to make one thing very plain to you." He glanced over his shoulder to see where Aunt Alice was. "Nothing would get me to move out of my modern, unpaid-for, centrally heated, four-bedroom house in Blackrock to a cold hillside far from the delights of town." As I stared at him, shock vying with relief, he went on. "I'm Maeve's husband, and while she's a darling girl an' all, she will get caught up in those rainbow schemes of her mother's."

"What we're trying to say," put in Gerry on my other side, "is that we know what *she's* about," and he nodded his head toward his mother, busy talking (and nodding in my direction) to two new arrivals."And you're not to worry. Never a soft word for Irene in her life, plenty of tears at the wake, oh my yes, and a different sort of noise altogether when the will was read."

The letter! "Oh, you're the Gerry who's to have the Mercedes," I said, suddenly recalling Aunt Irene's instructions.

"Oh, no way. You're the Irene that still has the Mercedes."

"No, I'm Rene."

"Praise be! It's got so the very word 'Irene' puts any decent one of us running in the opposite direction. Seriously now, Rene, that car is a gem. Kieron did give back the carburetor, did he not?"

"Aunt Irene specifically said . . . " I can stick to the point too.

He shook his head firmly. "This is not a day, either, for repeating what Irene said . . . though God bless the woman . . . " and he tilted his glass in a quick toast, as did Jim Kenny. Were these the "young" people she'd wanted to help? "We've all been Irened to the death of us. *This* is the day to meet your cousins over the waters, chat 'em all up, and get stocious. Now, tell me how you like Ireland. How long do you plan to stay, and are those large young people really *your* children?"

I jumped at the opportunity to answer innocuous questions. (Hide *behind* the Image!) On top of my relief at discovering that these male cousins of mine were singularly unconcerned about the eccentric will of our mutual relation, I found that they were delightful company. Shortly, however (and I'd noticed the pair keeping a surreptitious eye on Aunt Alice), they maneuvered me out of the kitchen, away from her notice, and into the living room.

When I didn't see my twins among the assorted younger people—there was an incredible number of children of all sizes and descriptions—I got apprehensive, until one of the women said the twins had gone to inspect young Tom's new motorbike and wasn't the racket frightful?

It was all very pleasant but I seemed to be getting too many refills on that drink, so I was very glad when someone asked me if I wanted a bite to eat. Gerry guided me to the dining room, where there was a turkey and a ham, sandwiches, and bread and cake and cookies. A platoon of teacups stood ready on the sideboard. I was very much in need of something to sop up all that liquor.

Snow and Simon descended on the buffet with six young people, chattering a hundred to the dozen. Snow heaped an indecent amount of food on her plate, but others had collected as much if not more. My conception of ladylike teas went through another upheaval.

Snow sidled up to me in her best conspiratorial fashion. "Boy, have I got a lot of gossip for you, Mom." Then she got snatched away by a grinning black-haired boy before she could elaborate.

No sooner had the multitude been fed and tea-ed than the table was removed and chairs pushed back. A redhaired man started to fiddle a come-all-ye, and another man hauled out an accordion.

Gerry was all for seizing me for a wild reel, but I firmly held him off and asked where the ladies room was.

"I'll take you, Mrs. Teasey," said a soft voice beside me. It was the motorcycling receptionist. She'd been waiting for a chance to get me aside, I suspected.

"I hope you don't mind, Mrs. Teasey," she said as she threw the bolt in the bathroom door behind her, "but I've been trying all the evening to get to talk to you. I wanted to explain and to thank you."

"There's nothing to explain, really," I told her, wanting very very much to use the toilet.

She turned to the mirror and began to fiddle with her hair, giving me a chance.

"You see, my grandmother . . . "

"Oh Lord, *which* one is *your* grandmother? I'm hopelessly lost with all these relations."

"My grandmother's Alice Hegarty. I'm Maureen, Tom's daughter. Brian Kelley's my father's boss. I had orders to let him know when you got here. I had to do that, you see. I didn't want to, but my dad said I had to, and there'd be

no harm done. You do understand?" She was so pathetically conscience-stricken. "And you should've heard *them*
when she died! Parceling out *her* things, her money—*if
there was any.*" Her tone mimicked the original speaker.
"And they were so positively *glad* to turf Ann and Mary
out, you wouldn't believe!" Her eyes were sparkling with
remembered outrage. She gave a sharply expelled breath,
her expression both sad and cynical. "I know how people
can behave, because I've been in a solicitor's office long
enough, but when they're your own kin, and it was Auntie
Irene . . . " Tears sparkled in her eyes, but she controlled
them. "You'd better go out first, Mrs. Teasey."

"Oh, for Pete's sake, Maureen, we *are* related, please call
me Rene?"

She gave me a soggy smile and nodded.

"And come see us soon at the queendom. Please? I need
your help, for Aunt Irene's sake."

She agreed and I left the bathroom, much relieved on
several counts. Such a sweet child. She must have been one
of those my aunt had wanted to help and didn't dare: The
vultures would have descended instantly.

Gerry was leaning against the hall arch, a drink in each
hand. Beyond there was singing; the tune was familiar, but
the words escaped me.

"C'mon, you've to do your party piece," he said, taking
me by the arm and wheeling me toward the dining room.
Protests availed me nothing.

My Uncle Bob was in the middle of the floor, vigorously
directing the singing, his face flushed and sweaty with effort. His tenor was strong, if not precisely true; he sang
with enough vivacity and enthusiasm to overcome any
faults. He beckoned Gerry to lead me forth. The last thing
I wanted to do was sing in front of this audience.

"No, no, I couldn't sing," I said urgently to Gerry, and
held my glass up. "I'm too tight."

"Sure and what are the rest of us? What'll you sing? My
dad can play anything on that squeezebox of his."

Uncle Bob seconded Gerry's insistence, and the man
with the accordion obligingly came over, said he was my
Uncle Tom, and told me to sing anything I wanted in any
key and he'd do his best.

Snow came running up to me. "Oh, do sing, Mommie,"

she said sweetly (the traitor), but the message in her eyes amounted to a royal command.

I don't like to sing cold, without a chance to warm the voice up properly. And I hadn't done any real singing, except the other night with George Boardman, in such a long time that I knew I'd sound stiff. Then I saw the faces of Imelda and Alice, politely composed to endure listening to the visiting Yankee relative whom they cordially wished to the devil. Well, I'd show them.

"Would you object to a Yank singing an Irish song?" I asked.

"Not at all," the men assured me, and the accordionist ran a few encouraging chords as a guarantee.

I told him the key, and when he looked slightly blank, I asked for a chord in B-flat, which he understood. And began to sing "Kathleen Mavourneen," which, believe me, was the only Irish song I could think of at that particular moment.

The babble courteously died. Then, as the quality of my voice became audible, I had an accurate count of which relatives had heard my aunt sing. A small gust of gasps occurred behind me, and, turning, I saw Gerry staring at me as if I'd erupted from the grave. His father gave a startled squeeze on his instrument. Uncle Bob's jaw dropped a foot. Neither sister turned a hair, their faces still polite, exhibiting merely surprise that I could sing creditably, but Winnie Teasey began to cry.

"By golly," said Uncle Bob, his eyes moist, as he pumped my hand during the applause, "you sounded exactly like Irene."

Then everyone was clamoring for more, for me to sing this song or that ballad. I had—to myself—sung well, but I wouldn't be able to sing long before lack of practice showed up in faulty breathing and projection. But I wasn't allowed to leave the floor until they had coaxed, then threatened, half a dozen songs from me. Then I got away because I simply walked out of the dining room and out of the house.

Gerry followed me. "Do you know how much you sound like Auntie Irene?"

"Did you hear her, or just the recordings?"

"Once as a small lad I heard her sing. But it's incredible. Did she know?"

"She knew I'd sung in G and S."

He gave a funny laugh. "Well, it's no wonder—the name, the voice, and all."

"Oh God, not the will again."

"Now, not to worry, Rene," and I didn't hear hypocrisy. "They've precious little to do except gossip. I told them they hadn't a chance in hell of inheriting."

"You knew . . . about me?"

"Sure, most of Irene's friends did." Gerry had a rich laugh. Then he solemnly took my hand in his. "And look you, you don't know our ways here in Ireland, so ignore the half of what you hear and discount the other fifty percent."

"What on earth do you mean?"

He jerked his head back at the house. "That lot has come up with some pretty silly notions, and they've hatched another tonight." He stroked my hand and grinned down at me. "They've decided to try to marry you into the family."

"What?"

"Not to worry, not to worry."

"Who?" I was appalled, furious, and somehow it was all hilariously funny.

"Me," he said in a squeaky voice.

"That's right, you're the widower."

All humor left his face. "Irishmen make devilish bad husbands, Rene. Never marry an Irishman. We're spoiled rotten, self-centered, and hard on a woman. Sell up, rent out, do what you like with the queendom, but don't marry here."

I felt awful suddenly, and awkward, too full of drink to cope with any more shocks, surprises, or contretemps.

"Oh, Gerry . . ."

"I'm warning you so's you'll know not to worry. I like being single again!" And he grinned in the most engaging fashion.

All I could think of was my mother sending me off to Ireland because men were men here. They certainly were, and I began to wish that I could go off quietly somewhere and sleep, not have to be diplomatic with these incredible relatives.

"Come, pet, I'll drive you home. Can you come back in, just the minute, so's my mother won't take offense at the guest of honor's leaving so?"

"Oh, my children! I've got a pair about here somewhere

. . ." The fresh air was not helping my wits at all, an effect which became even more noticeable when I got back into the close, hot atmosphere of the kitchen. Gerry's masterful manner—or maybe the fact that the relatives were only too happy to have him escorting me someplace—got me through the leave-taking formalities. Suprisingly, considering their dread at coming to the tea, the twins begged to stay on a bit. I was informed that someone would see them home, and then everyone was kissing me, especially the men, only it wasn't offensive, and I was saying over and over that I'd had a lovely time, and then Gerry had me out in the fresh air again and in a car and I suddenly realized that I *had* had a lovely time.

Chapter XII

The next morning was not a lovely time. I felt slightly ill, my mouth tasted like last winter's unaired snowboots, my feet felt bloated and too heavy, and I had the general sensation that I'd slept both too long and not enough. To compound the injuries to my person, it was raining.

I groaned.

Snow appeared in the doorway as if conjured, with a glass in one hand and a bottle in the other.

"Alka-Seltzer, Mother," she said in a neutral-nurse tone, and popped the things into the water, swirling the glass to make them dissolve faster.

"Don't! They're noisy."

"Hmm . . . that bad, huh?"

She sat on the bed, and I protested.

"They didn't slip you any poteen, did they?" she asked, suddenly suspicious. "Nevil said they might try it."

"Who's Nevil?"

"A cousin, what else?" She made a face and then giggled. "He's cute. He drove me home pillion. It was tough, Mom."

"Pillion?" I roused myself, regretted it, sank into the pillow. "Oh, that's dangerous."

"Naw! Simon warned Nevil, and they followed us to pick up any pieces." Again the giggle.

"How did Simon get home?"

"He went pillion with Tommy."

"Tommy? Another cousin?"

"An*other* cousin. *Zzzhish*, Mom, I thought we had cousins by the dozens in the States, but here it's by the gross." She let out a whistle, but I clutched her arm to stop that frightful noise. "Ooops. Sorry! Poor Mommy," and she disappeared, returning a moment later on elephantine feet. With loving concern, she placed a cool cloth on my forehead.

"Where's Simon? It's raining."

"He's talking up a storm with Tommy and Jimmy Kerrigan and Mark Howard. Now you go back to sleep!"

The seltzer made me burp, and my stomach was pacified. The rain was soporific, and I lay there, listening to the soft sound and feeling the cool on my head, and went to sleep again.

When I awoke, I felt a lot better. I heard laughter below me in the kitchen, and the sounds of pots and pans being battered about. So naturally I felt guilty about lying in bed and got up.

The kitchen was not very big, and looked much smaller with the thousand and five youngsters crowded in it, sitting on the cupboards, the woodbox, the chairs. One was perched on the fridge. They were all watching Snow make hamburgers and chips. They were all on their feet with a *thud-thud* when I entered.

"Coffee, Mother?"

"Yes, of course, darling. Did I meet all of you yesterday, or is my memory really going?"

I was introduced to Jimmie and Mark Howard, and Simon (with a laugh) and Tommy, and the long dark-haired one was a girl cousin named Betty. I'd met all except Mark Howard, who was seeing Betty.

Lunch was good fun, and by the time I'd had a hamburger and french fries I felt considerably "more better than," as Snow used to say with ungrammatical expressiveness. Snow also tipped me the news that we'd very little left to eat in the house. Betty had to get home, as she was minding her small brothers and sisters; Tommy and Jimmie wanted to take Simon with them, and it appeared the whole group had a date that evening to listen to Tommy's latest record buys. It was rather breathless, but I was relieved to think that the twins would have friends—relatives, even—with whom to enjoy their vacation.

The kitchen was all tidied before the visitors left with Simon. That's when Snow remembered the mail which had been forwarded to us from the hotel.

One was a letter from Mother, the other from Hank van

Vliet. Both held basically the same tidings: Teddie was having fits about my taking the children away. He'd phoned Mother and then visited her, demanding to be told where his children were and what sort of a low bitch did she have for a daughter.

"I took a great delight in telling my ex-son-in-law where to go, Rene," my mother wrote, her sweeping pen strokes embellished by ballpoint smears, emphasizing her annoynace, "something I've wanted to do for some time, I assure you. I phoned Hank after Teddie got off my line. I'm having no more of that kind of nonsense, I assure you. Hank is writing you, but my advice is to stay on in Ireland no matter what else you intended—at least for the summer and/or until his rage has subsided. But don't worry, you've done nothing wrong or illegal. If you have a phone number there, send it to me and Hank but give it out to none of your other friends. You know how Teddie can extract info if he wants it."

Apprehensively now, with hands shaking because the itch had (damn it) been accurate, I opened Hank's letter, and learned why Mother had enjoined me not to worry. Teddie had had an injunction issued to prevent me from "surreptitiously and without his knowledge" removing his children from the continental USA. I'd left before it could be served on me.

Hank assured me that I was completely within my rights, and he was taking steps to have the injunction canceled, since both he and my mother could vouch for the fact that I had informed Teddie of my intentions. (I wished people would stop telling me not to worry, because it made me worry more.) Hank went on to tell me not to worry about any moves Teddie might make locally to try to coerce me to return to the States with the children. (Oh, good Lord, what on earth could Teddie do locally? Well, if he met up with Auntie Alice or Auntie Imelda . . . That made me laugh, because Teddie would have met his match and retired from the field with that pair.) Teddie had threatened all kinds of imprudent and impulsive actions—Hank couldn't leave me ignorant on that score—but my legal position was secure. After all, Hank could easily prove that Teddie had many times chosen not to exert his legal rights of visitation (particularly when there was a golf tournament or a weekend winging).

I sighed as I finished this worrying don't-worry letter. "Oh, dear!"

"Daddy being a dastard again, Mother?" asked Snow, peering over my shoulder at Hank's concluding paragraphs. "Hmmm. Thought as much."

"What do you mean, 'thought as much'?"

Snow shrugged. "Well, he put on such a heavy father routine that time on the phone . . ."

"What time on the phone? I didn't know your father had called you."

Again that insufferably diffident shrug. "Oh, we knew it would unnerve you, Mommy. Besides, you know how Dad can carry on, and it's only talk."

"*What* did he say?"

"Oh, some drivel about your dragging us some place completely unsuitable for *his* children, and you'd probably make us go to Mass, and oh . . . you know how Daddy goes on!"

"Why didn't you tell me?"

She gave me that round-eyed innocent look. "Because you'd've worried and worried, and we wouldn't have come to Ireland. And we wanted to come with you!"

"Is that why you two organized me out of the country so fast?"

"You said it!" Then she hugged me. "We told Hank about the call, and Gammy, and that's why—"

"Why I was on that plane before I had time to think what Ted might do."

"You got it, Mommy," she said in that I-know-best tone of voice which reminds me so much of my own mother that I tend to overlook how impudent it is in my daughter. Besides, she was correct.

"Why all of you think I'm not capable of managing my own life . . ." This protectiveness only underscored my private opinion that I *was* ineffectual.

She threw her arms about me, her lovely eyes full of remorse and repentance. "Ah, Mommy, don't look like that. You do just great as long as Daddy isn't involved. But when he is, you go all to pieces."

She took me firmly by the arm, handed me my bag and raincoat, and propelled me toward the door. "We've more important things to do right now, like get the shopping done and buy paint. Because if we're going to stay here until Dad cools off, we're not going to flip our wigs looking at this revolting decor!"

The paint cost a small fortune, what with brushes, rollers, paint cleaners, and sandpaper. But Snow took the bite out of the bill by informing me that we'd save a lot by doing the work ourselves. When I countered that it would take all summer, she pooh-poohed the notion, demanding to know how long I thought it'd take with half a dozen brush wielders.

"Which half dozen?" I asked, but knew the answer, because Snow invariably operated on the Tom Sawyer principle. A born executive, my daughter.

"Never mind, Mommy, the task is well in hand."

"That's why the sweet talk and all the hamburgers?"

She gave me a tolerant look and then smiled in her sweetest fashion. "That's how to manage a queendom. Only, Irene was her own prime minister and I just appointed myself yours. She recruited a labor force when necessary. Why not you?"

"Oh?"

"Yes, oh." Snow gave an admiring sort of snort. "She might have been philanthropic, but she was smart too. D'ya know that Ann Purdee qualifies as a lady tailor? She whipped up Irene's clothes. We know that Kieron is a first-rate carpenter. Mary Cuniff is a bookkeeper, she only cashiers because the hours are better while Molly is young, and old Mrs. Slaney was chief cook and bottle washer until she got so crippled with arthritis. Oh, Aunt Irene had her queendom, but her courtiers were carefully selected."

"What about Sally Hanahoe?"

"Typist, but she has better hours as a supermarket clerk."

So our next stop was Sally's supermarket, where I wished she could have got a commission on the tremendous total we ran up. After that large outlay of cash, a visit to the bank was necessary, to cash more travelers' checks. The bank manager was so charming and helpful (he'd known my great-aunt, of course) that I ended up opening an account—much more sensible than carrying around large amounts of cash.

As we drove back to the house, Snow let out a satisfied sigh. "Now tomorrow we should turn this heap in. It's costing us a fortune."

"Not as much as all this paint."

"Paint's an investment, Mommy, and the Mercedes runs, so why *waste* money running this?"

A very good point.

"But we have to tax the car and transfer your insurance. I don't think the American policy is good here."

"How do you know so much?" I asked my daughter.

"Oh, I asked Nevil and Mark. Your best bet for insurance is—"

"Snow?"

"Yes, Mommy?"

"Are you managing your mother?"

She gave me her most charming smile. "Me? Whatever gave you that idea?"

"You!"

The phone was ringing as we entered the house, so I couldn't continue the argument.

"Mrs. Teasey, Michael Noonan here. Would it be inconvenient for me to stop by with some papers that require your signature?"

"Not more bad news?"

"More?" There was, thank goodness, a ripple of laughter in his voice, so his tidings couldn't be all that devastating. "I don't think so. Would half seven be too late . . . or too early?"

"No, no. You do know where I am?"

Again that ripple of amusement. "I'll see you then, so."

Snow was carrying in all the paint gear, muttering under her breath about Simon never being around when you needed him, the rain, and how heavy paint was. The next thing I knew, she was all set to start work immediately in the dining room.

"Not to worry, Mommy." How quickly my daughter got acclimated in language differences. "All the paint's latex, and there's no smell. Says so on the label."

"We have to strip the wallpaper off first . . ." I hadn't the words out of my mouth before Snow had seized a loose edge and *zip,* a whole panel came flying off in her hand.

"No problem at all."

If one is going to undertake a major task like painting a large room, there are certain preliminary steps that the careful workman takes: covering furniture, moving it away from the wall, putting cloths down to protect the carpeting.

We did none of those things, but somehow or other, three and a half hours later, we had a Wedgwood-green dining room, with ceiling in matching color, most of the easier-to-reach trim had been done, and we had got the groceries put away too.

"There! Now doesn't that make you feel better, Mommy?"

"I'm not so sure about ivory draperies, though . . ."

"Hey, Mom!" Simon returning from any absence manages to inquire after me in the roar of a bull calf, a summons guaranteed to pierce the unwary eardrum. "What have you gals been up to—Like, hey! Wow!" He whistled admiringly, absently giving me his customary hug and kiss. "You didn't waste much time, did you, Snow? Why didn't you wait for me? And that trim's not done."

"We left something for you, dearest brother of them all," she said, rubbing green paint into her nose. "I'm starving of the hunger."

I was too, and we had just finished when the doorbell wheezed.

"You could fix that if you felt constructive," Snow told Simon as I made for the front door.

Mr. Noonan, looking far too clean and dapper, smiled at me expectantly.

"I forgot all about you!" Not the most tactful remark to make, however honest, and I groaned. (Destroy the Image!)

He laughed and told me not to worry and what had we painted and could he see, and Snow took over while I washed paint off my arms so I wouldn't Wedgwood-green important documents. I returned to find that she had initiated an inquiry about the Mercedes, and Michael Noonan confirmed that I could apply for insurance.

"Now, as to these." He rustled papers and eyed my daughter in such a way that she took quick steps in another direction. "This is for the Trust Fund, now standing at five thousand four hundred thirty-two point thirty-four pounds. The estimated death duties are four thousand two hundred thirty pounds, give or take the odd pound and pence. As soon as probate is accomplished, you will have these funds unfrozen," and he passed me statements from the same bank I had dealt with that morning, one for a savings account, the other for the checking: a total of another nine hundred forty-five point sixty pounds.

"I can't use that until after probate?"

"That's right, but you can use the trust fund."

"And all the just debts are paid?"

He slipped another sheet in front of me. "These small accounts were settled, and of course your aunt had paid for her funeral before the event."

"Pay now, go later?" I couldn't have stopped the words had I smothered saying them, and the pair of us burst out laughing. "Oh, forgive me. It's just that—"

"Don't apologize," said Michael Noonan. "You've the same humor as your great-aunt, too. She'd've loved that. Pay now, go later. Seriously, though, Mrs. Teasey, it is an established custom here to pay for your funeral ahead of time."

Well, with £800 in a savings account and another £145-plus in a checking account, my aunt had not been hungry.

"Mr. Noonan, there's one thing that has puzzled me. There was nothing left in the cupboards when we got here . . ."

"Great Scott, Mrs. Teasey, I told Ann Purdee to clear everything out of the larder, to keep rats and suchlike out of the house."

"Oh, thank heavens."

"No, Irene Teasey never wanted for food, not with Ann and Mary Cuniff and Kieron about." His eyes screwed up with some humorous recollection. "Sides, she had a sort of sideline, I guess you Yanks would call it, that always guaranteed her petty cash."

"She did? What?"

He grinned but refused to answer. "Later. Now let's look at that Mercedes."

We all went out to examine our vehicle. Michael peered thoughtfully under the hood. I always suppose that men instinctively understand automobiles but apparently Michael Noonan knew doodly-squat about motors. Just then someone called from the front of the house.

"Sounds like Shay Kerrigan," said Snow, and I could have choked her. "I'll go bring him around. *He* knows from cars."

"Snow!"

"Well, she's the right of it," Michael said with a grin. "I don't. And Kerrigan does."

"You know him well?"

Michael grinned at the squeak in my voice. "You'll find that Dublin is a very small town, Mrs. Teasey, and everyone knows everyone else."

Shay greeted the solicitor as affably as if they were long-time friends. And then Kieron Thornton joined the board of experts. Some may say that the Irish will talk a thing to death before they lift a finger. Not so, or maybe it was the Mercedes. I don't care. What matters is that before I could protest, Shay and Michael were taking the tires to the nearest gas station to be filled, and had said they'd get me a proper battery until the existing one could be charged. They brought back filled tires, petrol, and a battery, and spent the next hour happily setting the car to rights, and off its blocks. And even helped me "sort out" the insurance and tax thing.

There were striking anomalies in the way Irish men treated their women, I thought, with the examples of Sally, Mary, and Ann, the blackmail tactics used against young Maureen. Yet here were three very attractive men worrying and arranging to take care of my very minor problems. Or was it just another case of minor problems being fun and the long-term monotony of marital bliss unendurable? Gerry *had* told me never to marry an Irishman. Then I found myself contrasting these men with Teddie. Depending on his mood, Teddie would have 1) assumed that I was too stupid to handle the insurance/tax/negotiations, 2) complained bitterly as he assumed the burden, or 3) sneered so at my ineptitude that, out of spite, I'd've done the job—and quaked with nervousness that I'd somehow goofed. These men made no assumption of ignorance; they were being courteous and helpful. It would have been churlish on my part to refuse their aid.

Once all the necessary documents were assembled and placed on the small hall table under the rifle (Had I got my license for that? No? Well, that could be done when I got the Garda to sign the taxation form . . .), Shay turned to the others and suggested that now a few jars were definitely in order.

"You lot," he said to Snow and Simon, "are all right on your own, aren't you?"

"We've our own engagement this evening," replied my daughter haughtily. Then giggled. "You get my mother in early. She's had a tiring day."

I was told to go wash the rest of the paint off my face and be quick about it. Anomalies all considered, this was a much nicer brand of male superiority than I was accustomed to, and I flew obediently up the steps to wash and change.

Mother would have been ecstatic, and Betty would have remarked drolly that that was the sort of singles club she preferred for me.

We went to a nearby pub where a blind pianist held forth ably, often singing songs of his own composition. Not that I had much time to listen to him with the good-natured teasing and talking that went on. I was ensconced on a bar stool, and the three men loomed about me. Heady stuff, and very, very good for my ego. For the first time, no Shadow-Teddie lurked in the background, casting poisonous looks if I appeared to be enjoying myself in another male's company. And this trio was outrageous. I laughed until my eyes teared and my ribs ached.

I had such a lovely evening that I actually let out a cry of disappointment when the barman called time. My three musketeers saw me home, none of them (they all declared) trusting the others to do so. It was fun until I passed the dark cottages where Ann, Sally, and Mary lived. All-that-glitters evening, I sternly reminded myself.

As I lay in bed, very tired, my mind churning with the evening's good fun, I had only a brief wakeful moment to wrestle with another anomaly: All three men appeared to like each other, so why had my aunt turned so against Shay Kerrigan?

Shamus Kerrigan was also well known, and seemingly well regarded, by the Gardai at the Cabinteely station. I was told not to worry when Shay explained about the Mercedes, the necessary yellow form was instantly produced, and the matter of the gun license would also be attended to immediately.

Shay had dropped Jimmy off at the house to help the twins prepare the living room for painting, so we chatted affably about the redecoration all the way into town.

"If you need to pick up the odd piece of furniture, the auctions here are excellent for that," said Shay.

"Oh, I'll go to a secondhand furniture dealer."

"That's what I was suggesting. They call them auction rooms here. Much more dignified."

Indeed it was. And we talked about the differences in terms and my struggle with the car-registration forms, and then he mentioned that he'd been in the States the previous year. He'd been particularly interested in building methods and restrictions. He'd been amazed to find out how much timber is used in America for building; American lumber is much better, whereas it would be horribly expensive in the States to build so exclusively out of brick and cinderblock. We talked about city planning and had a real laugh, since Dublin's appeal for me was its lack of planning, with awkward turns in the city-center streets and one-ways where they were the most inconvenient (so Shay said), I found Dublin more and more charming, so un-big-city-ish.

The insurance company occupied an old barn of a building on Wolfe Tone Street. There I ran into an unexpected difficulty in giving the proper information to the poor young clerk. About the only thing I had in order were the car's papers. Mine were all in my married name, and when I filled in the form I had to explain about now using my maiden name.

Then came the question of my husband. The clerk insisted on knowing his name, and I insisted that he didn't need it.

"Why, he doesn't even live in this country, so what good will his name do you?"

Utter confusion, and he went away to consult with a superior.

"Well, it doesn't do him any good," I told Shay. "Teddie wouldn't pay for a postage stamp I used now, much less car insurance. Though he's had the accidents, and I've never scraped a fender."

The clerk was back. "Any accidents, miss . . . oh, missus?"

"Never!"

I was so positive that he didn't belabor the point. I paid him my thirty-odd pounds, and then we had to wait about while they typed up a certificate.

"You know," Shay said as we waited, "I don't think you

answered a single question according to his not-so-distant training. Obviously," and he gave an exaggerated sigh, "you Yanks exist to bemuse, confuse, and confound us poor peat farmers."

Thirty-three pounds made eighty dollars, reasonable in the light of New Jersey fees, but Shay tsked-tsked all the way to the tax bureau over the atrocious rate. To my relief, getting the car taxed was nowhere near as much of a problem, nor as expensive as I'd thought, the way he carried on.

So we drove back in triumph, taxed and insured. The Mercedes had been washed, polished, and shined in our absence, an accomplishment which brought lavish praises from us both. I insisted that Shay drive the kids in the Merc while I took the Renault back. I was glad I had listened to Snow, for the bill put a substantial dent in my dwindling cash reserves. We tried to persuade Shay to stay for lunch, but he had an engagement. Jimmy was going to help us paint.

"I don't know why you should help us," I said to him over the sandwiches we hurriedly fixed.

He flushed a little, and became engrossed in the texture of the bread.

"I'd just like to, Mrs. Teasey."

"Every free hand is gratefully accepted," said Simon, giving me the "leave it there" look.

Jimmy proved to be a slow but exceedingly careful worker. Almost too slow. As if . . . the notion crystallized in my mind . . . as if he was afraid of doing something wrong. Fortunately, Simon was also a methodical worker, while Snow tended to slapdash through things, good for the overall effect but not for details. As Simon was quick to tell her.

"Well, I don't take all day to do a square inch," she said, flaring at her brother.

"The inch I do doesn't have to be done over," replied Simon, indicating the fireplace he was trimming.

"Well!" and I could see that Snow was taking umbrage.

"Do you help your father, Jimmy?" I asked, trying to find a neutral topic.

"My father? Oh, yes, in the garden. My dad's a keen gardener."

"You should see the greenhouses they have," Simon said. "All kinds of crazy plants and flowers—and grapes."

"Do you like gardening?" I asked Jimmy.

He finished a delicate stroke. "Well, yes."

I laughed. "The 'well yes' that means 'no.'"

"No," he said defensively. "I do. It's just that . . ."

"Just that sometimes you don't do things exactly the way your father thinks they should be done?"

Jimmy sighed with relief that I'd said it, and nodded.

"The same old story," said Snow, drawling her words out. "I guess dads are alike the world over."

They took up the comparisons game. I listened because I was hearing what Jimmy wasn't saying, and that was a situation that repeated itself all over the world too. He had three sisters and three brothers, and his father was a very busy barrister.

I began to see why Jimmy found us so fascinating: I was far more available to my children than his parents were to him, although there wasn't a hint of criticism in his comments, merely resignation to the-way-things-are. He was a fair ways toward substituting Shay as an active father-figure in place of his own. I wondered if Shay was aware of this. According to Jimmy, Uncle Shay was brilliant, always ready to listen, and quite pleased when Jimmy'd drop in unexpectedly. Uncle Shay had the keenest flat in Blackrock, with a super view of the harbor and all modern conveniences.

"Yes, but what does your uncle *do?*" Snow asked. I'd wanted to ask, so I had to stifle my surprise when Jimmy replied without reticence.

"He buys up land for development, and he's got an auctioneer's license, and he owns a pub in Monkstown and a garage in Glasthule. My father says that Uncle Shamus ought to get married and settle down." Jimmy laughed at such an outrageous future. "Uncle Shay says he'd rather stay single and act married than be married and act single, like some guys he knows."

There was rather a lot of wisdom in that statement.

"Irish men marry late," Jimmy went on. "Or they used to. My father was thirty-two before he married." Obviously that advanced age bordered decrepitude.

"How old's Uncle Shay, then?" asked Simon.

"He's thirty-five—I think. He never says, but he's the youngest in my father's family, and my next oldest uncle is thirty-eight. Mother says she wishes Shay would marry.

Then her friends would leave her alone with their match-making." Jimmy snickered.

"I have the feeling that Irishmen don't make reliable hus-bands," I said, thinking of the women in the queendom.

"That's what my mother says," replied Jimmy, and then frowned, painting a few thoughtful strokes. "Though she doesn't mean my father."

We finished the living room by evening, although now the tiles around the fireplace looked dirty. Jimmy declined to stay for dinner, explaining that he ought to get home so his mother wouldn't say he was overstaying his welcome here and prevent his returning the next day.

I was frankly pretty tired by then and took a bath—not quite as hot as I liked, but we'd used some of the hot water for the dinner dishes. Snow dragged Simon off to watch her ride Horseface.

Judging by the sounds I heard as I drifted off to sleep, she'd managed to get Simon aboard the horse too.

Chapter XIII

I wasn't all that happy the next morning, though. I woke early, refreshed, and lay listening to the birds warbling away, half my mind trying to match bird and sound, the other half feeling miserable about Shay Kerrigan and the access.

I didn't abuse myself with the notion that he had been so courteous because he liked my big blue eyes, or that he had fallen hopelessly in love with me at first sight. He was being attentive and helpful so that I'd weaken and give him the access. And yet . . . he was going about the process with such subtle courtliness and charm that . . .

What *had* Aunt Irene against him? Why did she rescind it? Did Michael Noonan really know and wouldn't tell? "It involves someone else's good name" had been Aunt Irene's words. Well, maybe no one except Aunt Irene and that "someone" really knew.

Did Ann Purdee know? But wouldn't tell so as to not cast any of her stones? Now maybe Mary Cuniff wasn't as reticent. She'd been fairly outspoken on Sunday. Ann had too, come to think of it. While I hated to put the kids up to doing my dirty work, Snow could weasel out a lot of information without seeming to. No! I'd best try Mary.

Just then my right hand began to itch, inconveniently in the palm. Oh Lord, what now? That was the trouble spot. I tried valiantly to keep from scratching, as if thus to ward off the foretold trouble. To divert myself, I resolutely rose. But when I was washing my face, I found myself scrubbing the facecloth into my itching palm. Oh, that would never do!

To create a diversion, I sat myself down with a cup of coffee in the living room, the un-paint-smelling, clean living room, planning how to redecorate it around the existing pieces of furniture. By the time I realized that it was getting late and dashed down to Mary's house, it was locked up tightly.

"Mary's away by half eight, you know," Ann Purdee said. She had come up from the direction of the main road, leading a sleepy-eyed, yawning little girl.

"Is that one of your daytime charges?"

"'Tis indeed. She was asleep upstairs t'other day," and Ann smiled reassuringly down at the pretty thing, who wasn't at all sure about me. "Say hello, Meggie."

"'Lo" came out in a whisper. Eyes cast down, the small person locked herself against Ann's leg.

"She doesn't see many people." Ann swung the girl up into her arms, at which point Meggie buried her head against Ann's neck rather than be gazed at by a stranger. "Now, now, love, that's bold. You remember Auntie Irene, don't you?"

There was a frantic denying motion of the head.

"Sure and you do, pet."

"Don't bother, Ann. She's half asleep."

Ann craned her neck toward the Slaneys' house. "You know, I've not seen the old lady in two days now."

"Is that unusual?"

"Yes, when it's sunny as it's been. She likes to sit out in the sun."

"You don't suppose it's because I frightened her?"

"Sure now and Mary and I told her how it was on Friday, and she seemed to understand and all."

Ann went to the nearest of the dirty windows and peered in. Without a word she handed me the child, who struggled only briefly. Ann pushed at the front door, but it was locked.

"What's wrong, Ann?"

"She's there, sitting on the bed. Just staring straight on." Ann's voice had a frozen sound, and when she turned toward me her face had gone white. "I'm going for Kieron." And she was away like the wind.

Kieron came back with her, at a run. He pushed at the

window frame, and the wood disintegrated around the catch with very little pressure. He took one good look inside, and we didn't need to see his face to know the answer.

"Oh no!" murmured Ann, both hands to her mouth. She began to wring her hands, tears welling in her eyes. She was one of those fortunate women who can cry without turning all red and blotchy. Kieron gathered her into his arms, and I had a sudden revelation about Mr. Kieron Thornton and Mrs. Ann Purdee. His face, when he looked toward me, reflected none of the tenderness he directed toward Ann.

"Rene, I think you'd better call the Gardai."

"Not a doctor? Or a priest?"

"It's too late for either of them."

"Oh dear!"

"No," said Ann in a muffled voice, "she'd want Father O'Rourke."

When I got to the house I discovered that I still had Meggie in my arms. Snow was coming down the stairs, so I thrust the bewildered little girl at my daughter and told her to cope.

"What's the matter? What's happened?"

My hands were shaking so that I couldn't turn the thin telephone-directory pages.

"What has happened?" demanded Snow, but she was also jigging Meggie on her knees to keep the child's pout from becoming a full-blown howling session.

"Listen and you'll learn," I said, finally finding the page with *GA.* "Oh God, there're so many stations . . . ah, yes . . ." I dialed the number, my fingers shaking. Why were they shaking over the death of a woman I hadn't even met? They were shaking because I felt a sense of guilt that her fear of me had been the cause of her death.

I did manage to tell the Garda what had happened, and had enough presence of mind to ask him to give me the priest's phone number. There'd be so many O'Rourkes in the phone book that, in my state, I'd never find the right one.

"Good Lord! The poor old thing," Snow said when she'd heard the salient points, and trotted herself and Meggie upstairs.

Father O'Rourke was saying Mass, but his housekeeper promised to give him the message directly he had finished and I wasn't to worry, the poor old soul had gone to the peace of the grave, thanks be to the Virgin Mary. She'd had the last rites during her bad spell in May, and Father would do the necessary, sure and he would.

That done, I stood indecisively in the hall, holding the receiver, wondering if there was anyone else one had to call in Ireland. I suppose that's why I didn't think it odd of Kieron to ask me to phone the police first. Simon came thudding down the steps, buttoning his shirt. Snow may take an inordinate delight in relieving you of all depressing details, but the bare facts were enough for my son. He went to the kitchen and returned with two glasses. He handed me one and told me to drink as he began dialing a number.

"Uncle Shay? I think you'd better get here on the double, if you can manage it. There's been some trouble." Then he put the phone down and sat me on the first step. "Now drink it, Mother. Won't do you any good in the glass."

I took a good mouthful, and the whiskey burned all the way down.

"Ann'll need one too," said Simon.

I watched the tall, broad-shouldered back of my dearly beloved son retreating from the house and mused that the young could have a lot of common sense. Or maybe at his age he still had enough sanity to act on instinct rather than conditioned social reflexes.

My stomach had stopped fluttering and there seemed to be bones in my legs again when Snow appeared, chattering away to the enchanted Meggie.

" 'Scuse me, Mom, but I think I'd better volunteer as baby-sitter." And she exited, rear door.

I didn't want to be alone, so I followed her and found Simon and Kieron standing over Ann, who was making very slow work of the whiskey. Then we heard the awful noise that emergency sirens make in this country.

"Simon, take Ann to the cottage, will you?" said Kieron. His face was bleak as he turned to me. *"You* wanted to speak to the old lady. You couldn't get an answer and asked me to investigate. Right?"

"Well, yes, but does it matter?"

"Kieron," said Simon, stepping beside me, "I'm not sure Mother's up to—"

"Your mother's a foreigner, Simon," said Kieron in a flat cold tone, "and she's the landlady, and there're other reasons. Just take Ann up to her house, and she wasn't here this morning."

Simon didn't argue and I couldn't, because the police car came up the lane as Kieron assured me he'd explain later.

I should have insisted that Kieron could very easily have played the role he was scripting for me, but there I was. Simon and Ann had disappeared into her house. However, the Gardai were so very courteous, sympathetic with my distress and confusion, eager to make all easy for me, that I didn't think beyond the immediate problem. I hadn't a clue why Ann mustn't be involved in the death of an old woman, but Kieron scotched an attempt at honesty when the Garda asked if any of the other neighbors were about.

"Mrs. Cuniff, who lives next door, is at work and her daughter at school. There's no one in the house on the other side," said Kieron.

"And what about that cottage?" the Sergeant asked, pointing his pen toward Ann's.

"Haven't seen them abroad this morning. The tenants have small children and keep very much to themselves."

Just then the Garda's partner came out of the Slaney house.

"You just opened the window, Mr. Thornton?" he asked.

"That's all."

And I knew then that Kieron knew why the police had to be called.

"She's got a hole in the side of her head you could plant your fist in."

I let out a gasp and, I think, a shriek, because Kieron and the Garda were both quick to support me to the nearest of the dilapidated car seats in front of the Faheys'.

"Now, now, not to worry, Mrs. Teasey."

"Not to worry?" I glared at the Garda. "When that poor old woman's been murdered? Why didn't you tell me that's what you saw?" I demanded of Kieron. But I could see why he didn't want Ann involved, and I wondered if she had seen that dreadful sight too.

"Now, now, no one's said that she's been murdered, missus," said the Garda rather firmly.

"With a hole in her head?" I grabbed at Kieron's hands. "I thought she'd just died of . . ." I nearly said "fright."

". . . Old age."

The other fellow was using the radio in the patrol car. I

began having visions of my queendom jampacked with reporters and homicide people and sensation seekers. AMERICAN INVOLVED IN GHASTLY MURDER: That'd be the headline. All I had to do was inherit Aunt Irene's queendom, and instead of applying American common sense, I got it embroiled in a murder case.

"Have you seen Tom Slaney about?" Kieron was asking, in a very conversational tone, I thought, for the circumstances.

"He's back, is he?" and the Garda was very alert.

"I turfed him onto the road the other night," said Kieron.

The Garda turned to the man on the car radio. "Find out if Tom Slaney's in the nick," and then he moved off toward the car.

"If it is murder, we can't keep Ann out of the picture," I said softly to Kieron. "They'll be on to just everyone."

"We can try," said Kieron back to me, softly but fiercely. "Her husband's in town, looking for her. He can't find her. He mustn't find her."

"Can't you explain?"

"I— Now what the hell is he doing here?" exclaimed Kieron, and I saw Shay's blue Jag careening up the lane. It slithered to a tire-slicing stop right by the black Gardai car.

"Simon called him."

"Simon is being—" and Kieron shut his mouth.

"If you please, sir," the first Garda said, stepping in front of Shay Kerrigan.

"And if I don't please, Sean? Now that's a rich one. Mrs. Teasey phoned me to come by. She said there was some trouble."

Garda Sean began to clear his throat, but that hesitation was sufficient for Shay to slip by him and come to me.

"Old Mrs. Slaney's dead," Kieron began.

"With a hole in her head," I finished, and then dissolved in horror at the rhyme.

"Kerrigan, take Rene up to the house. This is too much of a shock for her."

"Ann?" asked Shay very quietly. He and Kieron stared at each other for a long moment.

"Rene found her," Kieron said in measured tones, and Shay inclined his head understandingly.

"Paddy's back in town, I'd heard," he said. "And this is

where I can help, Thornton. Won't be a minute, Rene," he went on, as if a snap of the fingers was all he, Shamus Kerrigan, needed to set things right. He went over to Sean the Garda and began talking in a low voice. The policeman nodded, seemingly acquiescing. Shay wasn't a moment when he came back to say, "If they have to take a statement, they'll diddle the name. But likely it's Tom hit his mum once too often. He's been up for that before now, you know. Irene didn't let him get away with anything."

"Reporters?" I asked.

Shay grinned as if I were missing the obvious. "And this a private lane and all? Thornton, do you have something we can put across the entrance? And you can mount guard, once the Gardai leave." Then Shay pulled me gently to my feet and started me toward the house.

"Where're your children?"

"With Ann. Oh, we'll have to warn Sally."

"Sally?"

"Yes, Sally Hanahoe. She lives with Ann, and Ann takes care of her baby while she works."

"What?" Shay began to laugh. "Not another one in the queendom."

"What do you mean?"

"You might say that Irene made a specialty of deserted mothers and children." He wasn't mocking.

"Aren't there any agencies that help unwed mothers?"

"Sally's unwed to boot? Poor kid. Yes, there are nursing homes that take such girls," and his face and eyes were hard. "And make them feel like pariahs. Has anyone told Mary?"

"I don't think—"

"Call the Hotel Montrose. But first I want to give Michael Noonan a shout." He steered me in through the kitchen, pausing to plug in the electric kettle, and then marched me through to the telephone.

"Why Michael?"

"He's the one Simon ought to have called. Not me."

"Oh dear, I am sorry, Shay. Involving you in my problems when I can't . . ."

"Not to worry, Rene. Promise? Actually, I'm flattered that Simon thought of me." He dialed as he spoke. "I like that boy very much. They're both good youngsters. Hello, there, Noonan, there's been some trouble . . ."

Michael said he'd be out as soon as possible and I wasn't to say anything more until he got there.

Just as Shay started to dial another number, Sean the Garda appeared, very courteously, at the front door. "Here, Rene," said Shay, handing me the phone, "tell Mary . . ."

Mary was shocked and very upset.

"They think it was her son," I told her.

"I shouldn't wonder."

"Did you hear anything, Mary?"

"No. The walls are very thick between the two houses, thanks be to God. Oh, I ought to have called in. I knew he'd been drinking . . . on her bit of pension money, like as not. If only I'd gone over when I hadn't seen her out in the sun . . ."

"I think, perhaps, Mary, it's as well that I found her."

Mary's sharp intake of breath was confirmation enough. "They'll be on to me, I suppose, living next door."

"Michael Noonan's coming out. I'll ask what we should do and say."

"Rene, Ann's name mustn't get into the papers."

"We're doing something about that, Mary. Shay spoke to Sean the Garda."

She had to ring off. I phoned the supermarket to warn Sally.

Like Mary, she was horrified at the idea of Paddy Purdee's being able to find Ann. I explained that Michael Noonan would soon be around to advise us, and that Kieron and Simon would be watchdogs. But as I hung up the phone, I realized that I was by no means as reassured as I sounded, and fervently wished that somehow they could get Tom Slaney to admit he'd done it . . . horrible though it was to think . . . so that there'd be no fuss at all over the poor woman's death. I heard the kettle imperiously rattling its lid, and absently made coffee for myself.

Simon had snuck back in through the kitchen door.

"Ann's in hysterics, Mom," he said.

"Then go back and tell her that *I*, Queen Irene the Second, have admitted to finding the body. Shay Kerrigan's dealt with Sean the Garda, Michael Noonan will know how to protect her, I've told both Mary and Sally, *and* we're barricading the road against intruders."

"Not that I think it'll be necessary," said Shay, stepping into the kitchen with Michael Noonan.

"Hardly likely," said Michael, smiling reassuringly at me. "Not if Slaney's been drinking. As soon as the Garda have had a word with him, we'll know more." He looked wistfully toward the cup in my hand, so I asked who wanted coffee.

Simon said he'd get back before Ann had a stroke.

"Tell her I'll look in as soon as I can," Michael told him. "I can keep her name out of it." But he was thoughtful after Simon left, and spent a long time stirring the sugar into his coffee. "You know, closing off the lane is a very good idea right now. Not that Paddy has a chance of discovering Ann here in the south. She used to live in Santry."

"But what good would it do him to find her?"

Shay and Michael exchanged looks. "He is legally her husband. He could force his way in on her."

"How?"

"He's got the law on his side."

"Well, then it's a damned foolish law." I stared at them. "You mean, she has *no* protection from him? That he can just walk back in on her?" I was sputtering with indignation. "Why, that's outrageous. Why, in the States, a woman has some protection . . ."

"I told you things were different here in Ireland," Shay began.

"Different? They're archaic. Why, it's inhuman, it's—" I broke off because they were looking at me with the oddest expressions. "Well, what's the matter with you two grinning apes?"

"You sound exactly like your Aunt Irene," said Michael mildly. "She felt the same way, and so, I'll add, do I."

"Myself as well," said Shay.

"Then what are you going to do about it?"

Michael was looking at Shay rather strangely.

"Well?" I demanded again, because I was very, very upset. Bad as Teddie had been, I'd had sure legal redress once I'd made the decision to terminate the marriage. It hadn't ever really occurred to me how extremely fortunate I was.

"I'm doing what I can right now," said Michael. "Admittedly, it's only one isolated incident."

"What about making new laws? You're a solicitor. Or do barristers do that here in Ireland?"

"No, T.D.s—senators you'd call 'em."

"And why don't they?"

"It's not as easy as all that. You're in Ireland now, you know."

"Too well I know, and I thank my lucky stars that I can leave it."

"Now, now, Rene"—Shay's diffidence changed to alarm —"this is all very upsetting—"

"Wow! Understatement of the year!"

"Rene, did you warn Sally, and Mary Cuniff?" asked Michael, taking firm command of the situation.

I took his unspoken reprimand, because this wasn't the time to belabor the point, however morally unfair the situation was.

"They're both upset, but it's all for Ann's sake. Although I don't see that Sally's in a much better position. Or did the guy ever own up to paternity?"

Michael Noonan dropped his coffee cup. Had it been deliberate? He started making all the right noises, so I had to make light of the matter as I mopped it up.

Another siren heralded the arrival of some new official vehicle, and that gave Shay and Michael the excuse to leave. The next thing I knew, George Boardman was charging in, terribly upset, his silvery hair blown all over his face.

"Mary called me. What's this about old Mrs. Slaney being killed? And your finding her?"

At least my fable was becoming accepted as fact.

I gave George reassurances and a cup of coffee, and by the time he'd smoothed his wind-blown hair down, the front doorbell gave one of its asthmatic wheezes. The caller was the priest.

"Oh, but I've been here some little time now," he told me in a gentle voice, his eyes blinking so constantly that I wondered if he suffered from nerves or just an eye ailment. He started asking about requiem Masses. Fortunately, George not only knew Father O'Rourke but knew what to say about Masses, and the dear blinking Father went off in a gentle daze.

The Inspector arrived before Shay or Michael had a chance to warn me he was coming. They followed close behind, but even if I hadn't had three large male friends, and one of them a solicitor, I don't think I would have regarded this necessary formality with any dread—once it was over. The Inspector couldn't have been more courteous, and, after all, the facts, barring my fable, were so straightforward that the questioning didn't amount to much. He did say that he'd have to be back in the evening to take statements from Mrs. Cuniff and any of the other tenants who might have noticed something out of the ordinary. And he was gone.

"There's not much news, Rene," Michael said, "in an old woman found dead in her own home, not with Belfast claiming headlines and everyone's sympathy. However, I'll slip up and have a word with Ann Purdee." And he was away.

"Michael's right, you know," George said, combing his hair again with his fingers. "But I think I'll just collect Mary from the Montrose and give her some moral support. 'Bye now, and God bless."

I was getting messages rather loud and clear.

"I wonder, should I offer him Mrs. Slaney's cottage instead of Fahey's? Of course, maybe he's superstitious or something . . ." Then I caught Shay's expression. "Yes, I guess it isn't the time to make such a suggestion, is it?"

"My dear Rene, you amaze me more and more."

"Why? He certainly wasn't breaking his neck for worry over me. Though how I understand why an architect would be willing to live in a three-room cottage not big enough to house a drawing board. And Kieron Thornton's mad-crazy for Ann Purdee, and it wouldn't surprise me if Sally Hanahoe is still wildly in love with the guy what done her wrong."

"Sally who?"

"Sally Hanahoe, Ann's housemate, the unwed mother."

"Oh, yes. I haven't met that one. She must have arrived after I got in Irene's bad books." He slid into the chair at the small kitchen table, looking tired. I knew how he felt, and sat down opposite him. Then he gave a thoughtful snort, and gazed at me admiringly. At least, I preferred to take that interpretation.

"If you *knew* how much you sounded like Irene then, standing up for the poor, down-trodden Irish female . . ."

"Don't you mock—"

"I'm not, pet," he said, most seriously, and caught the hand I was brandishing. "I'm very much aware of how unjust the current laws are. But it's as much their own making."

"How? When a guy can beat up a little thing like Ann,

leave her without a penny to live on, and three kids, and then take up where he left off if he so chooses—"

"Wait a minute. You haven't been in Ireland—"

"Don't give me that old—"

He had both my hands and squeezed them hard. "Listen! I'm not defending the status quo, I'm explaining it, and you don't know it. Now, that's better, listen a minute.

"Simplifying the situation to absurdity, gay young lad sees pretty young colleen, falls madly in love with her wit and light feet, marries with pomp and circumstance and the fear of God from the local priest. All is still lightness and love. But gay young lad knows flipping little about the arts of love, and his pretty colleen even less, because they're good Catholics. So they ·fumble about, and before you know it she's pregnant, and sick, and he's tired of his pretty wife turned useless. He goes off to the pub for a few jars, where all his old buddies are drinking, and it's a big gas, and lots of fun down in the pub, with the peat fire and the Guinness and the telly and the dart board. And then the bahbee's born and he's a happy man and he's got a wife again, and whaddya know, she's pregnant again in next to no time. And he's off to the pub because her mother's with her, complaining that he's a lecher and a no good layabout and why doesn't he go off to the pub and leave the poor girl to rest. And so the poor girl, pregnant and exhausted, lavishes all her affection on her son, and pampers and spoils him as she'd like, perhaps, to pamper and spoil the man she keeps driving into the pub, and his friends, who are driven there for the same reasons. And then, guess what, the boy grows up, pampered and spoiled and used to seeing his old man go out every night to the pub with his friends, while his mother makes his sisters wait on them hand and foot because it's a man's world, pet, and the men get the best of the stick, and whaddya know. The boy grows up and marries the pretty colleen and gets her all preggers . . ."

"That wasn't the vicious circle for Mary Cuniff. And Ann's busted it."

"Ever seen how Ann treats her young son?"

I looked at Shay, because I hadn't seen Ann with the boy, but I could see that the pattern he projected could be terribly accurate. And it wasn't limited to Ireland.

"Is that why you don't marry?"

He gave my hands a final squeeze, winked one of his

very brilliant blue eyes, and sat back. "It could happen, and I'd hate it. I don't want a shrew and I don't want an innocent. I also don't want a woman who's gone too far in the opposite direction."

"You don't approve of women's lib?"

He snorted. "I'd prefer a woman who could speak out for herself. But I'd rather stay single and give joy to untold numbers of lonely females." He pulled himself up off the base of his spine.

"Aren't there *any* happy marriages in Ireland?"

"Law of averages says there have to be. No, seriously, Irene, Jimmy's father and mother are devoted to each other. Sheila's a wonderful person, but Dave got her." He sounded sincerely rueful. "You have been exposed to more of the exceptions than the average visitor."

"It's all so grossly unfair. These girls—Mary for instance—caught in the most ridiculous set of legalities! Can't anything be done for them, Shay?"

"Yes, Rene, they can stay on in the queendom and make their own way. They wouldn't be here otherwise. Irene wasn't impractical in her philanthropies. Which reminds me, Sheila told me of a candidate for Fahey's, once you can get that sorted out."

"Oh?"

Shay got slowly to his feet. "If I can make a humble recommendation?" When I assured him that he could, he went on. "You could even have her in on a caretaker basis. You can check with Michael about the mechanics."

"Who is she?"

"Another unwed mother. She was living with her sister, but the girl got married. Her son's three, so there's not so much work for Ann."

"She's practically got a playschool there."

"With Snow to help, it's no big thing."

"Hey, Mom," said my darling daughter, right on cue, but Shay gave me a quick sign to say nothing. With Snow's exuberant entry came the smell of freshly baked bread.

"Oh, heavenly!" I cried, reaching for the warm loaves. "However did Ann find time to bake . . . : today?"

Snow shrugged. " No problem." She was eyeing Shay Kerrigan oddly. "Ann feels that industry is the best cure for panic—and, Mom, she's panicky. No matter what Georgie-porgie and Mihall—"

"I wish you wouldn't, Snow."

"Huh, George doesn't mind!" My daughter gave me a grin, but her smile faded as her eyes swept past Shay.

"Maybe I could . . ." Shay began.

"No!" Snow's reply was emphatic enough to be downright rude.

I remonstrated with my daughter, but Shay smiled. "I don't know *what* turned young Ann against me, but I know where I'm not wanted." I could hear his bafflement as well as the hurt. "Anyway, I'd best be on my way. Look now, don't hesitate to phone if anything else occurs that worries you, or even if you just want moral support. Promise?"

I did, because Shay did reassure me in spite of all these unwelcome undercurrents and curious nuances. I must try to figure it all out one of these days.

Chapter XIV

Freshly baked brown bread, good butter, and honey made one of the most satisfying meals I've had. We ate completely through the loaf, even to wetting fingertips to lift the last remaining crumbs from the table.

"Why did you give Shay Kerrigan such a cold 'no'?" I asked my daughter.

She frowned. "I like Shay, but he was going to Ann's, and she said he'd never set foot in her house again."

"I've been given the impression that they've known each other a long time."

Snow gave one of her indifferent shrugs. "She was pretty positive, Mom. And she wouldn't say doodly-squat more than that."

"Doubtless you attempted to ascertain more details?"

"Sure did, and she warn't ascertaining nothing more. And when Ann Purdee has clammed up, Mom, the clamshell is shut." Snow frowned more deeply, because reticence is a challenge.

"Now, Sara, don't you go antagonizing Ann."

"Naw, I wouldn't do a thing like that," and she glared at Simon for his massive snort of disbelief. "I'm more subtle."

"I bet I find out more than you, and sooner," said Simon. "Man to man."

Abruptly Snow came out with the startling notion that we should forthwith tackle the hall's redecoration, idle gossip being an unconstructive way of spending time. Simon sourly remarked that we hadn't done the finishing in the living room yet. A wrangle developed, which I ended by suggesting that Simon finish the living room and we slop up the hallway. Snow took exception to my phraseology, and I had to put my foot down.

We did the kitchen. It was smaller. Ann came over as we were putting on the last of contact paper.

"Oh! How lovely it looks!" she said, but she was panting with exertion. She had a child on one hip, Meggie, her Tom, and Fiona holding on to her skirts. I'd thought she wore skirts so much to flatter a thin figure. Now I could see the practical aspect of many handholds for nervous children.

"What's the matter?" I asked her, because her worry was apparent. "Not that husband?"

"I saw Kieron holding back someone at the lane . . ." She was still breathless from hurrying. "And I just thought . . . that if no one was in my house . . ."

Snow was already hauling her into the room and smartly closing the door behind her.

"Well then, since you've a spare minute," said my daughter, "come see the rest of the first floor."

Ann was truly an encouraging person to show through a half-redecorated house. She was overwhelmed by the changes. Snow was urging her up the steps to the second story just as the doorbell wheezed.

Simon waved me back and advanced on the door. Not that Aunt Alice waited for him to open it. She barged past my astonished son.

"Why did you have to kill old Mrs. Slaney? Why couldn't you have stayed in America where you belong?"

I stared at her, unable to credit my ears.

"Now just a living minute," said my son. I'd never seen Simon so angry. "Where did you hear that nonsense? And how dare you accuse my mother of anything so vile?"

"I knew, I just knew, there'd be nothing but trouble and disgrace the moment I learned a foreigner had Irene's property. This never would have happened if Irene'd listened to me"

"Alice Hegarty, get the hell out of this house." Kieron came striding in. He took hold of my great-aunt by the elbows and bodily lifted her out the door, heedless of her enraged sputterings. "Rene no more killed Mrs. Slaney than you did. Tom bashed her once too often."

Alice Hegarty had grabbed the door frame. Her face was

contorted with a variety of emotions as she stared at me, but the hatred she emanated made me so ill that I sank to the steps, clutching at the bannister for support.

"He said she did it."

"Jasus!" cried Kieron. "And you're the gobshaw who'd believe him!" He laid a large hand on hers and pried her fingers from the wood, spun her around, and shoved her down the walk.

"You'll see, Irene Teasey, you'll just see!" Alice kept ranting as Kieron manhandled her into her car. He had no sooner slammed that door than another car came to a squealing halt.

"Merciful heavens, Alice, are you out of your mind?" It was Winnie, her voice fluting with distress. "Oh, Alice, how could you? Whatever will Rene think of us?"

"Winnie Teasey, you get that woman off this property."

"Who are you to give orders, Kieron Thornton?" said Alice in a penetrating shriek. "You're no better than any of the other floozies and strumpets on the place. Just you wait . . ."

"So help me, Alice, I'll thump you. And there's no one here who won't say you were hysterical and needed a clip on the jaw!"

Alice shut up in mid-vituperation, but the force with which she drove off set Kieron spinning to the side of the road.

"Oh, Kieron," Winnie was crying, wringing her hands in distress, "you wouldn't, you couldn't . . ."

"I didn't have to," said Kieron with a mirthless laugh, dusting his hands off, "but, oh Jasus, wouldn't I have liked to!"

The black Morris was bucking, stalling, starting, and jackrabbiting towards the main road. By the time it had paused there, I realized I'd been holding my breath and that I was trembling with reaction. I wished I'd never come to Ireland. I wished I'd never had an Aunt Irene. I just wanted to go up those stairs, pack my bags, and get the hell back to Westfield, New Jersey.

"Oh, Rene, I am so terribly, terribly sorry," Winnie was babbling, peering up at me through the railing. "The moment she rang off I *knew* she'd do something outrageous! But I never . . . I mean I drove as fast as I could to get here and stop her. I don't know *what* can have possessed Alice . . ."

"Greed," said Ann Purdee in a hard voice. "Covetousnous. She had her plans for this property, and well you know it, Winnie."

"Oh dear, but I thought she'd forgotten. Tom spoke to her about it." Winnie's face twisted, and she began to cry.

"Oh, do stop weeping, Winnie," Ann said contemptuously. "You'll start all the children."

"You're not responsible for your sister-in-law, Winnie," I said, because I couldn't stand her distressful bleating either. "It was good of you to come over."

"Where," demanded Simon, "did she get that garbled version?"

Winnie looked startled. "I couldn't tell you."

"The truth of the matter is," said Kieron, coming back into the hall, "that Rene went down to introduce herself to Mrs. Slaney and saw her sitting up in the bed just staring at the window. She was frightened and called me. The door was locked, so I opened the window and saw enough to realize the old lady was dead. So I asked Rene to call the Gardai."

"Then no one entered the house before the Gardai?" asked Winnie, her eyes round.

"Why?" asked Ann. "Because Alice had it that Rene was discovered throwing the poor old soul out of her house so she could let in some other floozy or strumpet?"

In Winnie's startled gasp we heard the truth, which she tried frantically to deny. I felt sicker than ever, and hugged myself against the venom of such a perversion. That settled it. I was in no way required to take this sort of slander. I would appoint a caretaker for the place. We'd make it a home for unwed mothers.

"Winnie, if you don't mind . . ." Kieron said, indicating the door.

"Oh dear, oh dear. I didn't mean to upset you, Rene," she said, coming toward me instead, but Ann firmly guided her out the door.

Suddenly Snow began to laugh. She wasn't hysterical, and I resented her capacity to find anything remotely funny about the past few minutes.

"Well?" I asked.

"But Mother . . . No one . . . would believe it. This scene . . . is . . . like wow!"

Simon's grim expression began to echo his twin's interpretation. By the time Ann and Kieron had returned, the two of them were rolling with laughter and the small children were giggling uncertainly.

"Will you two ghouls stop it?"

"My mother—the Irish murderess!" Snow made a dramatic pose. "A week in Ireland and she done Dublin dirty. Foul American Murders Ancient Crone She's Never Met!" Snow made banner gestures with her hands. "Westfield will never believe it of you, Mommy!"

It was nothing to mock at, and yet Kieron was grinning and Ann Purdee looked considerably less grim as the twins went on, falling into Batmanese. "Westfield Widow Witch! Will This Dastardly Deed Defy Dublin's Dauntless Detectives?"

"Look," Kieron said to me when the kids had somewhat subsided, "you get in that car and take yourself off for a nice long drive . . . away from here . . ."

"Go see the Lady Twins," said Snow.

"I don't want to see anybody."

I started up the stairs, but Simon blocked my way and Kieron marched me to the door, grabbing my handbag and keys from the hall table.

"Go down to the Silver Tassie and have a few quick jars. Go down to the Strand at Killiney and observe the shining sea!"

Getting away from it all did appeal strongly to me. I drove down the lane, each wheel revolution increasing the intense relief. I turned right and put my foot down on the accelerator. I took the next left-hand turn and got lost, naturally. I emerged at a signpost somewhere near Powerscourt, but stately homes were not soothing. Still, the drive was pretty, and I went on and on and on, and there were lovely mountains around me, with richly green growing things.

Power of suggestion and all that, I was at the bend in the Kilternan Road before the Brandel cottage when I recognized my whereabouts. I was determined not to stop, not to inflict myself on anyone or be forced to consider anyone else's troubles—and found myself flicking the turn signal.

Lady Maud was in the garden, in much the same spot as

we had first seen her, and Lady Mary appeared in the doorway as I closed the garden gate. It was such a repetition of
the first encounter that I momentarily wondered if they
might not really be dolls, timeless and immobile, until
opening the front gate started the action.

They'd already heard about Mrs. Slaney's death. They
wouldn't, however, talk about it until I was ensconced on
the loveseat, sipping tea and eating dainty sandwiches
which appeared magically. I *was* hungry!

"The one facet of today's episode which is completely
reprehensible," said Lady Maud when I'd related the day's
events, "is Alice's intrusion. I cannot, Mary, like the woman."

Lady Mary sighed. "Maudie love, you are a *very* astute
judge of *character*."

I said it without thinking: "Do you know Shamus Kerrigan well?"

Their smiles told me the answer. "He is *such* a charming
gentleman. *Always* punctual, and such a *good* heart."

"Then would you know why my aunt turned against
him?"

Lady Maud's brows creased in the tiniest of frowns, and
she looked down at her shoe tips as she reflected on my
question. Lady Mary sighed.

"*Truly* we *don't* know."

"Though we had been aware of Irene's sudden and
inexplicable dislike of dear Mr. Kerrigan."

"It seemed to *begin* after her *first* stroke, didn't it, Maudie?"

"Yes, I believe that's correct, Mary."

"But he *kindly* drove us to *visit* her in hospital, and
brought flowers and candy, and did *all* that was to be *expected* .... "

"I hate to press you, Lady Maud, Lady Mary," and both
Ladies nodded acceptance of my reluctance, "but you see,
he does want to use the lane to get into the land he
owns. Only, in her letter to me, Aunt Irene forbade it. And
he's been so charming to me and the twins . . . But I can't
go against Aunt Irene's *specific* instructions unless I *know*."

"Mr. Kerrigan comes from a *very* good *family*," was
Lady Mary's contribution. "County Meath."

"Irene could be very harsh with those who disappointed
her. But she was fair," said Lady Maud slowly.

"He says he doesn't have an inkling of what he did."

The two Ladies smiled at each other and then at me.

"Men often don't, my dear," said Lady Maud, her blue eyes twinkling.

"He's *so* charming"—Lady Mary took up the narrative— "that one would feel *obliged* to *forgive* him almost *any-thing.*" Then they beamed at me again.

"I expect it will all come out right in the end," Lady Maud added, in such a brisk manner that I realized this subject of conversation was now closed.

"Could you tell me how you heard about Mrs. Slaney, Lady Maud?"

"Actually, it was John the postman who told Mary."

"The postman?"

"In *Ireland* the *postmen* are usually the *worst* gossips of all," and Lady Mary tittered.

"Did he say where he'd heard it?"

"No, I don't recollect that he did."

I think Lady Maud would have been more surprised if he'd acknowledged his source.

"However, Pat the butcher knew it. But then, his wife has a cousin in the Gardai at Cabinteely, so naturally he'd know. And James would tell us, because he knows we're acquainted with Hillside Lodge."

I sighed in surrender, and the conversation turned to other things. They were delighted to learn that I had sung at the tea, exultant at the reactions. They learned that I had met George Boardman. (Oh, a charming young man . . .such a jolly right Pirate King, too . . .) And wouldn't I consider staying on and doing an audition for next year's show?

I started my usual disclaimer.

"Tell me, dear Rene," asked Lady Maud, "what sort of a life would you be leading in the States next fall?"

"Well, I . . . I mean . . . I'd be . . ." My voice trailed off as I reviewed my probable activities, dull indeed compared to what was already in progress here. There are certain advantages to being dull—safety from slander is one of them. But how much did I really want to feel safe? And how much more stimulating, if irritating, life seemed to be here!

Lady Maud smiled back at me, nodding, her eyes twinkling more merrily than ever, as if she realized the impact of that casual but shrewd question. I evaded any further answer by rising and suggesting that I'd taken quite enough of their time and I'd better get back to my twins before they listed me as missing.

I was never more sincere when I told them that tea had revived me: tea and these irrepressible, valiant, and sensible ladies.

As I drove into my lane (a sense of possession did a great deal to abet the restoration of my equilibrium), I saw that the roadblock had been drawn to the side. Then I was struck by the quiet. Horseface was grazing at the far side of his field, as if he wished to be dissociated from the goings-on in the houses, and there wasn't the least sign of activity. Not even the cheerful chimney plumes of smoke.

I was getting concerned when I saw the tail end of the blue Jaguar in my driveway. I parked hurriedly and almost ran into the house. Now what?

Shay Kerrigan was seated on the steps, looking quite at home, chatting on the telephone.

"Here she is now. Told you not to worry, Simon. Now go enjoy yourselves!"

He hung up, grinning so broadly that my half-formed suspicions of worse to come dissipated.

"We've cleared the whole lot off. Kieron and George have absconded with a veritable gaggle of females." From his expression, one was led to suppose an act of incredible heroism on the men's part. "Simon and Snow have been carried off by Jim-lad, Betty, and Mark Howard, and *I* am taking you away from all this."

He grabbed me around the waist and spun me about in such a vigorous fashion that I had to grab his arms to keep from falling.

"*Were* you at the Brandels'?" he asked, still whirling me despite my protests. "Simon said you'd likely end up there."

"Yes, yes. Now unhand me, villain!"

He stopped suddenly, and I clutched to keep my balance.

"Why should I?" he demanded in theatrical manner. "For the first time, I have you alone! In my power!"

His extravagant lightheartedness was an antidote to the morning's grimness—but then he kissed me! All part of the act—but I kissed him back! (Those reflexes—those yearnings—don't die easily.) And he kissed most satisfactorily. How long had it been since a man—an attractive-to-me man—had kissed me? The end effect, however, put my feet squarely under me, and I felt obliged to push firmly free of that embrace. I also felt obliged to laugh—no, giggle—as if I were a fair maiden alone and in his power.

"Sir James, your queen must garb herself afresh." I caught the look in his eyes and made myself whirl away in the best romantic Hollywood tradition. "Adieu, and for a little while adieu . . ."

I dashed up the stairs as if Alice Hegarty were behind me. I was rather surprised at the way my pulse was pounding as I flung open the wardrobe door to find something suitable to wear.

How could I have forgotten that kisses burn on the lips in afterglow? Yes, and how could I have forgotten that something turned my level-headed, fair-minded, friendly great-aunt against the charming Sir Shamus-James Kerrigan?

My composure restored, my make-up repaired, and my knees only a trifle jellyish, I minced back downstairs. Shay came out of the living room, smiling in appreciation at my quick-changery.

"My, my," and he meant the linen sheath I was wearing, "you certainly have wrought changes in the house. What next?"

"Today the kitchen! Tomorrow the hallway!" I made the appropriate grand gestures. "And then," I added, suitably prosaic, "the bedrooms!"

"That green in the dining room certainly sets it off. Were you an interior decorator in the States?"

"No, but I like doing houses up. The nest-building instinct."

"I thought you were a women's libber."

Before I'd thought to control the impulse, I turned to him. "Please don't label me. Please don't generalize like that!"

He raised his eyebrow at my fierce tone, and I relented. "I'm sorry. Teddie, the twins' father, used to do that."

"Well, I am sorry if I offended you, pet," he said.

"I know *you* didn't mean anything by it, I'm very sorry I took your head off. It's just that it seemed so like the beginnings of other evenings that I . . ."

He ushered me out the front door, still reassuring me— or was I reassuring him?

"Fair enough, Rene. All Americans are not rich, all women who have minds of their own are not women's libbers, all cats are not gray—"

"Don't be outrageous!"

"Why not? The night is young and you're so glamorous . . ." He opened the Jag's door with a series of complicated flourishes and a bow worthy of the Palladium on Royal night. "Seriously, though, Rene, you are doing wonders with the house. Have you ever considered doing it professionally?"

"No, I think I'd hate it then. It'd be a job. Take all the fun out of it."

"And you wouldn't do it just for fun, would you?"

"That wouldn't be wise. An artisan is worthy of his . . . or her . . . hire. I suppose it would be challenging to do a house or two, but I'd prefer to know the house and the people so the decoration would be *them,* not me or what the current 'thing' was in some magazine."

He looked slightly puzzled, so I explained the American magazine scene and how to decorate at little cost from old attic remnants and be clever, and laughingly quoted the Flanders and Swann song: "There's no place safe to dress!"

"I didn't think you Americans knew Flanders and Swann."

So we entered the dual carriageway to Bray singing a rousing chorus of "Mud, mud, glorious mud."

Chapter XV

We'd had our drinks in an old hotel in Bray, gone for a walk on the seaside, oblivious to others about us, had a delicious dinner—supper, Shay called it—at a seafood restaurant. We talked about nothing that mattered, and yet it seemed that we understood each other rather well.

As Shay drove me home, we were both silent, a tranquility born of a very companionable evening. A tranquility pierced by the fact that every light was burning in the occupied cottages and my house.

"Jasus, what's happened now?" Shay asked under his breath as we drove cautiously up the lane.

A figure came out of the gloom, brandishing a flashlight and the shotgun.

"Kieron?" I cried, sticking my head out the window.

"Not to worry, Rene," he said, stepping up to the car.

"Not to worry? With every light on in the place, and you running around waving that damned thing?"

"Someone's been lurking about the place. Snow saw him when she was getting to bed. Simon routed him out of the stable, he ran toward Ann's and then doubled back. You didn't see anyone running down the road, did you? Or a parked car?"

I hadn't been aware of anything but my peaceful feelings, the more fool me. Nor did Shay remember anything unusual.

"Well, so there we are!" Kieron shrugged. "Lock up everything well tonight, Rene. I'll go tell Ann the scare is over."

"Her husband?" I asked Shay as Kieron trotted off.

Shay shook his head. "He's not supposed to know where she is."

"That doesn't mean much, judging by the way news gets about in this town."

Shay laughed. "Don't sound so sour. Sure and *you're* news . . . ah . . . the rich American grass widow!" He was deft at teasing, all right. "Oh, you're news, Rene."

"I just hope it'll be as much news when I leave. Which I've a mind to do!" I'm appalled to admit that I flounced out of the car in a very bad humor. It just wasn't fair that our lovely time had been spoiled so quickly. It just wasn't fair!

Shay caught up with me at the front door, and kept me from opening it.

"Rene! Rene!" There was real concern in his voice. He took me by the shoulders and gave me a little shake, to make me look him in the eyes. "You can't abdicate." Another shake. "Not at the first sign of hostility. Not strong-backed Irish-American queens!"

"Why can't I? I only came here to get—"

"Away from what you were leaving behind?" He cocked his head to one side, giving me a long searching look. There was a slight smile on his lips, a cynical smile. "No one runs from trouble without it follows them, Rene. And you've a good defendable spot here, with loyal subjects." Another squeeze on my arms. "Who need *you* as much as you need them. Irene had great hopes for your succeeding her here."

"How would you know?"

The twilight was bright enough for me to see the hurt in his eyes, the earnest smile disappearing from his mouth, and I was instantly remorseful.

"Shay, I didn't mean that."

"Why should you mean other?"

"Shay, please, I really didn't mean that. You've been so wonderful, so considerate . . ."

"Having you on, my dear." I didn't blame him for sounding so bitter.

"Oh, Shay, I just don't trust anyone or anything, including myself."

"Including yourself?" He gave a funny little laugh and

then pulled me to him, bending his head to kiss me before I could struggle free.

It wasn't fair of him to kiss me that way. It wasn't fair because I had to kiss him back, wanted to go on being kissed and all that followed kissing . . . and loving . . .

"Especially myself," I said, ruthlessly pushing him away. "And thank you for a lovely evening," I added, shoving out my hand formally, because the door got yanked open behind me. By Simon.

"Hey, Mom, we had a prowler! Ann's scared it was her husband."

"Did you have fun this evening, Sim? How would *he* know where Ann is? Did you get a good look at him? And where are your manners? Say good evening to Shay. It was really a lovely evening, Shamus, thank you."

Shay had taken my extended hand in both his, fingers caressing it. And Simon was giving me his "what are you blathering about?" look.

"I said good evening to Shay earlier. We had a smashing time, Mom, and may we go swimming tomorrow with the group?"

"I see no reason why not."

"You'd better phone the Gardai and tell them about the prowler, Rene," Shay said, and then, bidding Simon good night, he disappeared into the dark shadows.

Simon gave a snort. "We did that already."

"Well, I don't know what else we can do, except go to bed."

Which is what we did.

The Garda came up the next morning and took full particulars from us and Kieron. When I tried to find out what had happened about Tom Slaney, I got a very polite and embarrassed evasion and Sean the Garda beat a strategic retreat.

"You don't suppose they think I had something to do with her death, the way Alice says?" I asked the twins.

"Ah, fer carrying out loud, Mom." Simon was disgusted.

The mailman came, quite willing to have a chat with me. I had about got used to the Dublin accent, but his, with flat broad A's and a curious nasal quality, had me so fascinated that I really didn't hear what he was saying—at first.

"She what?"

" 'Tis thought, missus, that the poor old thing died from her heart."

"Her heart? With that hole in her head?"

He dismissed that with a *"bosh!"* "I heard that the coroner himself said that 'twas her heart give out, missus, not her head."

"Then her son didn't kill her?"

"Now I'm not saying that, missus. I'm only telling you what I heard."

"She hit her head against something when she fell?"

Again he claimed ignorance. "Did you not get a good look at your prowler last night?" he asked.

"How did you hear that?"

He cocked his head at me, his bright brown eyes twinkling at my amazement. He patted his canvas postbag. "Not all the news that gets about is written, missus."

"Evidently!"

He had, however, a stack of mail for me. "All from Ameriky, I see. All airmail. Desperate the cost of stamps, isn't it?"

We discussed the weather then, and despite the innocent subject, I found I enjoyed the chat. As the twins had discovered their first time out, people took time to talk in Ireland, and they really seemed to be interested in what you were saying. The observation now had a double edge. I shook myself sternly as I watched the little postman amble back down my lane. Was I becoming paranoid? As Shay had said, the American was news.

I riffled through the letters. Most of them were for the children. I had letters from Betty, Mother, my sister Jen, and two bills. I'd a lot to tell Betty and Mother, certainly.

They had a lot to tell me first, however,

"What's the matter, Mother?" asked Snow, briefly interrupting her stream of "oh nos," giggles, and assorted monosyllables.

"Guess," asked Simon sarcastically, waving his own letter, his expression one of deep disgust. "Or maybe he hasn't bothered any of your friends yet?"

"Oh that!"

"What do you mean, Simon?" I asked, alarmed enough on my own account.

"Just that Dad's been to Pete Snyder, Doug Nevins, Popper Tracey, and—"

"Whatever for?"

"Ahhh, had they heard from me in Ireland, where was I, what were we doing there, and—"

"Oh, Mom, don't worry!" Then Snow made a face as she gave me a second, longer look. "Okay, what's Aunt Betty saying?"

"That your father has been phoning constantly, wanting to know what we were doing, what I was up to, taking his children away from him."

"I'll bet I know what Aunt Betty told him," said Simon, chuckling. He was very fond of Betty and her droll manner of speech.

"More or less," I said by way of agreement but without elaborating. I reread Betty's disturbing news:

> Teddie-boy seems positive that you have a) gone off with another man, totally unsuitable as a stepfather for *his* children, b) inherited a fortune, which is amusing when you consider that he had categorized the Irish as a shiftless lot of do-nothings, ignorant, stupid, and lazy. Between you and me, I hope you did inherit a fortune. Frankly, you may need it. Teddie was raving about withdrawing support money until you capitulated. So I took the liberty of phoning Hank. Then if Teddie is day-one late, Hank can leap on him. I won't tell you not to worry, because you will and do. But I want you to know that if there isn't a pot of gold, and Teddie-boy cuts off the support money, you need only wire Charlie and me for moral and financial assistance. I mean it, honey.

It was so like Betty to offer help. But Teddie couldn't . . . or would he? I didn't have all that much left in my checking account. I *knew* we shouldn't have spent so much on paint!

Being a glutton for punishment, I hurriedly opened Mother's letter. She had much the same news and suspicions as Betty, and had conveyed the same to Hank. I began to get angrier and angrier. Mother closed her letter by saying that I could always count on her for any financial help I needed to tide me over. And if I trotted obediently back to the States to placate Teddie-boy, I was no daughter of hers.

I was wondering where Ted had got his notion that I had inherited a lot of money when I opened Jen's letter and found out. Of course, she had known all along that I was to be Irene's principal beneficiary, and now I learned that Aunt Irene had even consulted Jen's lawyer-husband about American tax laws. Unfortunately, Jen had taken great pleasure in informing Teddie of my good fortune: "I told Teddie that Aunt Irene had left you enough to buy and sell his agency if you chose."

My dear elder sister occasionally gets carried away!

"I'd have Hank write him a letter, Rene, threatening him with a court injunction before he alienates all your friends. He's calling everyone, saying the most outrageous things about you and your reasons for going to Ireland. I used to think you exaggerated about that man. Now I know you didn't tell the half. So I owe you an apology."

I could just wish that she owed me the allegiance of silence, too. Jen always meant well.

When I lowered the last page of her letter, I saw that both my children were waiting.

"Your father doesn't seem to approve of our sojourn in Ireland."

"So . . . what else is new?" asked Simon.

"Has your father—"

"Missed anyone?" asked Snow sarcastically. "I doubt it. According to him, Ireland is the bog of iniquity, the cesspit of humanity, the modern Sodom and Gomorrah—gold-plated and shamrock-trimmed, of course. I mean, like, what is with the man, Mommy?" A hint of desperation had crept into her final question.

"When we were home," Simon said, "he only saw us if it rained and he couldn't play golf. Or if he was throwing"—Simon's expression turned very adult and hard—"one of his bashes and needed free butling and a . . . a cook."

"What did you start to say, Simon?"

"We *know* Snow can't cook that well!"

I knew that *he* knew that he hadn't fooled me. But I also realized that I wouldn't get him to explain . . . not yet, at any rate.

"Not to change the subject," Simon said, doing precisely that as he stood up, "I gotta answer some of these. With the expurgated truth. I don't have much time before our taxi arrives. You ready, Snow?"

"Will be. Now, Mother, you write Hank—if Gammy hasn't already talked his ear off. There must be something you can do to shut Daddy up." She rose, frowning at me. "And don't stand there wringing your hands. Take positive action. Write!"

I got my writing case, located a ballpoint that wasn't clogged with grease (other people's ballpoints always write better for me than my own), and settled myself at the little table in the living room. I'd a view of the front garden of my queendom, the rolling field beyond, and to the left up the hill . . . the hill that Shay Kerrigan wished to populate with . . . no, he'd definitely said they wouldn't be ticky-tacky boxes. And if he positioned them judiciously . . .

I forced myself away from the subject of Shamus Kerrigan. I was spending far too much time thinking about that charmer.

My hand had got a cramp by the time Mark Howard came up the lane to collect my pair.

"Now, don't worry about us if we're not back for supper, Mom," Snow said, kissing me. "You'll be all right, won't you?"

"If someone doesn't try to murder me, yes, of course." I meant to be funny but Snow's eyes got very wide. "For Pete's sake, Snow, go along. I'll be perfectly all right."

I was, and then again, I wasn't. I finished my letters and made myself some lunch, feeling a little lonely. Ah, well, I was truly delighted that the twins had met such an amiable group and were getting about.

I was drying my lunch dishes when I thought of it. If old Mrs. Slaney had died of a heart attack, then Tom would have been released from jail. And he might come back here.

Michael Noonan's line was busy, so I hopped down to Kieron's house, but he was out. Then I recalled that Shay Kerrigan was very friendly with Sean the Garda.

Shay Kerrigan told me not to worry—he was highly amused by the fact that I was worried, but he'd phone Sean the Garda right away and give me a shout back.

I was sitting on the steps, waiting for that reassurance, when I heard a car stopping in the lane. One thing certain, Tom Slaney had no car. I peered cautiously out through the glassed porch, because I also didn't wish to encounter any of those aunts of mine. From the angle of the window and the front porch, I could catch only a glimpse of masculine shoulders and trouser legs.

Never in my right mind would I have voluntarily opened the door for Brian Kelley, but it was he, smiling pleasantly, an exercise that only reminded me of Porky Pig in a winning mood.

"Yes, Mr. Kelley?"

"My client has requested that I approach you again, as he is willing to increase his original offer to you."

"Mr. Kelley, I can do nothing until probate is accomplished."

"Then you do intend to sell?" His eagerness was palpable.

I developed a case of the "smarts," as Snow would call it.

"I'm not at all sure I can abide remaining here," I said, and shuddered as I glanced toward Mrs. Slaney's cottage. Of course, he might not have . . . ah, but from the expression in his eyes, that leaping of porcine hope, I could see that he had.

"Most regrettable, most regrettable."

"Well, you can appreciate my position. Even if the coroner's verdict *was* heart failure . . ." He didn't know that. "However, if you could *assist* in speeding up the probate, and, of course, the price is right, I'd be most happy to see the last of this place."

"Oh, I'm sure that matters can be speeded up most satisfactorily," and he was rubbing his sausage hands together with anticipation. "Oh, that won't be a problem at all."

"Ah . . ." I stopped him as he turned to go. "You didn't mention how much higher your client was willing to go?"

"Well, I've managed to get him to offer thirty-five thousand pounds," he said, with the smug satisfaction of the wily entrepreneur.

"Yes, that would be a lot of money, wouldn't it?" I managed to sound impressed and wistful, although I knew the property was worth double that.

"And I can have a word with the odd man and see that there's no delay in probate." He leaned toward me with the conspiratorial subtlety of a sea lion.

"You would? I mean, I don't want to be stuck here in Ireland any longer than necessary."

"Nothing could be easier, my dear Mrs. Teasey. Particularly once my client is assured of your acceptance. Of

course, it wouldn't be wise to mention the fact that you'd
accepted. I mightn't be able to speed matters up if word got
about."

"Oh, of course, naturally. Mum's the word," and I started to ease the door shut.

He'd his hand raised to keep it open when the phone
saved me.

"Oh, I am sorry," I said, "you'll have to excuse me. And
do let me know if you're able to secure probate." I gave
him my most beatific smile and all but slammed the door in
his face.

Shay was chuckling as he told me that Sean the Garda
said that Tom Slaney was still very much in the nick, "so as
not to be an embarrassment to the nice American lady."

"He's not being accused or anything?"

"Well, I believe the fiction is that he is assisting the Gardai with their inquiries. In short, they're not quite satisfied
with his varied interpretations of the last interview he had
with his mother. But the cause of death was definitely heart
failure. The head wound hadn't bled sufficiently for it to
have happened before her death. Sorry about the details,
Rene," he said, for I'd given an audible gasp. "Still, Tom
wasn't your prowler, so Sean the Garda said they'd be
keeping a tactful surveillance on the lane for you. Could
have been a tinker for all of that."

We chatted a few more moments about the latest Kelley
encounter, and then he excused himself. I was a little disappointed that he hadn't asked if he could drop by that evening. Then I chided myself that he'd given up a good deal
of his time already to sorting out my problems. And further, I oughtn't to put myself under too great an obligation
to him.

Why had Aunt Irene turned against him? Or had he just
come on sweet enough to her to get access up the lane? No
—from what George and the Ladies had said, the friendship had been of long standing.

To take my mind off such dilemmas, I began to com-
mune with the house. Since I was now obliged to stay here
for the summer, I intended to make this house into *my*
home. We would need additional pieces of furniture. Simon
couldn't continue living out of a suitcase, and Snow
wouldn't stay happy long in her sparsely furnished room.

There was no reason why Hillside Lodge couldn't be turned into a very elegant Georgian farmhouse.

I found the previous evening's newspaper and scanned the announcements of furniture sales and auctions. I had seen auction room signs on my travels. Recently . . . I thought hard and remembered where, in Dun Laoghaire. So to Dun Laoghaire I repaired, notions of what to look for bouncing about in my mind.

The people in Buckley-the-Auctioneers were delightful and explained the whole thing to me: that you viewed the furniture on a Wednesday and up till 2:30 on a Thursday, and then waited until the lot number came up and put in your bid. If you were successful, you collected your new possession on the Friday. There were a few beautiful pieces on display in this section of Buckley's, but suitable only for rooms four times the size of my farmhouse. Still, I could see that I'd be spending a lot of time haunting auction rooms, looking for what the Buckley's people described as the "odd piece." I was beginning to appreciate the unique flavor of the Irish "odd."

The weather hadn't exactly settled out into a clear day, but it was bright, with tremendous clouds skittering across the sky, and black thunderheads that went innocently about their business despite omnipresent threats of deluge. And with such clear air, the views were superb—of sea on the one hand, a brilliant blue-green in the sun, and the hills, equally green and worthy of description, on the other.

I followed the "scenic route" until it fed into the main Bray road and then took an inspired right just before the town, toward Wicklow. When I was about convinced that there was nothing spectacular in this direction, I came to a dual carriageway, and the urge to try the Mercedes at speed was unbearable. Away I went, and the car could really travel. After a lunch at the Glenview Hotel, I found my way back via a different route.

Dublin summer evenings are blessed with a golden light, a clarity which lifts all out of the commonplace. The effect of so many rainbows? The leakages from a commensurate number of pots of gold?

I drove up my own lane, enjoying an unusually euphoric sense of well-being. Mary and Molly were gardening in the golden light, the scene positively idyllic. Mary beckoned me to join her. Trying not to behave like lady-of-the-manor, I parked my car in my drive and went back to join them. The only flaw in the scene was the closed door of Ann's cottage.

"Kieron took them all on a picnic up Ballycorus Hill," Mary said, smiling to relieve my anxiety.

The sense of tranquility returned, and I sat on the grass, plucking the odd (I was getting obsessed with the word) weed from the border.

"Ann was that worried, I know she didn't sleep last night," Mary told me. "For all of that, neither did Kieron." She laughed a little. "He'd've done better to sleep across her threshold instead of sitting up all night at the gate."

"Do you think it was her husband last night?"

Mary shrugged. "Who can say? I'd guess no, for surely, as I remember the man, he'd've been back as soon as all was quiet again, trying to sneak in the window."

"He'd be that persistent?"

She gave me a piercing look, as if I were a trifle lacking in wit. Then she gave a little sigh. "Of course, you've never met him, so you'd not know."

I shook my head vigorously and was restored to her good opinion.

"I suppose because this is a Catholic country, divorce is out of the question?" Mary nodded. "But isn't there *something* she can do?"

Mary yanked fiercely at a small innocent buttercup. "Stay out of his reach!"

"Not even if she can prove . . . what do they call it . . . oh, 'irreconcilable differences and breakdown of the marriage'?"

Mary shook her head again.

"Well, at least she has Kieron to help her." My observation may have been casual, but it had the effect of a casual bomb on Mary.

"She wants no part of Kieron Thornton! Or any man!" Mary's savage tone didn't apply to just Ann.

"You feel that way about George Boardman?" It just popped out.

Poor Mary. I seemed to be saying all the wrong things and distressing her no end. She looked frantically about her as if the fuchsia hedge had sprouted transistorized "bugs."

"You just got here last week!" she exclaimed, which confirmed my suspicions about Mary and George.

"My ex-husband used to say that I was magnetic for disasters and secrets. The rule of Rene—anything that can possibly go wrong will."

She touched my hand with quick remorse. "I didn't mean it that way, Rene."

"I know. And I'm generally the last person to see subtleties of any kind. It's just that I saw the look on Kieron's face when Ann discovered . . ." and I gestured toward Mrs. Slaney's empty house, noticing that someone had boarded up the window Kieron'd broken. "And then George comes haring in here wild-eyed and bushy-haired for you and Molly, so it was obvious to me. Why are you worried that others would see it? I think George is a doll . . . and . . . oh, but you're not married and not divorced. What the hell, what difference does it make?"

"I know what you're thinking, Rene," said Mary with a sad smile. "You don't understand Ireland."

"You're certainly right there. So I'll be bluntly American. George Boardman wants to buy one of those two cottages. He plans to enlarge it and live there. I assume it's for proximity to you and Molly. Do I refuse him for the sake of Ireland? Or do I remind you that you have a right to some happiness, and that I'm quite willing to sell him Mrs. Slaney's place and I won't ever ask to know which walls he knocked out? And, since I'm blowing off steam, do *you* know what Aunt Irene had against Shay Kerrigan?"

She did. I saw it in her eyes.

"You might just as well tell me, because I'll find out." Please, God, just once let my bluff work! "In the meantime, it's just possible that there's another stupid impasse. Oh, blast! I don't mean that you and Ann are being stupid . . ."

"I do know what you mean," and there was a terrible undertone of sadness in her voice.

"This is my queendom now. I've the ordering of it in some respects. Oh, I know Shay's been buttering me up something shameful, all to get access up that lane. He won't get it if I feel my aunt's reasons for denying it were valid. If she had good cause, then I'll just forget about him entirely. But he's been damned sweet and helpful these last few days . . ."

Mary looked me squarely in the eyes. "Do you mean you would turf him out?"

"I do." I wasn't really that sure, but . . .

"I shouldn't be saying it, but you *have* the right to know. He's the father of Sally Hanahoe's baby."

That was not what I expected to hear. I know that she had to repeat it because I stared at her with such blank astonishment.

"Who says so?"

"Sally!"

Well, it's true that Sally ought to know the father of her baby.

"But Shay doesn't know Sally!" Of that I was positive.

"Did you ask him?" Mary was aghast.

"No, but he doesn't. Not unless he goes about getting girls whose names he doesn't know pregnant. You see, I've mentioned Sally to him, and he didn't recognize the name."

"Are you *sure?*" asked Mary with bitter cynicism.

I thought back. And I was certain. I would have distinctly heard an evasion or studied ignorance.

"I'm sure. I'm as sure as I'm sitting here pulling weeds with you that Shamus Kerrigan doesn't know Sally Hanahoe."

"But she described him! Big blue car, sandy hair, smooth talker, beautiful dresser."

That could describe quite a lot of other men I'd seen, even in the brief time I've been in Ireland, and I told Mary so. A look of disbelief and distrust passed over her face.

"No, Mary, I'm not saying it because I believe what Shay Kerrigan says. I believe what I haven't heard him say. But now I know what he's supposed to have done—I'm sorry, Mary, the irresponsible-lecher role doesn't suit Shay Kerrigan. Well, maybe I can find out. But that's why Ann Purdee won't let Shay in her house? She's afraid Sally will see him?"

Mary nodded.

The rest of Sally's pathetic story, which I got from Mary, only reinforced my belief in Shamus's innocence.

Sally's Shay K. had given her a lift one miserable rainy evening; he'd asked to meet her the following Friday at the Hotel Wicklow. Mary told me the place was rather well known for "casual encounters" (a fact which strengthened my belief, because Shay Kerrigan would not operate in such a fashion), and he'd wined and dined her frequently, leading up to a seduction one night when he'd got her very drunk. She'd gone with him until she discovered her pregnancy, three months later. She'd been living in a bedsitter in Rathmines. She'd no idea where he lived; he'd always contacted her at her office. The man hadn't talked about his origins or background, never mentioned family (considering how often Shay spoke of his nieces and nephews, another point in his favor). He had mentioned deals in land, and that he owned a garage.

When Sally had confessed her state to him, he'd flatly told her that marriage was out of the question, because he *was* married. He'd railed at her for being too stupid to be on the Pill. She'd threatened him with the Gardai, and he'd only laughed, taunting her with the fact that he was already married and she'd have to prove it was his baby. What good would that do her? Then he'd left her.

She'd tried to find him, revisiting the places where they'd gone, pubs they'd frequented, but she was unsuccessful. Abortion was repugnant to Sally, morally and religiously, and impossible financially. She took a cheaper bedsitter, a closet, Mary described it, and saved every penny she could to support herself when she was no longer able to work.

"What about her family?" I asked Mary, who snorted with scorn.

"Down-country farmers, like mine. Her father would have beaten her to death for the shame she'd brought his name." Mary scowled bleakly. "So Sally never told them."

"Brothers and sisters?"

Mary shook her head. "By the galore, but no help. You don't know how it is in Ireland."

"So . . . she had her baby?"

"Yes. First she went to a house for unwed mothers, but she said it was so awful with all that repentance that she felt twice as bad as ever before. She wasn't a criminal, after all," and the look on Mary's face made it obvious that Sally had given her a lot more detail than I was getting. "She left in her seventh month and got a summer job minding a baby for a woman having her eighth. She had a bed in the room with the four younger children, she ate as well as anyone in the family, and the woman was very kind. She put Sally in touch with the Deserted Wives and Unmarried Mothers' Association. That's how she met Ann, and they got on like sisters." Mary smiled at that.

Molly had finished her chore of weeding on the other side

of the garden, and came over to sit inside the crook of her mother's arm.

"And you? How did you meet Aunt Irene?" I nodded toward Molly in case Mary didn't feel like answering at that moment.

"Oh, I came through a regular channel. This house had fallen vacant and Irene had advertised it. 'Low rent' "—Mary laughed—"which I had to have, 'in exchange for services.' I phoned to inquire what services"—again the cynicism in Mary's voice—"and found out that Irene wanted someone with bookkeeping experience. Did you know that your aunt made a lot of money on pools and horses?"

"No! How marvelous of her! A racetrack tout!"

"Well, hardly." Mary's disclaimer was amused. "No great amounts at any time, but the odd tenner here and there. What I didn't know until later was that she'd had answers by the galore but she was looking for the right tenants, someone like Molly and me." She broke off. "Would you like a cup of coffee?"

"I always like a cup of coffee."

The rooms inside their very neat little cottage were larger and more cheerful than you'd think from the outside, and I was sure Kieron had been busy in Mary's kitchen too.

Pretty though the house was, the evening beckoned us out again to the small front garden. We sat on the grass and compared our respective countries—in superficial terms. I'd guessed that Mary's time for confidences was over. Molly was yawning fit to pop her jaw when we realized with astonishment that it was half past ten, with the sky still bright.

"I wonder where my children are," I said as we rose.

"Enjoying themselves, I'm sure. Not to worry, Rene."

For once, I didn't. I went home and got ready for bed. Bright skies made it difficult to think of sleeping, so I read for a while until I heard a car pulling up and the cheerful courtesies of the twins, the responses of their friends.

They'd had a ball, Snow assured me, and a grinning Simon began to relate the details, but I soon sent them off to bed. Such energy at the end of a long, hectic day is so enervating!

Chapter XVI

Despite a reluctance generated by ignorance of the protocol and a malaise in any funereal circumstances, I attended Mrs. Slaney's requiem Mass and burial. Fortunately, the Irish are very sensible about such matters, and the ceremonies were conducted without unseemly dispatch or excessive emotion.

Tom Slaney was there, accompanied by a burly plainclothesman. The Ladies Brandel arrived and took their places beside me along with Shay Kerrigan, who had chauffeured them. Ann and Mary came with Kieron Thornton, since Snow and Simon had volunteered to keep all the children. Ann was so bundled up in a huge coat and head scarf that I barely recognized her, which I suppose was what she'd intended. There was also a handful of bent head scarves, and two men sitting at the back of the church, obviously not there for the proceedings.

Slaney kept, or was kept, well away from me, and disappeared with his escort as soon as the brief graveside service was completed. Ann was very nervous too, and couldn't wait to get home. But I didn't really want to be alone, so I was glad when Shay asked me to deliver the Ladies back to their cottage. He'd a business deal that was requiring a good bit of time right now, he explained. I wondered how truthful he was, because Ann had been giving him very cold glances.

The Ladies were delighted to accept my invitation and were effusive in their thanks to Shay, as if to offset Ann's manner. So we all drove back to my house. The Ladies couldn't have been more flattering in their comments over what we had already done, and they had the most charming way of making suggestions: They'd remind each other of the decor in houses of the same period. Their knowledge of antique and period furniture was far more secure and exhaustive than mine; they'd grown up with the real items firmly ensconced in appropriate settings for several generations.

Snow appeared with Ann's flock, and much was made of the children. Meggie responded shyly, without much coaxing, as if she'd finally found someone her own size.

I'd noticed that Ann had begun to relax the moment that Shay had left. I believed I could now understand her distaste for his company, but if she'd known him so well, how could she believe that Shay Kerrigan—no matter what Sally had said—would do such a shabby thing? He was not the sort of moral coward to take refuge in the obvious lie about being married. And I felt that if he had got a girl pregnant, he'd at least be gentlemanly enough to see her through the ordeal. I resolved to achieve a confrontation between Sally and Shamus at the earliest possible moment.

Of course, Rene's Law instantly came into effect. I should have counted on that, but I forgot to.

The Ladies Brandel looked fatigued, and I suggested that perhaps I'd better drive them home, as it had been a trying morning. I took a quick look into the fridge and decided I could use some more food from Sally's supermarket *and* start my plan.

I delivered Lady Mary and Lady Maud to their cottage, promising faithfully that we'd all drop by for tea in the very near future. They overthanked me and again praised what I'd accomplished in the house.

"Much as we *loved* Irene, she'd a better eye for a *horse* that a *house*" was Lady Mary's succinct remark.

They were such old dears, and I sensed that they had attended the funeral as much to support me as to add to Mrs. Slaney's few mourners.

I had to cash a large check, but the bank manager, no doubt thinking with black-ink visions of my incredible balance, was charm itself. But he'd been equally obliging before the trust-fund money appeared in my account, and I can't honestly resent such charm when it makes life so pleasant.

Sally was on one of the registers, so I patiently waited on her line to speak with her and discover her work schedule. I had planned to invite Shay Kerrigan for dinner on a Thursday, when she worked late. I would discover that I'd forgot an important ingredient that could be got only at her store, and so confront him with Sally. But it was a bit awkward, I decided. I ought to be able to contrive something better. Maybe if I asked Snow . . . except that I couldn't very well do that without disclosing the whole game. Snow knew all about illegitimate children and affairs and that sort of thing—she could hardly remain ignorant in this day and in the society in which she had moved—but my scruples prevented me from enlisting the aid of a fourteen-year-old girl.

Well, something would occur.

I got as far as calling Shay to issue the dinner invitation. His voice answered the phone, but before I could plunge into my carefully rehearsed invitation, his voice continued in an inexorable way to inform any listener that he was away on business and if the caller would leave a message after the beep, he would attend to the matter on his return.

I let the silly recording repeat itself because I was so astonished. He hadn't said anything to me about going away. I tried not to be hurt. After all, he had a legitimate grievance with me for holding up the development of his property.

I got busy in the kitchen, putting away groceries and sternly directing my mind away from Shamus Kerrigan. (Charming rogue? No, Shay Kerrigan *wasn't* a rogue!)

Simon came in with Jimmy, both predicting imminent death due to starvation. I made lunch and then realized that it was nearly two and I would have to rush to make the auction at Buckley's at half past.

"Auctions are fun," Jimmy told me. "Mom loves to go even if she's not in a buying mood."

"Are they worth it, though?"

"Sure, if you know what you want and don't pay more than it's worth," he replied, shrugging. He gave me a mischievous grin. "Sometimes Mom says people go out of their minds bidding against each other when they wouldn't buy the thing brand-new at a shop for the price they end up paying."

The items for auction were all numbered, and after a

look in the back room, where the auction had started with depraved lawnmowers, disabled washing machines, kitchen chairs, and the like, I toured the main floor and the balcony. One delightful wardrobey thing, called a compactum, fascinated me. It would solve Snow's closetless-room problem. If it took my fancy, it would probably take others' as well, but still . . .

The mob from the back room surged in, led by a man in a violent-purple shirt. He was followed by a youngish man with sandy sideburns (*he* answered Sally's description of her seducer, too), who was carrying a clipboard. A couple, about my age, smilingly edged in beside me. The woman, in an elegant tweed skirt and cotton blouse, eased herself onto the bureau against which I was leaning, then gave me the nod to follow her example, indicating it would be easier on the feet. I then noticed that other people were casually making themselves comfortable on auctionables. So I did. My friend had a list in her hand and now turned to show it to her husband. I was, in view of my fairly jaundiced experience with Irish married folk, rather astonished at the overt affection in the look he gave her, and the sweetness of his smile as he bent his head to review her list.

Then the bidding began.

I might not have noticed the couple had I not been beside them, but I could only be forcibly struck by his courtesy and her deference. He did the actual bidding; she anxiously followed the rise of price and, with an almost imperceptible shake of her head, indicated when the cost had gone too high on the chest she had wanted. His moue of regret for her disappointment was humorous and good-natured. I couldn't help but contrast them with Teddie and myself in a similar situation. He'd have bid until he got the item, no matter how outrageous the final sum, and would have been furious with me had I suggested an overbid.

I did fancy a little velvet-covered Victorian dining chair. But it reached £11 before I could even raise my hand. And sold for £15.

"That's overpriced," said the man beside me to his wife.

"Dreadfully. Why, we got our four for twenty pounds, didn't we?"

He nodded and caught my eye as he did so, giving me such a pleasant smile that I had the nerve to ask them why a chair would bring such a price.

"Sometimes the owner's here pushing the bid up," he said in a low voice. "Sometimes it's dealers who see a chance to finish a set, or maybe it simply strikes some party's fancy. Is this your first auction?"

I nodded, and was suddenly conscious that the man just beyond the couple was leaning in as if to catch the conversation. I'd remarked to myself on his utter boredom with the auction proceedings, his silence through all the bidding, which now made his sudden attention to our conversation the more obvious. The moment he saw me looking at him, he straightened up and looked away. I had the feeling that I'd seen the fellow before, although I couldn't place the circumstance.

Then the auctioneer called loudly for silence and a bid of £5 on the next item. Once again I became intent on the proceedings. The nosy character had eased away, so I thought no more about him.

Suddenly the auctionables had all had their chance, and people began to file out the front door.

"Better luck next week," the friendly woman said to me as she and her husband moved off.

I half wished that I could have become acquainted, but I didn't want to be considered pushy. Maybe they'd be here next week, too. Still, they had worked their magic on me and given me some perspective. I really had tumbled into an exceptional scene with Ann, Sally, and Mary. Then there was the fact that my great-aunt had been a confirmed-by-choice spinster. She would hardly have attracted the happily-marrieds as company. Certainly she'd performed a much-needed service in succoring girls in real distress, who'd been *done* by rascals. And, I reminded myself as I unlocked the Mercedes, I wasn't exactly the most unprejudiced observer on that count.

Besides which, there was George, dying to marry Mary; Kieron, gone on Ann, despite her not admitting it; and give Sally a chance and she'd probably fall in love with someone a good bit more reliable than the wayward Shamus Kerrigan—*her* Shamus, not mine. (*Mine?*)

I nearly braked at the subconscious use of the pronoun. Shay Kerrigan was not mine, nor was I his, nor did I . . . or did I? His kissing . . . had been *so* satisfactory, his presence so reassuring. His—great heavens above, Irene

Teasey! You only met him two weeks ago, he's under a cloud, he's after something, and you're . . .

I turned off the main road up my lane and glanced into my rear-view mirror as I slowed. The car behind me was driven by Nosy! Well! That was a coincidence. Or was it? Was he following me? Ridiculous notion! Supported by the evidence that, as I turned up Swann's Lane, his car continued on.

"That for your fancies, my girl," I told myself sternly.

Mr. Corrig, the postman, was pushing his bike up the hill toward my house, so I pulled over. I could save him a few steps.

"And a good evening to you, missus," he said, all affability, touching his cap brim: a salute which made me feel so very lady of the manor . . . and awkward. "Did your man ever find you?"

"My man?" I had a second's horrible terror that Teddie had arrived in Ireland.

"Yiss, missus. He was after asking me who owned the field there, so I told him 'twas yourself, and he wanted to know where you lived, and your name, so I gave him your direction. He seemed desperate anxious to see you."

"No one came, but then, you see, it was Mrs. Slaney's funeral today, and then I was out this afternoon."

"Poor old body," said the postman, shaking his head and clicking his tongue. "Many there? Not that I suppose she'd many friends left living, asides from yourselves."

"Why, yes . . ." and then I stopped. Nosy had been one of the men sitting way back at the service! "Yes, the Ladies Brandel came, Mr. Kerrigan drove them over. And, of course, all of us here. Mr. Corrig, the man who wanted to buy my land—what did he look like? I mean, I think he's been by before . . . when I wasn't at home. My son mentioned something . . ." Not the best of prevarications, but Mr. Corrig didn't seem to notice.

He wasn't very reassuring, either, because it was Nosy he described. And if Nosy *had* wanted to buy my property and had seen me turning into the lane, why didn't he "find me"?

"So maybe he'll call on you later. Here's your mail, missus." He passed over rather a staggering bundle. "The most I've delivered up Swann's Lane in many a year."

"I'm very sorry, but we've had so much to write home about."

"Not to worry, not to worry. Used to enjoy the odd chat with herself, I did, when she was still about."

I murmured something appropriate, and Mr. Corrig beamed at me.

"Good evening, missus, and God bless." He turned his bike around and whizzed off down the slope.

I riffled through the letters—more from my mother, and, oh no, another from Hank, some forwarded from my apartment, several for Simon, and two for Snow. Quite a clutch. Suddenly, I didn't want to open Hank's letter or Mother's all on my own. What bad news they might have to tell me was fortunately three thousand miles away. I could ignore it—for a while. I couldn't ignore Nosy, who was right on my doorstep, so to speak, and I didn't want him any farther in. Whoever he was! So I wanted very much to have a few words with Kieron . . . and I could give Simon his mail at the same time.

Simon wasn't with Kieron: He and Jimmy had gone off to Blackrock, Kieron told me. He invited me into his house to explain.

"I'd an old bike in the shed, just needed some adjusting and two new tires, so the lads went off to get them."

"Good Lord, did Simon have enough money?"

"Sure and they did, between them and me. You take milk and sugar, don't you?" he asked, for his kettle was just boiling.

"As Snow would say, constantly."

"Well," said Kieron, sitting himself down opposite me in the rocking chair, "what's troubling you?"

I groaned, distressed that I was so transparent.

"You forget how much like Irene you really are."

"Forget? I only wish I knew . . ."

Kieron frowned blackly at me. "Now don't you start greeting over what you couldn't help," he said, then sighed. "I've had enough of that from Ann."

"Did the funeral upset her?"

"No, but the *going* did." He was much annoyed.

"She can't honestly be that afraid of her husband finding her?"

"Oh, I fault your aunt on that score, Rene. She drummed it into Ann's head that she was safe here, that she should never leave, but by God, I know Irene didn't mean never set foot out of the place. How the hell would Paddy Purdee know Ann was here in Kilternan? When he married her, he'd two rooms in Finglas. They lived there"—he gave a short bark of mirthless laughter—"until he deserted her the first time."

"The first time?"

"Forgot you haven't had all the whole sorry story of it."

"True," I replied, a bit stiffly, "it's not something even the brashest American just blurts out and asks . . . particularly not of someone like Ann." I sighed with real regret. "She's such a wonderful person, coping . . . Oh, I know . . ." I had noticed his apprehension. "The Anns of the world prefer to do it their way and the hell with the helping hand."

Kieron nodded, the sorrow in his eyes adding to my sense of impotence.

"You do love her, don't you?" I asked.

Kieron glanced sharply at me for a long, almost uncomfortable minute before his face relaxed and his very charming smile parted the moustache around his lips.

"Yes, I do love her—not that it does me any good," he said with resignation, and stirred his coffee into sloppy turbulence.

"You mean, because of Ann or because she's married and Ireland doesn't have divorce?"

His head came up in surprise. "Sure now, you can get a divorce in Ireland . . . of a kind," he amended, pleased by my astonishment. "No, my problem is Ann. Because one man's been a bastard to her, she'll have nothing to do with any other. She won't believe that men come in different sizes, shapes, and temperaments." Kieron was very bitter. "And it's such a flaming waste!" He propelled himself so forcibly out of the rocker that it nearly overtilted. "And that's no thanks to Irene, sure it's not. Much as I loved the woman, she did me no favors with Ann. And she could have done."

"But I thought Aunt Irene liked you! You're *here!*"

"Oh, she liked me well enough, she did. I had my uses," and his gesture took in the furniture, the kitchen cabinets. "And I'd come back to take care of the old mother when I found my sisters had turfed her out. She was too old to help with the housekeeping," he explained, noting my horror. His laugh was bitter. "The mother, you see, favored the boys in the family, now hadn't she, said the sisters. So let the boys care for her when she couldn't work for her keep. The men aren't the only bastards in Ireland, Rene. Not that I really blame the girls: tiny houses, bad husbands, no money. They really couldn't keep her, even with the old-age money to help out. Mrs. Slaney found her tottering along Kilternan Road late one November evening, and cold it was. Irene took over, of course. There was a letter in Mam's handbag from me. Irene cabled. I was doing a tour of cabarets in the States. I decided that I'd better come back myself to see all was well. Although Mary and Ann *were* very kind to her."

"Doesn't that prove to Ann what sort of person you are? You gave up everything . . ."

Kieron's laugh was amused now. "I gave up nothing, Rene, but it was good publicity. It's best to leave when you're on top. I do as well here, all things equaled."

"But Ann isn't convinced?"

"Not at all. It only serves to show her how unreliable I am, without a regular job, working as it pleases me. Sure and I make more in one night's work than Paddy Purdee did in a week when the trawling was good."

"Surely Ann—"

"Ann doesn't, Ann won't, Ann can't. She's as hidebound as her mother before her, and that bugger hurt her, like her dad did her mother, and he's beat her and bred her and bolluxed her so badly that she doesn't know what she wants . . . except never another man in *her* house or in her life. Not that she ever *had* a man anyhow . . ." He glared defiantly at me for what he implied in that phrase. "No pleasure. She was never *married* to that bastard!"

I held my reaction to a sympathetic nod, but I could see why he felt Ann was wasted. She was so lovely, and there was so much more to loving than bedding. Ann didn't even know what she'd missed. I did, and . . .

"You said the first time he left her?" I asked Kieron, grasping for a subject to distract my own line of thought.

He glared at me ferociously, equally distracted by my abrupt backtracking. "Yes. A fortnight after the wedding he left her to go fishing. He got a chance at a berth on an English codder and took off for three months. He'd got her pregnant, and she was poorly when he got back, so he took off again for another three months. When he got back from that trip, she was in hospital with a threatened miscarriage, so he disappeared. He returned a week after Fiona was born . . . he must have had her in the hospital, because Tom was born nine months later. That's when she moved, but he tracked her down, beat her up every night he was home, and by the time he'd signed on another boat she was pregnant with Michael!"

My appalled expression seemed to mollify Kieron, for his fierceness lessened as he shoved his hair back from his forehead with impatient fingers.

"I can't imagine Paddy Purdee roughed her up before she married him," I said, "so Ann must think the change in the man is related to marriage. Why *should* she want it? But, Kieron, you said he deserted her, and yet you said he was . . ."

"Deserted her, yes, in the true sense of the word. He gave her no money to live on, she didn't know what ship he'd sailed with, how long he'd be gone or anything."

"No money? Even when they were first married?"

"The first time he went off, she thought he'd be back on the weekend, and she waited. She'd some money of her own, left over from wedding presents. She managed. Then one of his mates told her he'd signed on the codder, and she got her old job back. Once Fiona was born, of course, she couldn't work. As far as I ever heard, Paddy never gave her any money the whole time he was married to her."

This was much worse than anything I'd imagined for Ann. "But that's a psychological nonconsummation, isn't it? Or a lie, entering marriage under false pretenses? I mean, you're supposed to endow your wife with your worldly goods, cherish, honor, and support, and if he did none of those things . . . why, he never married her! But, Kieron, why can't she get an annulment or a divorce or something, so that at least she doesn't have to live in dread of his forcing himself on her again?"

He cocked an eyebrow at me, and I more or less answered my own question.

"No money!"

Kieron nodded. "Nor wish. So long's Paddy can't find her here, she's content enough."

He was obviously not. "Oh, really, Kieron, surely there's a Legal Aid Society which helps the . . . no? Good Lord. We are in the Dark Ages. I mean, when she's too scared to attend . . ." A sudden thought struck me. "You know, if he lived with her so little, would he even remember what she looked like?"

Kieron did a double take and then chuckled. "*You* tell Ann."

"Which reminds me, Kieron, have you seen a man around here, saying he's looking to buy my field?"

"There was a man nosing about yesterday."

His choice of phrase was a bit unsettling.

"You know," Kieron went on, staring off in a middle distance for a moment, "I've seen that lot before . . . in the church . . . today!"

"I went to the auction today, and I saw him *there*. He followed my car. If he really wanted to buy that property, as he told the postman, why didn't he turn in after me? Do the police really believe what we told them? Or do they think I bashed Mrs. Slaney in the head?"

"Jasus, no, Rene."

"Well, that man is obviously shadowing me."

"I'll give Sean the Garda a shout, just to clear it up."

Any clearing up got postponed then by the return of Simon and Jimmy, festooned with bike parts. I'd only time to beg Kieron not to mention Nosy when the boys were in the door. Nothing then would do but that they get the bike set to rights. "So I've got transport of my own, Mom. Isn't Kieron the greatest?"

I handed Simon his mail, concurring with his opinion while Kieron grinned sardonically. We all went out to Kieron's workshop. I still didn't want to open my mail alone, so I perched on a convenient surface and stoutheartedly slit Mother's envelope.

Mother had received my news, dismissed the sisters with a choice qualifying remark, and advised me to enjoy the male companionship with a free heart (I thought that "free" had been penned in a broader, admonitory line) and to look into the matter of a good school for the twins in Ireland. She'd heard rumors that Teddie-boy was still acting the fool.

Hank's letter was brief: Teddie-boy had not paid this month's support money, and a telephone conference with his lawyer disclosed that the omission was deliberate, so Hank was taking instant action.

I wasn't as depressed by these newses as I'd thought I'd be. I supposed that I'd half expected Teddie to stop the support money out of pique. The joke was on him, however, if he thought that action would force me back to the States. Sometimes Teddie had a hard time recognizing the Empty Gesture.

I stuffed the letters into my handbag, and was then asked to admire the newly refitted bike.

Chapter XVII

As I cooked dinner, I found my mind doing some "what-ifs," mainly financial ones. The days when I could cheerfully or reluctantly refer the matter to the man of the house were long gone. Like Harry Truman, the buck now stopped with me. And the loss of this month's support money disorganized my careful plans. I had, fortuitously, it now appeared, paid the July rent on the apartment before I left, but I'd be down to a nervous-making $10.75 in the checking account. I did have my half of the sale money of the "matrimonial" home, but that was in mutual funds sacred to college for the twins.

Although Hank had already set in motion the legal machinery to force Teddie to pay the support money, better best I not count on that money. Which left me nibbling away at the trust fund. I didn't like that sort of pilfering any better, because if Rene's Law came into effect the death duties might well turn out to be more than the trust fund. Still, for Teddie's benefit, I was finally ahead of the game. I chuckled to myself.

"What's so funny, Mom?" asked Snow, busily writing letters at the dining table, which I was setting.

"I'm winning."

"Huh?"

I was, but I didn't explain it out loud. Yes, I was really overcoming Teddie's latest machination. Stopping the support money was only going to land him in trouble. After all, I *could* work the caretaker routine.

I'd better contact George Boardman in the morning for a

firm answer. Michael, too, because I wanted to know what to do about Mrs. Slaney's house. And the place should be cleared of her belongings—not a task I relished, but it had to be done before I could arrange something for George. I should also find out what could be done about bribing Fahey out of his place and leaving the way clear for Shay's candidate for . . . what could I call it? investiture . . . into the queendom.

"How much should I bribe Fahey to leave?"

Simon looked up from his letter-writing and exchanged a meaningful twinnish glance with his sister. I wish I could interpret those cryptic exchanges: I'd know what was going on in their little minds.

"Well, Mom, I'd ask Shay or Michael or Kieron. Not us. But I'm really glad to hear it."

"Why?"

Simon had that "I won't answer you now" look on his face.

"Why?" I repeated, coming back into the room with our dinner plates. I was a little irritated with my obtuseness and their subtlety.

"Oh, because . . ." Snow began, paused, and then added, "it's good you're involved enough here to get him out. *He* drank. Almost as much as—" Then she did shut up.

"As Daddy?" I finished for her. I didn't miss the look, which needed no interpretation, between Simon and his sister. (SHUT UP, SIS.) "Both of you used to love your father." They were eating at a rate guaranteed to fill their mouths too full for answers. "You used to love doing things with him. What happened?"

They ate in deafening silence.

"All right, kids, something happened at the Harrisons' party . . ." Not even a look passed between them. "I know your father got stoned drunk that night. Did he embarrass you?"

"You can say that again," muttered Snow.

"Mom," began Simon in that "let's be reasonable" tone, "do you really need chapter and verse on Dad drunk?"

I caught the shudder Snow gave, and the revulsion on her face. I knew that something very deep and disturbing had happened.

"Let's just say, Mom," Simon continued, "that he was the worst he'd ever been."

"I'm your mother. I have certain rights. I can't protect you . . ."

"You did," said Snow in an implacable voice. "You divorced him. If you hadn't . . ."

What I heard then shocked me: *They* would have left. I knew that they couldn't have maneuvered me into divorce; that distressing solution had been in my thoughts long before the Harrisons' party. But it was after that night that I'd noticed a distinct reluctance in the children to do anything, go anywhere, even chat with their father. And he had become almost defensively insistent on their company, lavish with his gifts and affectionate demonstrations. I suppose their attitude toward him had been a subconscious factor pushing me toward divorce.

"Well, I did divorce him, and that's that." Even a clod could have have felt the relief in the room, and I decided not to press the subject further. We finished our dinner in a less awkward mood.

"Say, Mom," Snow asked in a more normal voice, "has Daddy stopped the support money?"

"However did you guess?" There wasn't much point in hiding that fact, although I wouldn't have been so frank half an hour ago.

Snow giggled. "It figgers."

"Will it matter much, Mom?" asked Simon, worried.

"Not in terms of eating . . ."

"Don't you dare knuckle under to that kind of blackmail," said Snow, hard-voiced again, scowling at me.

"Hank's already applying pressure."

"That'll annoy Dad," said Snow cheerfully.

I couldn't reprimand her—that would have been sheer hypocrisy—but I sighed. I had refused to have it on my conscience that I had turned Teddie's children against him. (Try to Preserve the Image!) However, I didn't have to worry: He had done the job all by himself.

"Mommie, what if Hank doesn't get Daddy to pay?"

"*If* that should happen, there is more than enough in the trust fund to get us home and maintain us come September. You do have to be back in time for school, you know."

"What? And let Daddy think you caved in?"

Humph! I hadn't thought of that aspect.

"Yeah, we know," said Simon, grinning. "And there are good schools here in Dublin."

"You've been checking?"

"Sure." Simon's grin got broader. "Why not? Plan ahead!"

I leaned back in my chair, as if the inanimate wood could give me moral support.

"Now look, you two . . ." Even as I framed it, my argument about continuity in education/friends/homes seemed weak . . . opposed as it was to the fact that Teddie-boy would think he'd won the game.

"Yes?" drawled my children encouragingly.

"*You* may like Ireland but *you* haven't been accused of murder, or gaining an inheritance under false pretenses. *You* don't have to bear the brunt of outraged elderly aunts and—"

The doorbell wheezed.

"Speaking of outraged elderly aunts," said Snow maliciously, "what odds will you give me on our caller?"

"I wouldn't," and I listened fervently for a friendly voice. The male mutters I heard were encouraging. Shay? I half rose in expectation, berating myself soundly for that notion. I was both pleased and disappointed to see Michael Noonan, tall and very attractive, striding into the dining room.

"I was hoping to find you home, Rene. Can I persuade you to have a few jars with me this evening? I couldn't reach you by phone this afternoon."

I heard that Michael wanted to talk to me, away from the ears of my adoring children.

"I'll change and be right with you. Snow, show Mr. Noonan what we've done with the living room and the kitchen."

You know, it was really fun at my age to dress up for an unexpected date, without resorting to the pretenses of indifference or keeping him waiting, so as not to appear unpopular.

I slipped quickly into the lemon-yellow sheath with the matching sandals that Snow had bludgeoned me into buying, found the strand of wooden beads that Snow said "made" the ensemble, pulled a brush through my hair, dabbed on scent, eschewed the eye shadow despite what Snow said about the absolute necessity of that, and was back down the stairs in seven minutes flat. Wishing it were Shamus Kerrigan who awaited me.

"Mom, practice makes perfect," said my daughter, casting an appraising eye on my costume.

Michael's expression told me he agreed. Then Simon stepped forward with an exaggerated swagger.

"Now, Mr. Noonan, I don't want any fast driving, she's our only mother, and you're to be home directly after the pubs close. Otherwise we'll worry. Now have a good time, dear."

Michael was at first nonplussed, until he recognized the reversal of roles. He made conventional responses in a mock-solemn tone of voice.

"What a pair!" he said as he guided me to his car, a dark blue Spitfire.

"I'm sorry to let you in for that."

"I'm not," he replied, with laughter in his voice.

"I guess they'd be considered bold here in Ireland. Or cheeky!"

He gave me a sidelong look as he started the car. "They're not disrespectful for all they're vocal, Rene. Then, of course, knowing they're Yanks changes one's perspective." He was not above needling me.

Michael had turned his car toward Dublin as we stopped at the dual highway. He was glancing in his rear-view mirror, waiting to get out into the traffic, which was fairly steady on the main road.

"Any favorite pubs?"

"I haven't done much searching yet, but I rather had the notion you wanted to *talk*."

He took off down the highway, easing in between two rather fast-moving vehicles with what I thought was a dangerous want of driving discretion. He appeared pleased with his maneuver, but I hoped he didn't continue to drive like this. But he did. At the lights in Cabinteely he took an unexpected—though he signaled—right and then almost immediately a left into the parking area for the Bank of Ireland Computer Building. He pulled on the brakes, doused the lights, and glanced back over his shoulder at the road. A car came tearing past the entrance, and almost immediately we heard it braking. I cringed for a crash-bang-shriek.

"Kieron was right. You *are* being tailed. C'mon."

"Tailed?" I said it to his closed door as he came round the Spitfire to help me out. "Was that what that wild driving was about?"

"I don't normally scramble, Rene."

Just as we got to the roadway, a car backed up past us,

braked again, and then angled into the one free roadside
parking space, its lights briefly full on our faces.

"Is that the man?" I asked, but Michael told me not to
look, and hurried me across the street to the pub.

Unexpectedly, the pub was luxuriously appointed, with
thick carpets, paneled walls, deep armchairs, and a cheerful
fire on the hearth.

"D'you mind sitting here?" Michael asked, gesturing to a
table whose chairs had a discreet view of the door.

"Under the circumstances, no."

We were giving our order when the door opened and in
came . . . Nosy.

"He just arrived," I told Michael, leaning forward as if to
flick my ash, then nonchalantly glancing up.

Michael sat back, rubbing his chin reflectively. Then he
adjusted his glasses. "You do have a tail: one of our good
private detectives."

"Does he know you?"

"He might." Michael sounded doubtful, although he gave
me a cheerful grin. "Much of our work deals with estate
management, wills, sales . . ."

"But wasn't he hired by my relatives?" Even as I said it,
the notion didn't sound plausible. How could a private detective's checking my movements help to contest the will?

"It couldn't be about old Mrs. Slaney?" He shook his
head. "My ex-husband?"

He nodded.

"But why? Why now? I've divorced him. What I do is
not his business any more—" I broke off because Michael
had that anticipatory look, like someone waiting for the
players to hit on the right syllables in charades. "He's trying
to revoke my custody of the children? Trying to prove me
immoral or something? He's out of his ever-loving mind!
Just because I came to Ireland for the summer?"

Michael had kept nodding agreement with my various
points. "I don't know the man, of course, but I understand
that he was not in favor of your holidaying here. In fact, if
I may be candid, I've heard from your American solicitor,
Mr. van Vliet, asking my advice on custody laws here."

"*What?*"

Michael patted my hand soothingly. "The Irish courts
would uphold your custody unless wilful and excessive neg-
lect of the children could be proved." I was sputtering with

indignation. "And that would mean you'd have to stop feeding them completely, keep them locked up in substandard rooms without toilet facilities, et cetera, et cetera. Or if you were proved guilty of some felony."

"Good God! How could Teddie have heard of Mrs. Slaney?"

Michael merely nodded in Nosy's direction.

"You mean, you think I've been followed since I got here?"

Our drinks arrived then, and I took a long, long pull. Michael, noticing, indicated to the barboy to bring two more.

"That impossible, incredible man! How could he do such a thing?" Very easily, I realized, remembering the unserved injunction to keep us from even leaving the States. What maggot was possessing Ted Stanford now? "Well, I'm glad you didn't mention this in front of the twins. They'll be livid."

Michael's eyebrows went up. "You're going to tell them?"

I sighed, thinking back to that earlier conversation. "Neither of them is stupid. Sooner or later they'll see Nosy, and it doesn't take them long to put facts together."

"You Yanks!"

"Yeah," I said, with no enthusiasm. "But what *can* he do?" I asked, in a fine state of agitation.

"Legally," Michael said in a forceful way, "nothing. I understand from van Vliet that at their ages your children have some say in the choice of parent." He shrugged as if that solved my problem entirely. "I'd hazard the guess that the man is merely trying to ruin your holiday."

"He's got company."

"I beg your pardon?"

"I was thinking of the aunts," I said, with a heavy sigh.

"Now, now, Rene, cheer up. After all, you *haven't* murdered anyone." He said it to shock me out of my depression, and he did.

"Speaking of Mrs. Slaney," I began brightly, "how much would it cost me to get Fahey out *now*? I really don't need any more unsavory characters on my queendom."

"I'll sound him out. How high would you go?"

"Well, I refuse to be milked, but I don't want anything to do with a man like that. More important: Does Tom Slaney have any legal right to squat in that cottage now that his mother's dead?"

"Tom Slaney's legal rights are nil as far as the cottage goes."

"Is there an inquest coming?" I asked.

"As it happened, her physician had seen her the previous week, and her heart failure was no surprise."

"What about the hole in her head?" I'm not a vindictive person, but the appalling nature of her final injury made me wish that her son would suffer something in the way of justice.

"Ah, yes, well, she *died* from the heart attack. Slaney admitted to her collapse, said she struck her head on the hearth—I understand there's corroborative evidence—and he put her in the bed. He was, on his own admission, drink-taken. It's been proved that he came back to her cottage Friday night to get money from her, since her pension had just been paid. At any rate, according to the barman, when he returned to the pub he had money enough to drink himself stocious. He did end up spending the night in the nick."

"While his poor mother lay dead . . ."

"Legally one could split hairs on this, and I don't know yet if there will be a prosecution. She died first, you see."

"Of fright, terror, disappointment . . . And where is that creature"—I preferred to call him "murderer"—"now?"

"He's still in custody. He won't bother you, and as far as the cottage is concerned, it has reverted to the landlord—you." Michael patted my hand reassuringly. He had such nice hands.

He started to recount a case he'd been briefed with which was so outrageous and improbable that I had to keep my mind on it. Then he regaled me with several more highly amusing incidents so that "Time, ladies and gentlemen" caught me completely by surprise, and with some dismay.

"Hungry, Rene?" asked Michael as we left the pub.

I naturally glanced over my shoulder to see if Nosy was there. Michael gave me a little shake.

"All aboveboard," he said. "If we can make it to Stepaside by half eleven, we can eat *and* drink. Might as well spend your ex-husband's money on Nosy's expenses . . . huh?"

"Hey, great!" I laughed. Michael was giving me the proper perspective.

As he drove off this time, it was at a circumspect speed.

"Speaking of ex-husbands, Michael, couldn't Mary Cuniff get an annulment and then be free?"

"Of course."

"How much does an annulment cost, then?"

"More than Mary can manage to save."

"Not more than George would be willing to spend, though?"

"Hmmm. My dear girl, you are remarkable. But are you so certain that Mary would jump out of one fire into another?"

"George is different! I know she really thinks so."

"Does she?" His question hinted at others unasked.

"Why?"

"Irene . . ." and then he stopped, and took a rather sharp curve carefully.

"I've a suspicion," I began, to relieve his conscience, "that my Great-aunt Irene had some blind spots in her philanthropy. I feel that George is right for Mary. Why must she be condemned to this sort of half life, this sense of being trapped, or Molly, for that matter? It just perpetuates the problems in the next generation."

"And you a divorced woman?"

I sighed. "My marriage to Teddie failed for very understandable reasons. But that doesn't mean that I couldn't and wouldn't make a second marriage work. In fact, I'd be better at it. I know so many of the pitfalls."

"Oh?"

Michael's reply was too bland, and I realized how my attitude had suddenly polarized. In spite of what I'd seen of Irish marriages, and in spite of what I knew about the high divorce rate of American marriages, I was essentially a romantic, cock-eyed optimist. And I really did like having a man about the house. Domestic by temperament, I liked to "do" for a man. I'd missed that these past eighteen months. While it was enthralling to have a queendom of my own, while I was enjoying the redecoration, I was also more and more aware that a good bit of such industry is doing it for a particular man: to please him, to give him a reason to boast to his friends about his home and his wife, and to give him a valid reason for coming home at all.

"Yes, 'oh,' " I said tartly, in answer to Michael. "There are some areas in which the resemblance between my great-aunt and me fails completely. Another thing: How can Ann Purdee get a legal separation? I'm willing to finance it. I can *always* say it was Aunt Irene's wish."

Michael gave a snort. "Irene did not like her protégés . . ."

"Succumbing?" I asked testily, when he couldn't find an appropriate verb. "Will or will not a legal separation give her protection against that husband of hers?"

"Yes, it would," Michael said. "I have suggested it. But the separation has to be made by mutual consent."

"And you don't see Paddy Purdee consenting?"

"Consenting, no. But he'd do anything for a price."

"You know him?"

"Yes. Irene tried to put the fear of the law and the Lord into him."

"Then why is Ann Purdee scared?"

"Irene Teasey is dead. He was afraid of *her*."

I thought of my aunt's diminutive stature. "Good heavens."

"Irene in an angry mood was . . . formidable, Rene." Michael was both amused and respectful. "She tore strips out of him."

"She met him?"

"In my office. I arranged the meeting."

"Then he'd know who and where . . ."

"I doubt it. For starters, your aunt's name was never mentioned. And the interview was attended by one of Irene's very good friends in the Gardai. Unfortunately, that gentleman has also passed on. We'll just hope that Purdee is still fishing a long trip and hasn't heard."

Undoubtedly Rene's Law applied to Ann, and Paddy Purdee would run into some person who knew about Irene Teasey, where she lived, and Ann's situation.

As we turned into the parking lot of the Stepaside Inn, Nosy wasn't far behind us, and I sighed deeply. I too did *not* like being followed. Once more I was visited by the irresistible desire to cut stakes here instantly and go back to my own country. But that would be cowardly, and worse, Teddie would think he had won.

We were lucky to find a table, for the Inn was rather full. As Michael pointed out, it was one excuse to keep on drinking past licensed hours and to get a solid base of food for more drinking at home.

"There's one more business," I said after we'd given the waitress our order.

"Yes?" he said encouragingly when I faltered.

"Do you know why my aunt turned against Shay Kerrigan? I mean, exactly why?"

Michael gave me the blank look which I suspected he found useful in courtrooms.

"Oh, c'mon, Michael, *I* know even if Aunt Irene shoved it under the convenient heading of protecting someone innocent. *Was* she explicit to you? The thing is, I don't think she got the right man. And it would alter matters considerably if I could prove it."

"Oh?" Again that horribly bland response.

"Really, Michael. You're infuriating. And it's not betraying a professional confidence to tell me if she was explicit. You have only to say that much and I'll reveal what I've found out."

Michael took ages to make up his mind. "She said, as nearly as I can remember her exact words, that she had been bitterly disappointed in Shay, that he had abused her confidence and lost her respect; he deserved no assistance from her."

"Then she never confronted him?"

"She absolutely refused to see him."

"That wasn't fair."

"Does 'fair' enter into it?"

"I think so. He's supposed to have fathered Sally Hanahoe's baby."

That was as much a shock to Michael as it had been to me. He blinked and stared at me as if he doubted his ears, strengthening my own belief in Shamus.

"Yes, and furthermore he's supposed to have told Sally that he was married and covered his tracks so well that she couldn't find him. She had to have the baby on her own."

Michael had begun to shake his head from side to side.

"I don't believe it either," I went on. "And for good reasons. One, Shamus made no secret to me of the fact that he's not married, nor likely to marry. Two, he has a keen sense of family responsibility. Look at his kindnesses to his nephew, his courtesies to the Ladies Brandel. They're damned good judges of character. But it fits in with what

I'm beginning to understand about Aunt Irene. She would
think the worst of a man, any man, without bothering to
ask yes, no, or maybe. Furthermore, when I mentioned Sally Hanahoe's name to him it didn't, absolutely didn't, ring a
bell. I'd stake my life on it." Michael gave me a knowing
glance, which I dismissed angrily. "I hear things when people are dissembling."

"He's got a good barrister in you. Too good!"

"Oh, nonsense, Michael. I simply can't stand injustice
and . . . and . . ."

"You're feeling guilty about the access?"

"Well . . . Oh, I *know* he was making nice-nice when
he thought he could wheedle the right of way out of me
but . . . he's gone on being . . ." The waitress fortuitously arrived with our suppers, and when we spoke again, the
subject of Shay Kerrigan did not come up. I heard that
somehow Michael preferred not to discuss him any more.

The lights were on at my house when Michael turned up
the lane. (My lane.) We were halfway to the door when it
was flung open and my children stalked out to intercept us.

"Where have you been, Mommy?" demanded Snow, worried and angry.

"Oh, good Lord, I'm so sorry. We went on for a bit to
eat and—"

"It's my fault, Simon, Snow," Michael interrupted, with
suspicious meekness. "I know I promised to have her back
after closing time . . . but we're only forty-five minutes
late."

Snow began to giggle, and Simon's frown disappeared.

"Aw, Mom, we're not that way," he said.

"No, it was inconsiderate of us," Michael said. "It won't
happen again."

"Ah, fer Pete's sake . . ."

Then I sensed Snow's unspoken anxiety.

"What's happened, honey?"

Beside me I could see Michael tense, and we exchanged
glances. But Nosy had been following me . . .

"Gerry . . . you know, your cousin . . . Alice's
son . . . was here with the motorcycle girl . . ."

"And . . . ?" I prompted, silently complimenting Simon
on his diplomacy.

"They wouldn't *tell* us." Snow was miffed. "But they're
very anxious to see you. Like then!"

"Gerry said he'd give you a shout tomorrow morning."

"Well, that's that, then." I turned to Michael, extending my hand. He held it in such a way that, for some obscure reason, I was very glad of my children's presence. Oh dear, what was wrong with me? Michael was so nice, and yet . . . I thanked him profusely for the lovely evening and the business we'd done in the pubs, and he said that he'd check into matters and ring me later next week.

Chapter XVIII

I did not sleep well, which was surprising with all I'd had to drink: anxiety over Teddie's next ploy, I supposed. But at five thirty, I finally admitted to myself that I was in the thralls of sexual frustration.

I missed Shamus Kerrigan! I missed him for himself, his easy charm, the warmth of his rather boyish smile, the reassurance of his presence in my vicinity, visible or invisible. Not that Michael wasn't charming too; he did have an easy way about him, a nice smile, good hands, but I *relied* on Michael, and I most certainly hadn't wanted to be kissed by him. Which had been very much on his mind during the later part of our evening together.

I was thwarted, too. Michael didn't believe Shay Kerrigan would be irresponsible toward a girl he'd got pregnant but it was Ann Purdee I had to prove that to. Because if I didn't, I lost any chance of influencing Ann. She wouldn't trust me, and I had to be in her confidence to deal with Paddy Purdee for her sake.

But clearing Shay would serve several purposes: One, I'd get in good with him by being able, with a clear conscience, to give him access up the lane; two, it would show Ann that Irene could be wrong about a man or men; three, it would put me in a damned good light. (Preserve the Image!)

I snorted at my conceit. I'd done such a good job of managing my own life that I should give someone else pointers? C'mon, Rene, be honest. The only point of the three is that you'll ingratiate yourself with Shamus Kerrigan. But what if he really is only buttering you up to get that access? You give it, he goes off his merry way, and then where will you be in Ann's and Sally's eyes?

Well, if *that* should happen, I'm wrong about Shamus Kerrigan's character, even if I do prove him innocent about Sally, and I'm well rid of him.

Now there's a dilemma for you to ponder, Rene!

I pondered . . . and woke, disgustingly refreshed, at eight o'clock, the clean fresh air blowing in my window like an intoxicant. There wasn't another sound in the house, but out-of-doors was as busy as could be. Birds, bees, other talking things . . . and loud clanking noisy things . . .

I sat bolt upright as I identified the noise. Bulldozers? I ran to the window, but I couldn't see up the hill past the screening trees. I threw my spring coat around my shoulders and dashed down the steps and out the door. I had to get into the lane before I had any view. A huge yellow bulldozer was on the hill, charging and roaring like its namesake, pawing pieces out of the meadow.

I glanced down my lane: no tracks.

So the dilemma had dissolved last night. I felt defeated. Shay must have bought the access rights in from Glenamuck. Was that the business deal which he'd been busy with? Had he really been away from his office these last few days? Or avoiding any calls from me?

Be fair! How can you blame him, with your shillyshallying?

Despondently I made myself coffee. I didn't even get a chance to mope in solitude. Snow came charging down the steps at such a pace that I yelled at her not to break her neck.

"There's a bulldozer in the field?" Her words were half query, half accusation. "Did you give—"

"No, I didn't." I didn't add that I wished I had. "And there isn't a mark on the lane."

Snow flounced into the other chair. "Then how? Levitation?"

"There was a possible way in from the other side."

"Hey, Mom," and Simon joined us. "What's with the—"

"He came the other way," said Snow.

"Oh!" Simon was also disappointed and uneasy. Oh dear, if Shay's action disillusioned them too, I'd have more than Ann, Sally, and Mary to worry about.

A more somber trio never ate without tasting. It occurred

to me as I put limp eggs and soggy toast into my face that the twins were even more upset about this revolting development than I was.

"It's Friday," said Simon for no reason.

"Yeah!" his sister agreed.

"Why?" I asked, to prove I was listening.

"Gotta come sometime, I guess," said Simon logically.

"Okay, Mom, like you always tell us," said Snow, "when you're down in the dumps, look up. There's a lot of work to be done about this place. Let's do it."

That's how we came to sort out Mrs. Slaney's cottage that Friday. I couldn't get more depressed than I already was.

I was, naturally, wrong, but at least I had company. The tired, tattered bits and pieces that had furnished the poor lady's home ought to have been interred too. Nothing seemed worth saving.

Ann concurred when she came over to see what we were doing. "But you've got to remember that Tom Slaney's entitled to it, rag, bag, and bucket. And he's the sort would create trouble if any's missing."

"What'll we do with it, then?" I asked.

"You've a world of space in the barn," Ann suggested.

"We can make a list, Mom," Snow said, "itemizing everything and having Ann sign it."

"Would he accept that?"

"And Mr. Corrig, the postman."

"I'll get some cartons from Sally's store," I said, relieved at an excuse to leave for a few moments.

By the time I returned with the largest cartons that Sally's obliging store manager could find me, Jimmy had arrived and Molly was abroad. Snow, with a clipboard and lists (two carbons), was organizing everyone, even Meggie, Tom, and Fiona. Before noon we had all but a wardrobe cleared out and stored in the haybarn.

"Eat now, scour later" was Snow's dictum, and we four repaired to my kitchen.

I had managed not to look up the lane at the bulldozer, but my resolve weakened when I passed the phone. While the kids were bickering over who used the john first, boys or girls, I dialed Shay's number. My ridiculous heart gave a leap at the sound of his rich voice on the other end, but sank as the recorded message idiotically reported back. I hung up quickly as Simon came thudding down the stairs with Jimmy.

We tackled the cleaning problem after lunch, and I tried to keep firmly in mind that the poor old lady mustn't have been able for many years. We used a big box of Flash, three cans of Ajax, wore out I don't know how many rags, sponges, and Brillo pads, but the fusty odor of decay had definitely been blown out of the cottage—had she ever opened the windows?—by late afternoon.

"Slaney's may be clean," Snow said as we drooped on the grass, "but it only makes Fahey's look worse."

As one, we glanced to the left. Jimmy sighed audibly.

"Not today," I said, touching his shoulder. "And you are in no way obliged to join our madness."

"No, honest, Aunt Rene, I *like* working with you and the twins. It's fun!"

Tired as he was, he meant it, and I was about to elaborate on my appreciation when Mary returned home in George Boardman's car. Soon Kieron put in an appearance, and while the men were occupied with storing the heavy wardrobe, I hemmed and hawed with Mary Cuniff, trying to find an adroit way of suggesting my plan. My progress was nil, because Mary was feeling conscience-stricken about not having looked in on old Mrs. Slaney over that fatal weekend, and not having offered to do any of the household tasks.

"It's a mercy the poor old thing's in her grave, Mary Cuniff," said Ann bluntly. "She'd've been long gone and welcomed it if that doctor hadn't been such a sanctimonious twit. My, the place looks nice now." Then Ann's gaze fastened on Fahey's, and her mouth tightened.

"Michael's going to buy him out as soon as possible," I said brightly, as a lead-in to my ploy. "Did Michael, by any chance, phone you today?" I turned to George.

"No, he didn't." George looked surprised and, curiously, uncomfortable. "I wasn't in the office, you see."

I wondered fleetingly if his ardor for Mary had cooled, but I had my opportunity. "Well, I'd like to have a man in that cottage, with Tom Slaney floating around."

"He's not likely to come back," said George firmly.

"Michael said something about your applying for planning permission, so if you still want to buy it . . ."

That touched off the reaction. No, it wasn't indifference

on his part, or Mary's. I heaved an internal sigh of relief. This playing the lady bountiful/arch meddler can lead to temptation: just one little shove in the right direction . . . Only how was I so sure that my direction was right?

I was tired.

That's what Kieron and Mary said, and Ann and George dutifully agreed.

"I'll cook dinner, Mom," Snow said, "and Simon and Jimmy can help." She flashed them warning glances.

Jimmy said he *had* to be home for tea tonight: His mom was getting narked. He put himself out of temptation's way by flinging himself on his bike and beetling off.

"I'll have a word with you, Ann-girl," Kieron said, taking her so firmly by the arm that she was too surprised to break away.

The rest of us were rather amazed at his masterfulness, but Ann, instead of an outburst of independence, meekly let herself be led toward her cottage.

Mary and I broke into a series of nervous inanities before we all dispersed. I wondered why George kept looking so worried. Did he know what Kieron was up to?

"Hey," said Snow as we walked toward the house, "what's with the strong-arm Kieron's using?"

"I haven't a clue," and I wished I had. Something was up.

The phone's ringing interrupted Snow's supposition. We all ran to catch the call, with me hoping fervently that it might be Shay Kerrigan.

It was Gerry Hegarty, sounding very relieved to hear my voice.

"I've been phoning and phoning, Coz," he said.

"Oh, Lord!" I'd forgotten the twins' message about him.

"We've been housecleaning down below . . ."

"Where? Oh, old Mrs. Slaney's?"

"Yes." Why did that interest Gerry Hegarty?

"Rene, are you free this evening? Maureen and I'd very much like a chat with you."

I couldn't come out and bluntly ask him if it was about the free cottage. So I said he'd be welcome and I'd love a chance to talk with Maureen again.

I worried all through supper about how to let them down gently. It wasn't that *I* didn't want to oblige Gerry (he couldn't help having Auntie Alice as a mother—maybe that's why he was so nice) or Maureen. It was just that . . .

Gerry and Maureen had both been in the house before. They seized on the subject of our redecorations as though I'd done something incredible. At least, Gerry did more of the talking; Maureen just looked apprehensive. The second time the conversation strangled to death, I rediscovered blunt speech.

"Now that I know you approve of my redecorating," I told them, "what is *your* problem?"

Gerry glanced at Maureen, and she, all but squirming, passed the buck back to him.

"Has Brian Kelley been at you again to sell?"

"The figure's gone up to thirty-five-thousand pounds. And if I agree to sell he'll use his influence to assure probate."

Gerry cleared his throat. "I've reason to believe that it's my mother trying to buy the property."

I couldn't help it. I let out a whoop. "But she objected to Aunt Irene buying it!"

"According to the latest," Gerry told me with a sardonic grin, "it was on my mother's advice that Irene purchased the land. Because land south of the city was sure to appreciate."

"The old——! So now, of course, that's why she should be left the land?" Gerry nodded. "Okay, would she have that kind of money?" Again Gerry nodded, and I whistled.

"Mother's rather shrewd with property."

"City property," Maureen corrected him.

"Then why the subterfuge? I mean, working through a clown like that Kelley character? And forcing Maureen to let him know when I arrived? And his besieging me?"

"For starters," Gerry said, still slightly embarrassed, "she assumed that you only came over here to sell the property. . ."

"And if she could get to me first, I'd sell and disappear forever? And then she could say that Irene *had* left her the property after all? That another will had been discovered?"

Maureen stared at me. Gerry gave a short laugh.

"I thought you'd only just met my mother!"

"I can't blame it on genetics, because it's from Mother's side of the family, but I've got an aunt in the States . . ." I didn't elaborate, because she *was* his mother.

"Do you *have* to sell?" Gerry asked. He glanced at Maureen. "Because if you *have* to . . ."

I scored a large plus for Maureen: She had not betrayed any confidential information about the trust fund.

"As it happens, Gerry, I don't. At least not precipitously. And, well, my affairs have taken such a turn that I'll probably stay on longer than I'd originally intended."

That news pleased them. Maureen actually smiled, with an air of relief that finally permitted her to relax on the chair.

"Say, mind my asking, but how *did* you find out your mother was bidding for the queendom?"

"Something I overheard at the house the other day matched what Maureen had told me about Brian Kelley," said Gerry, with an affectionate and amused glance at his young niece. "You're sure you're all right, as far as death duties are concerned? What I'm saying is, I personally would like to see Irene's queendom remain as she wished it. So for want of the few odd pounds, don't feel you have to sell it."

"That's extraordinarily nice of you, Gerry . . ."

"The least we can be, with my mother carrying on the way she has."

"And the first thing she'd do, did she own it, would be to turf Ann, Sally, and Mary out," Maureen said bitterly. "And the only one who's paid her any heed is Maeve. It's all very embarrassing," she finished, in a muffled voice.

Gerry leaned over and patted her hand. "I told you Rene would understand, pet."

"I truly didn't know it was Auntie Alice that Mr. Kelley was representing. And Ann and Sally and Mary have had such a desperate time—you don't *know* what can happen to women in Ireland . . ."

"Yes, well, I'm beginning to. I'm arranging a caretaker tenant for Thrush cottage . . . and then, bluntly, I'm bribing Fahey to vacate completely." Ah yes, there was a reaction there. "I'll look for suitable clients in the best traditions of the queendom. Did you by any chance know of someone?"

Gerry saw through that bland question with a chuckle, but Maureen looked surprised, hopeful, and apprehensive.

"I told you she was a downy one, Maureen. And, yes, Rene, we do."

"So does Shamus Kerrigan." What imp made me come out with that?

"Shamus?" Gerry frowned, confounding me. "Which Shamus Kerrigan?"

"She means Shay Kerrigan," said Maureen, "the one who was such a good friend of Auntie Irene's."

"How many Shamus Kerrigans do you know?" I asked Gerry.

He gave a chuckle. "Several, two of whom I hope you never meet. Two of 'em live in Dublin, as well."

I cut through the beginning of his next remark with an urgent question of my own. "Would your mother know Shay Kerrigan, the one who was friends with Irene?"

Gerry glanced at Maureen for confirmation. "Sure and she would. He developed property Dad owned in Ballybrack."

Well, that sort of tied in with another great unanswered question about Shamus: Which relative had given him that bogus permission to use my lane? So my dear Great-aunt Alice had been *that* positive she'd own the queendom? I wondered if she'd socked him a bundle for that one transit. And if he'd got his money back.

"Would you really consider helping someone, Rene?" asked Maureen, almost timidly.

"I sure would. Is she deserted, abused, or unwed? Oh dear, and I'm *not* being snide."

"She's married, been deserted, and has a small boy. Her name's Sheevaun Donnelly, and her man took the boat, which is just as well, as he'd been a bit too free with his employer's money," Maureen said in a rush. "She runs a hairdressing business in Rathfarnham, but the person who's been taking care of her little boy is altogether unreliable."

"We could get our hair done free?" That imp of misplaced humor made me say it.

"Oh, I'm certain Sheevaun wouldn't mind at all," Maureen said, a little stiffly.

"Honest, I'm pulling your leg."

Gerry's laugh was more reassuring than my words, and Maureen began to grin slowly, her eyes still on mine, and hopeful. However, now I could see their strategy in confessing Aunt Alice's abortive attempt to secure the queendom. Ah, well, theirs was the nicer axe to be ground.

"Sure now, Maureen, you know how Irene was in acquiring useful tenants. She liked the old gratitude bit, noblesse oblige," Gerry was saying.

"To be frank, however, I'd prefer less personal service and a bit more rent," I said. "Several pounds a month is—"

"Oh, Sheevaun would be able to pay more than that, Rene," her sponsor said quickly. "She's paying twelve pounds a week for two horrid little rooms now."

"Look, I have to get the cottage back first. But, yes, if I get it back, I'll definitely consider your Mrs. Donnelly. I hadn't actually committed myself to Shay's candidate."

Such a decision called for coffee, at the least, and then we ambled down to watch Snow riding Horseface. As nearly as I could tell, my darling daughter was improving. Ann shouted instructions from the center of the pasture's improvised ring, but she came over to the fence to greet Maureen and Gerry. Maybe she was on very friendly terms with them anyhow, but Ann was unusually expansive. I wondered what on earth Kieron had said to her. The girl was practically beaming at me with goodwill when she suddenly frowned and tensed.

Following her anxious gaze, we all observed a Mini Minor cautiously drawing up the lane. Ann ducked under the rail, about to fly toward the house, when a woman poked her head out of the window.

"Could you tell me if the Stanford children are still here?"

"Yes, they are," I told her.

Her head vanished as she turned off the ignition and got out.

"Are you taking care of them?" she asked pleasantly. "I'm Mrs. Melton of the ISPCC."

She extended her hand, so of course I shook it.

"Im Irene Teasey," I said, since that information seemed proper. What was the ISPCC?

"It's very good of you to take on such a responsibility," she went on, mystifying me more.

"No responsibility, really. I am their mother."

"Their mother?" The cordiality died in her eyes, and her whole attitude became wary. More than that I couldn't hear.

"Yes, I'm Irene Teasey Stanford, but I resumed my maiden name when I got my divorce."

"Divorce?" For the amount of information she was getting from me, she was giving poor return.

I looked about, toward Gerry, Maureen, and Ann. Gerry obligingly stepped up beside me.

"Yes, Mrs. Melton, I divorced Teddie Stanford. It was final about seven months ago now."

"Oh!"

"What is this all about, Mrs. Melton?"

"I told you. I'm from the Irish Society for the Prevention of Cruelty to Children."

"You've come for a donation?" An odd sales pitch.

She brushed that aside irritably. "Was there a death here recently?" She looked past me to Gerry.

"My great-aunt, who was also Irene Teasey, died in March," I told her. Or didn't she trust anything I said?

"No, no. Within the past few days?"

"If you mean old Mrs. Slaney," said Gerry as he pointed to the now clean cottage, "she died of a heart seizure this week."

"Heart?"

Mrs. Melton's habit could get on your nerves.

"Yes, sure now and the old dear'd been hanging on to life as if it was worth living," said Gerry, very smooth. I guess he had come to the same horrid conclusion I had. "Rene, here, my cousin," and his emphasis was slight, comforting to me, and noted by Mrs. Melton, "made the sad discovery. Quite a shock it was for her, seeing as how Rene had never laid eyes on the old dear before."

"Oh."

It must have been as plain to Gerry as it was to me: Auntie Alice had spread her "murder" bit about me with a lavish hand. But why on earth she'd bothered the ISPCC . . .

"May I see your children, Mrs. . . ."

"I'm legally Mrs. Teasey."

"Mrs. Teasey. They *are* here?"

"Yes, you may, since you're here. But I think someone has grossly misinformed you and your agency, Mrs. Melton."

She looked sternly at me. "Such a serious complaint has to be investigated, Mrs. Teasey."

"What complaint? As their mother and legal guardian, I have the right to ask."

"I am required to verify their whereabouts, the care

they're receiving, and their mental and physical well-being."
Her glance passed over the three cottages, settling too long
on the mess in front of Fahey's.

"There's my daughter, Mrs. Melton," I said, and waved
toward Snow, who was bouncing about on Horseface's back
with what seemed like bruising efficiency.

"The girl? The one on the horse?"

"Yes, if you'd like to speak to her while I call my son.
He's helping a neighbor with his motorcycle."

Her stunned expression told me that she had expected
babes in swaddling, or at least toddlers. So it couldn't have
been Auntie Alice. It had to be Teddie-boy.

"Simon!" I roared to release some of my spleen. And
bless him, the bullcalf roared back in a matter of seconds.
"Yeah, Mom?" He came running at an admirable sprint.

"Mrs. Melton, this is my son, Simon Stanford."

"How do you do, young man?"

"A bit greasy, thank you ma'am," he said, "so I'd better
not shake your hand." He gave me a "What's up?" quirk of
his eyebrow, which I countered with a mute warning of my
own.

"The girl on horseback is this lad's twin sister?"

"Yes, she is. I agree, they don't look much alike, but I
didn't have any say in the matter."

My levity went down badly with her, but it cheered me!

"They also don't look fourteen," said Mrs. Melton, as if
that *were* my fault. She was very put out. "Since I'm here,
perhaps I'd better see where you are all living." She turned
toward the cottages, with reluctant distaste.

"If you'll step this way, Mrs. Melton," and I couldn't
help making a grand gesture as I indicated the house.

"I'd like a few words with your son and daughter, if I
may."

I told Snow to give Horseface to Ann and come up to
the house immediately. Simon must have given her the private sign, because she too turned very dutiful, sliding off
Horseface. Ann, Maureen, and Gerry gave me a "Help
you?" look, which I appreciated but dismissed with a grin
behind Mrs. Melton's stiff back.

She sat, rigidly erect, on the little settee as the twins
ranged themselves close to me.

"Mrs. Teasey, my office received urgent communications
from the American Red Cross, the American SPCC, fol-

lowed by a request from the Embassy to trace your children. We were given the distinct impression that *infants*
had been illegally removed by you from the continental
U.S.A. and were being kept in substandard conditions by, I
will not mince words, a dangerously unstable woman unfit
to have the care of small children, and under suspicion of
committing a felony."

"Daddy couldn't have!" Snow's explosive denial blended
insult, indignation, embarrassment, and fury. "Mrs. Melton,
I'm so sorry. I could die! Why, you must be livid, being
dragged out on a fool's errand on such a lovely evening.
Oh, Mother, can't Mr. van Vliet do *something* about Daddy? I mean, this is the end!"

"Sara!"

"Mrs. Melton," Simon began, and he was so incensed
that his voice cracked a little, "our *mother* has done nothing illegal. She has the custody of us. Dad knew where we
were going and when Because Snow and I told him. He's
just—"

"Simon!" I felt I'd better call the children to order or
some of Teddie's ridiculous accusations might bear weight.
"I too apologize most profusely, Mrs. Melton. I can't think
what has possessed the children's father. You see, I'd inherited my great-aunt's estate . . ."

"Twelve acres, four cottages, and this lovely old house,"
said Snow at her most guileless, "and that lovely old horse
—would you believe that he's twenty years old?"

The frost receded a bit more from Mrs. Melton's attitude.

"It seemed a good idea," I went on, "to inspect the inheritance and for the children to meet our Irish relatives."

"We love Ireland," Snow said enthusiastically, "and I'd
never get a chance to ride horseback where we lived in the
States." My darling daughter made it sound as if we'd come
up considerably in the world to inherit an Irish Georgian
farmhouse. "We're just started with redecorating—would
you like to see what we've done?"

Mrs. Melton rose. "Thank you, my dear, but I have seen
all that I need to."

"Then you won't have to send us back to Daddy, will
you?" The fear on Snow's face was not sham.

"No, my dear. There's no need to. The facts of the situation were grossly misrepresented to my agency."

I would have escorted her back to her car, but at the front door she turned to me and held out her hand.

"Thank you, Mrs. Teasey, and I apologize for intruding."

"Oh, no, the apologies are all on our side, Mrs. Melton."

"It is scarcely your place to make any apologies, Mrs. Teasey," and when Mrs. Melton smiled, she was a very different, totally likable person. Then she shook her head, stern once more, and walked briskly away.

What had been fulminating within my savage breast during the interview had now reached boiling point. How I had been able to keep my cool while Mrs. Melton was in the house, I don't know. I suppose I must have realized how important it was for me to be pleasant and conciliatory, and give the appearance of being well-balanced.

"What time would it be in America right now, Simon?" Not that it made any difference, because I was picking up the phone and dialing for the overseas operator.

"You're calling Dad?" And the anger on his face turned to gleeful anticipation.

"No, I'm calling Hank. I couldn't hear your father's voice right now without foaming at the mouth. Hank's got to start proceedings or whatever to keep that man from harassing us. First he has me watched—" Whooops!

"Watched?" Both kids leaped on that one.

"You can call Hank if you want to," Simon said through clenched teeth, "but I'm calling my father. And I'm telling my father—"

"Not if I get the phone first, Brother," said Snow, in every bit as quiet a tone. "Watching *you* or us, Mommy?" she asked.

"Me." I suddenly wanted them to go easy on their father, but my answer didn't please them.

"Why? To open a custody case or something?" asked Snow and there was a sort of look on my daughter's face that was going to haunt me: It was too remorseless, too adult, too cruel.

"Well, he hasn't a hope in heaven," she went on. "You tell Hank that, and we'll tell our doting daddy."

For a wonder, Hank was actually in his office. Feeling my veins bubble again, I gave him a rundown of the recent indignities of surveillance, harassment of the children's friends in the States, plus the nice lady from the ISPCC. Hank blew his cool all the way across the Atlantic. At an

inverse ratio, I began to calm down. I even began to see the
amusing side of this.

"When I get through with Theodore Teddie-boy Pre-
serve-the-Image Stanford, there won't be anything left in
the mirror of his narcissism to reflect an image. He'll—"
Hank broke off, inarticulate for once. "What time is it
there, Rene? I'll phone back as soon as I have something in
train."

I told him, thanked him, and rang off. Simon took the
phone out of my hand. And I walked out of the room. I
wanted to hear what they said so badly that I couldn't listen. I kept right on walking, as much to work off the energy
of that excessive spleen as to quit the scene of combat. To
my surprise, because I'd forgotten all about them, Gerry
and Maureen were still at the pasture fence, chatting with
Ann. Horseface was grazing contentedly, reins looped
about his neck.

"It seems," I said as I joined them, "that my ex-husband
said his children were being lodged in substandard conditions, cared for by a murderess. The only agency he doesn't
seem to have called on to find his poor lost infants is the
U.S. Marines."

"Infants?" Gerry and Ann had exclaimed as the words
were out of my mouth. Gerry grinned more and more
broadly as I went on with my explanation. Maureen just
stared, but Ann's face got darker and darker.

"It never stops, does it?" asked Ann when I finished.
"Whether you're American or Irish, the man persecutes
whenever he feels like it and gets away with it."

"Oh, no he doesn't," I said firmly. "And not all men. Just
certain thoroughly spoiled immature temperaments who've
never got it through their thick heads that you can't win
'em all with charm and a sweet smile." Some of my own
anger cooled before the hopeless look on Ann Purdee's
face. "Besides which, I can't really uphold the theory that
says all men are bad, or all women nice. Look at Auntie
Alice for a bad example—Oh Gerry, I'm sorry. Kieron's
sisters, too." That comparison was hardly better chosen.

"But there's no way of knowing, is there?"

I blinked at her vehemence, rueing the disappearance of
that happy, relaxed Ann of a scant half-hour before.

"Not one hundred percent sure, but you do have clues,"

and I thought of the kids' theory about hands. "Ann, how old were you when you got married?"

"I was nineteen."

"I was only nineteen when I married, too," I told her. "Just took me a little longer to realize what a mistake I'd made."

"Your case is different," Ann began, almost belligerently, her eyes sparking.

"I know," I said, with all the rue I could put into my voice. "In my country, there are legal mechanics to solve the problem."

"Can you do something about *that?*" asked Ann skeptically, jerking her head to mean the recent visitation.

"My solicitor is handling the matter with due legal process."

"Then, girls," Gerry said, spreading his hands wide, "you should always marry Americans." A wide grin kept the remark from being snide. Nonetheless, I sensed that the tone of the conversation did not please him, wherever his sympathies might lie with the present company, or whatever he had told me about never marrying an Irishman.

"Good old Yankee know-how," I said with a self-deprecating grin, and heaved an exaggerated sigh. "Well, my sense of proportion is operating again, and I fervently hope that the twins are putting their paternal parent straight."

"The twins? Their father?" Ann was astonished.

On cue, the "infants" appeared among us. Their father had not been in his office and was not expected in, and they were mightily disappointed.

I also felt let-down and cheated. And yet, funnily enough, I was relieved. Some inner scruple in me wanted a good relationship (if not the image) preserved between the twins and their father:Children should love and be able to respect both parents, if possible.

"I know three gals who stand in the need of a jar or two," said Gerry.

"Oh, I couldn't . . ." Ann physically stepped away from the invitation.

"Nonsense," said Snow, who had started to unsaddle Horseface. "You *never* go anywhere—except to funerals! And the kids are all asleep, so don't weasel out because they'd cry if you weren't there."

"There's safety in numbers," Gerry said, teasing. Maureen added her urgings.

"He can't have spies in every pub in Dublin, now, can he?" I argued. "And when was the last time you went anywhere? Without kids . . . without . . ."

Ann muttered something dark about Kieron, stopped, and glanced apprehensively at his cottage.

"He's free to come too, you know, though it cuts the odds for me a bit." Gerry's grin was calculated to egg her on.

Ann found one last, feeble evasion—her clothes—but Maureen asked since when had one had to dress formally to drink a jar with friends?

"I've a pair of huge dark glasses you could wear," said Snow, all enthusiasm, "and that floppy hat. You'd look just like any other Yankee tourist."

"Oh, what will Sally—"

"Sally's got a date tonight, and you know it," said Snow, with disgust at her protestations. "What're you aiming for? Sainthood?"

For some reason, that taunt decided Ann, and we all linked arms to march over to Kieron's cottage. He gave Ann one long searching look after his initial astonishment.

"I'll just wash my hands," he said, and did so.

Then we all clambered into Gerry's blue Humber and jackrabbited away in a cloud of dust.

"You know, we should have got Mary and made it a residents' association meeting," I said, suddenly in the best of good spirits.

"She and Molly've gone out with George," Ann said, nervously peering out the car window before scrunching down in the back seat.

Did she really think that that husband of hers would pop out of the hedges to waylay her? Speaking of popping out of hedges, I noticed when Nosy's car edged into sight behind us. I opened my mouth to comment on that, then decided against it. Ann might see Paddy Purdee's hand in that too.

I don't remember what we talked about that evening, since so much happened later of more importance, but I remember what a fine time we all had—even Ann, once she got used to the notion of enjoying herself out in public. Not that she was public in the back of the dark booth with her hat and glasses on.

As usual, time was called all too soon. The jars we had
poured into Ann Purdee gave her sufficient Dutch courage
to sit straight up by the window in the back seat—well, as
straight as she could with Kieron's arm about her. Maureen
adroitly joined Gerry and me in the front seat. I was feeling
good too, and for some reason or other which I can't now
remember, we kept singing the unexpurgated version of the
Colonel Bogey song. Kieron knew the most scandalous
variations! A very merry carload pulled up the lane, right to
Ann's doorsteps. My two were deep in books, and there
hadn't been a sound upstairs, they told Ann.

I felt very good about the world and the future of man-
kind as I undressed for bed. Surely Ann would emerge a little from her man-hater's view of the world. As I drifted off
to sleep, it occurred to me that my Great-Aunt Irene *hadn't*
really been *all* that liberal in her views.

Chapter XIX

I wasn't deeply asleep—I'd had a shade too much, or too little, to drink—when a sudden sharp noise woke me. I lay there in a sort of rosy doze with my mind idly bouncing from one topic to another, like those word-cuers in a sing-along film. But I couldn't identify the noise in my dozy state. I suppose that's why I roused further. And *thought* I heard a man swearing softly. It was that sort of a still night, clear, breezeless, on which sound can carry.

My first thought was, *good Lord, doesn't Nosy ever sleep?* And then, *is he making sure where I'm sleeping?* It amused me to think that he'd have to break and enter this house to be certain. And then I wasn't amused. After what Teddie-boy had already done, he was capable of doing anything.

With that notion rankling in my no longer sleep-soothed breast, I went to the window. And *thought* I saw a shadow pass in the lane.

Well, if Nosy or anyone was now prowling my purlieu, I was going to give him a rude surprise. I'd had it with this nonsense. And who but Nosy had told Teddie about Mrs. Slaney? I slipped on my loafers, grabbed up my top coat, since navy blue is *the* color for skulking after skulkers (Preserve the Image), and padded downstairs. I removed my trusty fouling piece and proceeded in search of a target. I giggled a bit at the notion of actually firing the shotgun, although the thought of creating some mayhem of my own did have a certain shining appeal. I even checked to make sure the damned thing was loaded. Because if it wasn't Nosy, and was Tom Slaney, or even that Fahey creep . . .

If I was to skulk properly, I'd have a less impeded vision if I came up the lane from Ann's. I'd meet him head on, since he was proceeding down it. So I scooted along the back path to Ann's and came around her house by the kitchen door.

He was there! Trying to get in. Trying to force the door. And it wasn't Nosy. It was, I realized, in a blaze of outraged perception, Paddy Purdee! Next to Teddie-boy, he was the man I most wanted to meet on a dark night with a loaded shotgun in my hands.

"What are *you* doing here?" I cried in a stage whisper. If Ann found out he knew where she was . . .

"Huh?"

He whirled at the sound of my voice, and in the clearness of the night his white eyes stared at me in fright. His jaw dropped and his hands—they were nasty big porkfingered paws—went up in an automatic defensive gesture.

"Who-who's that?"

I was surprised but very pleased at the real fear in his voice.

"How did you find Ann? Who told you where she was?" I demanded, still in my hoarse whisper. If I could just scare him away . . .

His hands were raised now to his eyes, and he started to step backward, away from me.

"No! No! Go away! Go away! You're dead! She said you were dead. She *told* me you were dead."

Wow! Hey, I'd better preserve that image! He thought I was Aunt Irene.

"Didn't I tell you once that you were never to bother Ann again? Didn't you promise me? Did you think I wouldn't remember that promise?"

I advanced, keeping in the shadows of the house, backing him up the lane as I spoke, trying to sound as sepulchral as possible. I hoped he wouldn't realize that, though I sounded like my great-aunt, I was five inches taller. Or that ghosts don't generally carry shotguns.

I shrugged off the topcoat, because my nightgown was long and filmy and shroudlike.

"Paddy Purdee, you have sinned. You have sinned

against Ann. You have broken your sworn oath. Your soul
is in grave mortal danger. And I, Irene Teasey, will not rest
until you have paid for your faithlessness."

He'd stopped stepping backward, and was running, trying
to put distance between us. Although wife-beaters are
usually bullies, I wouldn't have thought him such an arrant
coward.

"No, she *is* dead. The old woman wouldn't lie."

"Irene Teasey is not dead . . ."

"It's a trick. That's what it is. It's a trick!" He started for
me, his voice getting firmer as his confidence returned.

There's nothing like having your bluff called when you're
playing ghost. How the hell could I disappear convincingly?

"A trick is it? You fool! This is Irene Teasey. But Irene
Teasey is dead. Whose voice is speaking to you if not Irene
Teasey's?" Ghosts use cryptic language, don't they? To con-
fuse the people they're haunting?

"Rene? Irene, is that *you?*" cried a woman's voice in the
night. It came from Mary Cuniff's cottage. "Oh, Rene, what
are *you* doing here?"

The real panic in Mary's voice was sufficient to loosen
Mr. Purdee's tenuous grip on common sense. He turned on
his heels and sped down the lane as fast as his legs could
pump, yelling at the top of his lungs.

"But she's dead! The old woman told me she was dead!
She's got to be dead!"

The light went on in Mary's coattage, and her front door
sprang wide.

I ran toward her, trying to keep her from rousing everyone, particularly Ann, when I tripped over the nightgown. I
went down, and the last thing I heard was a huge *bang!*
right by my head.

Suddenly, there seemed to be an awful lot of light in my
face. And someone was weeping bitterly in the background.
I heard several male mutters and Snow's chirp. When I
opened my eyes, only Mary was in my room, busily wringing out a cloth in a basin of water. My head hurt.

"I'm here again," I said, with what I felt was some origi-
nality. I did know where I was. "And I shot off that
damned gun, didn't I? I hope no one was hurt."

Laughter and concern warred in Mary's face.

"Yes and no."

"Oh? You mean that I hit the right person but not fatally?"

Her laughter bubbled up. "That was buckshot, you know, and it has a wide range."

"Right persons?"

She nodded encouragingly.

"I must've got Paddy Purdee." She nodded again, egging me on. "*And* Nosy?"

She agreed with considerable enthusiasm and then, rising, went to the door.

"She's conscious. I told you she'd only knocked herself out."

Ann Purdee, her face streaked with tears, rushed into the room. Kieron was right behind her, with Simon and Snow a poor third and fourth but looking righteously smug. Sally Hanahoe hovered tentatively by the door. And I could see a blue hulk and the shadow of a hat that suggested a Garda in abeyance.

"Oh God, not the police again!" I groaned, before I caught his smiling face.

"Well, sure now and you can't go around shooting everyone in sight without the Gardai taking some sort of notice," said Kieron. He too looked immensely pleased.

"Oh, Rene, you *are* all right, aren't you?" cried Ann.

I grabbed her hands, which were ice cold and shaking. "Of course I am."

"But he might have hurt you. He might have—"

"Him? That lousy coward? Running from a ghoulie-ghostie . . ."

"Who went bang in the night!" finished Simon with a loud crow.

"Well, if you've been afraid of that poor excuse of a man all this time, Ann Purdee, you ought to be ashamed."

The Garda tactfully cleared his throat and rocked on his feet in and out of the doorway.

"Please come in. I am decent and well chaperoned," I told him. "Besides, if I tell you the story in their presence, then everyone will know and I can get some sleep. My head is splitting." It wasn't, not badly, but my ear hurt. And my left arm and knee!

"Well, now, missus," the Garda began, taking out his notepad.

So I told him that I had spotted an intruder, that we'd

had other intruders, that I knew I was under surveillance by a private investigator sicced on me by my former husband, and about the ISPCC, and Paddy Purdee deserting his wife for the last few years (I could see the Garda knew all about that), and my voice being like my aunt's (he recognized it too), and so I thought I'd put the fear of God in Paddy Purdee, and I'd about chased him away with Mary's inadvertent assist when I tripped on my nightgown and the silly gun had gone off. And had I killed anyone?

His eyes were twinkling as he gravely assured me that both men had taken only minor injuries. "Not where a *man* would wish them, missus," which figured if the two were hightailing it.

My intervention had been timely, because Purdee had jimmied open the lock on Ann's door and had been about to enter.

At that point there was a wheeze from my front doorbell, and Simon went clattering down, muttering something about the doctor.

"Good Lord, I don't need a doctor for a lump on the head."

"And a few lacerations," said Snow.

"If it's the doctor," said Kieron, beginning to steer Ann out, "we'd best be off." Sally, grinning mischievously at me for my evening's work, started to follow them.

Ann got no farther than the door and stopped dead, all color draining from her face. She shot such an apprehensive glance behind her that I thought for a moment that some idiot was making her confront her husband. But Shamus Kerrigan walked through the door.

"Are you really all right, Rene?" he asked, brushing past Kieron, Ann, and Sally. He reached my bedside in a swift stride and took my good hand in his warm, firm, and very comforting grip.

I was so terribly, terribly glad to see him that I nearly burst into tears. I was trying to reassure him and not disgrace myself, or count too much on the unnervingly anxious expression on his face, so that I didn't really see the byplay until Kieron spoke.

"Sally, have you ever seen that man before?"

Kieron was pointing at Shay even while Ann was trying to lug Sally out of the room.

Sally peered obediently at Shay, who looked around, mystified. I recovered my wits.

"This is Shay Kerrigan, Sally. Shamus Kerrigan."

Sally's hand flew to her mouth, but there was no recognition in her eyes as she and Shay looked at each other.

"Well," said Sally after a very taut pause, "he's not the Shamus Kerrigan *I'd* like to meet in a dark lane with a shotgun."

There was a little moan from Ann.

"Thanks, Sally," I told her, but I felt no triumph now. In fact I felt sick because of the terribly sad look in Shay's eyes as he turned back to me.

"Is that why Irene turned against me so?"

"It wasn't fair!" I cried. "I knew it couldn't have been you. I only just *heard* what it was, but you'd gone away and I couldn't *tell* you and . . ." I started to cry. Reaction set in: some pain, intense relief, and that sick feeling in the pit of my stomach for the injustice.

I was being held against a comfortable masculine chest which smelled reassuringly of fresh linen and ironing and soap and shaving lotion, with gentle hands stroking my hair and patting my shoulder, and a vibrant male voice muttering soothingnesses in my ear, so that it was scarcely surprising that I wept up a storm. And mumbled all kinds of inanities in between sobs.

"She should have *known*. And you've lost so much money, and I ought to have given you permission, because the twins said you had hands and they liked you and *they're* smart enough to know. Only you didn't come back and I was—"

"There, there, Rene. Don't distress yourself so, pet. Now, do be a good love and stop crying. There, there!" My sore hand and arm were being gently kissed, and then he had the inspiration to put his hand on the nape of my neck, and, like a kitten, I sort of shook myself and sagged into silence.

"Oh, my God, my face. I look such a sight when I've been crying," I said, sort of knowing it wouldn't matter to Shay at this juncture, and caring all the more because it didn't.

A cool facecloth was tenderly pressed against my eyes and hot cheeks while suitable reassurances were conveyed in that heavenly voice.

"Oh, Shay," I had such a budget of things to tell him.

"I don't know why I have to time my entrances like this," said a man from the doorway.

It was some minor comfort that, with this gross interruption, Shamus seemed as reluctant to release me as I was to be released.

"You don't *act* concussed, Mrs. Teasey," the doctor continued, swinging his heavy bag to the bedside table. He looked tired and disgruntled. I couldn't blame him. I felt the same way.

He gave my injuries a quick glance, grunted, made with the light in the eyes, remarked on the sites of probable contusions for the morrow, and complimented me on my markswomanship. He then forced me to take some little white pills "because you look as if you would benefit from a good night's sleep," and glared at Shamus, who had been hovering in the hall. Then the doctor turned out my light and firmly closed the door behind him. Leaving me alone. I could hear Shamus protesting, and then the doctor's firm "Come along now, it'll all keep till morning!" And two heavy treads going down the steps.

I lay there, appalled, annoyed, and aching. Wondering if Shay had meant all those comforting, lovely things, and being finally able to relax in his innocence. Honestly, how *could* Aunt Irene have ever suspected him?

Whatever the doctor had given me was working with extraordinary speed . . . my legs were numb and my hands and arms. I must really ask him for a few more . . . less potent . . . Shay's voice and Snow's and Simon's . . . damned birds outside heralding a dawn that came at 3:30 in the morning in Ireland . . .

Chapter XX

I woke slowly, aware of the sweet scents of sun-warmed air, the myriad little muted sounds which meant that ordinary events hadn't waited for me to wake. I moved, found myself stiff, and . . . remembered.

I did not shoot bolt upright in bed. First I had to struggle to get up on an elbow, then move myself around carefully before a judicious shove raised me somewhat. My head didn't ache, but my ear (had I hit the ground ear-first?) felt bigger than it should, hot and pulsing. So did my elbow, hand, and knee.

I did make it to the loo, and fearfully inspected my face. Which looked just as it ought to: sleepy. Washed, it looked perfectly normal, which was reassuring.

I peered out the bathroom window and saw Shay's blue car parked in front. Ridiculous waves of relief coursed down my spine and into my tummy.

"Good Lord, glad Nosy isn't about! That would have been provocative . . ."

"Mom? You conscious?" Snow's dulcet tones floated up the staircase. She sounded anxious.

"Yes indeed." I leaned down the railing and grinned at her. "Any coffee?"

"Sure thing. You just pop right back into bed, Mommy."

I had that precise intention, because breakfast on a tray, when Snow is in a good helpful mood, is a real treat. But if Shay's car were outside my door, I didn't want to miss another opportunity.

I shucked my nightgown, slipped into panties, and was

fastening my bra when there was a knock at the door. I said, "Come in," even as I thought that it was odd of Snow to knock. I turned, and there was Shay, balancing a tray on one hand. We stared at each other for a moment, me horrified, him just . . . just taking me all in.

He said, "Don't please," as I reached wildly for my discarded nightgown. He put the tray on the bed, kicked the door shut, and came toward me with both arms outstretched and a look on his face which rearranged a lot of my resolutions instantaneously.

His hands closed most proprietarily about the bare skin at my waist, and slid up around to my shoulders to hold me sensually against him. At the same time, he was kissing me in such a devastating way! And bare skin, compromising situation, and impropriety notwithstanding, I was kissing him back with all the longing that had been building up in me, with all the conflicting emotions that had dominated our relationship since the bulldozing day we'd met.

We both sort of had too much at the same time. He released me, his hands still caressing my bare back, but holding me slightly from him so that we could look into each other's eyes.

"You'd better put that thing on, Rene," he said unsteadily, and dropped his hands to his side. "I'm sorry," he went on, turning about, one hand jammed in his pocket, the other nervously combing his hair back. "Snow said you'd gone back to bed . . . Hell, I am not sorry!" He circled abruptly back to me, his eyes dark with an expression I knew I reciprocated.

But I'd managed to get the gown around me while I rummaged in my closet for the dressing gown. He let me put that on and then reached for my hands, drawing me back into his arms.

"God, you're pretty," he said, smiling down at me, and he didn't mean my face. "Long and slender." His fingers walked down my back to my waist. Then he took a deep breath and spun me toward the bed. "Get in there, safely, get that tray on your lap. Your darling daughter sent me up with your breakfast, but she'll be up in a minute or two or my name isn't Shamus Kerrigan."

"Wasn't that a bit of luck last night?" I said, seizing on any topic to divert my torrid thoughts.

"Huh?"

"Sally being here and all, so we could prove to Ann that you really weren't *that* Shamus Kerrigan."

Shay gave me a long keen look. "And *that* was what Irene—and Ann—had against me?" His tone was bitter and resigned. "I can credit Irene, but not Ann. I thought she trusted me."

"It may be that she felt Irene had the right of it, and I gather my great-aunt was a trifle difficult to argue with . . ."

"But for Ann to think that I'd abandon a pregnant girl to the mercies of Ireland? Jaysus!"

"I don't fault Ann, considering her experiences with Paddy Purdee, as much as I fault my aunt. She was older, wiser, and presumably a far better judge of character than Ann. *She* should have known that you—"

"No, Irene had no use for men at all."

"Oh yes she did." I contradicted him, because it was pointless for us to be arguing on the particular sides we'd chosen. "Look at George and Kieron and even Fahey . . . Oh, as long as a man was *useful* . . ."

"And the Queen's courtiers had to be without flaw, sin, or blot on their escutcheons." And Shay smiled in a bitter nostalgic fashion. "She was *such* a fascinating woman . . ." His gaze went beyond me and the room to some memory. "She was the most charming woman I've ever met . . . she could get you to do the most tiresome jobs for her . . . while you'd wonder how you got yourself talked into it . . . Oh, Irene Teasey knew how to manage people."

"Well, then, she had no right, if she was so smart, to accuse and find you guilty without ever letting you speak in your own defense."

"Not to worry, pet."

"And if you think I'll let you blame Ann—"

"I said not to worry, pet," he repeated, capturing my gesturing hand and smoothing the skin across the back, his fingers lightly caressing.

"*That's* enough to make me. However, now I know she was wrong, and Ann won't have a conniption fit, I can—" I broke off. "It was Auntie Alice who gave you that bogus permission to use the lane, wasn't it?"

Shamus let out an embarrassed "Whuff."

"Wasn't it?" I persisted. "Because she thought all she had

to do was wave twenty-five thousand pounds under the nose of the usurping American and I'd grab it and leave! Why didn't you tell me? It worried me so. Oh, well, that doesn't matter now," I added before he could speak, "because now you *can* have the access."

"Hold it, Rene. *I* have something to say."

"But—"

His fingers stopped my lips. "I don't need the access any more."

I thought of the bulldozer cheerfully working away on the tract, and I thought of the sort of man I knew Shamus Kerrigan to be, and I thought . . .

"You've sold it!"

He looked sheepish. "Well, I considered that solution, I can tell you. I'd a lot of money tied up and—"

"Oh, Shay, will you ever forgive me?"

"Pet, not to worry." And he laughed at me. "As I said, I seriously considered that possibility. Then I realized that the next owner might just build those ticky-tacky boxes you were so narked about. So I swallowed my pride and bought access in from Glenamuck."

"At five thousand pounds?" I was aghast at what I, and Irene, had cost him over that hideous farce of names.

"I'm mortgaged to the hilt, all right." He didn't seem depressed.

"Can't you renege or something? I can give you free access now."

"And always wonder if I married you for that?"

"Oh, Shamus . . ."

"You will marry me, won't you?" He was dead serious and dead worried. "I know I'm rushing you. I'll wait—we only just met, but I've waited for some miracle like you."

"Oh, Shay . . ."

"Look." His grip on my hands was painful, he was so intent on persuading me. "I know you've seen horrible examples of Irish marriage and husbands, and I've no way of proving that I can be any better, but honestly, Rene, I'd do—"

"Will you let me talk?"

He paused, mid-word, his blue eyes darker by several shades, and the expression on his face making it rather difficult for me to breathe, much less think or talk.

"I'm not nineteen, Shay, and neither are you. And I

think horrible examples are necessary, to know the pitfalls to avoid. Anyway, we've as good a chance at making a marriage work as anyone. I think I'd like to try. I try very hard if given any encouragement."

"I'll encourage you constantly," he said, and his lips slid over mine with exactly the kind of encouragement that was liable to lead to . . .

"We can't do that now. Snow . . ." and then I groaned and my pretty bright bubble of hope burst all around me.

"What's the matter, pet?"

"There's Simon and Snow . . ."

"But I like your kids. I really do, and they seem to like me."

"They do, Shay, or why would Simon phone you the minute the least thing goes wrong? No, it's Teddie."

"Teddie? Who's he?"

"Their father. My ex-husband."

"Oh, him! Well, he certainly doesn't have to approve your second husband. Oh, I see—he might not approve of me as stepfather?"

"No, no . . ." I couldn't articulate my nebulous worry.

"I didn't think his approval would be required."

"No, but look at what he's done already, with Nosy, and—"

"Pet," and Shamus put his strong and compelling hand on the back of my neck to hold my head straight because I was bouncing around on the bed, I was so agitated. "If you have custody of those kids and they wish *you* to be custodian, there's nothing that ex of yours can do about it. Now, I've already been on to Mihall this morning about that clown—the twins told me about the ISPCC—and I do believe that between us we can sort him out. Now, if you've no other objections to me of any significance . . ."

Our glances locked, and I heard so much that he wasn't saying, felt so deeply the beautiful bond growing so swiftly between us now, that more words were redundant.

"Rene?" His rough whisper was exciting. "Thank you, pet." He leaned down to kiss me, and my urgings got the better of common sense. I reached up to unbalance him when his hands grabbed my wrists. "My dear girl, you know what could happen . . ."

"Uh huh." I returned the challenge candidly.

Just then Snow raised her voice in argument with Simon

in the kitchen below, and all my sensuality drained out of me. Shamus saw the change and laughed.

"Will you be less the mother when you're my wife?" he asked in a soft, teasing voice. He picked up the tray. "I'll get you some hot coffee. And this time . . . be dressed?"

I was, but for insurance's sake he brought Snow and Simon with him, both beaming from ear to ear. Snow embraced me, muttering happy things, and Simon gave me a suddenly awkward boy-kiss.

"What a relief, Mom," he said, flopping onto the stool. "It'll be nice to have moral support. You don't realize what you're letting yourself in for, Shay. I mean, I had to grow up with it so I'm used to it—"

"Huh!" said Snow with a contemptuous snort. "You poor abused child. Say," she added, in a complete change of pace, "you can give Mommy away, can't you? And I can be maid of honor, can't I?"

"Now, just a living minute . . ." and I cast a worried eye at Shay. Many's the man who's fled before the too-eager bride.

Shamus only laughed. "Not so fast, you two. I want to give your mother plenty of time to change her mind—" He couldn't go on because of their protests. "Well, women do, don't they? And repersuading her can be so much fun."

"Shamus Kerrigan! You're shameless!"

"Shameless Shay-mus." Snow went off into one of her giggling fits, which was, as usual, mainly relief.

"Anyway, you two," Shay went on, "how could you tots know I'm the proper husband of her and stepfather of you?"

"Ha! We knew right off," Snow said with a toss of her head, her eyes twinkling. And I thought to myself that Shamus Kerrigan would at least have the handsomest pair of stepchildren in the Island. "You've got hands!"

"Hands?" Shamus looked at them, mystified. "Most people do."

"Naw, you don't know what we mean," and Snow was tolerant of his ignorance and quite willing to enlighten him at length.

"Look, children, that can wait."

"What?" Snow obviously felt the topic was of vital importance.

"Right," said Shay firmly. "We do have more urgent . . .

if not as fascinating . . . business to attend to this
morning. Mihall Noonan's coming over. He needs the
details about this visitation from the ISPCC, and also what
you plan to do about Purdee."

"What do you mean, what I plan to do? Like prosecute?"
Shamus nodded. He was serious.

"What about the buckshot? Couldn't they prosecute me?"
He shook his head. "You have every right to protect
your property from unlawful intruders."

"Invaders, you mean," put in Snow.

"And Nosy?" I wondered what sort of ammunition his
report would give Teddie.

Shay drew his face into a lugubrious expression. "You
had no notion you were under surveillance . . . which will
be removed, I can promise . . . so if you shot at one intruder and got two . . ." He shrugged.

"Nosy's removed anyhow . . . with a rear full of buckshot," said Snow, chortling. "Do you think he gets double
pay for risk?"

"But what about Purdee?" I said. "Ann won't have a
restful moment now that he knows where she is—" I broke
off. "And it was Auntie Alice who told him where she is."

"By Jaysus, you may be right," said Shamus, blinking his
eyes at my suspicion. "Winnie's in the fish business, after
all, and while she may babble like a brook, she doesn't say
much. But if Alice were interested, she'd know where to
look and who to ask about Paddy Purdee, sure and she
would."

"Great!" I said sarcastically. "Then as soon as he's well,
we can expect a return engagement."

"Oh, I don't know about that," replied Shay in the slow
way that I was beginning to realize meant he had a trick
unplayed. "Between ghosts and buckshot, and by the time
Mihall gets through with him . . . If you'll go along with
our strategy, he won't be likely to show himself."

"Yes, but will Ann believe that?"

"Sure and she will . . . if you say that you'll threaten to
prosecute him for breaking and entering *unless* he agrees to
sign a legal separation agreement for Ann."

"Oh, Shay, would that work?"

"Mihall suggested it. She can have legal custody of the
children and legal protection from his . . . physical presence. That's all she wants right now."

Snow cocked a sophisticated eyebrow and jerked her head toward Kieron's cottage. Shamus saw her.

"Make haste slowly, young Sara," he advised kindly. "You lot have upset quite a few barrows in the short time you've been in Ireland. Let the mud settle a while."

"Say, Mom, now that we know Shamus didn't father Sally's baby," Snow began, and I stared at my precocious daughter. She grinned knowingly.

"Snow, if you and I are to have a congenial relationship," Shamus began.

"This is for *your* good," she replied archly.

"I've got access to the property, Sara Virginia," he said, and took the wind right out of her sails. For one split second.

"Evidently, but does it have to be right in front of our house? Mom owns *that* field, doesn't she?" Snow gestured out the window to the meadow beyond Kieron's cottage. "Be smart, wouldn't it, to carve a hunk off the far side of that and have two routes into the development . . . all well away from us?"

It boded well for that same congenial relationship that Shamus took the time to consider that proposal, and the look he then turned on Snow was approving.

"I think I'd better listen to you, pet, when you come up with sensible notions like that."

"And it would make me feel a whole lot better about the Glenamuck thingie," I said.

"Oh, I'll make that outlay up in the purchase price of the houses," Shamus assured me blandly.

"Speaking of purchases, Mom," Simon said, "you forgot to get more coffee . . . and someone"—he looked at his sister—"ate the whole box of cookies and . . . "

"I'll spot you all to dinner at Lamb Doyle's tonight," said Shamus, and the offer was cheered.

"Could Jimmy come, too? I mean, like we are celebrating, aren't we," said Simon, eagerly, "and he's been in it from the first, so to speak."

"Speaking of whom, guess who just turned in the lane?" said Snow, and the twins nearly got jammed going out the door together, each vociferously claiming the right to tell Jimmy first.

"Oh, good Lord, Shay, should we broadcast it so soon?"

"Trying to back out on me already?"

There was that sort of a grin on his face as he folded his arms around me that made me want to see what would happen if I did.

"Think what a relief it will be to his mother and father," Shay went on in that low, deliciously teasing voice.

"And how distressing to half the female population of Dublin!"

"Each with a bastard under 'her arm?" he asked, his eyes glinting.

"You *know* I never believed that." I hadn't meant him to take that interpretation.

"Why not?" He wasn't about to let me get away with it.

"Because . . . because . . . because you've got hands! And *they* don't lie!"

Those same hands were arousing rather dangerous sensations in my body, so I grabbed one of them, to give him as good as I'd got, and dragged Shay out to the safety of the great outdoors.

There was no questioning Jimmy's reaction: all systems green and go. When the shouting died, Simon reminded me about "coffee, Mom, you'll die," so Shamus masterfully popped me into 'his car and took me off, muttering about falling into uxorious ways before the banns could be published.

We went to Sally's store and waited in Sally's register line-up, and Shay kept up the most ridiculous stream of patter with me, then Sally, nodding now and then to people he knew. He seemed to know rather a lot of people. Teddie had, too, but faces didn't light up when Teddie hailed them: They sort of closed up, like defensive clams.

"Good thing we're making it formal, Rene," said Shay with the devil in his eyes as we left the shop. "Or Nosy could really play hare and hounds with your reputation."

"What? Being seen grocery shopping with you?"

"Do American husbands go grocery shopping with their pretty wives?"

"Great American pastime." Of course, Teddie never had. "But we don't have to do it the American way, you know."

His left hand covered mine, and he shot me a brief amused look. "Not going to reform my feckless ways?"

"Good Lord, no. You're just the way I like a man to be."

"And from the back bench a vote of confidence!"

"I am not a reforming woman."

He chuckled. "Oh no?" And I heard his opinion of all I'd got myself into already in Ireland.

"Oh, dear."

"Rene, love," and his voice was tender, "not to worry." And for the first time, I didn't.

Chapter XXI

As soon as we pulled up behind my Mercedes, the kids piled out of the house for the groceries and a message for Shamus.

"Shay, the guy up the road, Mick somethingerother," said Simon, "needs you on the site."

"I'll leave the car here, if I may." Shamus grinned. "Now I've got a handy field office too. You see what a conniver I am?"

He didn't kiss me, but the pressure of his hands on mine was a promise.

"I thought you only went for coffee and cookies," said Snow as each of them hauled in a large sack.

"I was talking," I said haughtily, and suggested that she had better do the beds, as I was much too stiff to bend down. I made pointed comments to Simon about the length of the front-garden grass and wasn't there a lawn mower somewhere in this queendom? Actually, I wanted a few moments of silence so I could assemble my scattered wits. I also wanted to savor the elation of Shamus's proposal. I hadn't been so absolutely euphoric since . . . since the twins were born? Good Lord, fourteen years ago? Oh, no, I'd had some brief spells of happiness. Into each rain some life must fall?

I was, at this precious moment, happy, and I would wallow in the experience, knowing it might have to last me a bit. Disenchantment has a way of creeping up on you. I thought back to the day Teddie had proposed. Good God, I'd had to shop that day too. And he couldn't find the brand of tomato ketchup he preferred. You'd've thought the shop had not ordered it to spite Teddie. Of course, I agreed with him that day.

I shook myself. I was not superstitious. I said it out loud. I also told myself that Shay was a much more stable personality. I couldn't imagine Teddie patiently enduring Aunt Irene's ostracism of him. No, Shay was a man.

I'd thought Teddie was a man too, hadn't I? At nineteen who knows what's a man?

Maybe I *was* rushing into marriage again. I'd been separated two years, true, but my divorce was barely seven months old. The twins liked Shamus, but as a permanent fixture? But he did seem to know how to cope with Snow without steamrollering her the way her father had started doing.

And it's lovely to get swept off your feet in a romantic fashion, but . . .

Dully I found places for cans of beans and tins of fruit.

Shay really could be marrying me for the land. I'd have to be very cautious and keep the queendom in my name. Surely a wife could hold property in her own right in Ireland—and if Shamus Kerrigan was marrying me for me, he wouldn't object.

I heard a car driving up the lane: Michael coming to extricate me from my latest escapade. And he wouldn't be all that happy about the latest development with Shamus, now, would he?

I sighed and straightened my shoulders. Thinking pleasant thoughts, I went to admit my caller.

Teddie's angry face glowered down at me.

"What the hell are you still doing here?" demanded Teddie, his eyes popping from his skull and his face flushing violently, as it did when he was upset.

"Where else would I be?"

He rallied quickly, more quickly than his second wife did. Florence stared as if I were the last person she had expected to see. She also looked slightly embarrassed.

"Is this hovel where you've stashed my children?" he demanded.

"As it's an excellent example of Georgian farmhouse architecture, and I've already been offered seventy-five thousand dollars for it, it can't be classed as a hovel."

"Seventy-five thousand bucks for this?"

In the shock of seeing Ted Stanford on my once-safe Irish doorstep, I had responded with the first things that came into my head. By instinct, I had chosen the one effective stopper: snobbery. Teddie instantly reassessed the place, as did Number Two. She wasn't a bad thing, after all.

"So . . . where the hell are they?"

"The children?"

"I sure as hell didn't come three thousand miles to see your face again, Irene."

I didn't flinch under that old twisting sneer of his. I couldn't. I was frozen solid. He'd come to see the twins? That made as little sense as his coming three thousand miles to see me.

"I've got a legal right to see my own kids," Teddie went on. "Only don't try shooting at me, Annie Oakley, or you'll be in more trouble than you already are. They deport undesirable aliens, you know. And it is Saturday, the legally agreed-upon visiting day."

Because I was clutching the doorframe, I remained upright, and my mind parroted, *It is legal. He does have the legal right . . . but I don't want them to see him. It'll upset them terribly.*

"They've made other plans for the day."

"They can damned well unmake them. *I'm* here."

"Quod erat demonstrandum!"

An angry flush reddened his cheeks still more. "Quit the stalling, Rene. Where are they? And I'm warning you, I'm looking into this business of your firing a shotgun irresponsibly around minors."

"Speaking of firing, that Mayday you gave the ISPCC has backfired. They were looking for kids in their diapers."

"Oh?" Teddie affected smug innocence. "My secretary must have mistranscribed her dictation." He took a step closer to the door. "Simon! Your dad's here," he yelled. "Ready and waiting. Sara? Where are you, dollface? Your daddy's come to see you."

His yell was superfluous.

"I'm here." Snow's voice came from behind me. She was crouched on the stairs, her fingers gripping the bannister so hard that the knuckles were white.

"Dad." Simon's voice announced his presence right beside me. And I wanted to burst into tears at the sound of defeat in their subdued voices.

"Snow, honey, I can't see you. Come give your old daddy a big smacker." Teddie had executed one of those lightning changes of his. Now he was Ye Affable Sire, Doting Daddy, Popular Papa. He peered over my head toward the stairs, Eager Smile #3 splitting his face in two. He took another step, but I blocked his way. I did not want Teddie's aura to contaminate my house. As he moved to push me aside, Simon stepped into the breach, his hand formally extended to his father. Teddie shook hands absently, then frowned as he realized he was being prevented from entering the house.

"Simon! What a formal way to greet your old man after all this time!"

"I saw you three weeks ago, sir." Simon took a deep breath. "Sara and I resent the way you've been persecuting Mother."

"Persecuting her? Ah, now, Simon boy, I didn't persecute her." Teddie displayed incredulous, jocular denial.

"With a private detective watching us? With that nonsense of the ISPCC? You only thought that up to embarrass Mother."

I stared at Simon, as astonished as his father. Then I felt Snow's hand fiercely latching on to mine. She edged close between me and Simon, her young mouth taut and her face very pale.

"Not to mention embarrassing us with all our friends," she said, "with stupid questions they couldn't have answered. And what excuse do you have for hanging on to the support money? Mother didn't fleece you, as she should've. You're getting off easy and you know it. You laugh about it often enough with those precious friends of yours—"

"Snow!" I couldn't believe the way she was addressing her father.

Teddie gawked, speechless for once, at his daughter. His wife had eased herself away from the doorway, hoping not to become the next target.

"Why, you filthy bitch," Teddie said to me, his eyes blazing, his chest swelling with inhaled anger, "turning my own kids against me . . . What kind of—why, I'll—" His clenched fist lifted.

"I wouldn't do that!" said Simon, stepping in front of me.

I gasped at the unnatural sight of my son raising a fist to his father.

"My son!" exclaimed Teddie in a muted whisper. "My only son, ready to strike his dad! What have you done to my children? I'll have you in court for this! You can't corrupt two nice—"

"You're a fine one to talk about corrupting, Daddy-dear." Snow's strident voice was almost unrecognizable. She'd stepped up beside Simon, but she still held my hand in that bone-crushing grip. "Oh, you've got a nerve! Corrupting? Nothing's too good for the client, is it, Daddy-dear? Including your own—"

"SNOW!" Simon's shout was a warning and a command for silence, but I'd heard what she hadn't said. And Teddie knew. His face turned white, and he staggered back, away from the revulsion in his daughter's face and voice.

I clutched at the door frame, because everything was whirling about me. Of all the things I'd imagined might have happened that night at the Harrisons', this . . . this . . . was appalling. No wonder the twins had turned against their father! When I thought of all the platitudes I'd uttered . . . of how often I'd tried to build their father's image in their eyes . . . And then he'd pandered to preserve an account . . .

"I think you'd better leave, Mr. Stanford." Shay's calm voice broke the tableau. "It should be obvious, even to you, that your children do not wish for your company."

"But they've got to. I mean, I'm their father!" Teddie had a very curious notion about rights and prerogatives. "I mean, I've got to have a chance to talk to them. There's been a terrible misunderstanding. They got it all wrong. She's brainwashed them—"

"Simon, Sara." This time it was Michael speaking.

The shock which had engulfed me cleared enough for me to realize that we were scarcely alone in the front yard. Shamus and Michael stood on the left, with George and Kieron by the gate and Mary and Ann at the driveway: the loyal courtiers come to relieve the beleaguered queen.

"I'm Mrs. Teasey's solicitor, Mr. Stanford. I've been in touch with Mr. van Vliet."

"Good man, now we can settle this all legally." Teddie

turned with smug self-assurance to Michael, his hand outstretched. Michael evaded that issue by reaching into his
jacket pocket for some papers. Teddie redirected his hand
to his forehead in an exaggerated gesture of relief. "I came
here to avail myself of the visiting privilege granted me by
the court. I have the right to see my children every Saturday during the year and to have them for a two-week vacation in the summer. I have decided to take them on a European trip, since they're halfway there already"—Teddie's
attempt at a jocular laugh met with no responsive echo—
"and this morning we're going to discuss where they'd like
to go."

"No, Mommy, no," said Snow, clinging to me, once
more a child needing her mother's protection. Oh, God,
how I hoped that spitting demon of a few moments ago had
disappeared . . . forever.

A hopelessness had settled on Simon's face at Michael's
words, but now he was glaring intently at the solicitor.
Hearing something?

"Yes, sir, those are your legal rights," Michael said
agreeably. I felt as cold as Simon looked.

"However, your children are now over fourteen, aren't
they?"

"Well, yes, of course they are. Don't they look it?" asked
Teddie smugly, as if he were solely responsible.

"Under American law, and indeed under Irish law, they
do have certain rights at that age, which I believe Mr. van
Vliet explained fully to them."

All at once the taut spring in Simon's back relaxed, and
he turned to his father.

"Thank you very much for the invitation, Father, but we
decline," he said, quietly but decisively.

"You . . . you *what?*" Teddie's head jutted forward
from his body in utter astonishment.

"We don't want to go with you," Simon said, gathering
courage from the expressions of support on the faces of our
friends.

"Nothing would get us to go with you again, anywhere,
Daddy," said Snow, with a resurgence of that brittleness.

"But—but—"

"I think that's plain enough, Mr. Stanford," said Michael. "Your children do not wish to accompany you. I'd
suggest that you leave."

"Leave?" Teddie's eyes popped out again, his chest swelled, and his face reddened alarmingly.

It was a sight which had often reduced me to ineffectual tears and pleas for forgiveness. Now he only looked ridiculous. He was drinking too much again, I thought with utter detachment. He'd put on a lot of flab. She really ought to get him on a high-protein diet. He doesn't resist that.

"Yes," Michael was saying, "leave." He stepped up to Teddie with a gesture of dismissal.

"Now just a living minute!"

Teddie solidly planted his feet, and I knew he was capable of slugging everyone in sight.

"Where the hell did all of you come from?" he demanded, just then aware of the full audience.

"Sure and we're friends of the children and Mrs. Teasey," said Kieron in a dangerously soft voice. "Come to speed you on your way, since you're leaving."

"Why you little sawed-off Irish bastard—"

Kieron assumed a semi-crouch, which would have warned anyone not blind that the "little sawed-off Irish bastard" was prime for a rough-house.

"Oh, for God's sake, Ted, John Wayne you are not," said the second Mrs. Stanford in utter disgust. "And there are four of them! Let's clear out. If your two kids don't want to go, who needs 'em? I don't. They'll be sorry soon enough."

If she hadn't added that last remark, she might not have succeeded.

"It'll be too late then," said Teddie, drawing himself up with massive and sorrowful dignity. "I've missed our weekly get-togethers, kids. I've worried about you a great deal. One day you were safely in Westfield, where I could keep a good watch over you . . ." Even Teddie saw the inappropriateness of that line, because Simon's head jerked up and Snow's laugh reminded him of the kind of watch he had been keeping. "Well," and Teddie half turned, head bowed, "you always know where to reach me. You've my telephone number in case of emergencies. You're still my children . . . Good-bye."

I think the catch of his breath was sincere, but he spoiled it with a sideways glance to see how effective he'd been. We all held our positions until we heard his car start up.

Snow's eyes still flashed with anger and anxiety. "He'll think of some other ploy. He always does!"

"Perhaps," said Shamus with gentle amusement. Snow gave him a dark look, but his attitude evidently reassured her. Then he began to unhook my fingers from the door frame, and smoothed them out on one palm. "Holding the house up, Rene?"

"Vice versa," I managed to reply through a dry mouth. Would my legs work if I asked them to move me? Shamus now took my arm as if he heard. I leaned into him gratefully. "Thank God you appeared. If you hadn't . . . And Michael, you scared me to death for a moment. But how'd you know?"

"I sent Jimmy for the Marines," said Simon, with a ghost of a grin on his anxious face, "the moment I saw Dad coming up the walk."

Michael took my other arm and led me into the living room. "I thought Henry van Vliet had explained your rights to refuse," Michael said to Simon and Snow. "He told me that you'd both asked about that on several occasions."

"What?" I stared at the twins. "You never told me . . ."

"We don't tell all," said Snow facetiously.

"But you always went . . . you made no protest . . ."

"Because he'd've made things tough on you, Mom," said Simon, at his most conciliatory, "if we hadn't gone."

"But we *never* went with him in the *evening*," said Snow, her blue eyes blazing again, "not *ever* again!"

"Oh, my darlings, if you'd only told me!" My chest was constricted in anguish for what they had endured.

Snow took my hands in hers and, sitting beside me, kissed me sweetly, reversing our roles for a moment.

"Mommy, it's all right. It's all over, and nothing actually happened. Simon made like big brother."

I decided not to think more about *that* right now . . . or I'd be actively ill. I felt Shay's hand sliding comfortingly around my shoulder, and I was mightily relieved by the thought that he'd now be able to protect Snow.

"What I don't understand is why Hank didn't warn us . . ."

"Actually," Michael said, clearing his throat, "I had a cable from van Vliet this morning . . . came in late last night, in fact . . . warning me that Stanford was on his way with the avowed intent of taking the children. Ostensibly on a European tour, citing the vacation clause of the custody agreement, but van Vliet was convinced that Stanford would fly them to the States and let you battle to get them back."

"That fiend! He can't do that! He can't!" My last vestige of control slipped.

Very calmly, my daughter fetched me a sharp little slap across my cheek. "If there's anything more revolting than a dramatic dad, it's a moaning mom."

I thanked her profusely, tears streaming down my face, but the incipient hysteria didn't overwhelm me, as my children comforted me.

"We can prevent him, Rene," Michael said firmly.

"We bloody well already have," Shay said, laughing.

"But Snow's right," Simon told them. "He'll try."

Shay was looking steadily at Michael, who nodded slowly. "Then, I think, Rene, well just sort him out right now," Shay said.

"Jasus, yes," said Kieron. "We've only just lifted the siege on one lady's demesne." He handed me a glass and told me to drink it, not to spill a drop, mind.

Whatever it was burned all the way down, but the quivering of leftover nerves subsided instantly and the pressure of tears behind my eyes eased.

"All right, then," I said, getting more of a grip on myself. "I really do not wish to box myself or the twins up on this queendom like"—I glanced hastily around for fear Ann was in the room—"but I shamefully confess that's my intense desire."

"Nonsense, Rene," said Kieron sharply and with startled concern. "You've shown Ann a thing or two."

"Me?" A poorer example I couldn't imagine just then.

Shay grinned. "You're quite an antidote to Irene, pet, though you start at the same point."

That was too devious for me right then, but at least they approved, and I didn't want to lose their approval. Shay gave me another squeeze on the shoulders and moved away from the couch. My instant courage dissolved as fast.

"Don't leave . . ."

"Sure now, Rene, that ex of yours can't regroup his forces that fast. Most of your bodyguard will stay."

"But where are *you* going?"

"For reinforcements, love."

With that I had to be content.

"Two to one Teddie knows somebody who's buddy-buddy with the Ambassador," I said, determined to be pessimistic.

"All we need," said Snow in an oddly muffled tone, "is for Daddy to meet up with Auntie Alice."

"Oh, for Pete's sake," I exclaimed in sharp disgust, "you come up with the most extraordinary ideas."

"You might say I've had practice, Mommy," Snow replied, propelling herself off the settee and out of the room.

I started to tell her not to leave the house, then realized how silly that was, but Simon, gesturing to Jimmy, went after her. As long as the three were together, they were safe. Jimmy knew who the Marines were in this battle.

"I think if you'll review the situation carefully, Rene, you'll realize that you may be unnecessarily anxious," said Michael.

I heard him thinking that Snow's weren't the only ridiculous ideas. "Humph." I had to get my wits together. "*You* didn't live with that man for fourteen years. His pride has been bruised . . . badly. He'll feel he *has* to reinstate himself with his children, if only to prove they were wrong about . . ."

"What can he do?" demanded Kieron with irritable sarcasm. "Kidnap 'em? Your daughter's got the lungs of a pig-farmer, and Simon's no way weak."

"I suppose you're right." I began to believe them. And what on earth was that heavenly smell?

Ann walked briskly into the room with a tray, and the three musketeers were right behind her, falling over themselves to keep up with that tantalizing odor.

"You've had a shock and all, Rene, and Snow said you'd no breakfast. So, as the bread was just baked . . ."

Kieron and Michael were quite as willing to be fed as I, and once that lovely, still-warm-from-the-oven, violently fattening, delicious brown bread found my stomach, I did indeed feel considerably more like facing whatever other challenges the day presented. We all did.

"Stop fussing with things now, Ann," said Michael, pointing authoritatively for her to be seated by me. He gave me a look, and I suggested to Snow and the boys that they'd better clear the empty bread tray.

"I stopped by to see both Rene and you, Ann. As you

know," said Michael, flicking a look at Kieron, "you can
get a legal and binding separation from Paddy."

Ann opened her mouth to protest.

"It's no more than the cost of my time in drawing up the
proper agreement." Ann kept opening her mouth, and Michael kept waving her silent. Then Kieron grabbed her
hand, and she subsided to a low fume. "This is the first
time we've had Purdee where we could catch him for a signature. This is the only way in which you can achieve any
legal protection against him for just the sort of thing he attempted last night. You can also have sole and legal custody of the children. You can also require him to pay support
money—"

"I don't want his money!" cried Ann fiercely.

"Sure and you don't think he'd pay it?" said Kieron with
a laugh. "It's only another way of insuring he stays away
altogether."

"If he'd sign at all." Ann held no hope for that occur-
rence.

"Oh, that's no problem now," said Michael, his eyes
twinkling at me. "I'm sure Paddy'll sign if Rene is willing
to drop charges of trespass."

"Oh!" Clearly Ann hadn't considered that possibility.

"You'd be free to come and go as you please then, Ann,"
Michael assured her. "He'd need your written permission to
enter the house or see the children. And if he so much as
grabs your arm, you can have him up for assault."

"Sure and it would cost the earth," she said in a flat
voice.

"Oh, for Pete's sake, Ann, don't worry about money," I
began. Kieron and Michael flashed me warning glances. "I
mean, you've the fees for taking care of another child. I
doubt Michael'll starve in the meantime and—oh hell, after
what you've been through, this is what you need . . ." I
kept fighting with myself not to play Lady Bountiful.

"Are you certain, Rene?"

Then I heard the root of her anxiety: Was it *right* for *her*
to achieve this freedom?

Right in whose eyes, I wondered. Hers, Irish society's,
Aunt Irene's? *Had* Aunt Irene suggested a legal separation
before? And had Ann refused? Or had Ann not been
pushed to the breaking point? Divorce, even among Irish

Protestants, was not yet totally accepted, so perhaps divorce
had been "dirty" in Aunt Irene's lexicon. But if reassurance
was all Ann needed, I could give her that courtesy and be
quite honest about it.

"Yes, Ann, I'm positive the separation is right for you.
It'd be far better, of course, if you could get a full divorce.
You've got nothing to lose, certainly. And you've been ex-
isting under . . . under . . . what amounts to a house ar-
rest!" I became exasperated with and furious for her.
"You're so young! Live a little! Enjoy." Then, because I felt
I was getting too intense, I added with a laugh, "They al-
ways say that in the States, 'Enjoy!', but never what."

The quip rated a laugh from the men and a slight, worried smile from Ann.

"Look, you've even forgotten how to smile! Say," and I
turned to Michael, "does Paddy Purdee still think it was
Aunt Irene's ghost after him?"

Michael ducked his head to hide a broad grin, and Kieron chuckled openly.

"Well, he's not all that certain," said Michael. "The Garda told him Miss Teasey's niece shot off the gun at intruders, but no one's told him that you're an Irene Teasey too,
or that you sound exactly like your aunt."

"I like it. I like it," I said. "Do him good. Might even
give him some religion."

"It won't do that," Ann said, but, for a wonder, there
was a gleam of amusement in her eyes.

"That must be Shay back," said Michael as we all heard
the sound of a car braking in the drive.

I hurried to the door, eager to see whom Shamus had
brought. The last people in the world whom I would have
anticipated! Shay carefully handed out first one, then the
other, Lady Brandel.

I was given lavender-scented, silken cheeks to kiss, and
soft little hands seized mine while I was beamed upon.

"We were so overjoyed to see dear Shamus, Rene," said
Lady Mary, tucking her hand under my right arm while
Lady Maud claimed my left. "He's *told* us *all* the happen-
ings. My dear Rene . . ."

"He's also told us how we can help with a few words to
the right person," said Lady Maud, "so if we may have permission to use your telephone, Rene . . ." She hesitated

before the phone just long enough to receive my dazed acquiescence.

"There are *moments* when a *telephone* is so very *useful*," said Lady Mary, folding her hands in front of her as she took a place beside her sister.

"Whom do *they* know?" I whispered to Shamus as Lady Maud unfolded a tiny notebook and carefully found the page she wanted. She pressed it flat on the table, ran her fingers down the entries, paused, peered, frowned at the number, and then, picking up the receiver, dialed very carefully, silently enunciating each numeral.

"Oh." Her face, serious from the delicate business of dealing with the unfamiliar instrument, brightened. "And good afternoon to you too. Is it at all possible for the Colonel to have a few words with Lady Maud Brandel? The matter is rather urgent . . . Yes, thank you, I'll wait." She turned her head to smile pleasantly at me, all cool, composed Grande Dame. She ignored Lady Mary, who was hovering rather breathlessly.

"Colonel who?" I hissed at Shamus. He signaled me to be patient and listen.

"Oh, Dermot, how good of you! Yes, thank you, I'm quite well. Yes, so is Mary. I trust that Derval and the children are well? Oh? Another grandson? How pleased you must be! Well, I'll come to the point if I may, for I know you're a very busy man. But one of my dearest friends"— she acknowledged that accolade to me with a courtly bow of her head—"is being harassed by an American in the most unpleasant way. Totally unnecessary. Her solicitor is standing by me, and I'm sure he can explain the pertinent details. You will then be able to judge the merits of the case. Yes . . . She's Irene Teasey's niece. You remember Irene, of course. Rene, that's the niece, has inherited Irene's property, you see, no problem that way, but you must know Michael Noonan? Well, let me just put him on to you . . . But I'm sure you'll see that something must be done directly. I know you won't disappoint me." She rose and handed the phone to Michael.

"Noonan here." A stunned look came over Michael's face, and unconsciously he stood straight, all attention. "Yes, *sir!*"

"I'm positive that Dermot can oblige," said Lady Maud

as she and Mary drew me into the living room. Shamus gave me a push from behind.

"That *dreadful* man!" Lady Mary was saying. "When Shamus *told* us, we were *appalled* to think of the *ordeal* you've been through . . . How distressing for our twins!"

"Shay, did you tell them *everything?*"

"Oh, Rene, we'd've *heard* it *soon enough* anyway, you know," said Lady Mary reassuringly, and she peered across me at her sister for confirmation.

"Pleasant to have the truth of a matter from a competent source" was Lady Maud's reply as she smoothed her skirts out on the couch.

"You see, *we* know *just* the person to *assist* you."

"Who?" I asked bluntly.

"Let's just say, a high-ranking official at the Castle," said Shamus. "I don't think he'll care for official thanks."

"Well? What's going to happen, then?"

"Oh," and Shay's eyes got wide and devilish. "I would suspect that shortly several officials will call on your ex-husband at his hotel and suggest, very politely, that his presence is unacceptable to the Irish Republic. He will be politely escorted to the airport and put on the first available flight out. And I don't think he will ever get back in again."

"But—but—" That was more than I'd counted on. "Can they *do* that?"

"You're in Ireland."

"But—but—"

"It's such a relief," said Lady Maud at her most placid, "to know that we could perform a little service for you . . . and Irene . . . after all you've done for us."

Her expression was guileless—like Snow's—but I wondered then, as I've wondered often since, if Lady Maud and Lady Mary were quite as ignorant of the origin of their trust fund as everyone assumed.

"Now, what is this that Shamus has been telling us about you two, dear Rene?"

I could not deny it in the face of their obvious delight and pleasure.

"And *how* could dear Irene have *so* misjudged Shamus? *You* barely *knew* him and yet *you* realized that he was *incapable* of *so* ungentlemanly a *deed.*"

I stared at Shay, who grinned and shrugged. "They *are* over eighteen, pet."

"As I've had occasion to remark to you before, Rene," said Lady Maud, putting a conciliatory hand on my arm, "we are aware of the ways of the world, whether we chose to follow them or not."

Simon, Snow and Jimmy came traipsing delicately in at that point, tray-laden. Before I knew it, I was eating again, drinking tea with the good Ladies. Michael joined us rather absently, and soon rose abruptly. "I have some legal tying up to do," he said. "If anything develops, I'll ring you this evening, Rene. Lady Maud, Lady Mary," and he bent with graceful dignity over each daintily extended hand. "My respects!" His grin indicated that he'd recovered his composure.

One day, I'd find out who had impressed him so!

"Don't panic, Mihall, if we don't answer here between seven and midnight," Shamus was saying as he and I escorted Michael to the door. "We've some celebrating to do, if Rene feels up to it."

"Of course Mommy'll feel up to it," said Snow emphatically. "She's going right upstairs now and rest."

"I'm being bossed."

The Ladies Brandel said that they would have been prostrate with exhaustion and wasn't I clever, and it was so nice to know that my lovely children and I were staying on in Ireland. They'd really get to know us. And I was going to sing with the Rathmines group now, wasn't I? Carrying on in Irene's tradition?

Michael then offered to drive them home, as it was on his way. Which seemed a neat ending to the day's activities.

As usual, Irene Teasey spoke too soon. No sooner had Michael's car pulled out into the main road than another came slithering over the loose gravel at the entrance.

"Good God, now what?" I complained, moving closer to Shamus in alarm. "I've seen that car before. It's Aunt Alice!"

"Good!" said Shay. "I've a crow to pluck with the old cow."

As well he was primed, because Auntie Alice Hegarty came charging out of her car, her face suffused with the blood of angry vengeance. It was me she headed for. Shay's hand was strong and warm against the small of my back. Not that I would have retreated. I was (Preserve the Image!) too proud.

"You'll sell now, won't you? You promised!"

"Sell?"

"And you!" She wheeled on Shamus, brandishing her rather heavy handbag. "Your check was stopped. You had no right to stop it!"

"All the right in the world, you old phony. You had no right to sell me access up the lane. Then or now. I think I'd better have a word with Tom."

"Tom doesn't enter into this matter at all!" She was defiant, and scared.

Oh, Tom was her husband, Gerry's father. The big-bear man who played accordion. But *he* scared Alice, even if he appeared innocuous to me.

"Perhaps not, Alice Hegarty. I could of course prosecute you for illegally selling rights you did not possess."

"Prosecute me?" She took another backward step. "I won't go to court. No Hegarty has ever been dragged into court." She got her second wind too quickly for my liking. "*You!*" The purse swung round to me. "You! You said you'd sell once the will was probated."

"I said I couldn't sell until the will was probated, Mrs. Hegarty." I took a deep breath. "And I certainly wouldn't sell to you."

"You'll be glad enough to be quit of Ireland when that fancy man of yours finds you and takes your brats away."

"He's been and gone," Shay said, his voice treacherous as silk, because I was bereft of speech. "And I'd say it was yourself told Paddy Purdee where to find Ann?"

"Of course it was," and the angry red returned to Auntie Alice's face. "I'll have the whole lot cleared out of here . . ."

Two more cars came tearing up the lane. Winnie Teasey popped out of the first one, in such a state that the car stalled with a buck. The other driver was Gerry, his usually affable face set in hard, angry lines.

It became a Donnybrook of words: Alice raging with frustration, Winnie wringing her hands. Shamus was adding some trenchant remarks about illegal permissions. Winnie said that he shouldn't upset poor Alice this way with talk of courts and suing. Shamus wanted to know what else could he do. Alice raved about his stopping checks when he'd made a strictly business arrangement . . .

"What check?" asked Gerry, in such a roar that everyone shut up.

"Why," said Shay, completely at ease, "the money I paid her for the use of this lane, which she didn't have the legal right to lease."

Gerry turned slowly to his mother. She drew her small stout self up against his scrutiny.

"This property is mine, Gerard. You *know* Irene meant to leave it all to me . . ."

"I know nothing of the kind, Mother. Now get in that car and drive home. Unless you want me to tell Dad that you've been meddling again?"

She didn't want to go. She opened her mouth to protest, but Gerry took her firmly by the elbow and marched her to her car. Winnie had been reduced to sobbing, wringing her hands and murmuring, "How could Alice? How can she be this way?"

When his mother's car swung on to the main road, just missing a truck, which honked a loud, continuous blast, Gerry turned to his aunt.

"Now, you calm down too, Winnie. Get along home, and we'll say no more about this."

She was being deftly inserted into her car by Gerry. Bucking and stalling it, she did manage to turn it around and leave.

"I *will* have to tell my father, I think," Gerry said to us. "I can't even say she means well, Rene," and Gerry sighed. "But we'll sort her out. Not to worry. I'd better go after her, if you'll excuse me. And forgive?"

I hastily assured him I did, and then he was away, leaving a cloud of dust to settle on the well-used lane.

"Well, will he?"

"Will he what, pet?" asked Shay, guiding me back to the house.

"Contain her."

Shamus chuckled. "Sure enough. Once Tom hears of this, Alice will be mild for months. There are, you know," and he smiled affectionately at me, "some good reasons for Irish men to beat their wives. Now and then only, of course —for the good of their souls and the peace of the neighborhood." His hand gently pushed me into my house. "Now, you're to go upstairs, alone, and get some rest. You've had enough on your plate."

"The twins?" I knew it was silly, but I was apprehensive.

"I won't take my eyes off them," he said, capturing my

waving hands and drawing me close to him for a very satisfactory kiss. Very satisfactory because I was thinking that
the twins were big enough to keep an eye on themselves,
and I wanted his on me.

"Oh!"

We broke away, or rather I tried to, at the soft exclama-
tion of dismay.

Ann was in the doorway to the dining room, looking flustered and utterly dismayed at our carrying-on. Blankness
came over Shamus's face.

"We'd better all be friends," I said to neither in particular, "and let bygones be. You'll be seeing a lot of Shay
again, Ann."

"A lot?" Shamus challenged my qualifier.

Ann's lips met in a firm line of disapproval.

"Yes, Ann, a lot. In fact, you might say a continuous
performance, if he hasn't changed his mind after all the tu-
mult and shouting today."

Shay's hand crept up my shoulders to rest on the back of
my neck in the most caressing and possessive of gestures. I
felt feline enough to want to wiggle with delight at that touch.
But Ann was there, and I should Preserve the Image.

The hell with that! I'd preserved, destroyed, tried on
enough Images for one person for the rest of her lifetime.
From now on I was going to be me, Irene Teasey
Stanford . . . God willing . . . Kerrigan.

"I've discovered that *I* can't function properly without a
man in my life, Ann," I said, looking at her unapologeti-
cally as I pressed closer to Shay. "I like having a man to
take care of, who'll return the courtesy by taking care of
me. And yes, I made a mistake, and I may make many
more."

"Not with me, pet," murmured Shay, so fervently that
Ann stared at him in a startled fashion.

"But I'm not about to close the book of my life for one
mistake, and you shouldn't either, Ann Purdee."

She looked so stricken at my attack that I relented and
reached out to her.

"Ann, honey, it's right for me, for the way I am. I know
it is now. I wouldn't have thought so even three weeks ago,
believe me. I'd finished with men. But I'm not too proud or
too stubborn or too stupid to change my mind for a good

reason. And now that Paddy Purdee's off your back, you can look around a bit too."

She shuddered at a notion still abhorrent to her. I now appreciated my friend Betty's wry smile.

"That's what this is all about, Ann, your being here. It's probably what Aunt Irene really wanted for you, in good time. It's what women's lib is all about—you, me, Mary, Sally, the Ladies Brandel, everyone having a chance to find their own way to . . . Oooops, I'm sorry. I'm the last one who should sermonize anyone! Enjoy! Enjoy, Ann, let yourself enjoy even a little!" I broke free from Shay's insidious proximity and rushed halfway up the stairs in my embarrassment at having spouted so intensely. "If you want to pick up the pieces about seven, Shay dear, I'll be ready. But right now I have to regroup my energies, as Snow used to say."

"At seven, then, your courtier will await thee, Queen Irene!" Shamus swept another of those ridiculously involved, flourishing bows. "She makes a bloody good queen, doesn't she, Ann?" I heard him say as I clattered up the rest of the steps.

"Sure and she does!" replied Ann, so firmly that I knew I *could* rest awhile. My queendom, for the moment at least, was in good hands!